ROBERT BELLMON. The spit-and-polish officer. He and his men would face off against Hitler's crack Afrika Korps.

BARBARA WATERFORD BELLMON. An Army brat, a barracks bride, she was a woman bound to the fortunes of war.

CRAIG LOWELL. The blond American aristocrat, too rich and too handsome to be taken seriously as a soldier.

ILSE VON GREIFFENBERG. The beautiful daughter of a German count—Craig Lowell found her selling love in the midnight streets.

RUDY MACMILLAN. Winning the Medal of Honor made him an officer, and, he sometimes thought, ruined his life.

SANDY FELTER. His Jewish background made him the odd man out. Until, on a lonely Greek hillside, he proved himself part of the

BROTHERHOOD OF WAR

By W. E. B. Griffin
from Jove

BROTHERHOOD OF WAR

The Lieutenants

BROTHERHOOD OF WAR

BOOK I

BY W.E.B. GRIFFIN

A JOVE BOOK

BROTHERHOOD OF WAR series was written on a
Lanier "no problem" word processor.

THE LIEUTENANTS

A Jove Book / published by arrangement with
the author

PRINTING HISTORY
Jove edition / September 1982
Second printing / December 1982

ISBN: 0-515-05643-X

Jove books are published by Jove Publications, Inc.,
200 Madison Avenue, New York, N. Y. 10016. The words
"A JOVE BOOK" and the "J" with sunburst are trademarks
belonging to Jove Publications, Inc.

PRINTED IN THE UNITED STATES OF AMERICA

For Uncle Charley and The Bull
RIP October 1979

And for Donn.
Who would have ever believed four stars?

BROTHERHOOD OF WAR
THE LIEUTENANTS

I

On 14 February 1943, strong German armored units sallied forth from passes in south-central Tunisia on the front of the II U.S. Corps, commanded by Major General Lloyd R. Fredendall, in an attempt to turn the flank of the British First Army (Lt. Gen. Kenneth A. N. Anderson) and capture the base of operations that the Allies had set up around Tebessa. In a series of sharp armored actions, the Germans defeated the Allies and forced a withdrawal by American troops all the way back through Kasserine Pass and the valley beyond.

American Military History 1607–1953
Department of the Army, July 1956

(One)
Near Sidi-Bou-Zid, Tunisia
17 February 1943
Two tanks, American, which showed signs of hard use, moved slowly down a path. The terrain was undulating desert. Not sand dunes, but arid, gritty soil, with crumbling, fist-sized

rocks and sparse vegetation. The dips in the land were just deep enough to conceal a tank. The high spots did not provide for much visibility. You could see for a mile, perhaps more, but a tank could be concealed in a dip a hundred yards away.

Major Robert Bellmon, riding in the open turret of the lead M4A2 "Sherman" tank, his tanned body outside the hatch, was a tall and rangy young man who had graduated from the United States Military Academy at West Point in 1939. He wore the Academy ring, a simple gold wedding band, and an issue Hamilton watch. The issue band had rotted, and had been replaced by a band stitched from the tail of a khaki shirt by the battalion tailor.

Bellmon wore a khaki shirt, a cotton tanker's jacket with a zipper front and knit cuffs and collar, wool olive-drab trousers, and a pair of nonregulation tanker's boots, which looked like a combination of dress low quarters, field shoes, and combat boots; their uppers reached ten inches up his calves. He also wore an old style tanker's helmet, which was like a football helmet to which earphones had been riveted. A Colt Model 1911A1 pistol was suspended half under his arm in a shoulder holster, and a pair of Zeiss binoculars, inherited from his father, hung around his neck.

Although he had stopped the tank and carefully searched the desert three minutes before, and only thirty seconds before had ordered Sergeant Pete Fortin, the driver, to get moving, he did not see the Afrika Korps Panzerkampfwagen IV until the muzzle blast of its 75 mm turret cannon caught his eye. A half-second later the tungsten-steel projectile slammed into the hull of his M4A2.

The Sherman shuddered. There was an awesome roar, followed immediately by the horrible screeching sound of tearing metal, lasting no more than a second. The M4A2 turned to the right, halfway off the track it had been following, and stopped dead. It had moved no more than eight feet after being struck.

The impact of the armor-piercing shell threw Bellmon against the edge of the commander's hatch, catching him in the rib cage. It bruised him severely, knocking the breath out of him, and almost throwing him out of the commander's turret.

He heard a groan, which sounded somewhat surprised, from inside the tank, but couldn't tell who it was. When he looked down, dense black smoke had already begun to fill the tank's interior. Without really thinking about what he was doing, acting in pure animal reflex, he hoisted himself out of the turret. There was a wave of pain.

He just had time to curse himself for getting out of the turret—his duty clearly was to have gone into the hull to help the others—when an intensely hot spurt of flame erupted upward from the turret. He knew what had caused it. Pieces of metal from the projectile, and pieces torn from the hull itself, had ripped into the brass cases of the 75 mm cannon ammunition, slicing them open and spilling their powder. Then the powder had caught fire. When unconfined powder burns, it does not explode. The explosion came a moment later, as intact shell cases and gasoline fumes detonated.

Bellmon felt himself flying through the air. He landed on his back upon the rocky ground, his shoulders striking the ground first, throwing him into a backward somersault, and knocking what was left of the wind in his lungs out of him. When he came to rest, he was conscious, but was incapable of movement.

He was dimly aware of a second shot from a tank cannon, a sharp cracking noise, followed immediately by a heavier thump. Despite the pain in his ribs, he tried to get control of himself. He forced himself to take a deep breath, and then another. And another.

Finally he was able to roll onto his side to see what had happened to the second M4A2, the other tank which had come out with him "to locate and assist the 705th Field Artillery Battalion." It was immobile. There was no one in the turret, and oily smoke oozed out around the fuel tanks and the turret ring. No one had gotten out of that one.

He heard the sound of a tank engine. He let himself fall slowly onto his face. He would play dead, though it was a slim chance at best. The crew of the German tank would more than likely give him a burst with the 7.93 mm machine gun. Prisoners were a nuisance in fast-moving tank warfare.

He closed his eyes, and tried to breathe very slowly. His only hope was to make them think that he had been killed when his tank blew up. If he tried to surrender, all he would do would be to give them a better target.

The PzKwIV ground to a halt near him. It was now the standard German medium tank, an efficient killing machine, into which had been incorporated all the lessons the German Panzertruppen had learned in France and Russia and here in Africa. Bellmon would have been willing to admit, privately, that it was a better tank than the Sherman.

He knew the German tank commander was watching him. Then he heard the crunch of footsteps on the gritty soil.

"Was ist er?"

"Ein Offizier, Herr Leutnant. Mit einen gelben Blatt."

"Ein Major?" the first voice said. "Is he dead?"

"No," the self-confident voice above him said, matter-of-factly. "He's breathing. Playing dead."

Good God, is my pretense that transparent?

There was the sound of more booted feet on the gritty soil.

"Please do not make it necessary for me to kill you, Herr Major," the first voice said.

A hand grabbed his shoulder, and rolled him onto his back. Bellmon opened his eyes and found himself looking into the muzzle of a .45 Colt automatic. It was in the hands of a young, blond, good-looking lieutenant of the Afrika Korps. He wore the black tunic of the Panzertruppen above standard gray Wehrmacht trousers. He smiled at Bellmon. Then he reached down with his free hand and took Bellmon's .45 from his shoulder holster.

"You may sit up, please, Major," he said. His English was British accented. "Are you injured?"

Bellmon sat up. The lieutenant handed Bellmon's .45 to the soldier with him. Another nice-looking, clean-cut, blond-headed boy, Bellmon thought.

"Will you also give me, please, the holster?" the lieutenant asked. Bellmon pulled it over his head and held it out. The soldier held his Schmeisser 9 mm machine-pistol between his knees, took Bellmon's shoulder holster, and put it over his head.

"Make sure that isn't loaded," the lieutenant cautioned. The soldier took the magazine from the butt of the .45, saw that it was full, emptied it, and then put it back in the pistol, and then slipped the pistol into the holster.

"The Colt is a very fine pistol, Major," the lieutenant said.

Bellmon didn't reply.

"Help the major to his feet," the lieutenant said.

"Are you going to see to my men?" Bellmon asked, getting painfully to his feet unaided.

The lieutenant actually looked unhappy as he made a sad gesture toward the two American tanks. They were both burning steadily. There was the smell of burned flesh. Bellmon willed back a spasm of nausea. He would not, he vowed, show weakness before his captors.

The soldier took his arm and led him to the PzKwIV.

"Please to get inside, Herr Major," the lieutenant said.

Bellmon climbed over the bogies, the wheels around which the track of the tank moved, and by which it was supported. A two-piece hatch in the side of the turret was open. The sweat-soaked face of an older man—probably the platoon sergeant, Bellmon judged, because there was something about him that told him he wasn't an officer—looked out at him. Bellmon lowered his head and started to crawl into the turret.

"Nein," the face said to him. *"Fuss vorwärts."*

Bellmon pulled his head back out, turned around, and backed into the turret hatch.

Inside the hull, which was more cramped than the hull of an M4A2, he was motioned to sit down on the floor. One of the crewmen (the driver, probably, he thought) came up with a length of field telephone wire. He looped it around Bellmon's ankles, and then around his wrists, and tied his wrists to his ankles.

Then he climbed out of sight. In a moment, there was the clash of gears, and the PzKwIV turned on one track, then went back in the direction from which it had come, to the east, toward the German lines.

I am alive, Bellmon told himself. Bruised, a little groggy, but not really injured. This is where I am supposed to think that I will live to fight another day.

He became aware that tears were blurring his vision and running down his cheeks. Was it shock? Was he weeping for Sergeant Pete Fortin and all the others? Or because the worst thing that could happen to an officer, capture, had happened to him? Did it matter? He lowered his head on his knees so that his captors would not see him crying.

(Two)
Hq, 393rd Tank Destroyer Battalion (Reinforced)
Youks-Les-Bains, Algeria
24 February 1943

The command post was built against the side of a stony hill, facing away from the front lines and the German artillery. At the crest of the hill, four half-tracks, two mounting 75 mm antitank cannon and two mounting multiple .50 caliber machine guns in powered turrets, were dug in facing the front.

On the ground, on the friendly side of the hill, two more half-tracks with multiple .50s faced the opposite direction. A half-moon of barbed wire with sandbagged machine-gun emplacements guarded the command post dugouts. The dugouts were holes in the side of the hill, with timber supporting sandbag roofs.

Two jeeps, traveling well above the posted 25 mph speed limit, approached the 393rd CP from the rear. Each held three men, and an air-cooled Browning .50 caliber machine gun on a pillar. The front jeep had nonstandard accouterments: the seats were thickly padded leather, instead of the normal thin canvas pad; a hand bar had been welded to the top of the windshield; and a combination flashing red light and siren of the type usually found on a police car was mounted on the right fender. It had been painted olive-drab, but the paint, here and there, had flecked off the chrome. An eight-by-twelve-inch sheet of tin, painted red and with a single silver star in the middle, was placed above the front and rear bumpers. Communications radios were bolted to the fender wells in the back seat, and their antennae whipped in the air. Spring clips had been bolted to the dashboard. Each held a Thompson .45 ACP caliber submachine gun.

The driver of the lead jeep was a master sergeant in his thirties, a pug-nosed, squat, muscular man with huge hands. He wore a tanker's jacket and a Colt .45 automatic in a shoulder holster. Beside him sat a firm-jawed, silver-haired, almost handsome man in his fifties, wearing an Army Air Corps pilot's horsehide jacket, with a silver star on each epaulet. A yellow silk scarf, neatly knotted, was around his neck. He also carried a .45 in a shoulder holster. The man in the back seat was young, clean-cut, and dressed like the general, the only difference being the silver bars of a first lieutenant on the epaulets of his pilot's horsehide jacket.

The second jeep contained three enlisted men, a technical sergeant and two staff sergeants, armed with both Garand M1 rifles and Colt pistols carried in holsters suspended from web belts around their waists. Their helmets had "MP" painted on their sides.

As they approached the gate to the command post of the 393rd Tank Destroyer Battalion (Reinforced), the master sergeant driving the lead jeep saw that the road was barred by a weighted telephone pole suspended horizontally across the road. He reached down and flipped the siren switch. The siren growled, just long enough to signal the soldier at the gate to raise the telephone pole.

He did not do so. The two jeeps skidded to a stop.

The master sergeant at the wheel of the lead jeep started to rise in his seat. The general, with a little wave of his left hand, signaled him to sit back down.

"It's all right, Tommy," he said.

This wasn't garrison, and the guard was not ceremonial. The German advance had been stopped a thousand yards away.

The guard was a very large, six-foot-tall, very black PFC, carrying a Garand rifle slung over his shoulder. He stood at the weighted end of the pole, examined the passengers in the jeep carefully, and then, satisfied, stood erect, grasped the leather sling of his M1 with his left hand, saluted crisply with his right, and then pushed the weighted end of the pole down. The barrier end lifted. The guard then waved them through. He stood at attention until both jeeps had passed, and then he quickly cranked the EE–8 field telephone at his feet.

"General officer headed for the CP," he said. "Porky Waterford."

By the time the two jeeps had reached the bunker with the American flag and the battalion guidon before it, a very tall, flat-nosed Negro lieutenant colonel whose brown skin was somewhat darker than his boots had stepped outside the bunker. He was dressed in olive-drab shirt and trousers, with a yellow piece of parachute silk wrapped around his neck as a foulard. He carried a World War I Colt New Service .45 ACP revolver in an old-fashioned cavalry-style holster (one with a swivel, so the holster would hang straight down even when mounted).

The guard at the door to the CP carried a Thompson .45 caliber submachine gun. He saluted the moment the jeep stopped, and the brigadier general in the front seat jumped out.

The lieutenant colonel, whose features and dark skin made him look very much like an Arab, took three steps away from the door, came to attention, and saluted.

"Lieutenant Colonel Parker, sir, commanding," he said.

The brigadier general returned the salute, and then put out his hand.

"How are you, Colonel?" he asked. The handshake was momentary, pro forma.

"Very well, thank you, General," Lt. Col. Philip Sheridan Parker III said. "Will the general come into the CP?"

"Thank you," Brigadier General Peterson K. Waterford said.

Colonel Parker waved him ahead into the CP. Someone called "Attention."

"Rest, gentlemen," General Waterford said, immediately.

The command post was crowded, but neat and orderly. One wall was covered with large maps and charts, overlaid with celluloid. There was a field switchboard, communications radios, folding tables equipped with portable typewriters. A large, open, enameled coffee pot simmered on an alcohol stove. There were perhaps twenty men, officers and enlisted, all black, in the room.

"Would the general care to examine our situation?" Colonel Parker said, gesturing toward the situation map.

"Actually, Colonel," General Waterford said, "I took the chance that you would have a minute or two for me on a personal matter."

"Perhaps the general would care to come to my quarters?" Lieutenant Colonel Parker offered.

"That's very kind of you, Colonel," General Waterford said.

"Captain," Parker said to a stout, round-faced captain, "would you brief the general's aide?"

The captain came to attention. "Yes, sir."

Colonel Parker pushed aside a piece of tarpaulin that served as the door to his quarters, an eight-by-eight-foot chamber hacked out of the hill. Inside were a GI cot, a GI folding table, two GI folding chairs, a GI desk, and two footlockers.

"Will the general have a seat?" Colonel Parker inquired. When Waterford had sat down, Parker knelt and opened one of the footlockers and took out two bottles, one of scotch and one of bourbon. He looked at General Waterford, who indicated the scotch by pointing his finger. He poured scotch into one cheese glass, and bourbon into the other. He handed the general the scotch, then tapped it with his glass of bourbon.

"Mud in your eye, Porky," he said.

"Health and long life, Phil," the general replied. They drank their whiskey neat, all of it. Parker asked with raised eyebrows if Waterford wanted another, and Waterford declined with a shake of his head.

"I'm really sorry about Bob Bellmon, Porky," Colonel Parker said. "I was going to get my thoughts together, and then ask if you thought I should write Marjorie."

"What are your thoughts?" Waterford asked.

"I'll tell you what I know," Parker said. "We were withdrawing. That's a week ago today. About three miles from Sidi-Bou-Zid, we came across two shot-up M4s. I had a moment or two, so I went and looked. The bumper markings identified them as belonging to 73rd Medium Tank. Numbers two and fourteen."

"Tony Wilson took the time to tell me what he knew," Waterford said. "Bob went out in number two. He was trying to link up with the 705th Field. Two lousy tanks was all that Tony could spare. Tony said Bob convinced him that they had to try with what they had. Neither of them knew, of course, but the 705th had already been rolled over."

Lt. Col. Philip Sheridan Parker III felt sorry for Lieutenant Colonel Anthony Wilson, who commanded the 73rd Medium Tank Battalion. Losing men was always bad. Having to explain how they were lost in person to a man who was simultaneously the father-in-law, a general officer, and an old friend must have been very rough indeed.

"Both tanks had been struck with something big," Parker said. "I'd say a high velocity tungsten-cored round from the Mark IV Panzer. Both had burned. One of them had exploded."

"Which one?" Waterford asked.

"I'm sorry, I don't remember which one," Parker said.

"That's all right," Waterford said. "Did you get a body count?"

"They burned and blew up, Porky," Colonel Parker said. "And I didn't have much time. We were under intermittent fire."

"But?"

"I hate to say this, because it might give hope where there is none," Colonel Parker said. "But I have a feeling that one man may have gotten out. And that he was carried off as a prisoner. There were Mark IV tracks, and footsteps. But they may just have been looking over the hulks."

Waterford sat with his shoulders bent, examining his hands.

"Yes, of course," Waterford said, after a long silence.

Parker poured an inch and a half of scotch in the cheese glass and handed it to Waterford. Waterford took it and tossed it down.

"I'm sorry, Porky," Parker said, gently, "but that's all I have."

"When we go back," General Waterford said, retaining control of his voice with a visible effort, "the Graves Registration people will probably be able to tell us something. They're really quite good at this sort of thing."

"If Bobby didn't make it, Porky," Colonel Parker said, "he went out quick."

"He went out too young. Bobby was . . . *is* . . . twenty-five," Waterford said. "God, I hate to write Barbara."

"That's what I've been doing," Parker said. "Writing the next of kin."

"You came out of it better than most," Waterford said. "We got the shit kicked out of us, Phil."

"I lost seven officers and sixty-three troopers," Parker said.

"Equipment?"

"I put all the old 37 mm stuff out in front. I lost seventeen tracks. Nine from mechanical failure. I blew them."

"I repeat, you came out of it a lot better than most," Waterford said.

"Are they going to relieve Lloyd Fredendall? That's the rumor."

"Probably," Waterford replied. "He lost the battle."

"Who's going to get the Corps?" Parker asked.

"I hope Seward. That'd put me in line for the division. But I suppose Georgie Patton will get it. Eisenhower still calls him 'Sir,' when he's not careful."

"I hope you get it, Porky," Parker said.

"No, you don't, you bastard. You're just saying that. You're jealous."

"Of course I'm jealous. But if you get the division, maybe you'll take us with you."

"If I get the division, Phil, you can bank on it. You've got some fine troops."

"I think so," Parker said. "None of mine ran."

General Waterford stood up. "I wish I could say the same thing," he said. "You know what the history books are going to say: 'In their first major armor engagement of World War II, at Kasserine Pass, Tunisia, the Americans got the shit kicked out of them. Many of them ran.'"

"They call that blooding, Porky," Phil Parker said.

General Waterford stood up, put his arm around Parker's shoulder, and hugged him.

"Thank you for your time, Phil," he said.

"I'm sorry I wasn't of more help," Parker said.

"I didn't ask, Phil," Waterford said. "Where's Phil?"

"A sophomore at Norwich. He'll be in the class of '45."

"Maybe we can wind it up by then," Waterford said.

"God, I hope so."

(Three)
Carmel, California
28 February 1943

Barbara Waterford Bellmon, a lanky, auburn-haired, freckle-faced brunette of twenty-four, stood by her locker in the ladies' locker room of the Pebble Beach Country Club and held out her hand for her winnings. She had gone around in 82, four over ladies' par, and they had been playing for a dollar a stroke. She had just won thirty-three dollars, and it was important to her that she be paid.

As the losers searched in their coin purses and wallets for the money, Barbara thought again that she really didn't like women. Women, she thought, were really lousy losers; they paid up reluctantly. She knew that the other members of her foursome would have preferred not to pay up at all, to let the settling-up slide until it was forgotten. It wasn't the money. These women were all well-to-do. It was some quirk of the female character.

"All I've got is a fifty," Susan Forbes said, examining the contents of her wallet, but not offering the fifty dollar bill. Susan was a long-legged blond, who looked considerably younger than her thirty-three years. Barbara took a twenty and a ten from her wallet and held it out.

"Oh, here's a twenty," Susan said.

As if you didn't know, Barbara thought, and snatched it from Susan's hand. Surprise, surprise.

"Thank you very much," Barbara said, sweetly. "Next?"

"The least you could do is buy us lunch," Patricia Stewart said, as she passed over a crisp ten dollar bill. Pat, whom Barbara thought of privately as the archetypical Tweedy Lady, was, at thirty-six, the oldest of the golfers. Barbara handed her a dollar change.

"I have a date," she said.

"Sounds exciting," Susan said. "Anyone we know?"

"He's tall, dark, handsome, and a Catholic priest," Barbara said.

"Shame on you," Susan said.

Standing on one leg, Barbara took off her golf shoes, put them into her locker, and then stuffed her golf socks into her purse. Finally, she slipped her bare feet into a pair of loafers.

They went through what Barbara considered the ludicrous routine of making smacking noises with their lips in the general vicinity of each others' cheeks. Then Barbara walked out the ladies' locker room, back onto the course rather than into the clubhouse itself, and went around the building to the parking lot.

She got behind the wheel of her mother's car, a 1937 Ford convertible sedan. After performing the elaborate but necessary ritual it required to get going (pump the gas pedal twice, then hold it down while the starter cranked, release it instantly when it coughed, while simultaneously praying), she backed out of the parking slot and drove home.

Home was Casa Mañana, her parents' home, a rambling

Spanish-style building with red-tiled roofs set on ten acres overlooking the Pacific. There were three flagpoles set in a brick-lined patch of grass in front of the house. An American flag, just barely moving in the wind, hung from the taller center pole. The two smaller poles were bare.

Casa Mañana, roughly translated, meant the "house for tomorrow." For three generations, it had been the home to which the Waterfords planned to retire, and where their women waited when the men had gone off to war. It was at Casa Mañana that the family gathered, when possible, at Christmas, and it was a family tradition that the babies were christened according to the rites of the Episcopal Church of St. Matthew's in Carmel, no matter where in the world they were born. It was home to people whose profession saw them spending a good part of their lives in foreign countries or in remote military posts.

There was enough money to keep it open, staffed, ready for occupancy, when there was no member of the family closer than a thousand miles. Over the years, the Waterfords and the Bellmons had slowly and wisely invested their money, so there was now enough to live "comfortably" if unostentatiously.

Just inside the door, on shelves, were two red flags neatly folded into triangles. One of them bore a single silver star, and the other two silver stars. The single-starred flag belonged to the present owner of the house, her father, Brigadier General Peterson K. Waterford, who had inherited the house from his father, Major General Alfred B. Waterford. The two-starred flag had belonged to Bob's father, Major General Robert F. Bellmon, Sr. They'd buried Bob's father from Casa Mañana, taking the remains to the military cemetery at the Presidio of San Francisco. When they'd hauled his flag down from the pole for the last time, they had folded it up and put it beside General Waterford's flag, where it would be ready when it was needed again. Porky Waterford was almost sure to make major general soon, and then he could fly it as his own. Or it could just stay there until Bob, twenty years from now, was himself entitled to the red flag of a general officer.

The flags were well made; they'd last that long. General Waterford's flag had belonged to his father.

With long and almost masculine strides, Barbara walked through the house, in search of her mother. It must be noon,

Barbara realized. Mother and the kids were having their noon-time cocktail. Marjorie Waterford never took a drink until noon, and she rarely made it to twelve fifteen without one. She called it a cocktail, but it was invariably bourbon and water, one ice cube. The kids got ginger ale with a maraschino cherry.

"How did you do?" Barbara's mother inquired, asking with her eyes if Barbara wanted a drink.

"No, I don't think so, thank you," Barbara said. "I don't want to smell of it. When I come back." She smiled with self-satisfaction at her mother. "I went around in 82 and took them for thirty-three bucks."

"Good for you," her mother said. "Father Bob called. He asked if he could bring somebody with him."

"Did he say who?"

"No. He said he had two. He didn't give any names. I think he would have, if it was someone we know."

"Yes," Barbara replied, as if distracted.

"I had Consuela do a pork loin," Mrs. Waterford said. "I thought that and over-brown potatoes, and a salad."

"That will be very nice," Barbara said. "I don't know how he stands it, doing that, day after day after day."

"That's what priests are for," her mother said. "And he's probably used to it by now."

"I'd better get changed," Barbara said.

When she came out of the shower and was drying herself, she heard the kids' voices in her bedroom. She wondered if Bobby just wanted to be with Mommy or if Bobby was already developing a curiosity about females. He was hardly old enough for that, but on the other hand, he was Bob's son. She remembered the first time Bob had talked her into taking her clothes off. At Fort Riley. She remembered that very clearly. She was seven, so Bob must have been eight. A naked little girl and a naked little boy, staring at each other with frank curiosity. He had a thing, and she didn't.

The next time he had seen her without her pants she had been twenty and he had been a twenty-one-year-old second lieutenant. It had been in a room in the Carlyle Hotel in New York City on the first night of their honeymoon.

"Jesus Christ," Bob had said. "It grew a beard."

The bastard. So had his. And she'd told him so.

Barbara stuck her head through the bathroom door.

"Scram, Bobby," she said.

"Why?"

"Because boys aren't supposed to be around when ladies aren't wearing clothes," Barbara said. "Go wait for Chaplain McGrory."

"Is he coming *again?*"

"Yes, he is," Barbara said. "Now beat it."

When he had finally made a reluctant retreat, Barbara came out of the bathroom naked and got dressed. Eleanor, a year younger than her brother, sat in the middle of the bed and watched her get dressed, first a bra and pants and a half-slip and a garter belt and stockings (no girdle, not even after two kids), and then making up her face and doing her hair. Finally she put on a gray suit, and last, her jewelry: her wedding ring and her engagement ring, and the miniature of Bob's West Point class ring.

She always had a question in her mind about wearing the engagement ring on occasions like this. It was a four-carat, emerald-cut diamond. Worth a bundle. It had been Bob's mother's. When, to absolutely no one's surprise, she had come back from the Spring Hop at the Point and announced that she and Bob were going to be married the day after he graduated, General Bellmon had given Bob the ring to give to her. She hadn't even had to have it resized.

It had never been a problem with the enlisted wives, who either didn't notice it, or thought it was costume jewelry, or thought that all officers' wives had diamonds like that. But it had gotten looks from some of the officers' wives on whom she had made "notification calls" with Father Bob.

The army sent a chaplain, and an officer of equal or senior rank, and, if one was available (as Barbara inarguably was), a regular officer's wife to offer what help and comfort she could.

She had received some jealous looks, a jealousy born of the fact that she was an officer's wife whose husband was still alive, who wasn't being visited by a notification team. That entirely understandable jealousy, however, sometimes changed into material jealousy. She couldn't be blamed for bearing condolences, for being the visitor instead of the visited. But she could be resented for being rich, for being part of the aristocracy within the army: those with private means, those who waited for the men to come home in a fifteen-room, servant-filled house on ten acres overlooking the Pacific instead of a tiny rented apartment, those with four-carat, emerald-cut engagement rings worth a major's annual pay and allowances.

But she always ended up wearing it. It was a symbol. It had been on the third finger of an officer's lady's left hand for half a century, and one day, Bobby's lady would wear it.

Barbara stood on one foot again and slipped her feet into brown pumps. They were too tight. Her feet always seemed to swell after she played eighteen holes.

Then she gestured toward the door and followed as Eleanor toddled out of her bedroom and down the tiled corridor to the living room, a large and airy room full of books and souvenirs and General Waterford's collection of silver cups from polo fields and equestrian competition all over the world.

The Reverend Robert T. McGrory, S. J., Colonel, Chaplain's Corps, United States Army, got to his feet when he saw her walk in the room. Some chaplains looked like what they really were, clergymen in a uniform that was actually the antithesis of their calling. "Father Bob" was tall, red-haired, ruddy-faced, and built like a football player. His uniforms were impeccably tailored, and he wore them with every bit as much flair as General Waterford wore his; more, Barbara had often thought, than Bob did.

Every time she saw Father Bob, she remembered reading that the Jesuits had acquired a great deal of power by making themselves available to the nobility in Europe, and wondered if that was what Mac had really been up to all these years.

Normally, she called him "Bob." She was Episcopal, after all; and Bob had been in her life, on and off, as long as she could remember. Calling him "Father" seemed a little forced.

But today, he had brass with him. A bird colonel she didn't recognize.

"Hello, Father," Barbara said. "Handsome as ever, I see."

"Barbara, this is Colonel Destin," Mac said, putting his arm around her shoulders, and then stooping over to pick up Eleanor.

"How do you do, Colonel?" Barbara said, giving him her hand.

"Mrs. Bellmon," the colonel replied.

"Someone senior this time?" Barbara asked.

"I'm afraid so," Colonel Destin said.

I don't like the way that sounds, Barbara thought. Father McGrory put his arm around her shoulders again.

"Mrs. Bellmon," Colonel Destin said. "I have the unfortunate duty to inform you that your husband, Lieutenant Colonel Robert F. Bellmon, is missing in action and presumed to be dead after action near Sidi-Bou-Zid, Tunisia, as of 17 February."

"Oh, *shit*," Barbara Bellmon said. Without being aware that she was doing it, she balled her hands into fists and then smashed them together.

"It's only presumed, Barbara," Father Bob said.

"Save it, *Chaplain*," Barbara said, nastily. She took Eleanor from him, and held her as she walked to the window looking down on the Pacific. The child cuddled up close and didn't struggle to be put down. Finally, Barbara set the child on her feet. Then she sat down on the windowsill and looked at the two officers.

"Who's the other one?" she asked. Destin didn't understand what she was asking.

"A warrant officer named Sanchez," Father Bob said. "We got word that he died in a prison camp in the Philippines."

"Would you like a cup of coffee, or something to eat, before we go see her?" Barbara asked.

Father McGrory took a long time to reply.

"Are you sure you want to, Barbara?" he asked, finally.

"What else should I do?" she replied. "Sit around here and have hysterics?"

Fighting back the tears, she walked across the living room and down the corridor to the front door and outside. She looked up at the flag, and went to the pole and lowered it to half-mast. Then she looked up at it. She leaned her forehead against the flagpole, and fought back the urge to weep.

"What the hell am I doing?" she asked aloud, pushing herself erect. "I'll believe he's dead when I see his casket, and not before." Then she ran the flag all the way back up the pole again.

She wept a little later that day, with Mrs. Sanchez, but that was for Mrs. Sanchez, not for Bob or herself. She didn't weep again, not that evening at dinner, looking at her mother's face, nor that night, when she went to bed, nor the next morning when she woke up early and lay in bed and told herself that the way the army worked, the odds were that Bob really had bought the farm, and the only reason they hadn't come out and said so was because they hadn't found his body. And that meant that this was the first day of her life that she could remember that Bob wasn't going to be around.

She wept ten days later when they called from the Western Union office and said they had a telegram for her, and did she want them to read it to her. She knew what it would be, and she didn't want to hear it read over the phone, so she said she would be in the village and would pick it up herself. After she wept, she got dressed and drove the old Ford convertible into the village and picked up the yellow envelope in the Western Union office and carried it out to the car to read it.

WAR DEPARTMENT
WASHINGTON DC

MRS. BARBARA BELLMON
CASA MANANA
CARMEL, CALIFORNIA

A LIST FURNISHED BY THE GERMAN AUTHORITIES VIA THE INTERNATIONAL RED CROSS STATES THAT LT COL ROBERT F. BELLMON, 0–348808, IS A PRISONER OF WAR. NO CONFIRMATION IS AVAILABLE, NOR IS ANY OTHER INFORMATION OF ANY KIND AVAILABLE AT THIS TIME. YOU WILL BE PROMPTLY NOTIFIED IN THE EVENT ANY INFORMATION DOES BECOME AVAILABLE.

INFORMATION REGARDING PRISONERS OF WAR GENERALLY IS AVAILABLE FROM THE PERSONNEL OFFICER OF ANY MILITARY CAMP POST OR STATION. FOR YOUR INFORMATION, THE CLOSEST MILITARY INSTALLATION TO YOUR HOME IS: HUNTER-LIGGETT MILITARY RESERVATION, CALIFORNIA.

YOU MIGHT ALSO WISH TO MAKE CONTACT WITH THE PENINSULA INTERSERVICE OFFICERS LADIES ASSOCIATION, PO BOX 34, CARMEL, CALIFORNIA. THIS UNOFFICIAL GROUP OFFERS ADVICE AND SOME FINANCIAL ASSISTANCE IF REQUIRED.

EDWARD F. WITZELL
MAJOR GENERAL
THE ADJUTANT GENERAL

When she learned Bob was alive, then she let it out, right there in the car, and then she went home and told her mother that it would be all over Carmel that she'd been on a crying jag, right downtown.

(Four)
Bizerte, Tunisia
9 March 1943

The POW enclosure had its prisoners under canvas, much of it American, captured during the German offensive. The enlisted men were separated from the officers, and the company grade officers were separated from the field grade.

The squad tent in which Major Robert Bellmon was housed also held a lieutenant colonel of the Quartermaster Corps, who had been captured while looking for a place to put his ration and clothing dump, and an artillery major who had been captured while serving as a forward observer.

They had been treated well, so far, and fed with captured American rations. The camp was surrounded by coiled barbed wire, called concertina, and wooden guard towers in which machine guns had been mounted. There was no possibility of escape for the moment.

A Wehrmacht captain, accompanied by a sergeant, walked up to Bellmon's tent and called his name.

"Yes?" Bellmon replied. He looked up from the GI cot on which he sat, but did not rise.

"Come with me, please, Herr Major," the captain, a middle-aged man wearing glasses, said in thickly accented English. He gestured with his hand.

Bellmon walked out of the tent. The QM light bird and the artillery major looked at him quizzically. Bellmon shook his shoulders. He had no more idea of what was going on than they did.

The German sergeant took up a position behind him, and Bellmon followed the captain across the compound and through a gate. It had been cold the night before, but now, just before noon, the sun had come out, and it was actually warmer outside than it had been in the tent.

He was led to the prison compound office, a sunlit corner of a single-story building within the outer ring of barbed wire

of the prison enclosure, and separated from the prisoner area
by a double ring of barbed wire.

"The major wishes to see you," the captain said, pushing
open a door and motioning Bellmon through it.

Bellmon was faced with a question of protocol. The code
of military courtesy provides that salutes be exchanged between
junior and senior officers, even when one is a prisoner of the
other. For the life of him, he could not recall what was expected
of him, in his prisoner status, when reporting to a German
major. In the American army, he would not have saluted another major. He decided that if it was good enough for the
U.S. Army, it was good enough for where he was now.

He marched up to the desk, and stood at attention, but did
not salute. If he were British, Bellmon thought, he could have
stamped his foot as a sort of signal that he was now present
as ordered.

The major behind the desk was an older version of the
lieutenant who had stuck the captured .45 in his face the day
he was captured. A good-looking, fair-skinned blond German,
very military in appearance, very self-confident. The German
officer looked up at Bellmon, smiled, and touched his hand to
his eyebrow in a very sloppy salute. There was nothing to do
but return it. The German smiled at him.

"Major Robert Bellmon," Bellmon said. "0–348808. 17
August 1917." Name, rank, serial number, and date of birth,
as required by the Geneva Convention.

"Yes, I know, Herr Oberstleutnant," the German major said.
"Won't you please sit down?" He indicated a folding chair.
Bellmon recognized it as American. So was the bottle of bour-
bon on the major's desk.

"I have some pleasant news for you," the German major
said. "Herr Oberstleutnant."

"My rank is major," Bellmon said.

"That's my pleasant news, Herr Oberstleutnant," the major
said, and he slid a mimeographed sheet across the desk to
Bellmon. It could easily be a forgery, but it looked perfectly
authentic. It was a paragraph extracted from a general order
of Western Task Force, and it announced the promotion of
Major Robert F. Bellmon, Armor (1st Lt, RA), to the grade
of Lieutenant Colonel, Army of the United States, effective 16

February 1943—the day before he was captured.

"And I have these for you, as well," the major said. He opened a drawer in the desk and took from it a small sheet of cardboard, to which two silver oak leaves were pinned. The name of the manufacturer was printed on the face of the card. The insignia were American.

"Thank you," Bellmon said. "May I have this as well?" he asked, indicating the promotion orders.

"Certainly," the major said. As Bellmon folded them up and put them in the breast pocket of his newly issued olive-drab shirt, the major poured whiskey into two glasses. He handed one to Bellmon. Another problem of protocol, Bellmon thought. Is accepting a glass of captured whiskey from an enemy who has just presented me with a light bird's leaf and the orders to go with it considered *trafficking with the enemy?*

"I don't normally drink at this hour," Bellmon said.

"A promotion is a special occasion," the German said. "No matter what the hour or the circumstances."

Bellmon picked up the glass and drank from it.

"Congratulations, Herr Oberstleutnant," the major said, raising his glass.

"Danke schön, Herr Major," Bellmon said. His German was fluent.

"You will be given an extra POW postcard," the major said. "I've sent for one. I'm sure General Waterford will be pleased to learn that you know of your promotion."

"Bellmon," Bellmon said. "Lieutenant Colonel. 0–348808. 17 August 1917." He said it with a smile, but it reminded the major that he was not going to discuss anything that could possibly be of use to the enemy.

"While this is technically an interrogation, Herr Oberstleutnant," the major said, tolerantly, "I really am not trying to cleverly get you to reveal military secrets."

"I'm sure you're not," Bellmon said, pleasantly sarcastic.

"No, I'm serious," the major said. "We know most of the things about you that we try to find out. You're an academy graduate, seventeenth in your class, of 1939. Your father was Major General Bellmon. You are married to Brigadier General Peterson K. Waterford's daughter Barbara."

Bellmon just looked at him and smiled. The major took a

copy of the U.S. Army Registry and laid it on the table. Bellmon smiled wider.

"And we know where General Waterford is," the major said.

"I'm sure you do." Bellmon suddenly thought that if he was seeking information, he would have said where General Waterford was to get confirmation, or simply to check his reaction.

"And I really think, Herr Oberstleutnant," the major went on. "That I know more of the present order of battle than you do. You were captured during the fluid phase of the battle, and couldn't possibly know how things stand now."

"Even if I were not bound by regulation and the Geneva Convention," Bellmon said, "and could talk freely, I rather doubt there is anything of value I could tell you."

"Probably not," the major said. "Front-line soldiers either know very little of interest to their interrogators, or have entirely the wrong idea of what's really going on."

What he's trying to do, Bellmon decided, is lull me into making some kind of slip. But what he says is true. I don't know any more about the order of battle of the II U.S. Corps than a cook in a rifle company.

"But just between us, Colonel," the major went on. "What do you think of we Germans, now that we have met on the field of battle?"

Bellmon didn't reply.

"Certainly someone who speaks German as well as you do can't believe we're savages?"

Damn it, why did I speak German.

"Not all of you, certainly," he said, in English.

"Some of us, you will doubtless be surprised to learn, are civilized to the point where we scrupulously obey the Geneva Convention," the major said. "And adhere rigidly to the standard of conduct expected of officers."

"I'm very glad to hear that," Bellmon said.

"Rank has its privileges," the major said, "even in confinement. You will be flown to Italy, and possibly all the way to Germany. Majors and below are sent by ship."

"I see," Bellmon said, with a sinking feeling in his stomach. He had had a desperate hope that the Americans would counterattack, and that he would be freed.

"We make a real effort to insure that once senior professional officers are out of the war, they stay out of the war," the major said. "You can conscript soldiers. Staff officers and battalion commanders cannot be trained in six months."

"I have to agree with your reasoning," Bellmon said.

A sergeant knocked, was told to enter, and laid a POW postcard on the major's desk. The major took a fountain pen from his tunic and handed it to Bellmon. There was space for name, rank, serial number, and a twenty-word message, one blank line provided for each word.

Bellmon filled it in, addressed it to Barbara Bellmon in Carmel, California, had a moment's painful mental image of the house there, and then wrote his message: "Alive, well, uninjured. Kiss the children. I love you. Bob."

He wondered when he would see them again. He capped the fountain pen and handed it and the card to the major.

"Thank you," he said.

"My pleasure, Herr Oberstleutnant," the major said. He put out his hand. "Good luck, and may we meet again under different circumstances."

Bellmon took his hand. He told himself that if the circumstances were reversed, he hoped that he would behave as the major had behaved toward him: correct, and compassionate. He realized he had been dismissed. Thirty minutes later, he realized that he had given the enemy information. He had confirmed that he was indeed Porky Waterford's son-in-law. He should not have gone even that far. He didn't know how they could use that information, how valuable it was to them, but he knew he should not have handed it to them on a platter the way he had.

(Five)
Friedberg, Hesse
12 April 1943

The bunker had been excavated under the castle at Friedberg, which stands at the crest of the ring of low mountains ringing the resort of Bad Nauheim, thirty-five miles north of Frankfurt am Main, in Hesse. The excavation had been conducted with the secrecy and the disregard of costs associated with anything that had Adolph Hitler's personal attention.

The bunker itself was beneath at least twenty feet of granite, and where there had been an insufficient layer of granite, reinforced concrete had been poured to provide the required protection. Siemens had installed an enormous communications switchboard, which provided nearly instantaneous telephone, radio-telephone, and teletype communication with Berlin and the various major commands in the East, West, the Balkans, and North Africa.

A battalion of the Leibstandarte Adolph Hitler, augmented by a reserve regiment of Pomeranian infantry and a regiment of Luftwaffe antiaircraft artillery, provided security.

Camouflage netting, placed twenty feet off the ground in the thick groves of pine which surrounded Schloss Friedberg, concealed the fleet of cars and trucks necessary to support a major headquarters. It was changed to reflect the coloring of the seasons. The Führer's train, when he was present, was protected from either view or assault by a concrete revetment, long enough to contain both his train and one other.

The bunker itself was an underground office building, four stories deep; access was by stairs for the workers and a private elevator for the senior officers. The Führer today was in Rastenburg, in East Prussia, so there was an acrid cloud of cigarette smoke throughout the bunker. When the Führer was in the bunker, smoking was forbidden.

The lieutenant colonel of the Feldgendarmerie, a portly, balding middle-aged officer, delivered his report to the generalmajor with assurance. He had been a policeman all his life, and thus trained to present facts—separate from conclusions and theory—to his superiors.

The Generalmajor, who was assistant to the chief of the Politico-military Affairs Division, asked several questions, all intelligent ones, and carefully examined the physical evidence which the Oberstleutnant of the Feldgendarmerie had brought in two bulging briefcases from Smolensk.

There were buttons from Polish Army uniforms; regimental crests; insignia of rank; identification papers; labels from uniforms bearing addresses of tailors in Warsaw; and a half-inch-thick sheath of photographs of bodies, open graves, and close-ups of entrance and exit wounds in skulls.

"There is no question in your mind, I gather, Herr Oberstleutnant, of what happened here?"

"There is no question at all."

The unspoken question was whether the SS could possibly have been involved. Both of them knew that the SS was entirely capable of an atrocity like this one. The unspoken question continued unspoken.

"If you will be good enough to wait for me, Herr Oberstleutnant," the Generalmajor said, "Perhaps we can arrange to route you via Dresden on your way back."

"I am at the Herr Generalmajor's pleasure," the portly policeman in uniform said.

The Generalmajor walked out of his concrete office, down a flight of stairs, and presented himself to a Generaloberst in his slightly larger office.

"I have the full report, Herr General," he said. "Together with some insignia taken from the bodies—"

The colonel Generaloberst stopped him, with a wave of his hand, from opening his briefcase.

"Has intelligence come up with the name of someone who can handle this matter?"

"Von Greiffenberg," the Generalmajor said. "For the moment, he's the only one readily available. He's on convalescent leave."

"And is he physically able to undertake the journey?"

"Yes, sir."

"His wife is a member of the Russian nobility," the colonel general said. "It will be suggested that he would believe the communists to be capable of anything."

"He was at Samur with General Waterford. It is considered important that Lieutenant Colonel Bellmon voluntarily inspect the site."

The Generaloberst shrugged. "What do you need from me?" he asked.

"Travel documents, and authority to take the American from the stalag."

"And if he won't give his parole?" the colonel general asked. But even as he asked it, he pushed a button which summoned a badly scarred Oberstleutnant, who stood at the door at attention. "The general will tell you what he must have," the Generaloberst said. "See that he has it, please."

He dropped his eyes to the documents on his desk, and then raised them.

"Let me know what happens, will you?" he asked, politely.

The Generalmajor clicked his heels, walked out of the office, and picked up the telephone on the Oberstleutnant's desk.

"Would you get me, on this number, Colonel von Greiffenberg at his home in Marburg, please?" he said, and then hung up and told the Oberstleutnant what he was going to need in the way of transportation, money, documentation, and supplies.

While the necessary arrangements were being made, the telephone rang. The operator reported that the Colonel Graf von Greiffenberg was not available, but that he had Frau Grafin on the line.

"My dear Frederika," the Generalmajor said, in Russian, which caused the badly scarred Oberstleutnant to raise his eyebrows. "Would you be so good as to tell the Graf that I would be very grateful to be received by him at half past two?"

The Mercedes was crowded. There were four flat-sided cans of gasoline in the trunk, filling it, and two more on the floorboard in the back seat. The fumes filled the car, whose canvas roof was up, and this made smoking impossible. There was salami and a half dozen tins of butter, captured from the English, and four cartons of American cigarettes. The Generalmajor's aide-de-camp rode in the back with the groceries under his feet and the cigarettes, wrapped in gray paper, on his lap. The Generalmajor rode in front beside the driver.

They drove north from Freidberg on the road through Bad Nauheim which took them past the rear of the Kurhotels that faced the large municipal park. In the old days, a *Kur* had meant bathing in the waters of Bad Nauheim and taking a salt-free diet. Now the *Kur* was for convalescent wounded. The roofs of the Kurhotels, small Victorian-era structures, were now painted with the Red Cross, and the streets and the park were full of soldiers, some ambulatory patients, some pushed in wheelchairs.

They entered upon the autobahn at Bad Nauheim, and drove fifteen miles until they turned off onto another country road—

sometimes cobblestone, sometimes macadam. This took them through Giessen. From Giessen, they followed the Lahn River to Marburg an der Lahn and drove to the center of town.

Marburg, one of the ancient university towns, was built up around the old castle which rose from the top of the rocky upcropping in the center of town. They were stopped by a Feldgendarmerie roadblock, and for a moment the General-major wondered if he should have taken the Feldgendarmerie Oberstleutnant with him. Embarrassing questions could be asked about the petrol and the food. He immediately decided he had made the right decision. The less the Feldgendarmerie knew about what he was doing with the information they had provided, the better. The Feldgendarmerie was entirely too cozy with the SS and the Gestapo. Tomorrow or the next day he would turn over what he had found to the Sicherheitsdienst, as a matter probably falling under their responsibility; but he would not let them know what the army was doing on its own about the situation.

They drove past Schloss Greiffenberg, which was several hundred meters off the road. Its steep roofs were also painted with the Red Cross. The Schloss was serving as a neuropsychiatric rehabilitation center.

Three miles beyond the Schloss, they turned off the highway onto a fairly wide dirt road that cut through a pine forest. A mile down the road they came to a cottage. There was a bicycle chained to a steel fence in the stone wall around the cottage, and the tiny garage next to it was open, revealing a tiny two-seater Fiat inside.

"This is the place," the Generalmajor said, when it seemed the driver was about to pass it up. The driver braked the car sharply.

"Help the lieutenant with the packages, and then put the gasoline out of sight in the garage," he said. "Hoarding" of gasoline was a serious offense, even for a man like Greiffenberg.

"Jawohl, Herr Generalmajor."

Colonel Graf von Greiffenberg came out from the cottage. He was a tall gaunt man with wavy silver hair, who wore a shabby tweed jacket, plus fours from some prewar golf-course locker, and a faded cotton plaid shirt.

"The Generalmajor will forgive me," he said. "I was walking in the woods, and just this moment got home." Peter-Paul von Greiffenberg was not at all pleased with the Generalmajor's visit. He believed that it had nothing whatever to do with a discussion of any future command. He suspected that it had something to do with airing dirty linen, and he was not at all interested in that.

"I believe, Colonel," the Generalmajor said, "that convalescent officers are encouraged to play golf and other sports, which will hasten their return to full physical capacity."

"I have been poaching," the Graf said, "not golfing." The remark was a hair's breadth away from insolence.

"Any luck?" the Generalmajor asked with a smile.

"Yesterday and today," the Graf said, wondering what it was that had made him try to provoke a lifelong friend. Possibly, he thought, because he finds me dressed like a peasant and living in a forester's cottage.

"A boar yesterday," von Greiffenberg said, now smiling. "For our lunch today. And a rehbuck today. For tomorrow." The Graf's eyes fell on the sergeant, who was busy taking fuel cans from the trunk. "The Generalmajor is more than kind. I especially appreciate the petrol."

"I have no idea what you're talking about, Colonel," the Generalmajor said. "Certainly you are aware of the regulations prohibiting the diversion of petrol to nonmilitary channels."

A tall woman and a thin girl of about fifteen were now in the doorway of the cottage. The woman had been born a duchess in what was once Petrograd. She had married a count. She carried herself like an aristocrat, the Generalmajor decided, but no one would have mistaken her for a duchess. Her clothing was worn and faded, and she wore neither makeup nor jewelry except for a thin wedding band. The girl, who curtsied as the Generalmajor approached, looked more like a forester's daughter than the product of the union of two ancient and noble families.

"You are soon going to be quite as lovely as your mother," the Generalmajor said. He bowed and kissed the woman's hand. "Elizabeth, you are as lovely as ever."

"Welcome, Herr Generalmajor, to our forester's cabin," the woman said. She spoke in Russian. "Ilse and I have gardening. Carrots and cabbage. No roses."

"Better times will come," the Generalmajor said. "We must believe that, mustn't we?"

"As we devoutly believe in the final victory," she said, with exquisite sarcasm. The Generalmajor thought that Greiffenberg was wise to keep his wife here in the country. She was unable to conceal that she held the Nazis in nearly as much scorn as she held the communists of her homeland.

"I must, I'm afraid, Frederika, pass up the great pleasure of your company at lunch," the Generalmajor said. "I must speak privately with Peter-Paul."

"Have you a command for him?" Frederika, Grafin von Greiffenberg asked.

"Not quite yet," the Generalmajor said. "The hospital has not seen fit to declare him fit for field service. But I need him to do an errand for me."

"Ilse," the Grafin said to the young girl. "Would you please remove two place settings from the table? And then you and I will take a walk in the woods."

"I am grateful for your understanding," the Generalmajor said.

"I am grateful that you are not sending my husband back to Russia," the Grafin replied, somewhat icily. "Perhaps there will be time for a glass of wine together?"

"Of course," the Generalmajor said.

When the wine had been drunk, and the loin of roast boar put onto the table, and the Grafin and her daughter had left, the Generalmajor decided that he would eat his lunch in peace before opening the briefcase and talking business. What was in the briefcase would ruin anyone's lunch.

(Six)
Near Szczecin (Stettin) Poland
15 April 1943

There were still patches of unmelted snow here and there on the ground, and it was cold in the rear seat of the Feisler Storche, but the sun was shining brightly, and it was evident that spring would soon bring green to the brown land.

Colonel Graf von Greiffenberg was in pain. His shattered knee hurt from the vibration of the four-hour flight in the small airplane. They had refueled in Leipzig after taking off from the

Luftwaffe's fighter plane airstrip in Marburg an der Lahn. Because he had been badly frostbitten in Russia, his toes, fingers, ears, and nose ached—in spite of his woolen socks and gloves and the woolen muffler wrapped around his head. From time to time shivers of pain swept through his body as if his fingers were broken.

He had waited all the previous day for the two Storches to show up. There had been some problem getting two of them at once. When they did finally shown up in Marburg just before dark, he had decided to wait until the following morning to leave. It was a question of his getting where he was going without problems. It would have been foolhardy to make the flight at night, although the pilots, two boys who looked as if they should still be in a Gymnasium someplace, were disappointed at his decision.

Their orders, marked SECRET, directed them to pick up the colonel in two airplanes, and fly him and anyone else he so designated anywhere he desired within lands controlled by the German state. Since they thought that what they were up to was quite different from the facts, they were eager to get at it.

They had taken off from the fighter base at Marburg, which was a one runway affair, built right down the center of what once had been a 160 hectare cornfield. This had been von Greiffenberg land, "rented" to the Luftwaffe for "the duration." Their destination in northern Poland was another fighter strip laid down on what, too, had once been a field owned by a landed member of the aristocracy.

As they approached the field, the colonel saw the stalag next to it. It contained a barracks, and to judge by the line of one-story stables off to one side, a cavalry barracks. There didn't seem to be an artillery park, so it must have been a cavalry barracks. It had once housed, perhaps, some of the Poles who had been sent out to challenge Panzerkampfwagen IIs and IIIs with sabers and glistening lances.

It was now a prisoner-of-war camp, Stalag XVII-B, surrounded by barbed wire, guardhouses, and probably, von Greiffenberg thought, a minefield. They had captured vast quantities of Russian and English mines early in the war, and there had been a period of madness when any flat surface which even remotely could pose a threat to the security of the German Army had been mined.

The pilot of the Storche was unable to establish radio contact with the field, so they flew over it once, to let them know they had arrived, and then landed. A bored junior Luftwaffe officer swaggered out to the Storche, then saw the colonel's insignia on von Greiffenberg's greatcoat, and snapped to attention.

The colonel, once a car had been arranged for him, gave the senior of the two boy pilots their ultimate destination and told him to prepare the most careful possible flight plan—with alternate landing fields and refueling sites. The second passenger must not be endangered in any way, von Greiffenberg told him.

He showed the major commanding the fighter strip enough of his orders to impress him with the fact that he was traveling with the highest priority under the authority of the Oberkommando of the Wehrmacht. And then he went out to the POW compound, taking a strange pleasure in seeing that he was right. It had been a cavalry barracks.

God, what a bloody shame, those horses! Some of the finest in Europe! Slaughtered senselessly.

The stalag commander was an elderly lieutenant colonel of infantry; his uniform carried wound stripes from World War I. A decent chap, von Greiffenberg decided on the spot, given this duty because he was too old for any other.

"How may I be of service to the Herr Oberst Graf?"

Von Greiffenberg produced his orders.

"I wish to confer with Lieutenant Colonel Robert Bellmon," von Greiffenberg announced. "I may take him off your hands for a few days."

That roused the commandant's curiosity, but he was a soldier of the old school. He would ask no questions. If he was to have an explanation beyond the official orders, it would be given to him.

"I'll send for him. And may I offer the Herr Oberst Graf a brandy and something to eat while he is waiting?"

"Yes, please," von Greiffenberg said. "And bring enough to serve Colonel Bellmon, too, if you would be so kind."

While he was waiting, von Greiffenberg left the food untouched—a plate of cold cuts, bread, and what looked like real butter; but he helped himself twice to the French brandy, wondering idly where the commandant had gotten it. The early days of the war, when there had been a good deal of French wine and perfume available to the services, were long over.

Lieutenant Colonel Robert Bellmon marched in, wearing a faded tanker's jacket and woolen olive-drab pants. He stopped before the desk and saluted.

"Lieutenant Colonel Bellmon reporting to the Herr Oberst as directed, sir." His German was fluent. He was a fine-looking officer, von Greiffenberg thought.

"I'm comfortable in English, Colonel," Colonel Graf von Greiffenberg said. "But please don't take that as a reflection upon your German. It's quite good."

"I have been working on it rather hard, Herr Oberst," Bellmon continued in German. "There isn't much else to do here."

"I daresay not," Von Greiffenberg said, in English. He unfastened the lower right-hand pocket of his tunic and took from it an envelope and handed it to Bellmon without explanation.

Bellmon opened the small envelope and took a picture from it. It was of the Colonel Graf von Greiffenberg as a young cavalry officer. He held a child, a girl most likely, of about eighteen months in his arms, beaming down at her with pure delight.

Bellmon looked at it, then at von Greiffenberg, and then started to hand it back.

"You don't recognize the lady, Colonel Bellmon?" von Greiffenberg asked. "I rather hoped you would."

Bellmon looked at the picture again without recognition, and shook his head. "Sorry," he said. "Never saw her before."

"You are married to the lady, Colonel," von Greiffenberg said. "That is Barbara Dianne Waterford Bellmon at age sixteen months."

Bellmon looked again. Now there was no question about it. The baby had Barbara's eyes. He looked at von Greiffenberg for an explanation.

"It was taken at Samur, the French cavalry school," von Greiffenberg said, "by, I recall, your mother-in-law. Your father-in-law was at the time—as he did frequently—cooking beefsteaks over an open fire. The usual result was meat charred on the outside, raw inside, and generally inedible. This never discouraged him in the least."

Bellmon had to smile, although in the back of his mind

there was a feeling that he had best be very careful dealing with this man.

"I am sorry, Colonel," Bellmon said. "But I don't recall my father-in-law ever mentioning your name."

"We last exchanged Christmas greetings in 1940," the colonel said. "After that, obviously, it was awkward."

"What is it you want of me, Colonel?" Bellmon asked.

"I had hoped to find that you were the sort of officer who does not hate his enemy," von Greiffenberg said. "Who is aware that there are some events which transcend the war immediately at hand. And I hoped that you would believe that despite our present situation, I regard Porky Waterford as a dear friend and colleague, and I dare to presume he feels the same way about me."

"I regret the war, of course," Bellmon said. "But I must in honesty tell you that I believe the government which you serve is morally reprehensible."

Von Greiffenberg neither reacted to that nor seemed even to hear it.

"Colonel, it has come to the attention of the High Command that the Soviets, in the Katyn Forest, near Smolensk, executed approximately five thousand Polish officers and cadets, who were their prisoners, and buried them in a mass, unmarked grave."

Bellmon didn't reply. It sounded like something from a propaganda movie. But Colonel von Greiffenberg was real. And unless he had lost all powers of judgment, he knew von Greiffenberg was dead earnest, not at all the sort of man who would be capable of invoking an old friendship for some propaganda gimmick. Bellmon looked at von Greiffenberg and waited for him to continue.

The colonel opened his briefcases and placed thirty or more large photographs on the desk and then, next to them, he laid out corroded and rotting insignia, identification papers, tailor's labels, the evidence that had been turned over to him in the forester's cottage outside Marburg.

"Identification of the remains is underway," von Greiffenberg said. "So far we have positively identified the remains of two general officers, sixty-one colonels, large numbers of other grades, and more than 150 officer cadets. Each was shot in the back of the head with a .32 caliber pistol. And each had his hands bound behind him at the time."

"Forgive me, Colonel," Bellmon said, trying very hard to keep his voice under control, "but how do I know this atrocity took place under the Russians?"

"At the site, at this moment, are fourteen forensic scientists, all from neutral countries. They are prepared to give their professional judgment as to how long the prisoners have been dead. Even given the widest latitude so far as the date of death is concerned, there is absolutely no possibility that German forces could have been involved. During the time of the atrocity, Soviet forces, and Soviet forces alone, held the area."

"Doubtless, you will make these facts known, via the International Red Cross, and other agencies."

"And doubtless, our accusations will be rejected as anti-Soviet propaganda," von Greiffenberg said.

"And that's where I come in?" Bellmon asked.

"I rather doubt that even you, Colonel Bellmon, would be believed outside the military establishment," von Greiffenberg said. "Our thinking is this. The honor of the German officer corps is involved. We want a member of the American officer corps, the son of a general, the son-in-law of a general, a man likely himself to become a general officer, to see this outrage with his own eyes. To spare him, if you like, from having to decide from secondhand information whether or not this is anti-Soviet propaganda."

"To what end?" Bellmon asked.

"That should be obvious," von Greiffenberg said. "What I would like from you, Colonel, what I beg of you, is your parole for whatever time it takes us to fly to Katyn, which is near Smolensk. There you will confer with the neutral physicians and scientists on the scene and then return here."

"If you're going to win the war, what difference does it make?" Bellmon asked.

Von Greiffenberg paused a long moment before replying.

"When we win the war, Colonel, I shall take great pleasure in bringing the barbarians who did this terrible thing to justice."

"But there is the possibility, which you must consider by now, that the war is lost," Bellmon said. "Is that it?"

"As a loyal officer, of course, I believe in the final victory," von Greiffenberg said.

"You understand, of course," Bellmon said, "that I could not make any statements of any kind so long as I'm a prisoner."

"Naturally not," von Greiffenberg said. "However, it is our routine practice to exchange the severely wounded and the dying, and routine practice to assign several officer prisoners to accompany the wounded and dying."

"If I go along, you're offering to have me exchanged?" He wondered if he was being bribed.

"It would be in our interests to do so," von Greiffenberg said. "And in yours. Should you become convinced this was a Soviet atrocity, as I believe you will by the evidence, you will then be in great danger should the fortunes of war see you come into Soviet hands."

"I'm sure you have considered the possibility that I would accept the offer to be exchanged, and then accuse your side," Bellmon said.

"The evidence is irrefutable," von Greiffenberg said. "And furthermore, Colonel Bellmon, I believe you to be an officer and a gentleman."

I am being soft-soaped, Bellmon thought. But then, he thought, what possible harm could it do?

"Very well," Bellmon said. "I will give you my parole. When do we leave?"

"Immediately."

(Seven)
Stalag XVII-B, Stettin
11 October 1944

There had been Christmas packages from the Red Cross. By some fluke in the distribution system, they had arrived in Stettin, in northwest Poland, a week after they had come into German hands in Sweden. The commandant had agreed to issue them immediately. The important thing was that for a few days there would be powdered coffee (*real* coffee) and chocolate and gloves and handkerchiefs and paperback copies of Ernest Hemingway novels. There was no sense in putting the packages into a warehouse for issue on Christmas Day. Christmas Day here would be 25 December 1944, no different at all from 24 December and 26 December, just one more day in a former cavalry barracks in northwest Poland.

Bellmon had made the decision that he would drink his powdered coffee full strength, black. He would not drink it all at once, but save it for when he really wanted a cup of coffee, and then have a real cup of coffee, strong and black. He would not try to stretch it, to make it last longer. He would have as many cups of strong coffee as there were in the tin, whenever he wanted one, and then he would do without.

He had never felt quite so alone, quite so fearful for his sanity.

Eighteen months had passed since his trip to the Katyn forest. During that time there had been thirty-one letters from Barbara, single sheets of paper which folded to make a self-contained envelope. Some of these had arrived out of sequence, and none had arrived on any sort of predictable schedule. He had once gone five months without any letters at all.

He kept the letters in a Dutch Masters cigar box on the table beside his bed. The cigars had come without explanation six months before, half a box for each officer. Before the cigars had come, he had kept Barbara's letters wrapped up in a sweater.

Bellmon was executive officer of the prisoner staff. The senior prisoner was an infantry full colonel who had never served in the infantry. He was a professor of art history at the University of Wisconsin who had been commissioned as a military government officer, and who had been captured in Italy. He was not a soldier, although he wanted to behave like one, and he vacillated between relief that he had a professional soldier on whom to rely for decisions, and resentment toward Bellmon, based on the fact that Bellmon's competence pointed out his own incompetence.

Bellmon had not told the colonel about Katyn, and he had not told him about the package he kept hidden within the thin cotton mattress on his bed. The package, according to a letter from Colonel Count Peter-Paul von Greiffenberg, contained twenty-four eight-by-ten-inch photographs of the horrors of Katyn. Others showed Bellmon at the site with the neutral forensic experts. It also contained identification papers, letters, and insignia taken from the corpses. It was sealed with a wax seal of the Oberkommando of the Wehrmacht, and beneath a sheet of acetate was a letter on OKW stationery, signed by Generaloberst Hasso von Manteuffel, stating that the package was in the possession of Lieutenant Colonel Robert Bellmon, United States Army, by direction of the OKW, and that it was neither to be examined, nor taken from him, by any member of the German military or security forces for any reason. The letter bore the seals of both the OKW and the SS. Bellmon could not read the signature of the SS official.

He was clearly being used by the Germans. And he had been tempted, more than once, to throw the package into the small cast-iron stove, to remove any suggestion at all that he was offering aid and comfort to the enemy.

But there was no question in his mind that the Soviet secret police, with the full support of the Red Army, had in fact taken 5,000 captured Polish officers—among them at least 250 cadets, some of whom were no older than fourteen—tied their hands behind their back, forced them to lie in open trenches, and then shot each of them in the back of the neck with a small caliber pistol.

There was no question in his mind, either, after seeing this atrocity with his own eyes, that at Katyn he had become one with Colonel von Greiffenberg and other Germans like him, and that now the Russian ally had become his enemy. Sure, war by its very nature was obscene, and there were atrocities on battlefields. He'd heard about those all his life, and he'd seen some in North Africa. Indeed, he had expected to be shot, instead of taken prisoner, when they got his tank.

But that was the battlefield. What the Russians had done was barbaric beyond understanding. They had decided to subdue the Poles for the future by wiping out their leaders, young and old, even their chaplains. Bellmon had identified with the dead Poles. Many of them wore cavalry boots. They were cavalry officers, captured probably as he had been, without real fault of their own. Because they had been taught to expect it, they would have expected the treatment required by the Geneva Convention. Instead, they had been slaughtered like cattle.

At first, he had told himself that when he was exchanged, as Colonel von Greiffenberg said he would be, he would wait thirty days to regain control of his emotions and of his ability to think clearly and objectively, before he turned the package over to the proper authorities.

But then it had become apparent that he was not to be exchanged. He didn't understand why, and there were fifty possibilities. But he had come to accept that he was not going to be exchanged, that there would not be thirty days' liberation leave to spend with Barbara in Carmel, at least not until the war was over. He had no idea what had kept him from being exchanged as von Greiffenberg had promised; but he sensed, somehow, that it had nothing to do with the German officer.

As executive officer of the prisoner staff he was ex-officio chairman of the escape committee. The escape committee was brave, enthusiastic, imaginative, and in Bellmon's professional judgment, incredibly stupid. There was no way that they could get out of Poland, much less out of German-occupied Europe. There was no underground here who could help them, as there was supposed to be in France. That was the primary reason the Stalag had been established in Poland. The Germans were not fools.

Of course, he questioned that judgment, too, wondering if he had lost his courage, or if he was subconsciously identifying with the German enemy because of what he had seen at Katyn, because von Greiffenberg had gone to the cavalry school at Samur with Porky Waterford and cradled Barbara in his arms.

He had imagined he'd get some sort of pressure from the Germans, at least a subtle pointing out that the Germans and the Americans were the same kind of people, functioning under a Christian ethic; that it was really absurd that they should be fighting each other, rather than the common, godless Soviet enemy; that Hitler, had after all, gone out of his way not to get into a war with the Americans.

But there had been nothing at all like that. The only propaganda to which he had been subjected was the magazines and newspapers in the Stalag library. And that was to be expected. There was nothing more reprehensible about providing captured American officers copies of the German Army magazine *Signal* than there was in providing captured German officers copies of *Yank*.

• • •

In September, the British and French officers who had been in the stalag with them had been transferred elsewhere. Stalag XVII-B was now entirely American.

That had posed certain administrative and logistic problems. Without Bellmon having paid much attention to it, captured British and French enlisted men had been the logistic backbone of the stalag. They were the cooks, the orderlies, the latrine cleaners, the laundry workers, the bedmakers.

When the British and French officers left, so did their enlisted men, and that left the kitchen and the laundry without people to operate them. There was a cook, a phlegmatic Bavarian, and a laundry supervisor, but no labor force.

Bellmon had crossed with the senior prisoner over that.

"What we'll have to do," the senior prisoner said, "is simply take turns. On a roster. Make it fair."

Bellmon was furious but kept his temper. If the colonel did not realize that the ' were not boy scouts out roughing it in the woods, he would have to teach him.

"We are officers," Bellmon said. "In many cases field-grade officers. We will not work in laundries. Commissioned officers of the United States will not be kitchen helpers. Commissioned officers will not clean latrines."

"Oh, for God's sake, Bob, we're prisoners."

"We're officers," Bellmon said. "You, Colonel, as a reservist, as much as me."

"Since you bring that up, Bob," the colonel said, without much conviction, "I *am* the senior officer. I could order you to do what has to be done."

"And I would obey your order. And the day we get out of here, I would bring you up on charges of conduct unbecoming an officer and a gentleman," Bellmon said.

"Who the hell would ever know if your precious officer's dignity was relaxed?" the senior prisoner demanded. When he said that, Bellmon had sensed he had won. The colonel was more afraid of him than of the Germans.

"The enemy," Bellmon said, gently. "That's the point, Colonel."

The commandant said that he had requested a contingent of enlisted prisoners to take over the housekeeping duties, but he had no idea when, or even if, they would be sent.

No officer details were sent to the kitchen, and none to the laundry. Two German soldiers were sent to the kitchen to help the cook. Officers carried their mess plates to the mess, ate, washed their plates and cutlery, and left with them. Officers washed their own underwear, and if they wanted clean outer garments, washed and pressed them themselves.

Bellmon spent long hours with a cast-iron clothes press, keeping his trousers, shirts, and tunic neat. He tested the principle of inspiring by example. It had a thirty percent effectiveness factor, he found. One officer in three followed his example and tried to look as much like an officer as he could. Two out of three let themselves go.

Bellmon stopped talking to the unpressed and unshaven, or even acknowledging them with a nod of his head. When they sought him out, mostly for his skill as an interpreter, or for his opinion on the legality of a move they planned in connection with an escape attempt, he refused to deal with them.

"Can I have a moment of your time, Colonel?"

"You need a shave, Lieutenant. And your uniform is foul."

They came back, shaven, in slightly more presentable uniforms. He told them what they wanted to know. He shamed the senior prisoner, who not only resumed shaving daily, but began a British-style mustache.

The slovenly percentage dropped to fifty percent and then below. Some of the shaven and self-laundered began to mock him with crisp salutes whenever they met him. He returned the salutes as crisply, with motions right off the parade ground at the Point. The mockery in the salutes gave way to casual touching of the hand to the eyebrow. But they were still salutes. Not to everybody from everybody, but from all the company grade to all the field grade, and from everybody to the senior prisoner and Bellmon.

He was in command. What good it would do, specifically, he didn't know. But he believed, devoutly, that the prisoner complement of Stalag XVII-B was a military formation, and a military formation must have discipline. Without discipline, a body of men becomes rabble. Rabble dies, either on the battlefield or in a POW camp.

Six weeks after the French and British left, a convoy of canvas-topped Hanomag trucks came through the heavy wooden gates of the compound and discharged four truckloads of American enlisted prisoners, twenty-two to a truck.

Bellmon heard the sound of the trucks and looked out his window and watched the troops get off. Some showed signs of long imprisonment (how he could tell, he didn't know, but he knew), and others had apparently only recently been captured. They were all dispirited. They sat in groups immediately to the side of the trucks that had brought them, and waited for whatever was going to happen to them. Many of them looked as if they really didn't care.

Bellmon buttoned his tunic, straightened his tie in the mirror he had carefully made by polishing a sheet of steel with ashes, and went out into the courtyard.

At first none of the prisoners reacted to his presence beyond looking at him expectantly. Bellmon put his hands on his hips and let his eyes fall on them, one at a time, looking carefully and without expression. He had looked at perhaps thirty of the prisoners that way when one of them suddenly got to his feet and walked over to him.

"Sergeant MacMillan, sir," he said.

MacMillan wore the stripes of a technical sergeant sewn to the gabardine tunic issued to paratroops. Bellmon could see where the insignia of the 82nd Airborne had been cut from it. The Germans regarded that insignia as a special souvenir, much as Americans were delighted to get their hands on the death's-head insignia of the SS.

MacMillan was a young man, stocky and muscular, a typical parachutist. Irish, Bellmon thought. Or maybe Scotch. But he sensed something about this noncom. Somehow he knew that this sergeant was a regular.

"Is that the way you were taught to report to an officer, Sergeant?" Bellmon asked, quietly. Sergeant MacMillan looked at him for a moment, then popped to attention. He threw his hand to his forehead, held it.

"Technical Sergeant MacMillan reports to the colonel with party of eighty-seven, sir," he said.

Bellmon returned the salute.

"Fall the men in, Sergeant," he said.

Macmillan did a precise about-face movement.

"All right," he bellowed. "Fall in!"

There was some stirring, and one or two men got to their feet, but there was no movement toward Sergeant MacMillan, no suggestion that they intended to obey this order.

MacMillan didn't move for a full minute. Then, very deliberately, he walked to the man sitting nearest to him on the ground. He bent over him, picked him up by his shirt front, and punched him in the mouth. The soldier, a buck sergeant, fell on his rear end and put his hand to his bleeding mouth.

None of the others moved at all, but one man spit.

"Get up," T/Sgt MacMillan said, softly, and pointed with his left hand, finger extended, to the spot where he wanted the man to stand. The buck sergeant backed away from MacMillan like a crab, but then got to his feet and walked to where MacMillan had indicated, and more or less came to attention.

"Anybody else?" MacMillan asked, looking at the faces of the others. No one moved or said a word. "Fall in on him," MacMillan said. "Three ranks."

Slowly, resentfully, the others formed on him. When they were all in place, standing at a position that charitably could be called attention, MacMillan did another snappy about-face and saluted again.

"Sir," he said, "the detachment is formed."

"Very good, Sergeant," Bellmon ordered. "Prepare the detachment for inspection."

MacMillan did another about-face movement, and gave the commands. "Dress, right, *dress!* Open ranks, *march!*"

Bellmon marched to the left-hand corner of the formation. MacMillan marched to join him. Bellmon went down the ranks, pausing to look at each man, giving each man a chance to look at him. Then he marched out in front again.

"Stand at ease," he ordered. "My name is Bellmon. I am the executive officer. The first thing we are going to do is feed you, show you where you will be quartered, and see that you have a shower. We have to fend for ourselves here. Sergeant MacMillan will appoint mess hall, shower point, and delousing details of six men under a noncom each." He looked at MacMillan, who was standing at parade rest in front of the formation. "First Sergeant," Bellmon called. "Front and center."

MacMillan walked up and saluted still again. Bellmon told

him where the kitchen and the shower were.

"When you get things running, come to my quarters," he said.

MacMillan nodded.

Bellmon raised his voice.

"First Sergeant, take the detachment," he said, and then did an about-face and marched back to his barracks building.

A group of officers had been watching from inside.

"Colonel, can I ask a question?" one of the captains said. Bellmon nodded. "What would you have done if they had just kept on sitting there?"

Bellmon felt anger sweep through him. It must have shown on his face, for the captain quickly said, "Sir, the question wasn't supposed to sound flip."

"That's a regular army sergeant out there, Captain," Bellmon said. "He would have been unable to leave them sitting there. An officer had called for them to fall in, and they would have fallen in, or somebody, maybe the sergeant, would have been dead."

He wondered how he knew, why he was so sure, that Technical Sergeant MacMillan, who was hardly more than a boy, was regular army.

When MacMillan came to his room, he gave him a cup of the real coffee.

"How long has the colonel been a prisoner, sir?"

"Since North Africa," Bellmon said. "Kasserine Pass."

"They got me about three weeks ago," MacMillan said. "Just before the goddamn war is about over."

"We hadn't heard the 82nd was engaged," Bellmon said. When MacMillan looked surprised that he had known his division, Bellmon explained he had seen where the patches had been cut off.

"Operation fucking Market-Garden," MacMillan said. "We tried to grab the Rhine bridges. Biggest fuck-up in the war. We got the shit kicked out of us."

"That's normally when they catch prisoners," Bellmon said. "Kasserine was a big fuck-up, too."

"How'd the colonel get caught, if you don't mind my asking?"

"I was in a tank. A PzKwIV got us. I got blown off."

"We went across this fucking river," MacMillan said. "Little fucking English boats. No fucking oars. Collapsible sides. They mortared the shit out of us in the water. And then when we got to the other side, there was no fucking ammo. No fucking ammo. How the fuck do they expect you to fight without ammo?"

"So what happened?"

"So we took it off the dead, and shot that, and when that was over . . . what the fuck was I supposed to do? Do a John Wayne? Charge with a fucking carbine bayonet in my hand?"

"What did you do?" Bellmon asked.

"I got out of my fucking hole and put my hands up, that's what I did."

"I tried to play dead," Bellmon said, aware this was the first time he had ever told the story. "But they saw me breathing, rolled me over, and stuck a .45 up my nose."

"So what happens to us now, Colonel?" MacMillan asked.

"We wait for the war to end," Bellmon said.

"We was nine days on the train, plus half a day on the truck," MacMillan said. "We're a long way from our lines. How far are we from the Russians?"

"I just don't know," Bellmon said.

"There's no sense in trying to get out of this fucking place now," Macmillan said. "There's no way we can get back on our own, goddamn it."

"MacMillan," Bellmon said, "there is an active, enthusiastic escape committee here."

MacMillan looked at him.

"If they ever reach the point where they're going to try it, I will order them not to," Bellmon said. "But in the meantime, I don't think you should let your opinion of the situation be known."

"Keep 'em busy, huh, Colonel?"

"If I had some whitewash, I'd have them painting rocks, Sergeant," Bellmon said. He laughed. He realized it was the first time in a very long time that he had laughed.

MacMillan grunted understandingly. They were smiling at each other now, two hometown people who had found each other in an alien land.

"Are there any more regulars here, Colonel? Or is it you and me?"

"Just you and me, MacMillan," Bellmon said.

"Ah, what the fuck, Colonel," MacMillan said. "If it wasn't for the war, you'd still probably be a first john, and I'd still be a corporal."

II

(One)
The United States Military Academy
West Point, New York
22 December 1944

Cadet Corporal Sanford T. Felter, of the class of 1946, sat at attention on the edge of a straight-backed, rather ornately carved wooden chair in the outer office of the Commandant of the Corps of Cadets. His rigid back was three inches from the rear of the chair, and he held his plumed shako in a white-gloved hand. He had been summoned from the dismissal formation following the formal parade immediately preceding the Christmas holidays.

He was small and slight, rather pasty-faced in complexion, and his face showed signs of the acne which had nearly cost him his competitive appointment to the Academy.

He was staring straight ahead at a portrait of a senior officer he had never heard of, but who apparently had done something sufficiently meritorious to have his portrait hung in the outer office of the commandant. He was going over in his mind what would likely happen inside the commandant's office, and what his responses should be. He was uneasy, but determined.

"If Felter is out there," a metallic voice came over the intercom, "send him in."

"You may go in," the commandant's secretary said.

Felter stood up. He put his shako squarely on his head, and picked up his M1 Garand rifle. As long as he had been at the Point, he had never before reported under arms to an officer indoors. He wasn't sure if he should march in with the piece at right shoulder arms, and then come to present arms, or whether he should march in with the piece at trail arms, come to attention, and render the rifle salute.

He decided, right then, to do it at trail arms.

He knocked at the door, waited for the command to enter, and then marched in, coming to a stop eighteen inches from the huge, polished mahogany desk. He came to attention, lowered the butt of the Garand onto the carpet, and rendered the first movement of the rifle salute. He moved his right hand across his body, fingers extended and stiff, so the fingertips of his right hand contacted the stacking swivel of the M1 he held in his left hand.

"Sir, Cadet Corporal Felter, Sanford T., reporting to the Commandant of Cadets as ordered, Sir," he said.

The major general behind the desk, who was the Commandant of Cadets, returned the salute. He was an athletic man in his late forties, who wore his gray hair in a closely cropped crew cut. He was the sort of man one *knew* had played football in college, and now spent as much time as he could spare on the golf course.

Felter completed the salute, snapping his right hand quickly back across his body to his side. He stared six inches above the commandant's head, at the knees of a portrait of General Philip H. Sheridan.

"Stand at ease, Felter," the commandant said. Felter moved the muzzle of the Garand four inches forward, moved his left foot six inches to the side, and put his left hand in the small of his back. The position was that of parade rest, but this was the commandant's office and the commandant, and he was a cadet corporal, and parade rest seemed to be the position to assume. In at ease it was permissible to look around. Cadet Corporal Felter lowered his eyes and met those of the commandant.

"I have your resignation, Felter," the general said. "You want to tell me about it?"

"Sir, I believe it speaks for itself," Felter said, without hesitation.

"Oh, no, it doesn't," the general said. "I want to know what curious line of thinking is responsible for it."

"Sir, I believe the war will be over before I would graduate," Felter said.

"And do you have some notion that you will be able to cover yourself with glory?" The general had pushed himself back in his chair, tilting it.

"No, sir."

"But you would like to get in, personally, on the fall of the Thousand Year Reich, is that it? You have a personal involvement?"

"If the general is making reference to my Jewish faith, no, sir."

"Then what the hell is it?" the general snapped, impatiently.

"Sir, I have decided that what I would learn in the active army during the last stages of the war would be more valuable in my military career than what I would learn here, as a cadet."

"Has it occurred to you, Felter, that your idea has been considered, and discarded, by a number of your superiors? It is their considered judgment, with which I fully agree, that the best place for a cadet at this time is at the Academy."

"Yes, sir."

"But you don't agree?" Now there was sarcasm in his tone.

"No, sir."

"You know what's going to happen to you, don't you? You're going to be sent to an infantry replacement training center, run through basic training, and put into the pipeline. Three months from now, maybe less, you'll be a rifleman in a line company."

Cadet Corporal Felter did not reply.

"I asked you if you knew what this resignation means to you, Felter," the general said, coldly. "Please pay me the courtesy of a reply."

"Sir, I very much dislike having to dispute you, sir," Felter said, forcing himself to meet the general's eyes.

"Goddamn you, you arrogant little pup, dispute me!" the general said.

"Sir," Felter said. "According to regulations, when a cadet who has completed two or more years at the Academy enters the ranks, he will be given constructive credit for basic training, sir, and will be eligible for further assignment."

"I presume you're sure of that," the general said. "I confess I didn't know that. But all that means is that they will hand you an M1 and a bayonet that much sooner. Goddamn it, Son, the army has invested two years in you. We don't want you killed off as a goddamned private."

"Sir, I have reason to believe that I qualify for one or two procurement programs."

"What kind of procurement programs?"

"There is a critical shortage of interpreters in German and Polish and Russian. There is a critical shortage of POW interrogators with fluency in the same languages. I'm not sure I meet the criteria for a POW interrogator, but I am sure that I am qualified as an interpreter. If the shortage still exists when I go in the ranks, I think it is reasonable to presume that I would be assigned such duties."

"And if they hand you a rifle and tell you go stick the bayonet in somebody?"

"That is the worst possible projection, sir," Felter said. "But even in that event, I believe that service as an infantry rifleman would be of more value to me in my future career than spending the next year as a cadet and missing active service, sir."

"You keep talking about your career, Felter. You are resigning your appointment. How is that going to affect your career?"

"I intend to apply for readmission to the Academy following the war, sir, under the regulations providing for the admission of regular army enlisted men."

"And what makes you so sure that they'd let you back in?"

"I don't feel that active service would be a bar to readmission, sir," Felter said.

"There used to be an offense, Felter, called silent insolence. That remark came pretty close to it."

"I beg the general's pardon. No insolence was intended."

"This whole goddamned resignation is insolent!" the Commandant of Cadets snapped.

"It is not so intended, sir."

"OK, Felter. I'm calling your bluff. I will give you precisely sixty seconds to reconsider your resignation. You may consult your watch."

Felter raised his wrist, watched as the sweep second hand completed a circle from seventeen seconds past the minute. Then he put his hand back to his side.

"Corporal, I now give you an opportunity to withdraw your resignation," the commandant said, formally, but not unkindly.

"Thank you, sir, but no, sir," Felter said.

"Report to your battalion tactical officer," the general said. "Tell him that your resignation is being processed, and that you will remain assigned to your company pending further action. You will not, repeat not, go on Christmas leave."

"Yes, sir."

"You are dismissed, Mister Felter," the general said.

Cadet Corporal Sanford T. Felter rendered the rifle salute, did an about-face, and marched out of the Commandant of Cadets' office. His stomach hurt, and he was afraid that he was going to be sick to his stomach.

The Commandant of Cadets put Cadet Corporal Felter's personal and academic records together in a neat stack, and then he asked his secretary to ask the General's secretary if the General could give him a couple of minutes. "The General" was the Commandant, the United States Military Academy at West Point, and the Commandant of Cadets immediate and only superior at the Point. He was a lieutenant general. The Commandant of Cadets was aware that there was something actually ludicrous in a situation where a twenty-year-old cadet corporal had backed a major general into a corner, where he had to go ask a lieutenant general what to do.

When the Commandant of Cadets' secretary called back a minute later to say that the General was free to see him, he picked up Felter's records and walked down the portrait-lined corridor of the building to the office of the Commandant, the United States Military Academy.

"Would you like coffee, Charley, or something a little

stronger?" the Commandant asked, when he had waved him
into his large, rather elegantly furnished office. The Commandant was a tall, thin, very erect man whose uniform hung
loosely over his shoulders. He was known to the Corps of
Cadets behind his back as either the Hawk or the Vulture.

"Strong, please, sir," the Commandant of Cadets said. "I
guess the little sonofabitch got to me. There aren't many people
I can't stare down."

"And you were probably thinking, Charley, 'If I can't go,
why the hell should you get to go?'"

"Christ, I suppose so," the Commandant of Cadets said.
"'What did you do in the war, Daddy? Why, I wiped noses
and changed diapers at the Academy, that's what Daddy did.'"

The Commandant chuckled. He handed him a scotch and
water.

"Thank you, sir," he said.

"Plus, of course," the Commandant said, "he's right."

"You really think so?"

"So do you," the Commandant of West Point said. "You
don't, you can't, learn about war sitting in a classroom."

"Christ, the whole class of '46 will try this, once it gets
out."

"Not necessarily," the Commandant said.

"I think they will," the Commandant of Cadets said. "Hell,
I would."

"They're not eligible for direct commissions," the Commandant said. "Felter is."

"He didn't say anything about a direct commission," the
Commandant of Cadets said, visibly surprised. "That's the first
I heard about that."

"He probably figured that would really make you blow your
top. But the fact is, he is eligible for a direct commission as
a linguist-interrogator. Two years of college, and fluency in
one, or preferably more languages on the short list. He speaks
Russian, Polish, and German."

"If he gets a direct commission, he could never come back
here," the Commandant of Cadets said.

"I disagree with you there. We're already starting to pick
up bright young reserve officers to run them through here. If
he's right, he could come back."

"Right about what, sir?"

"That the war will shortly be over," the Commandant said. "He may be wrong. This may be a lot longer war than we think it will be. We're getting the shit kicked out of us in the Bulge, Charley."

"Yeah, while you and I sit here drinking scotch whiskey, and watching that little Jew manipulate the system."

"If I thought he was manipulating it for his personal benefit, I would personally see to it that he wound up in a line company," the Commandant of West Point said. "But what I think we have here, Charley, is a perfectly bona fide case of devotion to duty."

"What do you want me to do, General? Discharge him from the Corps of Cadets and turn him over to his draft board?"

"No," the Commandant said. "What I want you to do, Charley, is to change the training schedule."

"Sir?"

"I want the reveille formation on 2 January 1945 to be in full dress. I want the band there, not just the drums and the bugles. I want the color guard. I want Felter there in pinks and greens. *You,* in your pinks and greens and all your decorations, will hold the Bible while I, wearing mine, swear him in. I want an adjutant, an officer not a cadet, to read his orders in a very loud voice. 'Second Lieutenant Whateverhisnameis Felter will immediately proceed to the Overseas Replacement Depot, Camp Kilmer, New Jersey, for priority air-shipment to'—a division in the field. Have him sent somewhere flashy, maybe the 82nd Airborne, or the Big Red One, or one of the armored divisions. You follow me, Charley?"

"Yes, Sir," the Commandant of Cadets said. "I see what you're doing."

"I want the flags flying, and the band playing 'Army Blue,'" the Commandant of the United States Military Academy said. "When the the Corps of Cadets marches by, at eyes right, I want every goddamned eye to be wet with emotion and green with envy. If I thought I could get away with it, I'd have the bugler sound the charge."

(Two)

First Lieutenant Wallace T. Rogers, Infantry (USMA '43) was Cadet Corporal Sanford T. Felter's tactical officer. A tactical officer is mixture of disciplinarian, mother hen, and observer of the cadets committed to his charge. He was having as much trouble with the resignation of Corporal Felter as was the Commandant of Cadets.

Lieutenant Rogers had volunteered for the airborne, and upon graduation had been sent to the Parachute School at Fort Benning, Georgia; and upon graduation from there, he'd been sent to the Airborne Center at Fort Bragg, North Carolina, where, on his very first jump as a platoon commander, he had been blown off the drop zone and into a stand of pine trees. He'd suffered a compound fracture of his left leg, just above the ankle.

On his release from the Fort Bragg Army Hospital to limited duty, he had been assigned to the United States Military Academy at West Point as a tactical officer.

His classmates, his friends, were in combat, commanding troops around the world, and here he was baby-sitting the cadets. And now Felter was trying to pull this resignation business.

Lieutenant Rogers, moreover, was aware that he did not like Cadet Corporal Sanford T. Felter. He was even willing to admit that there just might be an element of anti-Semitism in his dislike, but he really believed that it wasn't anti-Semitism but a personality clash based on chemistry. He just didn't like Felter's type.

Rogers was tall, Felter was short. Rogers was muscular, Felter was skinny. Rogers had had to really crack the books, Felter seemed to have a mind like a camera. He saw or heard something once, and thereafter could effortlessly call it forth from his memory. Rogers was gregarious, Felter was a loner. Rogers was a team player, Felter, as this resignation business proved, was completely immune to peer group pressure.

Wallace T. Rogers, aware of his personal feelings toward Cadet Corporal Sanford T. Felter, leaned over backward to make sure that not only did he treat Felter exactly as he treated the other cadets, but that Felter would never suspect that Rogers considered him to be a wise-ass Jewboy who had no business being in the Corps, or in the regular army.

When the word from the Commandant of Cadets had made its way down the chain of command to the company, instead of sending the charge of quarters to fetch Felter, Lt. Rogers told the CQ he was going to see Felter in his room.

Felter's door was open, and Felter was in the process of buttoning himself into his greatcoat. He sensed the presence of Lieutenant Rogers, turned, and snapped to attention.

"Rest," Rogers said, immediately, and smiled. "I seem to have caught you as you were leaving."

"Sir, I was going to the telephone."

"Then I'm glad I caught you, Felter," Rogers said, smiling. "I just got the word from the Commandant of Cadets. You are authorized Christmas leave."

"Yes, sir," Felter said. "Thank you, sir. Sir, may I ask if there is some reason they changed their minds?"

"They didn't say, Felter. I can guess . . ."

"Please do, sir."

"Well, I don't imagine with everything shut down for the holidays, that very much can be done about your resignation. And the commandant probably realized there was no reason you shouldn't be granted leave."

"Yes, sir," Felter said. "That seems logical. Thank you, sir."

Felter decided that what it really was was that the Commandant of Cadets was giving him another chance to think it over, that after his leave he would be given another chance to withdraw his resignation.

"You're going to have to hustle to make the 4:48, Felter," Lieutenant Rogers said.

"Yes, sir."

"Get your gear, and I'll run you to the station in my car."

"Thank you very much, sir."

There was no time for Felter to call home and tell them he would be late. He called home from Grand Central Station. His mother answered the telephone and told him that Sharon and his father had gone to Pennsylvania Station in Newark to meet him, and hadn't come back yet. He told his mother that he had missed the first train and would be home in about an hour.

On the train ride down the Hudson River to New York, he

had considered again what, if anything, he should tell his parents, and more importantly, Sharon, of his intended resignation. He decided again to tell them nothing about it until he knew for sure what would happen. There was no point in going through the explosion that would follow his announcement until he had to. He had no intention of debating the issue with them.

Felter took the Hudson tubes from Manhattan to Newark attracting curious stares in his long, gray, brass-buttoned greatcoat and brimmed cap with the brim precisely one inch over his eyebrows; and again there were stares on the bus from the station to the Weequahic section of Newark. There weren't that many West Point cadets anywhere, and there was only one in the Weequahic section of Newark.

Nice, upwardly mobile young Jewish boys from Weequahic tried to get in Yale and Harvard, not the United States Military Academy. Although some had rushed to the recruiting stations after Pearl Harbor, and there were as many blue-starred flags hanging from windows to announce a son or a father in the service in Weequahic as there were anywhere else, Sandy Felter was aware that he was probably the only individual in Weequahic who did not plan to take off his uniform as soon as the war was over.

When she saw him get off the bus, Sharon came out of the Old Warsaw Bakery, on Aldine Street, and let him hug her. The greatcoat was so bulky that he really couldn't feel any of her except the warmth of her back under his hands.

Inside the bakery over the cash register, there was a picture of him as a plebe in a small frame with two little American flags crossed over it. It rather embarrassed him. He knew the only reason his parents were happy that he was at West Point was because it kept him out of what his father called the trenches. His father had been a Polish conscript in World War I.

When he saw Sharon, and smelled her, and tasted her, he wondered if he had done the right thing. If he stayed, he would live. The war was going to be over. He and Sharon could be married the day he graduated, and then he would have the four years of his obligated service to convince her that being a regular army officer was just as good and just as prestigious a way of life as a lawyer's or a doctor's or some other professional's. Right now, Sharon, her parents, and his thought he was still behaving like a child.

He had, he realized, made the right decision about not telling them about resigning. It would have ruined Christmas. They were Jews, Polish and Russian Jews on Sandy Felter's side, and Czech and German Jews on Sharon's, but they celebrated Christmas anyway. Not in a religious sense of course, but with a Christmas tree and the exchange of presents and all sorts of Christmas baked goods from the old country. There was even a roast goose for Christmas dinner.

He couldn't ruin that.

On Christmas Day after dinner, when both he and Sharon were feeling the wine they'd had with the goose, Sharon's mother caught them kissing on the back stairs. He didn't know how long she had watched them before she made her presence known, but she hadn't seemed all that angry—even though Felter knew that Sharon's mother had taken great pains to make sure they weren't alone in circumstances "where something could happen." They even had to take Sharon's brother with them to the damned movies.

Whenever he could get Sharon alone for a moment to kiss her, he considered again that if he stayed at the Point, in eighteen months he could marry Sharon, and they wouldn't have to take her little brother with them anymore. He didn't believe that Sharon had the same thing happen to her that happened to him (his nuts ached), but he suspected, *knew* somehow, that she wanted to make love with him as much as he wanted to do it with her.

If he went off to the war, he was not only going to break his mother's and his father's heart, but he was liable to get killed, and then he would have died without ever having done it with Sharon.

On 28 December 1944, the field-grade duty officer at West Point telephoned the residence of Thaddeus Felter (formerly Taddeus Felztczy) in Newark, N.J., asked to speak to Cadet Corporal Felter, and told him, after he came on the line, that his leave had been cancelled and that he was to report back to the Academy as soon as possible.

Cadet Corporal Felter was not given a second chance to reconsider his resignation as he'd expected. He was ordered to turn in his cadet uniforms and equipment. He was then outfitted in an insignia-less olive-drab uniform, the "Ike" jacket and trousers now authorized for wear by both officers and enlisted men, and assigned a room in the Hotel Thayer.

He spent December 30 and 31 filling out forms and being fitted for uniforms. He ate a solitary dinner in the Hotel Thayer dining room on New Year's Eve. He called his parents and Sharon, separately, two calls, and wished them a Happy New Year, and told them that no, nothing was wrong.

At 0445 on 2 January 1945, Lieutenant Wallace T. Rogers came to the Hotel Thayer, his arms loaded with uniforms from the officers' sales store and a canvas Valv-pak with FELTER S.T. 2ND LT 0-3478003 already stencilled on its sides. He watched as Felter put on a green tunic and pink trousers and a gabardine trench coat, nodded his approval, and then delivered him to the quarters of the Commandant of Cadets, who fed him break-fast.

At 0615 on the plain, with a light snow falling, Sanford T. Felter raised his right hand and repeated after the Commandant of the United States Military Academy that he would protect and defend the Constitution of the United States from enemies, foreign and domestic, that he would obey all orders of the officers appointed over him, and that he would faithfully dis-charge the duties of the office he was about to enter. The Commandant of the United States Military Academy ('18), the Commandant of Cadets ('20), First Lieutenant Wallace T. Roger ('43), and the cadet colonel of the Corps of Cadets ('45) shook his hand.

A bull-voiced lieutenant colonel ('28), the sheet of paper flapping in his hands, bellowed, "Attention to Orders," and then went on.

"Second Lieutenant Sanford T. Felter, Infantry, Army of the United States, 0-3478003, having reported upon active duty will proceed immediately to the Overseas Replacement Depot, Camp Kilmer, New Jersey, for further shipment by military air transport, Priority AAA1, to Headquarters, 40th Armored Division, in the field, European Theater of Opera-tions."

He about-faced and saluted the Commandant of West Point and the Commandant of Cadets.

"March past!" the Commandant of West Point ordered.

The cadet colonel and Second Lieutenant Felter marched up onto the low reviewing stand after the adjutant. The band played "The Washington Post March," and the Corps of Cadets marched past the reviewing stand. When the color guard reached the reviewing stand, the band segued to "Army Blue."

"Eyes right!" the first battalion commander called out.

Four bandsmen struck four bass drums. *Boom*.

Everyone knew the lyrics.

"We Say Farewell to Kay-det Gray." *Boom*. "And Don the Army Blue." *Boom*.

The Commandant of West Point looked out the corner of his eye, as he held the hand salute, at the Commandant of Cadets, and Second Lieutenant Felter, and the cadet colonel.

"We Say Farewell to Kay-det Gray." *Boom*.

"And Don the Army Blue." *Boom*.

The Commandant of West Point's eyes were misty.

The band segued to "Dixie!"

That sonofabitch, the Commandant of West Point thought. The Commandant of Cadets was a goddamned Rebel, and he was always slipping the word to the bandmaster to play "Dixie." He'd have a word with him.

And then he had second thoughts.

This wasn't the first time the band had played "Dixie" on the plain when a cadet resigned his appointment to go off to a war. The band had played "Dixie" at the last parade for the cadets who had resigned their appointments so they could fight for the Confederacy.

The Corps of Cadets, forming a Long Gray Line, marched off the plain to the strains of "Dixie" to return to the barracks and change uniforms and go, three-quarters of an hour late, to class. Second Lieutenant Sanford T. Felter walked off the reviewing stand and got into the Commandant of Cadets' Ford staff car and was driven to the railroad station.

Lieutenant Wallace T. Rogers saw him onto the train.

"Good luck, Lieutenant," he said.

"Thank you, sir," Lieutenant Felter replied.

He was home just before three and his father wept and his mother shrieked and wailed as he thought they would.

Sharon told him just after supper, when they were left alone for an hour, that she had made up her mind that she wanted him to do it to her, but that her time of the month had come early and she was sorry that they couldn't.

He reported to the Overseas Replacement Depot at Camp Kilmer at fifteen minutes before midnight, and two days later the Transportation Corps people took him and eight other people by bus to Newark Airport and put him on a C-54 just about full of crates marked FOR MEDICAL OFFICER ETO WHOLE BLOOD RUSH.

(Three)
Stalag XVII–B
Near Stettin, Poland
3 March 1945

The regulation stated only that a photograph of the Führer would be "prominently displayed." It did not say that there had to be one in every room, or specifically that one be hung on the wall of the commanding officer, although the Führer's stern visage had frowned down from the walls of every commanding officer's office that Colonel Graf Peter-Paul von Greiffenberg could call to mind.

Nevertheless, he would be in this office for the indefinite future, and he simply did not want Adolf Hitler, the Bavarian corporal, staring over his shoulder in an obscene parody of paintings of Christ or photographs of the Pope inspiring the faithful.

He walked to the wall and unhooked the framed photograph. The photo had been hanging there for some time, and the outline of the frame was clearly visible. He could, he thought, hang a swastika large enough to conceal the frame's outline. Anything would be better than the Bavarian corporal.

There was a knock on the open door, and he turned to look at his adjutant, Karl-Heinz von und zu Badner.

"Der Amerikaner Oberstleutnant Bellmon ist hier, Herr Oberst Graf," the lieutenant said. Badner, a tall, erect Prussian with sunken eyes, had left his left arm in Russia, and his tunic sleeve was folded double and pinned up.

"Ask him to come in," Colonel Graf von Greiffenberg said. "I wish to see him alone."

"Jawohl, Herr Oberst Graf," the lieutenant said, and nod-

ded with his head for Bellmon to enter. He closed the door
behind him.

"How are you, Colonel?" Von Greiffenberg said. "It's good
to see you again."

"Very well, thank you, Colonel," Bellmon said. "May I
offer the hope that that isn't serious?" There was just the slight-
est nod of his head toward the colonel's left leg, which, obviously bandaged (and perhaps in a cast), stretched the material
of his trouser leg.

"It is recovering well, thank you," von Greiffenberg said.
"Some muscle damage. A piece of shrapnel. Enough to keep
me from field duty, I'm afraid. It has been decided that I am
fit enough to command this stalag."

"I see."

"I regret that I was unable to arrange your repatriation," he
continued. He wondered if Bellmon would react to that, if
Bellmon blamed him for still being here, when von Greiffenberg had as much as promised that he would be exchanged.

"So do I," Bellmon said, with a smile.

"It could not be arranged," von Greiffenberg said. "I made
inquiries."

"I understand, Colonel," Bellmon said, and then he gave
into the temptation: "I cry a lot, but I understand."

The remark surprised von Greiffenberg. It was not the sort
of jesting remark a professional German officer would make.

"You have the material I sent you?" the colonel asked,
formally. He did not expect Bellmon to have it. The risk was
too great, and disposing of the Katyn Forest massacre evidence
would have been simply a matter of throwing it in a fire.

"Yes, of course," Bellmon said, as if surprised by the question.

So he was an officer, an officer who kept his word even
when it was difficult to do so, even at the possible risk of his
life. Von Greiffenberg decided to reply in kind.

"I was wounded in the Ardenne Forest," he said. "I was in
command of a Panzer regiment. The plan was to capture Liege
and Antwerp, primarily to sever your supply lines, and, it was
hoped, to avail ourselves of your petrol and rations."

"I see."

"The plan, as I saw it, was audacious," the colonel went

on. "It had a fair chance of success." He watched Bellmon's face for his reaction. It was not customary for officers to discuss military operations with their prisoners.

"But apparently, it did not," Bellmon said.

"It was necessary for us to alter the plan, and reestablish our lines," the colonel said, either quoting or paraphrasing the official explanation for the failure.

"I see," Bellmon said again.

"What the plan failed to take into consideration was the capability of your logistic trains, and the limitations of ours. We were, regrettably, unable to maintain the force of the assault as long as necessary. On the other hand, your service of supply was equal to the demands put upon it. I understand that General Patton was able to disengage a six division force, move it one hundred fifty kilometers, and mount a successful counterattack on a six division front, within a total of six days."

That was not the official version of a defeat and Bellmon knew it. He took another chance.

"Do you know General Patton, Colonel?" he asked.

"I played polo with him—against him—in Madrid, sometime in the thirties," von Greiffenberg said. "He was at Samur two years before I was there. I believe he and your father-in-law are quite close, aren't they?"

"No, as a matter of fact, they're not," Bellmon said. "My father-in-law never forgave Patton for going back to the infantry after the first war."

"I wondered why Porky wasn't with Patton's Third Army, but with Simpson's Ninth," von Greiffenberg said. "You've answered that question."

"I think that's just the way the chips fell, Colonel," Bellmon said. "I don't think personalities were involved."

It was the first he had known where Major General Waterford was.

Von Greiffenberg shrugged his shoulders and went on.

"Our attack rather seriously drew down our reserves of forces and supplies," von Greiffenberg said. "A critical part of the plan was to capture Bastogne, a road and rail center. Much of our artillery was expended in an attempt to reduce your forces there. They held out much longer than it was thought they could, and they were ultimately relieved by elements of the 1st Armored Division."

"Bastogne did not fall?"

"After considering the fluidity of the situation," Colonel von Greiffenberg said, a light but unmistakable tone of bitter mockery in his voice, "the Führer decided that the capture of Bastogne was no longer necessary to the plans for final victory."

"And how are the Russians doing?" Bellmon asked.

"It has been necessary to adjust our lines across the Soviet Union and Poland." He paused for a moment, then resumed. "I understand it is the Soviet intention to take over this area within sixty days, although I am sure the Führer has plans that will thwart that intention."

"If the readjustment of your lines in this area is subject to revision," Bellmon asked, "are there any plans to insure the safety of the prisoners of war?"

"My primary duty as commandant of this stalag," von Greiffenberg said, "is to insure the safety of the prisoners. Generaloberst von Heteen felt it necessary to remind me of that when informing me of my posting. While I have every faith that the Führer will be able to stop the Soviet forces, I have, of course, made contingency plans for the evacuation of this stalag and its prisoners to the west."

"How long do you think it will take?" Bellmon suddenly asked.

Von Greiffenberg looked at him for a moment.

"You are not very delicate, Colonel, are you?" he asked.

"I beg your pardon, sir," Bellmon said.

"Sixty days," von Greiffenberg said. It was out in the open now. Bellmon obviously knew how the war was going. There was no real reason for him to be "delicate" either. "There is talk of a last-ditch defense in the Alps, but I think that is whistling in the dark."

Bellmon pursed his lips, and then nodded, as if what he had just been told confirmed what he already believed. But he said nothing.

"If it should come to pass that you should fall into Soviet control," von Greiffenberg said, "it would be very dangerous for you to be found with the Katyn material."

"Yes," Bellmon said, "I've thought of that."

"I release you from your word, Colonel Bellmon, to deliver

them to your appropriate superiors," von Greiffenberg said.

"I'll hang on to them," Bellmon said, flatly.

"Colonel, I'll spell it out for you. If the Russians find that material in your possession, you will die."

"Perhaps," Bellmon said, gently mocking von Greiffenberg's vaguely Biblical phraseology, "'it will come to pass' that I will be freed by American forces."

"That is very unlikely, I'm afraid," von Greiffenberg said.

"It is often darkest just before the dawn," Bellmon said.

"So the Führer has been saying," von Greiffenberg said dryly.

Bellmon looked at him. Their eyes locked. The American and the German smiled at each other.

(Four)
April Fool's Day, 1945

The commanding officer of Stalag XVII-B, Oberst Graf Peter-Paul von Greiffenberg sent Oberleutnant Karl-Heinz von und zu Badner to fetch Lt. Col. Robert F. Bellmon five minutes after he received the movement order. He spent three of the five minutes in thought, one in prayer on his knees, and one pouring himself and drinking a very stiff brandy.

The middle-aged sergeant major and the more than middle-aged corporal on duty in the office rose to their feet and came to attention as the two officers entered the outer room of the commandant's office. The corporal always jumped to his feet and stood at attention when an officer of either army entered the office. Colonel Count von Greiffenberg was a stickler for correct military behavior: corporals demonstrate respect to rank no matter what the army. The sergeant major was normally preoccupied when Wehrmacht officers below the grade of major or American officers of any grade had business in the office. But he rose and stood at attention for Colonel Bellmon.

"Guten Abend, Oberfeldwebel," Colonel Bellmon said, in fluent German, acknowledging the sergeant major's gesture with a crisp salute.

"Guten Abend, Herr Oberstleutnant," the sergeant major said. "The Oberst Graf will see you now." He pushed open the door to Oberst Graf von Greiffenberg's office.

"Herr Graf," he said. *"Herr Oberstleutnant Bellmon."*

Bellmon removed his overseas cap with the silver Lieutenant Colonel's leaf pinned to its front, and which he had worn in the manner of armored soldiers, cocked to the left. Holding it in his left hand, he saluted again.

"Come in, please, Colonel," the commandant of Stalag XVII-B said in English. And then, over Colonel Bellmon's shoulder: *"Du auch, Karl."* The intimate *"Du"* was magnified by his use of the Oberleutnant's Christian name. *"Und schliesse die Türe, bitte."*

Wordlessly, Colonel Count von Greiffenberg handed Colonel Bellmon and Oberleutnant von und zu Badner Stubberweg cognac snifters. He picked up his own glass, raised it to his companions, and then drank it down.

"I am in receipt, Colonel," the count began, "of movement orders which affect your officers." He spoke in English as if reciting from memory. "There have been certain temporary adjustments of the line, which make it necessary, in order to maintain the safety of our prisoners, to move them."

"I see," Bellmon said.

"Perhaps you might wish to examine the map," Colonel Graf von Greiffenberg said. He gestured—an elegant movement—toward his desk. Both Colonel Bellmon and Oberleutnant Stubberweg tried, and did not manage, to conceal their surprise at this offer. It is the duty of prisoners of war to make an attempt to escape. The most essential equipment in an attempt to escape is a map. Maps are therefore guarded with great care by the captors.

"If you are in any way uncomfortable, Oberleutnant von und zu Badner," von Greiffenberg said, "you may withdraw."

Oberleutnant von und zu Badner did not hesitate. He came to attention.

"With the Oberst Graf's kind permission, the Oberleutnant will remain in the hope that he might be of some small service."

"Thank you, Karl," von Greiffenberg said.

"It is my privilege, Herr Oberst Graf," von und zu Badner said.

"Very well," Colonel Graf von Greiffenberg said, pointing with a long, well-manicured finger to a point on the map. "We are here, Colonel Bellmon. Specifically, five kilometers from the center of Stettin."

Colonel Bellmon nodded, but said nothing.

"The temporary situation which requires adjustment in our lines," the count went on, in a dry, faintly mocking voice, as if he were once again addressing a class at the Kriegsschule, "involves certain pressures from this area." His thin finger pointed toward the direction of Warsaw. "Consequently, I have been ordered to effect a movement, which I am assured will be temporary, to the west, in this direction." His finger moved west and came to rest on the map near Berlin.

Bellmon leaned over the map, found the scale, and measured the distance with his fingers.

"At the moment, Colonel Bellmon, no transport is available for your officers," von Greiffenberg went on. "It will therefore be necessary for your officers to proceed by foot."

"I trust, Colonel, that arrangements have been made to feed my officers," Bellmon said.

"I am assured, Colonel," the count said, "that supplies and vehicles will be provided at approximately this point in our route," the count said, pointing with his finger.

"Peter," Colonel Bellmon said, suddenly deciding to take the risk, "we're not going to make the rendezvous point with the trucks, much less the Berlin area. Why don't we just stand pat and let the Russians roll over us?"

Von Greiffenberg involuntarily looked at Oberleutnant von und zu Badner to see his reaction to Bellmon's addressing him by his first name. He knew that the young officer was very much aware that he and Bellmon were more than prisoner and captor. But their public relationship had been correct. He didn't know how Badner would react when the prisoner suggested treason as the only logical thing to do, and he did nothing about it.

Karl-Heinz von und zu Badner said nothing, and it was impossible to tell from his face what he was thinking.

"My duty, as I see it, Robert," the colonel said, "is quite clear. In addition to seeing that you remain in custody, it is to protect you."

"Should our positions be reversed, Peter," Bellmon said, "should the fortunes of war see you in my custody, I would feel precisely the same way."

"Yes, I know you would," the count said. "But I have Katyn Forest in my mind."

"The Russians would get to you over my dead body," Bellmon said.

"Yes, they would," the count said. "I have reminded you of that very real possibility before." Now Badner looked confused. "Colonel Bellmon is rendering the German officer corps a very real service, Badner. I will explain that to you later."

"That is quite unnecessary, Herr Oberst Graf," the young officer said.

"You're in command, Colonel," Bellmon said.

"Yes," the count said. "For the moment. Perhaps you noticed, Colonel, that the message made no reference to your enlisted men."

"Yes, I did."

"Perhaps the thinking is that it is better to let the Russians have the enlisted men if that is the price for keeping the officers," the count said. "But in any event, I'm afraid your men are going to have to fend for themselves. Without instructions, I cannot move your enlisted men."

Bellmon looked at him for a long moment, trying to read his meaning.

"It has come to my attention, Colonel, that there is a good bit of neutral power shipping at Odessa," the count said. Bellmon immediately looked at the map. Odessa was on the Black Sea. He folded his three center fingers, put his thumb on Poznan, and stretched his little finger toward Odessa. The span was too great. He rolled his hand over, so that the palm was up, and laid his fingers flat on the map. Then, against the scale, he repeated the movement.

"That's more than 1,700 kilometers," he said.

"I understand," the count went on, "that an effort is being made to protect certain artworks and other treasures from the ravages of war by shipping them from the country in neutral ships."

"Oh?" Bellmon asked. He was obviously confused.

"Colonel, what the colonel means," Oberleutnant von und zu Badner said, "is that the SS, the regular SS, not the Waffen SS, is shipping their loot out of the country on neutral ships."

"Oh," Bellmon said again. He still didn't quite understand, but he didn't want to wait for an explanation.

"I understand, further, that the personnel situation is such that many such shipments are being shipped by truck without military escort," the count went on. "And I also understand that escaped prisoners of war are being summarily shot by the SS and some units of the Feldgendarmerie."

"I understand," Colonel Bellmon said.

"I further have reliably been given to understand that the Russians are often unable to make the distinction between Germans and escaped prisoners of war, and that when there is some question, they are prone to err on the side of their security."

"As they resolved the Katyn question," Bellmon said.

"So I have been led to believe," the count said. "And now, Colonel, if you will excuse us, Oberleutnant von und zu Badner and I have to see what we can do about rations for tomorrow."

Colonel Count von Greiffenberg made one of his graceful gestures, ordering the young officer to precede him out of the room. At the door, before he closed it, he said, "The Oberfeldwebel will see you back to your quarters, Robert. Please inform your officers we will march at first light."

Colonel Bellmon immediately picked up the map and started to fold it. Beneath the map was a Colt .32 caliber automatic pistol and a spare clip. The pistol was finely engraved. It was obviously Greiffenberg's personal weapon. He thought a moment, then jammed the pistol in his waistband. He put the spare clip in his sock.

Then he saw that the lower right drawer of Greiffenberg's desk was open, and he saw the dull gleaming metal. He pulled the drawer open. There was a Schmeisser 9 mm machine pistol in there, disassembled. He looked at it a long moment before reaching for it. He unfastened his belt and trousers. He slipped the machine pistol in one pants leg, and the three magazines in the other. He closed his fly, fastened his belt, flexed his knees. His trousers were tucked into the tops of his tanker boots, held in place by extra-long bootlaces.

It wasn't the most secure arrangement in the world, but it would have to do.

He took his overseas cap from beneath the epaulet of his Ike jacket and put it on his head. Then he opened the door to the outer office. The Oberfeldwebel came to attention.

"The Herr Oberstleutnant is finished?" the Oberfeldwebel

asked, politely. "In which case, I will escort the Herr Oberstleutnant to his quarters."

"I think that I would like to see Wachtmeister MacMillan before I turn in," Bellmon said.

"Whatever the Herr Oberstleutnant wishes," the Oberfeldwebel said.

When they reached the enlisted men's quarters, the German noncom saluted crisply and left him. Bellmon then rapped once on MacMillan's door and walked in without waiting for a reply. MacMillan jumped to his feet.

"Rest, Mac," Bellmon said. MacMillan, he saw, was freshly shaven and neatly cropped. His boots were even shined.

"How goes it, Mac?" Colonel Bellmon asked.

"What did old Von want?" MacMillan asked.

"We're being moved, on foot, at first light," Bellmon said.

"Shit! I was practicing to kiss my first Russian," MacMillan said.

"The enlisted men aren't going," Bellmon said.

"We're not?"

"You can take your chances, Mac," Bellmon said. "You can sit here and wait to get rolled over by the Red Army."

"Or?"

"I'll tell it the way I got it from von Greiffenberg," Bellmon said. When he had finished, MacMillan looked very carefully at him.

"You trust him, Colonel, don't you?"

"He's a regular, Mac, like we are," Colonel Bellmon said.

"What do you think we should do?"

"If you are caught by the SS or the Feldgendarmerie, you're liable to be shot. Under those circumstances, Sergeant, you have no obligation to attempt to escape."

"Just my fucking luck. Five combat jumps, and I'm going to get shot two weeks before the war is over."

"If you like, I'll insist that you be taken with us."

"Into Germany? No, thank you."

"I've got a map for you," Bellmon said. "If you want it."

"Von?" MacMillan said, taking and unfolding it. "That the route these loot trucks are taking?"

"Yeah. I'm not sure how current it is. As current, and as accurate, I'm sure, as von Greiffenberg can make it."

Bellmon took the Colt pistol and laid it on MacMillan's bed.

"Not, as I understand it, that anyone is paying a whole lot of attention to it, but possession of a firearm by an escaped POW is sufficient grounds under the Geneva Convention to use weaponry in his apprehension."

MacMillan looked at the pistol.

"Maybe you better keep that, Colonel," he said. He hoisted the front of his Ike jacket. Bellmon saw the angled butt of a Luger.

"How long have you had that?"

"Fritz gave me two of them," he said. "Two of them and two Schmeissers. A dozen clips. About thirty minutes ago. When he told me that Von had your marching orders, and they didn't include us."

"So what are you going to do, Mac?" Bellmon asked.

"I've got one guy who speaks German, and others who speak German *and* Polish," MacMillan said. "I've got two German uniforms, one of them a captain's."

"That'll get you shot as a spy," Bellmon said.

"If we can grab one of those trucks and put some distance between here and us, we might be able to make it."

"Who are you taking with you? How many?"

"There will be twenty-two of us. The rest want to wait for the Russians."

"Do they know what they're getting into?"

"I think so," MacMillan said. "If they don't, they'll damned sure find out soon enough after we're on our way."

They looked at each other. Bellmon sensed that this was the time he should have something to say to MacMillan. He could think of only one thing.

"Good luck, Mac," Colonel Bellmon said.

"Same to you, Colonel," MacMillan said. He grabbed Bellmon's hand and shook it.

"This is the second time since I've been a soldier I don't really know what to do," the colonel said.

It was a confession of inadequacy and MacMillan saw this. He was embarrassed for Lt. Col. Robert F. Bellmon.

"Yeah, you do," he said. "You gotta take care of those reservists. If you're worried about me, don't be. I've had enough of this POW shit. I don't want to get stood up against a wall without a fight."

"Thank you, Mac," Bellmon said, emotionally.

"Fuck it, Colonel," MacMillan replied, his own voice breaking. "Have the bugler sound the charge."

(Five)

At 0500 hours the next morning, the 240 officer prisoners of Stalag XVII-B formed ranks in the courtyard of what, long before, had been a Polish cavalry barracks. It was cold and damp, and many of them coughed rackingly and spit up phlegm. They were sullen, resentful, and disheartened.

Colonel Graf Peter-Paul von Greiffenberg appeared. Oberleutnant Karl-Heinz von und zu Badner called "Attention." Colonel von Greiffenberg stepped in front of the formation, and formally announced that a readjustment of German lines made necessary the removal of Stalag XVII-B to the west. He expressed regret that motor transport was not presently available.

"Colonel Bellmon," he concluded, "will you have your officers follow me, please?"

Bellmon saluted.

Von Greiffenberg walked to one end of the formation.

"Company!" Bellmon barked. "'Ten-hut! Uh-right-*face!* Forward, harch! Route step, harch!"

The prisoner complement, under armed guard, shuffled, rather than marched after the prison commandant. They went out the gate, and then turned toward Stettin.

Technical Sergeant Rudy MacMillan watched them move out. He waited until the last guard had had time to come from his watchtower. He waited ten minutes more to be sure. Then he formed his ranks where the officers had stood. A coal miner from Pennsylvania, dressed in the uniform of a Wehrmacht captain, and a steelworker from Gary, Indiana, in the uniform of a corporal, both carrying Schmeisser machine pistols slung from their shoulders, marched the twenty men in American uniforms, MacMillan second back in the left rank, onto the highway, and off in the other direction.

They marched for about forty-five minutes before the right

circumstances presented themselves. A Hanomag truck, its body enclosed in canvas tarpaulin, its front fender bearing the double lightning bolt runes of the SS, came down the cobblestone road.

"Take a left, Vrizinsky," MacMillan called out. The double column of men drifted across the road. The Hanomag truck squealed to a halt. The driver opened the door and shouted an obscenity. The SS Hauptsturmführer on the passenger side stood on the running board.

MacMillan, holding the Luger in both hands, and squatting halfway to give himself stability, shot him in the forehead. PFC Vrizinsky couldn't get his Schmeisser to fire. Private Loczowcza dropped his Schmeisser in his excitement. MacMillan jumped onto the running board and shot the driver twice in the back with his Luger.

The bodies were dragged off the road and stripped, while Private Loczowcza opened the Hanomag hood and pretended to work on it. The truck was full of wooden crates. As soon as MacMillan could change into the SS captain's uniform, which required that he search for and find a stream to wash the blood and brain matter out of the uniform cap, he supervised the off-loading of enough crates so there would be room for the men lying two deep on their sides, inside the truck, within a cavern of crates.

Outside of Wroclaw, four hours later, they came across a similar truck. Its crew was changing a flat tire by the side of the road. MacMillan had hoped to wait until the tire was changed before taking any action, but the SS Sturmscharführer in charge persisted in trying to engage the captain in conversation, and it became necessary to shoot him and the driver and to finish changing the tire themselves.

In twenty-four hours they were in L'vov, in the Ukraine. They picked up fuel and a few rations there and kept driving. The papers of the trucks were in order, and they passed through all but one Feldgendarmerie roadblock without incident. Near Podolskiy, Moldavia, an overzealous Unterfeldwebel of the Feldgendarmerie paid for his professional intuition that there was something wrong with this two-truck SS convoy with two 9 mm slugs in the back of his head.

Eight hours after that, they rolled into Odessa. There were

seven ships tied to a pier. It was necessary for MacMillan to walk down the pier to look at the port of call painted on the stern of the MV *Jose Harrez*. He did not recognize the flag of Argentina. When it said Buenos Aires on the stern, he decided that he had drawn and filled an inside straight. The MV *Jose Harrez* was loading cargo, and her booms would handle the trucks.

With Private Loczowcza marching behind him, he took the salute of the Service Corps Feldwebel guarding the gangplank and marched up the gangplank to the ship. An officer directed him to the captain's cabin.

The captain's name was Kramer. He looked like a German. He spoke German.

"Do you speak English?" MacMillan asked.

"Yes, Herr Hauptsturmführer," the captain said. "I speak English." If he was surprised to be addressed by a German officer in English, he didn't show it.

"There will shortly be two trucks on the dock," MacMillan said. "I want you to pick them up and put them in your hold."

The captain replied in German. MacMillan had no idea what he said.

"He said why should he do that, Mac," Loczowcza translated.

"Because I will shoot you right where you sit if you don't," MacMillan said. He unholstered the Luger, but held it at his side.

"Under those circumstances, I don't have much choice, do I?" the captain replied. He wasn't flustered.

"None," MacMillan said.

"If the German authorities learn that I am loading, or have loaded the trucks, would I be in danger?"

"From me, Captain," MacMillan said.

"I suppose you have considered that this, in effect, is an act of piracy, punishable under international law? Wherever we dock next?"

"If the Germans catch us now, we're all dead, right here," MacMillan replied.

"I was about to say British," the captain said. "But you're American, aren't you?"

"Yes," MacMillan said. "I'm an American."

"And to the victor go the spoils?"

"Spoils? You mean loot? You're welcome to whatever is on the trucks."

"Go get your trucks," the captain said.

The *Jose Harrez* sailed at four the next morning. It was to proceed via the Suez Canal for Dar es Salaam, Capetown, and Buenos Aires. The trucks were unloaded during the day and dropped over the side after nightfall. The SS and Wehrmacht uniforms went over the side when a launch flying the flag of the Royal Navy came out to the *Harrez* off Port Said.

Neither MacMillan nor the captain ever mentioned the contents of the crates, even though MacMillan knew they had been opened, and even though he and the captain had become rather friendly during the seven-day voyage from Odessa.

As the launch pulled alongside the *Harrez*, Captain Kramer handed MacMillan an envelope.

"It's all I can spare from the ship's funds without questions being asked," he said.

"Thank you," MacMillan said. It was obviously money, but he didn't count it. He just jammed it in his trousers pocket. His attention was on the crew of the launch. They were in whites. Short white pants, white knee socks, starched white shirts, with officer's shoulder boards on the shirts.

MacMillan, wearing a woolen olive-drab shirt, OD pants, and combat boots, saluted the moment the Limey officer stepped onto the deck of the *Harrez*.

"Sir, Technical Sergeant R. J. MacMillan, United States Army, reporting with a party of twenty-two," MacMillan said.

"I beg your pardon?" the Limey said. He did not return the salute.

(Six)
Cairo, Egypt
21 April 1945

The military attaché at the U.S. Embassy, Cairo, was an Air Corps full bird, an old one. He returned MacMillan's salute casually and handed him a message form. MacMillan was still wearing the tunic in which he had been captured.

"I don't know what to think of this, MacMillan," he said.

"But nobody seems to know about you." The colonel was an old soldier. He knew an old soldier when he saw one. There was a SNAFU someplace, but that didn't help matters.

WAR DEPT WASH DC
20 APR 1945

US EMBASSY CAIRO EGYPT
FOR MILATTACHE

REF YOUR TWX 49765 9APR45:
(1) WITH EXCEPTION MACMILLAN, PERSONNEL LISTED SUBJECT TWX AUTHORIZED PRIORITY SHIPMENT VIA MILITARY AIR TO ZONE OF INTERIOR. ALL PROVISIONS LIBERATED PRISONERS OF WAR APPLY. NOTIFY WAR DEPT DEPUTY CHIEF OF STAFF PERSONNEL BY PRIORITY RADIO HOUR AND DATE OF DEPARTURE AND ETA ZI RECEIVING STATION.
(2) NO RECORD EXISTS OF POW TECHNICAL SERGEANT MACMILLAN, RUDOLPH GEORGE ASN 12 279 656. PENDING SEARCH OF OTHER FILES AND INVESTIGATION BY COUNTERINTELLIGENCE CORPS PERSONNEL, YOU ARE DIRECTED TO DETAIN MACMILLAN. POSSIBILITY EXISTS HE IS GERMAN DESERTER.

> FOR THE CHIEF OF STAFF
> EDWARD W. WATERSON
> THE ADJUTANT GENERAL

"I'll be a sonofabitch," MacMillan said.

"I'll tell you what I'm going to do, Sergeant," the military attaché said. "Five minutes after your plane leaves."

"What's that, sir?" MacMillan asked. He was not unduly upset. He was an old soldier; he was used to fuck-ups. He was pissed, but not disturbed. He didn't think he was about to be shot by the U.S. Army as a German spy.

The military attaché handed him a message form.

FROM MILATTACHE USEMB CAIRO

FOR WAR DEPARTMENT WASHDC
ATTN DEPUTY CHIEF OF STAFF PERSONNEL

REFERENCE YOUR TWX 10APR45 RE TWENTY-THREE LIBERATED POWS. REGRET INFORM YOU ALL PERSONNEL MY BASIC TWX DE-

PART CAIRO BY MILAIR PRIORITY A1A 0700 HOURS 21APR45 FOR
ZONE OF INTERIOR. DESTINATION FORT DEVENS MASS. ETA 1800
22 APR45.

> BRUCE C. BLEVITT
> COLONEL, AIR CORPS
> MILITARY ATTACHE

"Thank you, Colonel," MacMillan said.

"If you're a German spy, Sergeant, I'm Hermann Göring," the colonel said.

Two agents of the Counterintelligence Corps met the C-54 which had come from Cairo, via Casablanca and the Azores, to Logan Field in Boston. They were both Jewish. They rather conspicuously carried snub-nosed .38 caliber Colt revolvers in small holsters attached to their trouser belts.

They came on the plane before any passengers were allowed to debark.

"Which one of you is Tech Sergeant Macmillan?" one of them asked.

"I am," MacMillan called.

They came to where he was sitting. One of them got in the aisle ahead of MacMillan; the other positioned himself so that MacMillan would be between them in the aisle.

"If you'll come with us, please, Technical Sergeant MacMillan," the one in front said.

"Jesus, Mac," Loczowcza said, "he's got a worse accent than Fritz the Feldwebel."

"You will kindly keep to your own business," the CIC agent said. "This does not concern you."

MacMillan got out of his seat and started to walk down the aisle.

"Achtung!" the CIC agent behind MacMillan suddenly shouted. MacMillan turned around very slowly, at first confused, and then realized that the CIC agent was trying to "catch" him obeying a command in German, and thus "proving" he was a German spy.

'Achtung!' yourself, Humphrey Bogart!" he said, laughing, not angry.

The CIC agent, flustered, angry, suddenly drew his revolver.

"Put the cuffs on him!" he ordered.

"Jewboy," Loczowcza said, firmly, not a shout, "you better put that thing away before Sergeant Mac makes you eat it. Or before I personally stick it up your ass."

The CIC agent spun to face Loczowcza. Loczowcza found himself facing a pistol. He slapped the CIC agent's hand, knocking the pistol out of the way; and the revolver fired. The sound inside the aircraft's enclosed fuselage was loud enough to be painful.

"Oh, shit!" someone shouted, almost a scream. "I've been shot!"

Loczowcza leaped from his seat and knocked the CIC agent down, and then pinned him to the aisle floor.

The other CIC agent, standing in the middle of the aisle, held his pistol in both hands and aimed it at first one and then another of the passengers, many of whom were getting to their feet.

"At ease!" MacMillan's voice boomed. "At *goddamn* ease, goddamnit!"

There was silence.

"Let him up, Polack," MacMillan ordered. Loczowcza backed away from the downed CIC agent.

"Everything's going to be all right," MacMillan said. "Just everybody take it easy." He turned to the CIC agent wielding the pistol. He put his hands out to be handcuffed.

(Seven)
Fort Devens, Mass.
22 April 1945

The general's aide-de-camp, a young first lieutenant in pinks and greens, opened the door to the general's office and nodded at MacMillan.

"The general will see you now, MacMillan," he said.

MacMillan, attired in brand-new ODs, their packing creases still visible, with brand-new low quarters on his feet and his Ike jacket sleeves bare of insignia, marched into the general's office. He stopped three feet from the general's desk.

"Sir," he snapped, as his hand rose in salute, "Technical Sergeant MacMillan reporting to the commanding general as ordered."

"Stand at ease," the major general, a plump, ruddy-faced man in his early fifties, said, returning the salute. That was a reflex, a conditioned response, as automatic as was Mac-Millan's instant crisp shifting of position from attention to parade rest. No matter what a general says to you, you don't slouch. When a general gives you "at ease" you go to "parade rest."

The commanding general of Fort Devens, Mass., looked at MacMillan as if he didn't know where to begin.

"Welcome home, MacMillan," the general said, finally. "I don't suppose anyone has said that to you here, have they?"

"Thank you, sir. No, sir, they haven't."

"If the incredibly stupid behavior of those two clowns from CIC didn't want to make you weep, if it wasn't for the trooper with the .38 slug in his leg, this whole mess could be funny," the general said.

"Sir, may the sergeant ask how Private Latier is?" MacMillan said.

"Very well. I checked on him right after I sent for you. I thought you'd want to know."

"Thank you, sir."

"Well, we've finally got this mess straightened out," the general said. MacMillan, still peering into space six inches over the general's head, stiff as a board, said nothing.

"You don't seem surprised," the general said.

"Sir, the sergeant knew that it would be straightened out in good time."

"You're not curious what happened?"

"Sir, it doesn't matter."

"If you're going to be an officer, MacMillan—" the general said, with a smile. "Correction: Now that you *are* an officer, you're going to have to learn the difference between 'at ease' and 'parade rest.'"

MacMillan's hands, which had been crossed in the small of his back, palms open, fingers stiff and together, fell awkwardly to his side. He made an effort to stand less at attention. His eyes looked at the general, and then snapped back to where they had been directed, six inches over the general's head.

"Ed," the general said to his aide-de-camp, "would you ask the sergeant to get Lieutenant MacMillan and myself a cup of coffee? And under the circumstances, I think that perhaps we might like to have a little character in the coffee. Sit down, Lieutenant MacMillan. On the couch."

MacMillan, half afraid this was some kind of incredibly detailed nightmare, walked stiffly to the general's couch, and sat down. A tech sergeant, crisply uniformed, obviously the general's sergeant, who just as obviously had been standing ready with the tray with the coffee pitcher and the cups and saucers and the Old Bartlesville 100-Proof Sour Mash Kentucky Bourbon, bent over the coffee table in front of the couch, lowered the tray, and winked at MacMillan.

"Perhaps the lieutenant," the tech sergeant said, "would like his character straight-up." He handed MacMillan a shot glass. Mac tossed it down. He felt the liquor burn his throat. This was no dream.

"As well as I have been able to piece this thing together, MacMillan," the general said, walking to the couch and sitting down beside MacMillan, "on 20 September 1944, acting on the recommendation of your battalion commander, the commanding general of the 82nd Airborne Division directly commissioned you as a second lieutenant."

"I don't remember anything about that, General," MacMillan said. "Colonel Vandervoort said I was in command, but I don't remember nothing about a commission."

"Obviously, you misunderstood your colonel," the general said. "When were you captured?"

"On the twenty-first," MacMillan said. He looked at the general with embarrassment, even shame in his eyes. "We were on the far side of the canal. We were supporting the 504th. We were out of bazooka ammo. We had one clip for the BAR. We were down to four guys, and two of them was bad wounded. General, there was more krauts than we had ammo!" He looked very close to tears.

The general snapped his fingers, then gestured "bring me" with his fingers. His aide-de-camp went to his desk, picked up a sheet of paper, and handed it to the general. The general put his glasses on. He began to read:

"Second Lieutenant Rudolph George MacMillan, 0-589866, then commanding reconnaissance platoon, 508th Parachute Infantry Regiment, 82nd Airborne Division, then engaged against

German forces in the area known as Groesbeek Heights, near Nijmegen, the Netherlands, suffered the loss of eighty percent of his command while leading them to effect a join-up with the 504th Parachute Infantry Regiment.

"Despite his own wounds, Lieutenant MacMillan personally took over operation of a rocket launcher, and ignoring a murderous hail of small arms, mortar, and artillery fire, personally destroyed five German tanks. His action prevented the enemy from forcing a breech in the ranks of the 504th Parachute Infantry Regiment, and consequently saved many American lives.

"Again ignoring his wounds, and without regard to his personal safety, Lieutenant MacMillan then personally carried two of his men through a murderous hail of enemy fire to medical facilities, during which activity he was again wounded. In order to make an attempt to save the lives of other members of his platoon, he returned a third time to his forward position.

"After expending his last rounds of rifle ammunition, and after having been wounded a fifth time, Lieutenant MacMillan was last seen advancing toward the enemy with a Thompson submachine gun, which he was firing with one hand."

"That's bullshit," MacMillan said. Tears were running down his cheeks. The tech sergeant touched his shoulder and when MacMillan looked up, the tech sergeant handed him another shot glass. MacMillan tossed it down, shuddered, and suddenly leaned forward and held his face in his hands.

"Why is it bullshit?" the general asked, softly.

"Well, I wasn't *wounded,* for one thing," MacMillan said. "Not really shot, or bad hurt. Just some scratches when I got knocked down by concussion, and fell down. You know what I mean. And that last part, about 'advancing toward the enemy with a Thompson.' Shit! What I did when we ran out of ammo was lie in that fucking hole until the krauts came and rolled over us and then I put my hands up over my head."

"I thought that paragraph was a bit colorful," the general said, dryly. He picked up the paper and resumed reading.

"Lieutenant MacMillan's actions were above and beyond the call of duty. His heroism, valor, and leadership characteristics are in the finest traditions of the United States Army and reflect great credit upon him and the military service. Entered the military service from Pennsylvania."

"Sir, can I ask, what is that you're reading, anyway?" MacMillan asked.

"This is what the military aide to the President of the United States is going to read aloud when the President hangs the Medal of Honor around your neck, Lieutenant MacMillan."

MacMillan looked at him in utter disbelief.

"There was some doubt as to whether you had survived the action," the general went on. "So award of the medal was held in abeyance until we should get some positive information about you. Or get you back. The records of Technical Sergeant MacMillan were closed. The records of Lieutenant MacMillan were flagged, so that if you should show up in one piece, we could roll out the red carpet for you. That's why there was no record of you when the military attaché sent his TWX."

MacMillan had two stiff drinks in him. He was relaxing somewhat.

"Well," he said. "Second Lieutenant MacMillan. What do you know about that?"

"First Lieutenant," the general corrected him. "Automatic promotion after six months."

"What happens now?" MacMillan asked.

"Well, either Tuesday or Wednesday, we'll fly you to Washington. We'll have your wife meet you there, of course. And on Thursday, you'll go to the White House. There are six people in the ceremony, as I understand it."

"What happens today?" MacMillan asked. He added, "Sir?" It was obvious that the announcement had, indeed, got to him. He had forgotten his military courtesy.

"It's Friday afternoon, I'm afraid," the general said. "There's not much that can be done. Get you moved into a BOQ, of course. Run you by the officer's sales store to be fitted for pinks and greens. They expect you at the hospital at 0730 tomorrow morning. Complete physical. Relax, Mac-Millan. For the next week or so, people will be doing things for you. And after Washington, you're entitled to a thirty-day liberation leave . . . not charged as leave, by the way. They've taken over the Greenbrier Hotel for that. Ever heard of the Greenbrier?"

"No, sir, I haven't," MacMillan said. "When do I get to see my wife?"

"I'm sure Second Army is already working on that. We'll

have her on hand when you get off the plane in Washington. Don't you worry about that."

"I want to see her as soon as I can," MacMillan said. "Tonight."

"I'm afraid that's quite out of the question, Lieutenant MacMillan," the general said, and Mac recognized the tone of voice. There would be no argument.

"Yes, sir," he said.

The general looked at his watch.

"Well, MacMillan," he said. "If you want to get yourself fitted, you're going to have to run along."

MacMillan stood up and popped to attention. "Yes, sir," he said. "Thank you, sir."

The general put out his hand. "It's been an honor to meet you, Lieutenant," he said. "Oh, there's one more thing I think I should tell you. I'm putting you in for the DSC for your escape."

MacMillan didn't say anything.

"And I'm sure, Lieutenant, that nothing more will be heard about the little administrative SNAFU, will there?" the general said. "It was just one of those things, wasn't it?"

"Yes, sir," MacMillan said. "That's all it was."

The general's aide-de-camp took MacMillan in the general's Ford staff car to the officer's sales store, where he was measured for uniforms. The enlisted man's uniform he was wearing was, at the aide-de-camp's insistence, pressed on the spot. It occurred to MacMillan that he could probably get out of turning the ODs in, and he would then be ahead one uniform.

There was a small problem about insignia. It could be cleared up in the morning, the aide-de-camp said, or by Monday at the latest. But for the time being, MacMillan would have to do without the embroidered insignia of the 82nd Airborne Division; without his Expert Combat Infantry Badge; without his parachutists wings; without, in fact, everything except the silver bars of a lieutenant and the crossed rifles of infantry.

"It'll be enough, Mac," the aide-de-camp said, "to get you into the officer's club to eat. And first thing in the morning, we'll turn you over to a team from PIO, who'll take care of everything while you're being briefed for the White House affair, and the press conference."

The aide-de-camp got him settled into the bachelor officer's quarters, and then left him, after pointing out the officer's mess, across the parade field.

There was a telephone in the BOQ and Mac got on it, and after several telephone calls learned that the guys, "except the one got hisself shot" had already been processed and were gone on liberation leave. A nurse in the hospital told him that the man who was shot on the C-54 could not be called to the telephone; his family had just arrived to greet him.

First Lieutenant Rudy G. MacMillan saw a small sign on the wall behind the telephone: OFF-POST TAXI 4550.

The dumb bastards, he thought, were convinced that he would be a good boy and stay sober and on the post because they hadn't paid him. He had the money, nearly a thousand dollars, that the captain of the MV *Jose Harrez* had given him at Port Said. He had seen no reason to share it with the others. For one thing, he knew they would be paid the moment they got to the States. For another, if it hadn't been for him, they would still be in Poland someplace.

He put his finger in the telephone and dialed a four, two fives, and a zero.

(Eight)
Boston, Mass.
22 April 1945

"Please deposit $2.35, sir."

Nine quarters bonged and a dime binged into the slots. He heard the number start to ring. On the third ring, somebody picked it up.

"Hello?"

His eyes watered and his throat tightened so much it hurt.

"Long distance is calling Mrs. Roxanne MacMillan."

"This is Mrs. MacMillan."

"Go ahead, sir."

Nine quarters and a dime dropped into Massachusetts Bell's coin box with a crash.

"Roah," MacMillan said. Goddamnit, he couldn't talk.

"Hello?"

"Roxy?"

"Hello?"

"Roxy, this is Mac."

"Mac?" There was disbelief in her voice.

"Honey, how are you?"

"Oh, Mac! Oh, shit, I thought you were dead! Oh, *Mac!*"

"Why did you think I was dead?"

"The army's been calling up here and at work, and they're supposed to call about now and come over. Mac, I thought they were going to tell me you were dead!"

"I'm áll right, honey," Mac said. "I'm all right."

"Honey, where are you?"

"In a railroad station in Boston."

"What are you doing there? When can you come home?"

"Can you borrow your brother's car? Can you come to New York?"

"Yeah, I'm sure I can. Tommy's home. He'll drive me."

"I don't want him to drive you. I want you to come by yourself."

"Where in New York, Mac?"

Christ, he hadn't thought about that.

"Where should I come, Mac?"

"You remember that hotel where we stayed when I was at Camp Kilmer? The Dixie?"

"Yeah, sure."

"I'll meet you there, Roxy," Mac said.

"What about the people from the army?"

"Take off right now, honey, before they get there."

"Mac, are you in some kind of trouble?"

"Just come, will you, Roxy, for Christ's sake?"

(Nine)
New York City, New York
24 April 1945

The desk clerk of the Dixie Hotel told the soldier that he was sorry, but they were all full up.

The soldier reached in the chest pocket of his Ike jacket and came out with a folded wad of money. He peeled off a twenty dollar bill, and then another.

"Like I said," the soldier said. "I'd like a double room, with a double bed, for two nights." He held the two twenty dollar bills up in front of him.

"Well, I . . ."

"You better take it," the soldier said. "That's all I'm going to put up."

"I think we just may have a cancellation, sir," the desk clerk said, and snatched the forty dollars.

While the soldier signed the registry card, the desk clerk looked around for the woman. He saw no one.

He examined the card, more than a little surprised that Lieutenant and Mrs. Smith had not just registered. The card read "1/Lt and Mrs. R. G. MacMillan, Mauch Chuck, Penna."

"Where's the bar?" Lieutenant MacMillan asked.

"Right across the lobby, sir. Your luggage, sir?"

"No luggage," MacMillan said.

"Then I'll have to have payment in advance, sir," the desk clerk said.

The soldier produced the wad of money again and paid for two days in advance. Then he walked across the lobby and went into the cocktail lounge.

An hour later, he reappeared at the desk and asked for his key. His face was liquor flushed, and there was a woman hanging tightly on his arm. She was a redhead, and her breasts overfilled the dress, straining the buttons.

"You got my key, Mac?" the soldier asked.

"Yes, sir. Eleven-seventeen. I'll get you a bellman."

"I don't need no bellman, just give me the goddamn key."

"Yes, sir."

The desk clerk watched them get on the elevator. As soon as they turned around, before the operator could close the door, the soldier dropped his hand to the redhead's buttock and gave it a little squeeze.

"Behave yourself, for Christ's sake," the redhead said.

And then the elevator door closed and took Lieutenant and Mrs. MacMillan to their floor.

(Ten)
Washington, D.C.
28 April 1945

"I understand, Lieutenant," the gray-haired man in the

glasses said to him, "unofficially, of course, that there was some doubt that you were going to find the time to come here today."

First Lieutenant MacMillan, his wife Roxanne hanging tightly on to his arm, could not form a reply.

"One of the things I learned when I was a battery commander, Lieutenant, was there was AWOL, and then there was *AWOL*. Are they giving you any trouble?"

"They were pretty mad, sir," Lieutenant MacMillan said.

"If they give you any real trouble, you let me know," the man in the glasses said. He lifted the medal suspended around MacMillan's neck on a starred blue ribbon. "That ought to be worth a weekend pass, anyhow. If they give you any real trouble, tell them the Commander in Chief told you that."

III

(One)
Kilometer 835, Frankfurt-Kassel Autobahn
Near Bad Nauheim, Germany
6 April 1945

A BMW sidecar motorcycle bounced up the median of the autobahn. It was driven by a huge black American T/4, an MP brassard on his arm. A three-by-six-foot American flag was just barely flapping from an antenna rigged as a flagpole, and a small passenger was hanging onto the lip of the sidecar cockpit.

Endless ranks of gray-uniformed prisoners marched listlessly down the median in the opposite direction. There were four tightly packed columns of American vehicles on the autobahn itself, on both sides of the median. On the left, moving northward in what were customarily the southbound lanes, was a slow-moving armored column and a second slightly faster-moving line of General Motors six-by-six trucks. The northbound lanes were jammed with a stopped double column of trucks.

The BMW motorcycle came to a bridge over a deep gorge. Its center span was blown and lay in a pile of crumbled concrete and steel two hundred feet below. The combat engineers had laid a one-lane Bailey Bridge over the gap, and a trio of military policemen directed traffic over it. Six tanks were waved across with impatient gestures, then six of the trucks from the columns on the left. The columns on the right were going to have to wait, and they had the message. Their drivers were sitting on the hoods of the GMCs. The line of prisoners wended its way down the far bank of the gorge and then up the near side.

The BMW with the sidecar had a siren, and the passenger shouted for the motorcycle driver to sound it as they approached the MPs. One of the MPs heard it, looked, stepped in front of it, and raised his hand. The passenger of the motorcycle waved his hand violently, imperiously, motioning the MP aside.

The MP swore, but he saw the MP brassard on the driver, and he thought he saw the glint of officer's insignia on the collar points of the passenger. He looked to his left. There was a fifteen-foot gap between two of the M4A3 tanks about to enter on the bridge. What the fuck, if they got run over, they could be quickly pushed out of the way. Without signaling the tank to stop or slow, he waved the motorcycle into the moving line.

First with a roar of the engine to pull ahead of the tank, then the squeal of brakes to keep from running under the tank ahead of it, the motorcycle pulled into line, and then bounced over the Bailey Bridge, somewhat cockeyed: the wheels of the motorcycle rode in the tread of the bridge, and the wheel of the sidecar was on the planks of the Bailey, six inches lower than the road.

When they reached the far side of the Bailey, they were going too fast, and the motorcycle lurched dangerously as it bounced off the Bailey and onto the undamaged portion of the bridge.

Five hundred yards off the bridge, a cluster of vehicles was parked in a field to the left. There were six military police jeeps, each with sirens and flashing lights mounted in their fenders and in their rear a machine gun on a pedestal. There were four half-tracks, each with a four-barreled multiple .50 on a turret in the bed. There were three M4A3 tanks, and half a dozen GMCs with van bodies, plus another GMC guarded by two MPs. Three flags were stuck into the ground beside its rear-opening door. One was the national colors, the second was the two-starred red flag of a major general, and the third carried an enlargement of the shoulder insignia of the 40th Armored Division, a triangular patch, yellow, blue, and red, with the number forty at the top.

As the BMW motorcycle turned out of the moving tank column with its flag catching the breeze, Major General Peterson J. Waterford came out of the van. He stopped at the top of the folding stairs and put a tanker's helmet on his head. The 40th Divisional insignia was on each side of the helmet, and there were two stars on the front. The general wore a fur-collared aviator's jacket (stars on the epaulets, the zipper fastened only at the web waistband) a shade 31(pink) shirt, shade 31 riding breeches, with dark suede inner knees, and glistening riding boots. A shoulder holster held a .45 Colt automatic, and there was a yellow scarf at his throat.

The general smiled. "Jesus, Charley," he said. "Get a load of that, will you?"

He had seen the BMW with the large black T/4 and the flapping American flag whose passenger was doing his damndest to hang on as the sidecar bounced him around.

The motorcycle slid to a halt, and that damned near sent the passenger flying out on his ass. The general was barely able to restrain himself from laughing out loud. The passenger stood up in the sidecar and saluted. That sight was too much. The passenger was about five feet five or six, and the helmet and the goggles nearly covered his head. He looked, the general thought, like a mushroom. The general chuckled loudly, almost a laugh, as he returned the salute. Fat Charley, his G-3, laughed out loud.

"General Waterford, sir," the saluting mushroom said, and scrambled out of the sidecar, bending over it to pick up a Schmeisser machine pistol, and then trotting up to the van steps. The mushroom saluted again. General Waterford saw that it was a little Jew, and that the little Jew had a second lieutenant's bar pinned to his collar.

"Lieutenant, where the hell did you get that motorcycle?" General Waterford demanded, with a broad smile.

"Sir, Lieutenant S. T. Felter requests permission to speak to the general, sir."

"Speak," Major General Peterson K. Waterford said, amused.

"Sir, I think we should speak in private," Lieutenant Felter said. "It's a personal matter."

"A personal matter?" General Waterford was no longer amused.

"A personal matter involving the general, sir," Felter said.

Waterford looked at him without expression for ten seconds. Then he turned around and stepped back inside the van, signaling for the lieutenant to follow him. Fat Charley, the G-3, stepped to one side to let the lieutenant pass.

The interior of the van had been fitted out as a mobile command post. There were desks and a half dozen telephones. On two of the walls were large maps covered with celluloid on which troop dispositions and the flow of forces had been marked with colored grease pencils.

"All right, Lieutenant," General Waterford said. "Who are you, and what do you want?"

The lieutenant took off the helmet, and pushed the goggles down over his chin, so they dangled from their strap around his neck. He rubbed the bridge of his nose, and then came almost to attention.

"Sir, I am Lieutenant S. T. Felter, attached to the POW interrogation branch of the 40th MP Company."

"And?"

"General, I believe I have located Lieutenant Colonel Bellmon."

"Which Bellmon would that be?" General Waterford asked, making an effort—and succeeding—to keep his voice under control.

"Lieutenant Colonel Robert F. Bellmon, sir. Your son-in-law."

"You're sure, Lieutenant?" Waterford asked. Fat Charley stepped into the van. "He says he's located Bob," Waterford said.

"How reliable is your information, Lieutenant?" Fat Charley asked.

"I would rate it as ninety percent reliable," Felter said. "I have three separate prisoner interrogations to base it on. One of the prisoners taken near Hoescht was a captain who was formerly assigned to Stalag XVII-B."

"I heard he was in Stalag XVII-B," Waterford said. "That's not news."

"The officer prisoners of Stalag XVII-B are being evacuated, on foot, from near Stettin," Lieutenant Felter said. "May I use the map, sir?"

"Go ahead," the general said. Felter went to a map of Germany mounted on the wall of the van, pointing out where Stalag XVII-B had been located near Stettin. Then he pointed out the route reported to be, and most likely to be, the one it would take if moving westward on foot.

Both the general and Fat Charley followed the map with interest.

"Have you any report on Colonel Bellmon's physical condition?" General Waterford asked.

"Yes, sir. He is in good physical condition. I understand he is the *de facto* senior prisoner."

"As opposed to *de jure?*" Waterford asked, half sarcastically. "Where did you go to school, Lieutenant?"

"Yes, sir. As opposed to *de jure*. I understand the senior prisoner is a full colonel suffering from depression."

Cocky little bastard, General Waterford thought. He wondered where he had come from. CCNY Jew, the general guessed. Then Harvard Law.

"I asked where you went to school," General Waterford said.

"I was at the Academy for two and a half years, sir," Felter said.

"West Point?" the general asked, incredulously.

"Yes, sir. I resigned."

"Well, then, Lieutenant," General Waterford said, "you will understand my position. While I am very grateful to you for bringing me this information, you will understand why I cannot act upon it. Why I must let things happen as they will. I cannot, as much as I would like to, send a column to free them."

"Yes, sir."

"Oh, for Christ's sake, Porky," Fat Charley said. "Why not? We have the assets!"

"I rather doubt that Colonel Bellmon would want me to," General Waterford said. "It would clearly be special privilege."

"It would be freeing prisoners. Bob's not the only one."

"The subject is not open for discussion, Colonel," Waterford said. He looked at Felter, then walked to the door of the van. As he reached it, he turned around.

"Charley," he said, "get the lieutenant's name, and write a letter of commendation to be put in his file. That was good detective work, Lieutenant, and you demonstrated a tact in presenting your information that becomes you. Thank you very much, and please keep me posted."

Then he walked down the steps of the van.

Fat Charley picked up a sheet of paper and a pencil and bent over the built-in map table.

"Name, rank, and serial number, Lieutenant," he said.

Felter gave it to him.

Then Fat Charley made up his mind.

He took a second sheet of lined notepaper and wrote on it. He gave it to Felter. Felter read it.

Phil: Porky says he will not order a relief column because it would be special privilege. Charley.

"Two point three miles beyond the bridge," Fat Charley said, "the one we fixed with a Bailey?"

"Yes, sir. I came that way."

"You will find the 393rd Tank Destroyer Regiment. I want you to tell the commanding officer, Colonel Parker, precisely what you told General Waterford."

"Yes, sir," Felter said. "Sir, if Colonel Parker is going to lead a rescue operation, I would very much like to go along."

"I have no idea, Lieutenant," Fat Charley said, "what Colonel Parker may do."

"Yes, sir."

"What I am going to do, Lieutenant, is telephone your commanding officer and tell him that I have pressed you into temporary duty here for a few days. General Waterford is a busy man, and I see no reason to bother him with any of this. Do you understand?"

"Yes, sir." Felter pulled the goggles back up over his chin and adjusted them. He picked up his helmet.

"Lieutenant, may I make a suggestion?"

"Yes, sir," Lieutenant Felter replied. "Of course."

"If you put a couple of handkerchiefs, or socks, or something, between the top of the straps and the inside of the helmet liner, it will keep your helmet from riding so low on your head."

"Really?" Second Lieutenant Felter said. He took two handkerchiefs from his field jacket pocket and jammed them into the helmet.

"There," Fat Charley said when Felter had put it on. "Now you'll be able to see."

"I never wore it much," Felter confessed. "But I heard the general was very firm about helmets."

"On your way, Felter," Fat Charley said, smiling. He touched Felter's shoulder in a gesture of affection as Felter walked past him. "Good luck."

(Two)
Kilometer 829, Frankfurt–Kassel Autobahn
Near Bad Nauheim, Germany
6 April 1945

The officers and the first grade noncoms (the regimental sergeant major, the battalion sergeants major, the first sergeants, and the other six-stripers, the S-3 and S-2 operations sergeants, the regimental motor sergeant and band sergeant) gathered in a half-circle around Colonel Philip Sheridan Parker III, commanding the 393rd Tank Destroyer Regiment.

Colonel Parker, in a zippered tanker's jacket, tanker's boots, and with his Colt New Service Model 1917 revolver hanging from a pistol belt around his waist, stood on the curved brick entryway to a mansion the 393rd had taken over as a command post three days before.

Built into the walls of the mansion, which looked more French than German, were flag holders. The American flag hung loosely from one, and the 393rd's flag, a representation of a tiger eating a tank, and which the colonel personally thought was more Walt Disney than military, hung from the other.

They didn't look like the Long Gray Line, in that some of them were fat, and some of them were short, and some of them were fat and short, and all of them were colored. But neither, Colonel Parker thought, as he often did when he looked at them, did they look like a Transportation Corps port battalion.

They looked like what they were, combat soldiers, who had proved themselves under fire, and knew they were good. Colonel Philip Sheridan Parker thought, all things considered, that his men were just as good as the Buffalo Soldiers, the 9th United States Cavalry (Colored) which had charged up Kettle Hill under Colonel Theodore Roosevelt and Master Sergeant Philip Sheridan Parker, Sr.

"Ten-hut!" his adjutant said, softly.

"Rest!" Parker said.

His noncoms and officers stood at a loose but respectful parade rest.

This was not, Colonel Parker thought again, the Fow-Fowty-Fow Double Clutchin', Motha-Fuckin' QM Truck. These were soldiers.

"Gentlemen," he said, "I think it is pretty clear that this campaign is about over. It is equally clear to me that we are at the moment about as useful to current operations as teats on a boar hog."

There were chuckles.

"It is my judgment that we have been committed to action for the last time. We may, and probably will, move again, but I think we have had our last action against tanks. The Germans seem to have run out of tanks, or at least out of any fuel to run the ones they have left.

"On the other hand, they are dug in here and there, and apparently haven't gotten the word the ball game is all over but the shouting. What I am attempting to do is paint the situation as one where we can, with our heads held high for doing our duty as well as anyone, just sit still and wait for the capitulation.

"It has, however, come to my attention that about 250 captured American officers are being marched on foot from western Poland into Germany. It is my intention to lead a column to liberate them. I have not, repeat *not*, been ordered to do so. I am proceeding under my general authority to engage targets of opportunity wherever and whenever encountered. I intend to engage whatever targets I happen to find in eastern Germany with two dozen tracks, ten jeeps, and thirty six-by-sixes, which will carry what supplies we need and whatever American prisoners we are fortunate enough to encounter.

"I will not ask for volunteers. However, those of you who would prefer to make the intelligent, rational, honorable decision to remain here until the war is over may return now to whatever you were doing before I called this officer and noncom call. Atten-hut. Dis-missed."

Not a man moved.

Colonel Parker waited until he was sure the lump in his throat had gone down sufficiently so that it would not interfere with his speaking voice.

"All of you obviously can't go," he said. "Officers may plead their cases to the exec, who is not going, and enlisted men to the sergeant major, who is. We obviously can't have a force made up entirely of officers and master sergeants. For one thing, it has been my experience that, as a general rule of thumb, such people make lousy track crewmen."

There was again the polite, respectful chuckling.

"I will not, repeat *not,* listen to appeals of the decisions made by the exec and the sergeant major," Colonel Parker said. "We move out in thirty minutes."

Lieutenant Sanford K. Felter was denied by Colonel Parker himself the honor of leading Task Force Parker into eastern Germany in the sidecar of his liberated BMW motorcycle. Parker felt the motorcycle was a good idea, and so was the flag flapping from its jury-rigged antenna (in fact, he ordered every American flag but one in the regiment carried along in the tracks, unfurled); but Lieutenant Felter was too valuable an asset for the operation to risk having him blown away while riding in the van in a motorcycle. Lieutenant Felter spoke Russian, and that was going to be necessary.

Lieutenant Felter rode in the third vehicle of the column, the first track, behind the motorcycle and a jeep, standing up in the rear, holding on to the mount of the multiple .50.

There was a military vehicle in the convoy that Sanford Felter had never seen before. It was constructed of aluminum and cloth and had an eighty-five horsepower engine. It was a Piper Cub. The 393rd's self-propelled 105 mm howitzer battery was considered to be separate artillery and thus entitled to its own artillery spotter, although the normal distribution of artillery spotters was one per battalion, three batteries of artillery.

Colonel Parker elected to employ the aircraft for column control. As they made their way through badly bombed Giessen and then wholly untouched Marburg an der Lahn, it flew ahead of the convoy reporting where the road was blocked by American units waiting to advance, and where secondary roads, often unpaved, would give them passage.

Beyond Marburg an der Lahn, at Colbe, the column turned dead east. Forty miles down that road, once they were in enemy-held territory, the Piper Cub began to report actual, or possible, or likely German emplacements and alternate routes to bypass them without a fight. The Cub, for which there were two pilots, landed at the head of the advancing column, swapped pilots, refueled, and was airborne again before the last of the tracks and trucks had rolled past it. The pilot now on the ground rode in Colonel Parker's track and pointed out on the map what he had seen from the air.

Task Force Parker averaged 16.5 miles per hour over the ground from the point of departure to the point of link-up with forces of the Union of Soviet Socialist Republics near Zwenkau, in Saxony.

This over-the-road movement time was calculated excluding the seven hours the first night Task Force Parker halted (forming its vehicles in a circle with the gas and food trucks inside, very much like a wagon train in the Wild West) and the six hours it stopped the second night on the crest of the hill overlooking Zwenkau. The convoy spent eight hours in movement the first day and fourteen the second, twenty-two hours of movement covering 363 miles on the road, about one half that distance as the crow flies.

At first light on the morning of the third day, a line of Red Army infantry skirmishers appeared, moving toward them from Zwenkau. Colonel Parker ordered one of the tracks, flying unfurled American flags, to make itself visible. It was immediately brought under heavy machine gun and small arms fire and withdrew with two of its crew wounded, but not critically.

Colonel Parker denied permission to return fire, and instead asked for two volunteers, one to drive the BMW motorcycle and the second to hold erect in the sidecar a white flag of truce. He denied Lieutenant Felter's offer of his services. Sooner or later, they were going to have to talk to the Russians, and he was the only one who spoke Russian.

The MP whose motorcycle it was insisted on driving the machine, and Lieutenant Booker T. Washington Fernwall, who had been associate professor of Romance Languages at Mississippi State Normal and Agricultural College for Colored, and who spoke French and German but not Russian, rode in the sidecar.

Watching through binoculars, Colonel Parker and Lieutenant Felter saw short, squat, gray-clad troops rise from the ground and intercept the motorcycle. And then Lieutenant Fernwall and the MP T/4 were seen being marched down the road into Zwenkau.

When they did not reappear in thirty minutes, Colonel Parker summoned Major L. J. Conzalve, who was functioning as a replacement for his bitterly disappointed executive officer who had been left with the regiment outside Bad Nauheim. He informed the major that he was going into Zwenkau in his track and that if he did not reappear or otherwise communicate in sixty minutes, the major was to move into Zwenkau with the remaining tracks, returning fire if fired upon.

Colonel Parker then ordered the multiple .50 mounts on the half-tracks to be pointed to the rear, so as to visually demonstrate a nonbelligerent attitude. Next he ordered his driver to move out. As they approached the stone fence which was obviously the outer ring of the Russian line, he motioned Felter to stand beside him in the front seat.

At that moment, a half dozen Soviet soldiers, in battle-soiled quilted cotton jackets, rough wool pants, and canvas and rubber shoes, stepped out in front of them, their submachine guns held menacingly.

One soldier stood in the middle of the road, blocking their passage.

They were, Colonel Parker realized with surprise, Orientals of some sort. And then he identified them: Mongols. He had heard that the Russians were using Mongols as their assault troops.

"Do not the soldiers of the Soviet Union salute a colonel of the United States Army?" Felter snapped in Russian. There was no reply and no salute.

"Get that man out of the road, or we'll drive over him," Felter went on. Then he told the driver to drive on. As soon as the gears clashed, and the engine revved, the Mongolian soldier stepped out of the way.

They rolled, past stone farm buildings into Zwenkau and came to the center of town, a wide marketplace with a flowing water pipe. An ancient church stood on the far side of the square. Lieutenant Fernwall and the motorcycle driver were standing by the motorcycle. There were three Russians with them, troops that somehow both Felter and Parker recognized to be company-grade officers. One of them walked up to the track and saluted.

"This is Colonel Parker, of the United States Army 393rd Tank Destroyer Regiment," Felter said. "Send for your commanding officer."

"I am the commanding officer," one of the Mongolian officers said.

"We do not deal with captains," Felter said.

"He spoke a little German," Lieutenant Fernwall said. "I think he sent for somebody."

"Ask him where the Americans are," Colonel Parker said to Felter.

"I don't think we'd better ask," Felter said. "I think we had better give them the idea we know where they are."

"All right," Parker said. "I've got to take a leak. Come with me."

He opened the door of the track and climbed down.

"Inform your superiors that the colonel is here," Felter said to the Russian officer. Then he followed Colonel Parker across the cobblestones to what had apparently been a tavern, a gasthaus. Parker, with intentional arrogance, pushed the door open. Half a dozen women, in torn clothing, cowered in a corner of what had been the dining room. There were two naked women lying on the floor, dead, one from a bullet wound in the face, the other slashed across the stomach.

"There is a 'Herren' sign," Felter said, "if you want the men's room."

Parker followed the nod of Felter's head. There was a urinal trough in the men's room, but there were feces in it and in piles on the floor already attracting hordes of flies.

"Savages! Savages!" Parker said. He relieved himself in the urinal. He looked at Felter. "Are you all right? You're not going to pass out?"

"No, sir."

When Colonel Parker had zipped his trousers, he marched back out of the gasthaus, looking at neither the bodies nor the women cowering against the wall. A jeep was now drawn up with its bumper against the bumper of the track, and a Caucasian officer standing beside it. His uniform was of much finer material than the uniforms of the Mongolians. He was not, Parker sensed, a combat officer.

"What is he?" Parker asked. "Do you know the insignia?"

"Major of military government," Felter said. "Either military government or service of supply."

The major saluted, and walked toward Parker and Felter.

"Good morning, Colonel," he said, in heavily accented English. "You seem to be lost."

"Good morning, Major," Felter replied, in Russian. "May I present Colonel Parker of the 393rd Tank Destroyer Regiment?"

"You speak Russian very well, Lieutenant," the major said, in Russian, looking at him with interest. "Are you perhaps Russian?"

"I am an American," Felter said. The major shook hands almost absent-mindedly with Colonel Parker.

"But then you must have Russian parents," he said. He switched to English. "I was saying, Colonel, that you seem to have lost your way."

"We are not lost," Parker said. "Quite the contrary. We have come for the American prisoners."

"What American prisoners?" the Russian major asked, innocently.

"The prisoners of Stalag XVII-B," Parker said.

"I'm afraid I have no idea what you're talking about," the major said.

"I'm very sorry to hear that," Parker said. "I had hoped you would be able to help us find our countrymen. Now we'll just have to look for them."

"This is the front line, Colonel," the Russian major said,

coldly. "It would be dangerous for you to move around very much here."

"Yes, it probably will be," Parker said. "But one has one's orders, and one does what one can to carry them out."

"As I say, I know of no prisoners—" the major said.

Parker interrupted him, calling up to the driver of the track. "Have Major Conzalve send a half dozen tracks down here, Sergeant."

"Colonel," the major said, in English, "I must insist that you withdraw."

"What did he say, Lieutenant?" Parker asked politely.

"I said," the Russian said, "I must insist that you not send—"

"Major," Felter said, in Russian. "Why don't you say what you want in Russian, and then I will translate for you."

"I said," the Russian said, now blustering, the Russian words coming out in a torrent, "that you must withdraw. This area is occupied by the Soviet Army."

"I don't quite understand what you mean," Parker said. "Withdraw? Withdraw where?"

The sound of half-track engines could now be heard.

"Please tell your colonel that I insist he withdraw his forces to American lines," the Russian said, furiously.

"Colonel," Felter repeated. "The major insists that you withdraw to American lines."

"Ask him what he means by that," Parker replied.

Felter repeated the question in Russian.

The major glowered at both of them, but said nothing. The sounds of half-track engines and the clanking of their tracks were now loud in the early morning quiet. The Americans were coming. The only way they could be stopped was by firing at them. The Russian major was not prepared to do that.

"Ask him where the prisoners are, Felter," Colonel Parker said, coldly, looking directly at the Russian major.

The first of the tracks became visible down the narrow street leading to the marketplace. There was a very large black officer standing up beside the driver, and its four .50 caliber Brownings were manned and pointing forward. Ten feet behind it came a second track, and ten feet behind that a third. When the tracks reached the marketplace, they formed a line, six abreast, and then sat with their engines idling.

"Ask the major, Felter," Colonel Parker said, "if he will lead us to the prisoners, or if he wants us to go find them ourselves."

"A protest will be made," the Russian major said.

"Tell the major what he can do with his protest, Felter," Colonel Parker said.

(Three)
Zwenkau, Russian-occupied Germany
8 April 1945

The two hundred and thirty-eight American officers, formerly interned in Stalag XVII-B, were in the huge and ancient timbered barn of a farm two miles east of Zwenkau. A detachment of soldiers assigned to the Military Government and Civil Affairs Division of the Red Army had laid a single roll of concertina barbed wire in a circle twenty yards from the barn. They had made clear the purpose of the barbed wire by firing a jeep-mounted machine gun into the ground ahead of a party of American officers who wished to pass the barbed wire while serving as burial detail.

The first German to die had been Oberleutnant Karl-Heinz von und zu Badner. One of the Russians who had overtaken the column of prisoners had knocked Colonel Graf Peter-Paul von Greiffenberg to the ground with the butt of his machine pistol. When Badner had tried to protect the fallen colonel from being kicked in the mouth, he had been summarily executed.

Thirty minutes later, just after the Americans were shoved into the barn, the rest of the Germans had been lined up against the stone walls of the building and machine-gunned. The Russians then denied the Americans permission to bury the bodies anywhere but in the barnyard under the manure. Then, as if to show there were no personal hard feelings, the Russians had pushed through the open barn gates a dozen German women, making their intentions clear with wide grins and the international hand language for copulation.

The females, ranging in age from thirteen to sixty-four, had already been raped repeatedly before being turned over to the Americans for their pleasure.

Lt. Col. Robert F. Bellmon had had to tackle and wrestle to the ground a previously quiet and mild-mannered Signal Corps major who had quite seriously announced his intention to take the Barisnikov submachine gun away from the Russian commander and blow his fucking head off with it.

If they were to break out of here violently, Bellmon thought, that wasn't the way to do it. The possibility that they should take some action was a very real one. He had Katyn in mind, and that, he believed, presented two duties to him. As the actual commander, he had a very deep responsibility to make sure that his officers did not wind up in a ditch with their hands bound and a .32 caliber bullet in the base of their skulls.

He also had the responsibility to get the documents of the Katyn massacre to the proper American authorities. That was a double responsibility; first, a general one as an officer, and second, a personal one to Colonel Graf Peter-Paul von Greiffenberg, who had been murdered here in Saxony.

He forced himself to think calmly, to think the problem through. They had been captured by front-line assault troops. If they were going to be shot down, chances were the front-line troops would have done it, and done it already. Front-line troops of any army were more prone to commit summary executions than the service of supply troops who followed them into an area. When the supply troops moved up here, the chances of the American prisoners being massacred would diminish. It was, of course, possible that they would still be eliminated. The Poles at Katyn had been murdered by rear area troops, but it would take an order to get service troops to do something like that; and with the war about to end, Bellmon thought that an officer would be less likely to take that responsibility.

What was most likely to happen would be that vehicles would arrive and transport them to the Russian rear. If there was a movement order, Bellmon was determined to resist it, although at the moment he had no clear idea how he could.

He had Greiffenberg's Colt .32 automatic. He had been stripped of the Schmeisser.

One little pistol against a hundred armed Russians was almost the same thing as being completely unarmed. A wild thought, holding the pistol to the head of the Russian commander, came to his mind. It was not a sound plan, but it was all that he had.

And his command was in bad shape, physically and mentally exhausted. More than a dozen of his officers were nearly catatonic. They were lice-infested, dirty, hungry, and weak. Many were bootless.

He had sent one of the lieutenants up the inside wall of the barn, to the peak of the roof, where an opening gave a partial view of the rest of the farm, but not of the road leading to it, nor of the barnyard itself.

"I hear tanks, Colonel!" the lieutenant called down softly.

Bellmon had a quick mental picture of a half-circle of T-34's turning their machine guns on his officers. He dismissed it, thinking first that the tanks were on their way to the front, and if they weren't, they were vehicles entirely suitable to accompany a force of two hundred and thirty-eight men being marched to the rear.

He heard the roar of engines now himself, and the clank of tracks. The vehicles were in the barnyard now, apparently forming up in front of the fifteen-foot-tall doors.

Then the engines were killed. There was the crack of backfires, the screech of steel treads on cobblestones. Then the sound of muffled voices. He had a moment's wild suspicion born of desperation, that he heard English. He forced that from his mind, desperately searching for a plan of action.

And then there was the sound of a trumpet, faint but unmistakable, through the heavy wooden doors. He didn't believe what he heard, because he was afraid that he had finally gone off the deep end and was hallucinating.

But in the last seconds before the ass-end of a half-track came crashing through the heavy wooden doors, he couldn't dismiss what he heard as impossible. Some sonofabitch out there *really* was playing, "When the Saints Go Marching In."

The knocking down of the barn doors with the track had set up a huge cloud of dust, which billowed outward into the yard. A man staggered out through it, his arms at his sides, and looked at the tracks. His uniform was in tatters, and he was skeleton thin. But there was an overseas cap on his head, cocked to the left in the tradition of armor.

Colonel Philip S. Parker VI pressed the button on his microphone.

"Bring up the trucks," he ordered. "We've found them."

A half dozen others staggered out after him, blinking in the sunlight, shielding their eyes.

The trumpet player, a fat, very black staff sergeant with tears running down his cheeks, put his horn to his lips and played again, not quite able to do what he was trying to do, play what the army called a "spirited air." It came out more like a dirge, but it was still "When the Saints Go Marching In."

The emaciated officer looked in the direction of that track, and half smiled, making a gesture with his hand. Then he saw the commanding officer of the detachment of soldiers from the Red Army, and advanced on him, his arms spread and bent, his fingers extended, violence obviously on his mind.

Two of the men who had followed him out of the barn started after him. One of them broke into a run.

One of the Russian soldiers fired a burst with his Barisnikov machine pistol onto the cobblestones before him. The officer stopped. A half-second later, the multiple .50 caliber machine guns on one of the tracks fired a second's burst. Forty .50 caliber bullets, eight of them tracers, slammed into the cobblestones in front of the Russians. One of the Russians, not the commanding officer, slumped to the ground, the top of his head and the back of his helmet blown away by a ricocheting projectile.

By then, Lieutenant Felter was out of his half-track, across the cobblestones, and standing in front of the officer with violence on his mind.

"Colonel," Felter said. "For God's sake!"

Bellmon looked at him, as if surprised to see him.

There was the sound of starters grinding and the whine of electric motors as the multiple .50 mounts turned to bear on the Russians.

"Goddamn you, Jamison!" Colonel Parker shouted at the gunner who had let fly with the burst.

Another track, racing, came around the corner of the barn, followed by a six-by-six, a T/4 at the .50 caliber in the ring turret over the cab.

Colonel Parker jumped out of the track and signaled where he wanted the line of trucks to go, and then he went over to where Bellmon and Felter stood facing each other.

"If there are any radios in that Russian jeep," he ordered Felter, "smash them." Then he turned to Bellmon.

"Bobby," he said, very gently. "We've got to load your people and haul ass," he said.

Bellmon looked at him without recognition for a moment. "It's Colonel Parker, isn't it?" he asked.

Parker, obviously having a hard time keeping his emotions under control, nodded. "Bobby," he repeated, "we've got to load your people right now."

"Yes," Bellmon said, dreamily, then seemed to regain some control as he said: "Yes, of course, sir." He turned and staggered back toward the door of the barn.

"Disarm them," Parker said, indicating the Russians. "Throw their weapons down a well. Lock them up in the farmhouse. Tie them up with commo wire." Parker ran back to his half-track, climbed in, and picked up the ground-to-air radio.

"We've had a little trouble down here," he said, calmly. "We're going to run back through Zwenkau. Check to see if they've tried to block the road."

The L-4 which had been circling overhead banked steeply, and flew low over the farmyard, as if the pilot was curious and wanted to see what was going on, and then flew off toward Zwenkau.

(Four)
57th U.S. Army Field Hospital
Giessen, Germany
11 April 1945

Carrying a bottle of Pinch Bottle Haig under his arm, Major General Peterson K. Waterford walked into a private third floor room in the neat, modern, airy hospital, which had been built for the Wehrmacht for the care of gastrointestinal illness.

"Can you handle this?" he asked, extending the bottle to the pale man with shrunken eyes, who sat on the edge of a hospital bed wearing a purple U.S. Army Medical Corps bathrobe and white cotton pajamas.

Lt. Col. Robert F. Bellmon nodded his head. General Waterford put out his hand, to shake that of Colonel Bellmon, and then suddenly changed his mind. His arm went up and around Bellmon's shoulders, and still clutching the bottle in his fist, he hugged Bellmon to him.

"I'm sorry," he said, when they had broken apart, "that I couldn't get here sooner."

"I understand."

"You are suffering from exhaustion and malnutrition," General Waterford said. "That's all."

"This is the neuropsychiatric ward," Bellmon said. "I'm surprised there isn't a sign."

"You have never been in the N–P ward," Waterford said. "The surgeon is an old friend of mine."

"I'm not really crazy, you know," Bellmon said. "Skinny, certainly, and my teeth seem to be falling out. And in a rage. But not crazy."

Waterford didn't reply. He walked to the bedside table and spilled some of the scotch into a water glass, then picked up the glass and handed it to Bellmon. "Drink that, Bob," he said.

Bellmon took the glass, and a mouthful, and swirled it around his mouth before swallowing it.

"First in a long time, huh?" General Waterford asked.

"No, actually, it's not," Bellmon said. "Philip Sheridan Parker III, in the sacred tradition of the cavalry, had a bottle in his saddlebags, when he sounded the charge and rode to the rescue."

"I have to tell you this, Bob," Waterford said. "If I had known what Phil Parker was planning to do, I would have stopped him."

"What the hell's the matter with you?" Bellmon exploded. "Don't hand me any of that noble, no special privileges bullshit. I wasn't the only officer there; and if Parker hadn't shown up when and where he did, two hundred and thirty-eight officers, including me, would now be pushing up daisies or on our way to a Siberian prison camp."

"I don't intend to debate the matter with you," Waterford said, coldly. "I just wanted you to know my position in the matter."

Bellmon looked at his father-in-law with ice in his eyes,

apparently on the edge of saying something. He said nothing.
Then he drank the rest of the scotch in the glass and helped
himself to more.

"What happens to me now?" he asked.

"I've got you a uniform. You'll put it on. And then you'll
be driven to Frankfurt. You'll be home in thirty-six hours."

"Thank you very much for the special privilege, sir," Bellmon said, sarcastically. "But if it's all right with you, I'll just
stay here and press charges."

"You didn't hear me, Bob," General Waterford said. "You
will be driven to Frankfurt, and you will be flown home. If
you are not in a mental condition to be able to obey a lawful
order when you receive one, you will be sent home in a padded
cell on a hospital ship."

"You're ordering me home?" Bellmon asked.

"You'd damned well better be grateful for special privilege.
George Patton is ordering you home. Eisenhower and all of his
staff want you locked in the booby hatch."

"Do you understand the nature of the charges I'm bringing?"
Bellmon asked.

"The counterintelligence officer you spoke to is another old
friend of mine. He came to me before he passed the story
upstairs."

"He wanted me to give him the photographs," Bellmon said,
"and the other evidence."

"I think you'd better give them to me," Waterford said.

"Over my dead body," Bellmon said. "This is not going to
be whitewashed."

"I want whatever you have, Bob," Waterford said. "I'm
asking for them as nicely as I intend to."

"You can have them taken from me, I suppose," Bellmon
replied. "But you'll have to use force. And that will force
Barbara to choose between us."

"Just what the hell do you think you can do with that stuff?
For God's sake, those allegations have already been considered
and dismissed as enemy propaganda."

"They're not 'allegations,'" Bellmon said, furiously. "Goddamnit. I was there."

"You were a prisoner, subject to enormous psychological
pressure."

"I was taken to Katyn by Peter-Paul von Greiffenberg," Bellmon said. "Did your CIC friend tell you that, too?"

"No," Waterford said. He was visibly surprised to hear that. "He did not."

"And did he tell you that the ranking officer of the group of Germans who had made themselves my prisoners, who our Russian allies stood against the wall at Zwenkau, shot, then made us bury under a pile of cow shit, was your old friend, Colonel Count Peter-Paul von Greiffenberg?"

"Good God!" Waterford said.

"I'm not crazy, Dad," Bellmon said. "Two hundred and thirty-eight officers saw what those bastards did."

"The Germans' hands aren't clean, Bob," Waterford said.

"What's that got to do with it?"

"One of my regiments ran over a place where the Germans took the Russians and Polish, and for that matter, their own Jews. They gassed them, Bob, by the tens of thousands, maybe even by the millions. Then, after they shaved off their hair and pulled their teeth for the gold, they burned them in ovens."

Bellmon looked at him.

"I can't believe you'd tell me something like that if it wasn't true," he said.

"It's true. I went and saw it myself," Waterford said.

"Then I suppose, under the rules of land warfare, we are going to have to try the Germans responsible for that, and hang them. As I intend to have the Russians responsible for Katyn and Zwenkau tried and hung."

"You can forget Zwenkau," Waterford said.

"Forget it?"

"It was a regrettable misunderstanding, with error on both sides," Waterford said.

"Because one Russian got himself blown away with a ricochet?"

Waterford nodded.

"Prisoners were taken from me," Bellmon said. "And shot down in cold blood."

"The Russian story is that they liberated you from the Germans, who were killed in the engagement."

"My officers will tell you different."

"The senior prisoner is mad," Waterford said. "Certifiably

mad. He is going home in a padded cell on a hospital ship."

"I had assumed command," Bellmon said. Waterford shook his head 'no'.

"Just for the hell of it, Dad," Bellmon said, sarcastically, "let me tell you about the little girl the Russians gave us. Pretty little thing. About thirteen, I would say. They had raped her, and then when they got tired of that, before they gave her to us, they stuck a bayonet up her anus. She died in the half-track on the way back. Because we couldn't stand the smell, we buried her by the side of the road. Her mother was so afraid of the Russians she begged us not to leave her. She wouldn't even get out of the half-track long enough to watch us bury her daughter."

"Oh, for Christ's sake, this is getting us nowhere," General Waterford said, impatiently. "Don't you think I've heard these stories before?"

"If you have, they don't seem to bother you very much," Bellmon said.

"I'll lay it out for you, Bob, and hope you can understand what I'm saying. You can continue making noise about this. You have my word it will get you nowhere. No matter what you say the Russians have done, the Germans have done worse. If you continue to make noise here, you will be sent home for psychiatric care. That would be the end of your career, and you know it."

"If this is how I am supposed to behave as an officer, I'm not sure I want a career."

"You can go home now and keep your mouth shut, bide your time, and decide in a year or so if you want to make a stink then. Get it through your head you cannot make a stink now. No one will listen. It would be an exercise in futility."

"Shit!" Bellmon said, and walked to the window of his hospital room. The sun was shining, and the trees just starting to turn green. But Bellmon smelled burned wood and stagnant water, perhaps even a faint odor of rotting human flesh in the air. He looked at the glass of whiskey in his hand, raised it to his lips, and drank it down. Then he walked back to the bedside table and poured more scotch in his glass.

"So what's your advice?" he asked, turning to face his father-in-law.

"I think you should go home, get your weight and your strength back, be with Barbara and the kids, and take time to make up your mind."

"My mind is made up!"

"Decide whether you can be of greater service to your country as a general officer when that time comes, or as a shrill, forcefully retired officer who went mad in a POW camp," General Waterford said.

"You're saying that no one will believe me?"

"I didn't say that," Waterford said. "I believe you. Patton believes you. That's why he's sticking his neck out for you. I'm saying that if you expect anything to be done, you're wrong."

"What did Colonel Parker do? I presume he got a speech like this."

"Patton pinned a Silver Star on him and then he got him out of theater before the chair-warmers around Ike could relieve him of his command. You owe Phil Parker, Bob. That operation he mounted to go get you cost him his star."

"What the hell kind of a war is this?"

"A shitty kind of a war," General Waterford said. "Do you know of any other kind?"

(Five)

Mrs. Robert F. Bellmon, her mother, Mrs. Peterson K. Waterford, and the Bellmon children were on hand at Andrews Army Air Corps Base near Washington, D.C., when Lt. Col. Robert F. Bellmon was returned from the European Theater of Operations by military aircraft.

The first thing Barbara Bellmon thought when she saw her husband walk stiffly down the portable stairway rolled up against the Military Air transport Command C-54 was that he was an old man.

All the returned prisoners were reunited with their families in a hangar which had been cleared of aircraft and support equipment on a semipermanent basis for that purpose.

The aide-de-camp to the commanding general of Andrews Army Air Corps Base waited until Lt. Col. Bellmon had a moment to embrace his wife, his children, and his mother-in-law; and then he went to him and gently touched his arm. When he had his attention, he quietly told Bellmon there was a car waiting for him outside the hangar, that it would not be necessary for him to ride with the others on the bus to the Walter Reed U.S. Army Medical Center. The commanding general of Andrews and Major General Peterson K. Waterford had been classmates at the Academy.

Lt. Col. Bellmon's children had no idea who he was.

Barbara Bellmon was sure that Bob would blow his cork when he found out that he would be required to undergo, for seventy-two hours a comprehensive physical and psychiatric examination before he could go on leave. But he said nothing at all about it, just nodded his head; and she wondered if there was perhaps something wrong with him mentally.

She had already been briefed by an army psychiatrist, who told her that she should prepare herself for significant psychological changes in her husband's behavior. Imprisonment was, he said, a psychological trauma.

On the morning of his fourth day home, he called her where she was staying at the Wardman Park Hotel.

"Have you got any money?" he asked.

"I don't know what you mean?"

"If I don't stick around here to get paid, I can leave now," he said.

"Come," she said. "Come right now."

Mrs. Waterford took the kids to the Smithsonian Institution, and said that she would probably buy them supper somewhere.

When he tried to make love to her, he couldn't.

"The psychiatrist warned me this was liable to happen," he said. "I'm sorry."

"Don't be silly, Bob," she said. "We have the rest of our lives to catch up."

It didn't seem to bother him, she saw with enormous relief. He immediately changed the subject.

He rolled away from her on the bed and handed her his copy of his physical examination. It had been determined, she read, that he was of sound mind and body, though showing signs of malnutrition. He had been warned to seek dental attention, since prolonged malnutrition made the gums shrink, loosening teeth and causing other oral-dental problems.

The very phrase "prolonged malnutrition" filled Barbara with pity.

"I'm on a thirty days' returned prisoner-of-war leave," Bob told her. "And we have reservations at the Greenbrier Hotel, at government expense. Do you want to go?"

"Do you?" Barbara asked.

"I don't know," he said listlessly.

"What would you like to do?" Barbara pursued.

"I'd like to buy a car," he said. "And take a long, slow drive to Carmel."

"OK," she said. "When do you want to look for a car?"

"How about now?" he asked.

Barbara got out of bed and started to get dressed.

Mrs. Waterford returned to Carmel with the children by train. Lt. Col. Bob Bellmon bought a 1941 Buick convertible sedan and started out with Barbara on a slow, cross-country drive. One of their stops was at Manhattan, Kansas, outside Fort Riley, where Colonel Bellmon presented his respects to recently retired Colonel Philip S. Parker III.

Later Mrs. Parker confided to Barbara that so long as they had been married, she had never seen her husband quite as drunk as he got with Bob Bellmon. The two women tried to determine what it was that had so gotten to their husbands. They each took what solace they could from learning that neither husband had chosen to confide in his wife.

Barbara Bellmon was tempted to inquire of Mrs. Parker if her husband was impotent, too. But the words would not come. Officers' ladies did not discuss that sort of thing among themselves.

It took them thirteen days to reach Carmel. Once there, Bob spent long hours working on the Buick, completely rebuilding the straight-eight engine and lining the brakes, all by himself in the garage. He took long walks, alone, very early in the morning along the Pacific Ocean, and ritually drank himself into a sullen stupor by five in the afternoon.

Barbara Bellmon concluded that it was a vicious circle. He drank because he was impotent; and because he was hung over and/or drunk, he couldn't get it up. After doing everything but appear in pasties and a G-string, she sensed somehow that the thing to do was wait.

He asked for, and was granted, a thirty-day extension of his leave. His orders, to the Airborne Board at Fort Bragg, N.C., came in the mail on the tenth day of the extension.

"You getting a little bored, honey?" he asked. "You want to report in early and see about getting someplace decent to live?"

"I think that would be a good idea," Barbara said.

Right after lunch on the day before they left Carmel, he began a frenzied search through his footlockers, which had been stored at Fort Knox during the war, then shipped to Carmel after his return. He took from them what he thought they would need in the first weeks at Bragg before their household goods arrived.

Mrs. Waterford had arranged a small cocktail party for old friends for five that afternoon. Barbara, afraid that he would be drunk when the party started, and afraid to say anything that would make it inevitable, nevertheless went to their bedroom; and under pretense of getting dressed for the party and helping him pack, she gave him company.

At a quarter to five, when Barbara was looking through already packed suitcases for a slip, she heard the lid of a footlocker slam and turned to look at him.

He was smiling.

"Finished?" she asked.

"Finished," he said. "Everything I won't need is in the one we'll take with us. And everything I will need is in the other one, which will arrive in time for Christmas, 1948."

"You'd better get dressed, then," she said, and bent over the suitcase again.

"That's exactly the opposite of what I have in mind," he said.

She didn't quite get his meaning until he had walked up behind her, pressed his erection against her rear end, and slipped his hand under the elastic of her panties.

She straightened, and pressed her head backward against his; and very slowly, very carefully, very much afraid that when she touched it, it would go down, she moved her hand to his crotch.

Then she turned around without taking her hand off him, pulled him toward the bed, and lay down on it. She pushed her panties out of the way and guided him into her.

The Bellmon kids had a ball on the drive to Fort Bragg from Carmel. They were left much to themselves. They even had their own room in the motels at night. About the only thing wrong with the trip was the embarrassment their parents caused them by constantly holding hands and smooching and not acting their age.

(Six)
Camp 263
Near Kyrtym'ya, Russian Soviet Federated Republic
21 June 1945

The German prisoners were ordered from the trains immediately on arrival. A detail was picked from them to load coal into the tender of the locomotive. Since there were no shovels, the loading was accomplished by a chain of prisoners between the coal pile and the tender. Each prisoner carried an eight- or ten-inch lump of coal and passed it along until it reached the tender. The locomotive was then detached from the string of cars and reattached to the other end. The train immediately left the siding. Since there was a shortage in Russia of both train cars and locomotives, the ones they had were kept moving as much as possible.

Bread and sausage were distributed among the prisoners. They had not eaten much in the past three weeks, and they fought over the food.

Portable barricades—sawhorses laced with barbed wire— were emplaced by prisoner laborers around the siding. Guard posts and a deadline were also established. More elaborate security measures were not required, for Kyrtym'ya was an island in the swamps, completely water-filled in the spring from melting snow. There was no place else for the prisoners to go, even if they had the strength.

The prisoners were kept where they had gotten down from the boxcars for four days, while the administrative processing was completed.

The records of some of the prisoners, and all of the SS, were immediately separated. These would be immediately put to work draining the swamp.

The records were also searched for prisoners whose skills were needed to administer the camp. Prisoners who spoke Russian were in great demand, and so were carpenters, foresters, tailors, and supply clerks. There was a surplus of food service personnel.

Some of the NKVD records were flagged. These prisoners had either actual or professed socialist and/or Russian sympathies; and after a period of time, it was contemplated that they might be of some use. These were to be assigned duties which would give them a greater chance—by no means a sure chance—of surviving a winter or two in the swamp.

Other prisoners' records were flagged in a manner indicating that they were to be kept alive. The phrase used was that "the physical condition and status of reeducation of this prisoner will be reported monthly." The NKVD expected to hear that the prisoner in question was not only alive, but that his reeducation was progressing satisfactorily.

One of the prisoners whose records were so flagged was identified on the NKVD records as Greiffenberg, Peter P. von (formerly Colonel), 88–234–017.

Number 88–234–017 was assigned to work as a clerk in the office of the logging master. It was inside work, and that was important in the winter in the swamp.

IV

(One)
Fort Bragg, N.C.
9 July 1945

There were twelve multicolored ribbons above the breast pocket of Lt. Colonel Paul Hanrahan's tunic, and above them was pinned the CIB, the Expert Combat Infantry insignia: a silver flintlock rifle on a blue background circled by an open silver wreath, and above that, parachutist's wings with two stars signifying two jumps into combat.

There were no ribbons above Lieutenant Rudolph G. MacMillan's breast pocket, just his CIB and his jump wings with five stars.

MacMillan walked into Hanrahan's office and saluted. There was a pleased smile on his face.

"How the hell are you, you kiltless Scotchman?" Hanrahan said, returning the salute casually, and then coming around his desk to warmly shake MacMillan's hand.

"Permit the lieutenant to say," MacMillan said, grinning broadly, "that the colonel, so help me God, even looks like a colonel."

"With one exception, Mac," Hanrahan said, waving him into an upholstered chair, "you don't look so bad yourself."

"What's the exception?"

"There's an order around here, Mac," Colonel Hanrahan said, "that officers are supposed to wear their ribbons."

MacMillan shrugged, unrepentant.

"You want some coffee, Mac?" Hanrahan asked.

"Please," MacMillan said. "What's this all about, anyway?"

In 1940, Hanrahan had been a second john, and MacMillan had been a corporal. They had made their first jump together, when the entire airborne force of the United States Army had been the 1st Battalion (Airborne) (Provisional) (Test) of the 82nd Infantry Division. They had been paratroopers together before anyone knew if the idea would work, and long before the 82nd Infantry Division had become the 82nd Airborne.

They had last seen one another in 1942, when First Lieutenant Paul Hanrahan had suddenly vanished from the 508th Parachute Infantry Regiment in 1942. Nobody knew for sure where he had gone, but rumor had it that he was on some hush-hush operation in Greece with something called the OSS.

"You are about to be counseled about your career by a senior officer of suitable rank and experience," Colonel Hanrahan said. "So pay attention." He handed MacMillan a china cup full of steaming black coffee.

"Thanks," MacMillan said. "Can you get me away from those goddamned historians? I'm losing my marbles."

"The day after one war is over, we start training for the next one," Hanrahan said. "The historians have a place in that. The presumption is that somebody who lives through a war must have been doing something right. So they will write down the Saga of Mac MacMillan, and force unsuspecting people to read it. You'll be immortal, Mac."

"Bullshit, is what it is," MacMillan said.

"Shame on you!" Hanrahan said, laughing.

"The division is coming home," MacMillan said. "Can you get me a company?"

"I could, but I won't," the colonel said, looking directly at MacMillan.

"Why not?"

"Can I talk straight, Mac, and not have you quoting me all around the division?"

"Sure," Mac said.

"If we were going to war, you'd have a company," the colonel said. "But we're going to have peace, Mac, and that's a whole new ball game. They don't want company commanders, even with the Medal, who quit school in the tenth grade." He looked at MacMillan to get his reaction. MacMillan didn't seem very surprised.

"The war is over, soldiers and dogs keep off the grass?" he replied.

"Don't feel crapped upon," Hanrahan said. "They don't want twenty-six-year-old light birds, either."

"They gonna bust you back?"

"They're trying hard," Hanrahan said. "I want to show you something, Mac." He motioned Mac to the desk, where he had MacMillan's service record open before him, and pointed to a line on one of its pages.

18Apr45 Returned US Mil Control, US Embassy Cairo Egypt
20Apr45 Transit Cairo Egypt via Mil Air Ft Devens, Mass
22Apr45 VOP 4 days lv
26Apr45 Transit Hq War Dept
29Apr45 Hq Ft Bragg Dy w/US Army Historical Section

"What the hell is VOP?" Mac asked. He could translate without thinking all other abbreviations, but VOP was new to him.

"I had to ask to find out," the colonel said. "It stands for Verbal Order of the President."

"That's funny," Mac said. "He told me when I was there, that when he was a battery commander, he found out there 'was AWOL and then there was *AWOL*.'"

"It's not funny, Mac," the colonel said. "That VOP is going to follow you around the army from now on. Forever, until you turn in the suit."

"What's wrong with it?"

"The bottom line is that you went AWOL," the colonel said.

"Not according to that, I didn't. I went VOP," Mac said, smiling, pronouncing it as a word, not as individual letters.

"You went AWOL and were pardoned by the President. *You went AWOL!* And every time somebody asks what the hell is 'VOP,' that story will be told. And what they are going to remember, because they will want to remember it, is that you went AWOL. That gives them a hook, Mac. And you better get used to the fact that the hook is going to be out for you from now on."

"What the hell are you talking about? I'm a goddamn hero. Didn't you read that bullshit citation?"

"Don't mock it. You *are* a hero. And that's your problem."

"I don't have idea fucking one what you're talking about," MacMillan said.

"Then pay attention. One officer in twenty gets into combat. Of the officers who do get into combat, maybe one in ten gets any kind of a medal, and one in what—ten thousand? fifty thousand?—gets *the* Medal."

"So?"

"So there's a hell of a lot more of them, Mac, then there is of you. Call it jealousy. 'How come that dumb sonofabitch, and not me?' "

"So they're jealous, so what?"

"So they will stick whatever they can—your lousy education, for example—up your ass whenever they can."

MacMillan didn't like what he had heard, but he trusted the colonel; they went back a long way. He decided he was getting the straight poop.

"What about me getting out and re-upping as a master sergeant?"

"No sense giving anything away," Hanrahan said.

"You just as much as told me I don't have what it takes to be a good company commander," Mac said. "I may not be. But I *know*, goddamnit, that I'd be a good first sergeant."

"I didn't say that you wouldn't be a good company commander, Mac," Hanrahan said. "You're not listening to me."

"Then what the hell *are* you saying?"

"You're a brand-new first lieutenant," Hanrahan said. "So you can forget about getting promoted for a long time. Five years, maybe six. Maybe longer."

"I don't find anything wrong with being a first lieutenant," MacMillan said. "But I thought you were just saying they'd try to take it away from me."

"What you have to do is pass the time doing something where you can't get in trouble, where there won't be too much competition for your job."

"That brings us right back to me commanding a company. Goddamn, airborne is what I know. Airborne is *all* I know."

Hanrahan was losing his patience. No getting around it, MacMillan was none too bright.

"Airborne is dead. It just doesn't know enough to fall over," Hanrahan said, patiently. "But for Christ's sake, Mac, don't quote me on that."

"That's a hell of a thing to say," MacMillan said. He was truly shocked. It was as if the colonel had accused Jim Gavin of cowardice.

"For Christ's sake, think. You were at Sicily. Look what our own navy did to us, by mistake. How many planeloads got shot down before they got near the goddamned drop zone? You made Normandy. Look how they tore us up in Normandy. And you jumped across the Rhine. That was a disaster, and you know it was."

MacMillan was looking at him, Hanrahan thought, like a hurt little boy.

"For Christ's Sake, Mac," Hanrahan said, "you were there. You were bagged there. And you don't understand what a colossal waste of assets and people that was?"

"I never expected to hear something like that from you, of all people," MacMillan said. "Jesus Christ, you and me started airborne!"

"I'm a soldier, Mac. Not an airborne soldier, not any kind of special soldier. I'm a soldier. My duty is to see things as they are, not how I'd like them to be."

"And you think airborne is finished? You *really* think that?"

"It's a very inefficient way of getting troops on the ground. And it will grow more inefficient every passing day. And it wastes a lot of talent."

"What's that supposed to mean?" Mac demanded. They were no longer colonel and lieutenant, or even lieutenant and corporal. They were friends and professionals. They were, in fact, comrades in arms.

"You've heard that an airborne corporal is just as good, just as highly trained, just as efficient a leader, as a leg lieutenant?"

"And I believe it," MacMillan said, firmly. "For Christ's

sake, if I had volunteered six months later, they wouldn't have taken me. I didn't have a high enough Army General Classification Test score."

"That's my point. They had almost as high qualifications for jump school as they did for OCS."

"Your goddamn right they did," MacMillan said, righteously.

"Then apply some logic. Extend the argument," Hanrahan said. "If a man is good enough to be a lieutenant, we should be using him as a lieutenant, not an assistant squad leader. If we're going to spend people, which is the name of the game, Mac, keep the price high. Every airborne sergeant we spent, dead before he hit the ground, probably could have kept twenty legs alive if he had been a leg sergeant."

"Jesus!" MacMillan said.

He walked to the window and looked out. Hanrahan saw that he was disturbed and was pleased. To get his point across, he was going to have to really shake MacMillan up.

MacMillan finally turned from the window and leaned against the sill, supporting himself on his hands.

"You're trying to tell me the whole airborne idea was wrong?"

"There were two mistakes in War II, Mac," Hanrahan said, gently. "Airborne and bombers."

"Somebody did something right. We won," Mac said, sarcastically.

"The navy did what it was supposed to do," the colonel said. "And so did the artillery. But the ones who really came through, on both sides, were the tankers."

Mac just looked at him.

"You ever wonder why we didn't jump across the Rhine near Cologne? You *know* why we didn't jump on Berlin?" Hanrahan pursued.

"You tell me, Red," Mac said. "I'm just a dumb paratrooper who apparently doesn't know his ass from a hole in the ground."

"Because when the tanks crossed the Rhine, they brought their support with them, and they brought firepower with them. Not some lousy 105 howitzers with fifty rounds a gun. The big stuff and all the ammo they needed for them. And we didn't jump on Berlin because the 2nd Armored was already across the Elbe."

"The Russians took Berlin."

"Correction. Three mistakes in War II. Ike giving Berlin to the Russians. 2nd Armored could have taken it. Eisenhower ordered them to hold in place."

"He did?" MacMillan had apparently never heard that before. "What for?"

"Political considerations," Hanrahan said, watching his tongue very carefully. He thought it was entirely possible that MacMillan had never considered why World War II was fought. The more he thought about that, the more sure he was he was right. MacMillan had fought in World War II, fought superbly, risked his ass a hundred times, simply because he was a soldier and somebody had issued an order.

"I didn't know that," Mac said. The colonel said nothing. "What are you telling me I should do, Red? Go to armor? I'm infantry. *Airborne infantry.*"

"No, you shouldn't go to armor. First of all, they wouldn't take you. And if they did, they'd eat you up worse than airborne would."

"They'd eat me up? I'm airborne. But the way you talk, *you* don't think of yourself as airborne," Mac said.

"I haven't been airborne since I left the 508th Parachute Infantry," Hanrahan said.

"I notice you're wearing two combat jump stars on your wings," MacMillan replied.

"I went into Greece twice," Hanrahan said. "Once out of a B-25, the other time out of a B-24. A combat jump is defined as a jump into enemy-held territory."

"I never thought about that," MacMillan said. "You know what I think of when I think of a combat jump? A whole regiment, a whole division."

"I've known you long enough to say this," Hanrahan said. "Without you thinking I'm just making an excuse for leaving the 508."

"Say what?" Macmillan asked.

"Mac, we jumped in four guys, five guys at a time. Sometimes just one guy. But we did more damage to the enemy than a battalion of parachutists, maybe a regiment. Maybe even, goddamnit, a division."

"You and three, four other guys?" Mac asked, in disbelief.

"We had more Germans chasing us around Greece than you

would believe. And every German that was chasing us wasn't fighting someplace else. That's the name of the game, neutralizing the enemy's forces, Mac, not 'Geronimo,' not 'Blood on the Risers.'"

MacMillan was made uncomfortable by the discussion. He realized that he really thought, at first, that jumping all by yourself out an Air Corps bomber wasn't really a combat jump. But then he carried that further. At least when the regiment had jumped, he hadn't been alone. Hanrahan's jumping had been more dangerous than even his own jumping in as a pathfinder had been, and the pathfinders had gone in a couple of hours before the rest of the division had jumped. Hanrahan, MacMillan realized, with something close to awe, had jumped into Greece *knowing* that there would be no regiment jumping after him.

"So what are you going to do, in this peacetime army we're about to have?" he asked.

"I'm going back to Greece," Hanrahan said.

"Why do you want to do that?" MacMillan replied, surprised. "I didn't even know we had any troops there."

"Because I like being a lieutenant colonel, for one reason, and they tell me that if I'm in Greece, I can keep it, at least for a while. I hope I can keep it long enough to keep it, period."

"What are you going to do in Greece?" MacMillan asked.

"Train the Greeks to do their own fighting," Hanrahan said. "We send in an experienced company-grade officer and a couple of really good noncoms, make them advisors to a company, or even a battalion. That's where it's going to be, Mac: for the price of three or four people, you get a company."

"Special people, huh? Regular soldiers, who really know what they are doing?"

"Special people, but stop smiling; you can't go."

"Why the hell not?"

"Because you're a *hero*, MacMillan. I keep trying to tell you what that means. It would be embarrassing for the army if we lost a Medal of Honor winner on some Greek hill in a war we aren't even admitting we're fighting."

"Fuck the medal, I'll give it back."

"Don't be an ass, Mac," Hanrahan said. "That medal is your guarantee of a pension at twenty years as a major, maybe even a light bird."

"I don't want to sound like damned fool, but I don't want to spend the next fifteen years as somebody's dog robber," MacMillan said. "I'm a soldier."

"For the next couple of years, until things simmer down and get reasonably back to normal, all you have to do is keep your ass out of the line of fire."

"Like doing what, for example?"

"Army aviation," Hanrahan said.

"You've got to be kidding," MacMillan said. "Army aviation, shit!"

Hanrahan lost his temper. His voice was icy and contemptuous when he replied, "Engage your brain, Mac, before opening your mouth."

MacMillan colored and glared at him. Hanrahan did not back down.

"OK," MacMillan said, after a long pause. "I'm listening. Tell me about Army aviation."

"Those little airplanes, and helicopters, too, are going to be around the army from now on. And it's going to get bigger, not smaller and smaller. The Air Corps is going to go after bigger and bigger bombers, and the army is going to have to fend for itself with light airplanes."

"What's that got to do with me?"

"It's a very good place for you to be," Hanrahan said. "There aren't very many aviators around who know their ass from a hole in the ground about the army. And don't underestimate your medal. You can be a very big fish in a small pond."

"You know, I don't believe any of this conversation," MacMillan said.

"I'm not finished," the colonel said. "I've got you a space at Riley."

"The Ground General School? Doing what?"

"For a fourteen-week course, after which you will be an army liaison pilot," the colonel said.

"You've got to be kidding," MacMillan said. "All those guys are is commissioned jeep drivers."

"Some of them are, and some of them are just as good soldiers as you are," Hanrahan said, coldly. Then he lightened his voice. "They get flight pay, which is the same dough as jump pay. What have you got to lose?"

"I'm supposed to spend the next ten, fifteen years flying

one of those little airplanes? An aerial jeep driver?"

"By then, you'll be a captain. With a little bit of luck, a major." He looked at MacMillan. "Airborne is dead, Mac. You either go to army aviation or you spend your time as a talking dummy for the PIO guys, giving speeches to the VFW. Believe me."

MacMillan looked at Hanrahan for a full minute before he finally said anything.

"Army aviation?" he asked, incredulous.

Hanrahan nodded his head.

"Oh, goddamn," MacMillan said. "Wait till Roxy hears about this."

"Happy landings, Mac," Hanrahan said.

(Two)
Sandhofen, Germany
16 February 1946

It was Major General Peterson K. Waterford's custom to receive newly assigned junior officers in his office at Headquarters, United States Constabulary. The headquarters was established in a Kaserne designed, it was rumored, by Albert Speer himself, and intended to provide the officer cadets of the SS with far more luxurious accommodations than those provided to officer cadets of the army, navy, and air force.

The office now occupied by General Waterford was the most impressive he had ever occupied. His red, two-starred major general's flag and the cavalry yellow flag of the Constabulary were crossed against the wall behind a desk. (The insignia of the Constabulary, sewn into the middle of the flag, was a "C" pierced by a lightning bolt, giving the irreverent cause to refer to the United States Constabulary, the police force of the United States Army of Occupation, as "the Circle C Cab Company.") The desk itself was twelve feet long and six feet wide. It was forty-four feet from the forward edge of the desk to the door to the office.

General Waterford lined newly arrived officers up before his enormous desk, and gave them a thirty-minute pep talk and "Welcome to the U.S. Constabulary" handshake, before sending them down for duty to the regiments and battalions and companies and platoons.

Twenty or thirty company-grade officers every week or so were gathered in the general's outer office by Lieutenant Davis, his junior aide-de-camp. They were given a cup of coffee, while the aide briefed them on what was expected of them when they passed through the door onto which was fastened a gleaming brass nameplate which read, MAJOR GENERAL PETERSON K. WATERFORD, COMMANDING GENERAL.

The aide-de-camp explained that the reception was designed to make them feel part of the outfit, to give them an understanding of the great privilege it was for them to be in the Constab, and under the command of Major General Peterson K. Waterford himself.

Lieutenant Davis briefed groups of junior officers so often that he hardly paid any attention to individual officers at all. The only reason that First Lieutenant MacMillan had caught First Lieutenant Davis's eye at all was because of what MacMillan wore on the tunic of his pinks and greens when he reported at the prescribed time to be received by the general. Everybody else in the room was wearing the ribbons representing the decorations they had been awarded. The general desired that every officer and trooper of the United States Constabulary wear his authorized ribbons. The general's desire was made known in the mimeographed Memo to Newly Assigned Officers furnished each newcomer.

Lieutenant MacMillan was not wearing any ribbons at all when he showed up in General Waterford's outer office. He did, however, have three metal qualification devices pinned to his tunic. On top was the Expert Combat Infantry Badge. Below the CIB was a set of paratrooper's wings, with five stars signifying jumps in combat, and below them he wore a set of aviator's wings.

General Waterford said nothing about MacMillan's defiance vis-à-vis the wearing of authorized ribbons, but when all the hands had been shaken, and the newcomers had been dismissed and were leaving his office, Major General Waterford said: "Lieutenant MacMillan, will you please stay a moment after these gentlemen have gone?"

It was Lieutenant Davis's firm belief that Lieutenant

MacMillan's first step in the Constab had been into a bucket of shit. He was going to have his ass eaten out, in General Waterford's legendary manner, for not having worn his ribbons.

And it had started out that way, too.

"Lieutenant MacMillan," the general said. "I am somewhat surprised to see that you are not wearing your ribbons."

MacMillan came to attention but said nothing.

Oh, you poor bastard, Lieutenant Davis thought.

"If I had your decorations, Lieutenant MacMillan, I would wear them proudly," the general said. MacMillan responded to that with a slightly raised quizzical eyebrow.

"Oh, yes, Lieutenant MacMillan," the general said. "I know all about your decorations, and how you came by them. It has also been brought to my attention that under stress, you are prone to use foul and obscene language to senior officers."

"Sir?" MacMillan asked.

"'Fuck it, Colonel,'" the general said. "'Have the bugler sound the charge.'"

MacMillan looked really confused now. The general allowed him to sweat for a full sixty seconds before walking up to him with his hand extended. "Bobby Bellmon's my son-in-law, Mac. Welcome aboard."

"Thank you, sir," MacMillan said.

"Take a good look at this officer, Davis," the general had said. "There are very few men who get so much as a Bronze Star without getting their ass shot up. MacMillan has never been so much as scratched. But if he were wearing all his ribbons, the way he's supposed to, he would be wearing that little blue one with the white stars."

"Yes, sir," Lieutenant Davis said.

"I don't know what the hell I'm going to do with you, Mac," the general said. "Bobby wrote and asked me to take care of you, and you know I'll do that. And I'll be damned if I'll have a Medal of Honor winner doing nothing more than flying a puddle jumper."

"Sir," MacMillan said, "if the Lieutenant may be permitted to make a suggestion?"

Waterford gestured with his hand, "come on."

"How about a company of armored infantry, sir?"

Waterford shook his head. "Bobby said you'd ask for one," he said. "But I don't think so."

"Yes, sir," MacMillan said.

"What did you do before, Mac? Before you started jumping out of airplanes?"

"I was a dog robber, sir."

"A dog robber? For whom?"

"Colonel Neal, in the old 18th Infantry."

The general looked thoughtful for a minute. Then he said, "Why not? That's a good idea."

"Sir?" MacMillan said.

"For the time being," General Waterford said, "you can be my *flying* aide-de-camp. I'll be losing my senior aide before long, anyway. You can be my aide *and* fly me around. How does that sound?"

"Whatever the General decides, sir."

"It's settled then," Waterford said. "Davis, see to his orders, and then see that he's settled down in quarters, will you?" He shook MacMillan's hand again. "In a couple of days, when you're settled, Mrs. Waterford and I would like to have you and Mrs. MacMillan for dinner. Just family, Mac. Bobby feels that way about you, and I'm sure we will."

Some time later, a friend in the office of the chief of staff told Davis that Waterford had written a letter to the War Department, urging the special promotion of Lieutenant Mac-Millan to captain, stating that in his present assignment he had "demonstrated an ability to perform in a staff capacity very nearly as well as his record indicates he can perform in ground combat."

MacMillan's "ability to perform in a staff capacity," Lieutenant Davis somewhat bitterly thought, was not quite what it sounded like on paper. MacMillan was an ace scrounger. If the Class Six (wine, beer, and spirits) weekly ration for the division included one case of really good scotch and really good bourbon, it appeared in the general's mess and in his quarters. When Mrs. Waterford gave a buffet dinner for senior officers and their ladies, it contained roast wild boar and venison, even if that meant a squad of soldiers had to be sent out into the Tanaus Mountains with orders not to return until they had boar and deer in the back of their weapons carriers. MacMillan turned up a Hungarian bootmaker in a displaced persons' camp and put him to work turning out handmade tanker's boots for the senior officers and shoes for their wives. He even found a deserted railway car once owned by some Nazi bigwig, and put fifteen people to work turning it into a private "rolling command post" for General Waterford. Waterford was permitted to roll into Berlin to visit an old classmate with all the splendor of Reichsmarschall Göring. He rolled around Hesse in a Horche that had once belonged to Rommel. MacMillan found it, and arranged for it to be put into like-new order.

There was nothing whatever Davis could do but nurse his ill feelings in private. Among other things, Mrs. Waterford's golf partner and crony was Mrs. Roxanne MacMillan. MacMillan had moved in, and he was squeezed out. He didn't like it, but there was nothing whatever he could do about it.

The only one who had been able to resist him at all was Major Robert Robbins, the division aviation officer. Robbins was that rara avis, a West Pointer who was also an army aviator. And he knew how to play the game. By constantly reminding the general that a general should have a field-grade officer to fly him about, rather than a lowly lieutenant, and by subtly reminding the general that Lieutenant MacMillan was fresh from flight school, where he had been flying since 1941, he had remained the general's personal pilot.

(Three)
The Frankfurt am Main–Chemnitz Autobahn
Near Bad Hersfeld, Germany
10 May 1946

The highway winds its way through pine forests and fields, its two double lanes often so far apart that one cannot be seen from the other. When there is no traffic, as there was none today, there is a pleasant feeling of being suspended in time and space.

The car was a Chevrolet, a brand new one, dark blue, which had been shipped as parts from the States and assembled at a General Motors truck factory in Belgium. It bore the license plates carried on personal automobiles of soldiers of the Army of Occupation, and a smaller plate identifying its owner as an enlisted man.

The driver was a hulking, square-faced man in his late forties, his hair so closely cropped that a six-inch scar on his scalp was clearly visible. There were four rows of ribbons above his breast pocket, and an Expert Combat Infantry Badge. On his sleeves there were the chevrons—three up and three down, individual stripes of felt sewn on a woolen background—of a master sergeant. On one sleeve were nine diagonal felt stripes, each signifying three years of service, and on the other were six-inch-long golden stripes, each signifying six months of overseas service during World War II.

Beside him on the front seat was a slight, gray-haired woman of about his age. She was wearing a skirt and a blouse and an unbuttoned sweater. Her only jewelry was a well-worn golden wedding band and a wristwatch. From time to time, she took a cigarette from her purse. Whenever she did, without taking his eyes from the road, the master sergeant produced a Ronson lighter and held it out for her.

The back seat of the four-door sedan was jammed full of wooden boxes and paper bags. The ends of cigarette cartons, soap powder boxes, and other grocery items could be seen, as could bloodstained packages of meat.

All of a sudden, when they came around a curve on the highway, two soldiers stepped into the road and signaled for the car to pull over. They wore varnished helmet liners with Constabulary insignia painted on their sides and leather Sam Brown belts; and they were armed with .45 Colt pistols.

"Oh, goddamnit!" the master sergeant said, when he realized they had been bagged by a Constabulary speed trap. Then, glancing in embarrassment at the woman beside him, he said, "Sorry."

"It's all right, Tom," the woman said.

He braked the Chevrolet and pulled to the shoulder of the road.

One of the two Constabulary troopers walked to the car. The master sergeant rolled down the window.

"Got you good, Sergeant," the Constabulary trooper said. "Sixty-eight miles per hour." The speed limit was fifty miles per hour and strictly enforced.

"Now what?" the master sergeant asked.

"Pull it over there, and report to the lieutenant," the Constabulary trooper said, pointing to a nearly hidden dirt road. Twenty yards up it three jeeps and a three-quarter-ton weapons carrier were parked, and a canvas fly had been erected over a field desk.

The master sergeant nodded, rolled up the window, and started up the road.

"I'm sorry about this."

"It couldn't be helped," the woman replied.

"What do you think I should do?" he asked.

"Pay the two dollars," she said, and laughed.

He stopped the car, pulled on the parking brake, then took his overseas cap from the seat, put it on his head, and got out of the car. As he walked to the fly-shielded field desk, he tugged the hem of his Ike jacket down over his trousers.

The lieutenant, the woman noticed, took his sweet time in making himself available to receive the sergeant; but he finally walked behind the desk, sat down on a folding chair, and permitted the sergeant to salute and report as ordered.

She saw him handing over his driver's license and the vehicle registration. Then the lieutenant swaggered over to the car.

"You German, lady?" he asked.

"No," the woman said. "I'm American."

"What have you got in the back?" the lieutenant demanded, and then, without waiting for a reply, jerked open the back door.

"Jesus Christ," he said. Look at this. What were you planning to do, open a store?"

"Hey, lieutenant!" the master sergeant called.

"What did you say? What did you say, Sergeant? Did I hear you say 'Hey' to me?"

"Excuse me, sir," the master sergeant said. "No disrespect intended."

"You just stand where you are, come to attention, and stay there until ordered otherwise, clear?"

The master sergeant looked at the woman. She made a slight gesture to him, warning him to keep his temper. The master sergeant came to attention.

"Just what do you think you're doing, Lieutenant?" the woman asked.

"What I think I'm doing, lady, is stopping your little black market operation."

"I wasn't aware that it was illegal to have commissary goods in a personal automobile," she said, reasonably.

"Who you trying to kid, lady?" the lieutenant said. "You got enough goddamned goodies in there to start a store."

"They're intended as a gift," she said.

"And pigs have wings," he said. He called to the troopers standing under the fly, and pointed out two of them. "You guys start unloading this car," he ordered. "I want a complete inventory."

"You are charging us with blackmarketing?" the woman asked.

"That's right," he said.

"Arresting us?"

"You got it," he said.

"May I make a telephone call?" she asked."

"No, you can't make a telephone call," he said. "You and your husband are under arrest. Understand?"

"I understand that when you're arrested, you are permitted a telephone call," she said. "I'm politely asking you to make that call."

He looked at her for a long moment before he replied. "Who you want to call?"

"Does it matter?"

"OK," he said. "Come on." He walked ahead of her to the table, on which sat a field telephone. She saw that the Constab corporal, a pleasant-faced young kid, was embarrassed by the lieutenant's behavior. "Get the switchboard for her," the lieutenant ordered. The kid cranked the field phone.

"Ma'am," he said, "this is the 14th Constab switchboard."

"You know how to work a field phone?" the lieutenant said. "You got to push the butterfly switch to talk."

"Thank you," she said. She took the handset and depressed the butterfly switch. "Patch me through to Jailer Six Six," she said.

The lieutenant looked at her with interest. Jailer Six was the Constabulary's provost marshal. Jailer Six Six, he decided, was probably the provost marshal sergeant. This guy had six stripes; it was therefore logical to conclude that he was an old buddy of the provost marshal sergeant. The Old Soldier Network. Well, she was wasting her time.

"Oh, Charley," she said to the telephone, "I'm so glad I caught you in."

Charley, whoever Charley was, said something the lieutenant couldn't hear. Then the woman went on: "Charley, Tom and I just got ourselves arrested. No, I'm not kidding. About ten miles out of Bad Hersfeld. Speeding, and I'm afraid we're guilty of that. But also for black-marketing, and I plead absolutely innocent to that charge."

"Yes, there's an officer here," she said. She handed the telephone to the lieutenant.

"Lieutenant Corte," he said, sharply.

"Lieutenant," the voice at the other end of the line said, "the correct manner of answering a military telephone, unless you know that the caller is junior to you, is to append the term 'sir' after your name."

Christ, she knows some officer.

"Yes, sir," he said. "I beg your pardon, sir."

"Let me get this straight, Lieutenant. I have been given to understand that you have arrested Master Sergeant Thomas T. Dawson and charged him with speeding?"

"Yes, sir. Sixty-eight miles per hour in a fifty mile per hour zone."

"Are you aware, Lieutenant, that Master Sergeant Dawson is the sergeant major of the Constabulary?"

"No, sir, I was not. But with all respect, sir, the sergeant was speeding and admits as much."

"You've also charged him with black-marketing, is that correct?"

"Yes, sir. Him and his wife. Their car is loaded down with enough commissary and PX stuff to start a store."

"His wife, did you say?"

"Yes, sir. The lady who called you."

"The lady who called me, Lieutenant," the voice said, "is not Mrs. Dawson. She is Mrs. Marjorie Waterford. Mrs. Peterson K. Waterford."

Lieutenant Corte's face went white, but he said nothing.

"Lieutenant, on my authority as provost marshal of the Constabulary, you may permit Master Sergeant Dawson and Mrs. Waterford to proceed on their own recognizance," the provost marshal said. "You will forward, by the most expeditious means, the report of this incident to Constabulary headquarters, marked for my personal attention. Do you understand all that?"

"Yes, sir."

"Then please let me speak to Mrs. Waterford again, Lieutenant," the provost marshal said.

Lieutenant Corte heard: "Oh, I didn't mind so much for myself, Charley, but what he did to Tom was inexcusable. I've never seen an officer talk to a senior noncom the way this one did to Tom as long as I've been around the service."

When she hung up, she turned to face Lieutenant Corte.

"I presume we are free to go, Lieutenant?"

"Yes, ma'am," Corte said. "Mrs. Waterford, if I had any idea you were the general's wife..."

"You miss the point, Lieutenant," Marjorie Waterford said. "A gentleman would have been just as courteous to a sergeant's wife as he would be to a general's lady."

"Ma'am?"

"You may legally be an officer," she said. "But I fear that you are not a gentleman, Lieutenant." She waited for a reply. There was none. "Good afternoon, Lieutenant," she said. She turned and thanked the corporal who had cranked the field phone for her, and then she went and got back in the car.

When they were on the autobahn again, Master Sergeant Dawson took his eyes from the road a moment and looked at her.

"You gonna tell the boss about that jerk, Miss Marjorie?"

"I've been thinking about that, Tom," she said. "And I don't think so. Fear of the unknown is worse than having the ax fall. I think it will be better to just let him think about it."

He chuckled. "Maybe you're right," he said. "But that wasn't right, what he did."

"I think he'll think twice before he acts like that again," she said.

"That he will," the master sergeant said, chuckling.

They drove into Bad Hersfeld, close to the dividing line between the American and Russian zones of occupation, and finally stopped in front of a four-story, walk-up apartment building.

With their arms loaded with bags and boxes, they climbed four flights of stairs and knocked at the glass window of a door.

A tall, gaunt, gray-haired man in a worn, patched sweater opened it.

"Hello, Gunther," Mrs Waterford said. "You remember Sergeant Dawson, of course?"

"Nice to see the general again, Sir," Master Sergeant Dawson said.

"Marjorie, your generosity shames me," the general said.

"Don't be silly," Mrs. Waterford said. "There's more in the car. Would you help Sergeant Dawson fetch it while I say hello to Greta?"

"Of course," he said. He raised his voice. "Greta, it's Marjorie Waterford, again."

Frau Generalmajor Gunther von Hamm looked no more elegant than her husband. Her clothing was worn and patched. Her face was gray, and her eyes sunken.

"Oh, Marjorie," she said. "You constantly embarrass us. We can make out."

"I know you can," Marjorie Waterford said, kissing her cheek. "Give what you can't use to someone who can." She reached into the bag she was carrying and came out with a bottle of scotch whiskey. "I don't know about you, but I desperately need a little of this."

It took Generalmajor Gunther von Hamm, who had been at Samur with Major General Peterson K. Waterford, and Master Sergeant Dawson three trips to unload all the groceries and conveniences from Dawson's car.

"Have one of these, Tom," Mrs. Waterford said, when they had finished. "You look like you can use it."

"Not now, Miss Marjorie, thank you just the same," he said.

"Have one, Tom," she said, smiling, but firmly.

"Yes, ma'am," he said. Marjorie Waterford understood that Tom Dawson was uneasy drinking with general officers and their ladies, but she was afraid that Gunther von Hamm would think he was refusing to drink with a former enemy. He wasn't, but Gunther was very sensitive, and having to accept the food and cigarettes and soap that she had brought was enough of a blow to his pride without being snubbed by an enlisted man.

Marjorie told them that Porky was starting up a polo team, and that seemed to please Gunther, for it brought memories of happier days. But the von Hamms' news for the Waterfords was not at all pleasant.

"Elizabeth von Greiffenberg killed herself ten days ago," Greta von Hamm said.

"Oh, no!" Marjorie Waterford said.

"We just found out yesterday," Gunther von Hamm said. "Poison."

"That's terrible," Marjorie said. She felt especially bad because Elizabeth von Greiffenberg's husband, Colonel Count Peter-Paul von Greiffenberg, had been commandant of the POW camp in which her son-in-law had been held. He had been killed right at the end of the war, shot down in cold blood by the Russians.

"She was not stable," Gunther said.

"I feel personally responsible," Marjorie said. "I should have done something to help her."

"What could you do, more than you have done?" Greta said, kindly.

"Something," Marjorie said.

"She wouldn't see you," Greta said. "She told me to leave her alone when I was there. She . . . she . . ."

"Was not stable," Gunther von Hamm filled in for her.

"What about the girl?" Marjorie asked.

Greta von Hamm shook her head.

"No one knows where she is," she said. "What everyone is afraid of is that she went to East Germany, where there are relatives."

"Oh, my God," Marjorie Waterford said. "The poor thing. How old is she? Sixteen?"

"Seventeen," Greta said.

"Excuse me, Miss Marjorie," Master Sergeant Dawson said. "We've got to get going."

"Yes," Marjorie Waterford said. "We do. It's a long ride, and we don't want to get arrested for speeding, again, do we, Tom?"

(Four)
Mannheim, Germany
11 May 1946

There were four Stinson L-5s lined up on the Eighth Constabulary Squadron's airstrip. They had the legend US ARMY and a serial number painted on the tail. The star-and-bars which identified all U.S. military aircraft was painted on the side of the fuselage. Immediately below the rear passenger seat was the "Circle C" insignia of the U.S. Constabulary.

A Horche sedan, which it was alleged had belonged personally to Field Marshal Rommel himself, pulled onto the airstrip behind a pair of MPs on Harley Davidson motorcycles with red lights flashing and sirens wailing. The open convertible was trailed by two jeeps each equipped with a machine gun and manned by three soldiers in chrome-plated helmets.

The convoy pulled up beside the nearest L-5. The driver of the Horche jumped out and opened the rear door.

Major General Peterson K. Waterford, attired in a highly varnished helmet liner with glistening stars forward and Constabulary insignia on the sides, stood up, clutching his riding crop. He acknowledged the salutes of the personnel in the area by touching his riding crop to the brim of his helmet liner. Then he descended from the Horche and marched toward the closest Stinson L-5. Major Robert Robbins saluted for the second time.

"Good morning, General," he said.

"Morning," the general said, touching his helmet liner with his riding crop. He climbed into the rear seat of the aircraft. Major Robbins took a red plate on which two silver stars had been mounted and slipped it into a holder on the fuselage, then climbed into the front seat.

Everything was in readiness. The plane had been gone over from propeller to tail wheel. Robbins threw on the master switch, primed the engine, and pushed the starter switch down. The starter motor groaned, and ground. The propeller went unevenly through several rotations, once sending a puff of blue smoke from the exhaust past the cockpit. The starter motor groaned and ground again. The propeller jerked spasmodically through its arc. The engine refused to start.

"Tell me, Major," General Peterson K. Waterford asked,

icily, "do you suppose that Captain MacMillan remembered to wind up his aircraft?"

"Yes, sir. I'm sure, sir, that the backup aircraft is operational."

"Good, good," General Waterford said, with transparently artificial joviality.

"I'm very embarrassed about this, General," Major Robbins said.

"Nonsense," the General said. "We all break our rubber bands from time to time, don't we, Robbins?"

"Captain MacMillan's aircraft is right next to us, General. But I don't see how we'll be able to take Captain MacMillan with us, sir."

"I do, Major," the general said. "We'll let Captain MacMillan drive, while you stay here and get another rubber band for this one."

General Waterford climbed out of the plane, snatched his two-starred plate from the fuselage, and strode purposefully to the adjacent L-5. He handed it to MacMillan, who stood by the aircraft. He looked him up and down.

"Does your airplane work, Mac?"

"Yes, sir, I believe it will," Captain MacMillan said.

"And have you been briefed on our destination?" the general asked.

"Yes, sir."

"Then I suggest we proceed," the general said. He climbed into the back seat and strapped himself in again.

Major Robert Robbins came to the airplane and started to get into the pilot's seat.

"I told you that I was going to go with Captain MacMillan," the general said.

"Sir, may I respectfully point out to the general that Captain MacMillan is a recent graduate of flight school?"

"I have it in reliable authority that whatever else Captain MacMillan may be, Major, he is not a fool."

"Yes, sir."

"If he believes himself to be safe flying this thing, I will accede to his judgment," the general said. "What are we waiting for now, MacMillan?"

MacMillan got in the pilot's seat.

He pushed the starter button and the engine coughed and caught immediately. The major stood just beyond the wing tip, nearly at attention, looking uncomfortable, waiting for MacMillan to taxi away. The general folded down the upper portion of the window-door and beckoned to him. The major, holding one hand on his hat to keep the prop wash from blowing it away, went to the window.

"I've never believed that *l'audace, l'audace, toujours l'audace* crap, Robbins," he said. "The boy scouts have got it right. *Be prepared,* Robbins. Goddamn it, Robbins, remember that! *Be prepared!*"

He closed the window. MacMillan looked over his shoulder at his passenger.

The general made a "wind it up" signal with his index finger. MacMillan taxied onto the runway, checked the magnetos, pushed the throttle forward. The little airplane slowly gathered speed. MacMillan edged the stick forward, so that the tail wheel lifted off. When he reached flying speed, he inched back on the stick. The little L-5 began to fly.

He made a circling turn, still climbing.

"To hell with that," the general's voice came over the intercom. "Fly up the autobahn."

MacMillan nodded his head to show he had heard the order.

"And don't get too high," the general said.

MacMillan nodded again. He leveled off at about seven hundred feet.

"What did you do to Robbins's airplane, Mac?" the general inquired. "Nothing, I trust, that he can blame you for."

"I didn't do a thing to it, General," MacMillan said.

"Bullshit," General Waterford said. "That was too good to be an innocent happenstance."

"He did look a mite embarrassed, didn't he, General?" MacMillan said.

The general chuckled.

"I wouldn't be surprised, when they examine the engine," MacMillan said, "if they find that somebody forgot to tighten the spark plugs."

"You sneaky bastard you. But what if it had gotten up in the air, and then the engine had stopped? With me in it?"

"I double-checked it myself, General," MacMillan said.

"You're damned near as devious as I am," the general said,

and then changed the subject: "Everything laid on at Nauheim, Mac?"

"Yes, sir. I was up there this morning. Everything's greased."

The autobahn, a four lane superhighway, was now below their left wheel. They reached Rhine-Main in a matter of minutes; then, on their right, the rubble of Frankfurt am Main appeared, and then disappeared. Thirty miles further along, MacMillan banked again to the right.

"I led the most powerful tactical force ever assembled up that goddamned highway," the general said in his earphones. "I was in the van of Combat Command A, and they were in the van of the division, and the division was in the van of the whole goddamned Ninth United States Army."

MacMillan nodded his head once again.

"The only thing I forgot was a brilliant and unforgettable remark for posterity," the general said. "You're one up on me there, MacMillan. I don't think I'll ever forgive you for that."

"Yes, sir," MacMillan said.

"Every time Bobby Bellmon tells the story of leaving you in the POW camp, I think about that. 'Fuck it, Colonel. Have the bugler sound the charge.' Great line, Mac. I would have had to clean it up, of course—you can't say 'fuck it' in history books—but I should have thought of something like that."

"There it is, sir," MacMillan said, gesturing to the right front.

They were over the municipal park in Bad Nauheim. There were a pair of goalposts set in a flat area, and a line of army trucks parked to the left of the field. MacMillan came in low and slow, and touched down. He slowed and taxied back up the field. A herd of horses grazed on the grass.

He braked to a stop at the head of the line of the army trucks.

A young lieutenant trotted up to the little Stinson. He wore golden ropes through his epaulets, and the two-starred shield of a major general's aide-de-camp on his lapels.

He saluted, and opened the L-5's door.

"I trust the general had a pleasant flight," he said.

"Once I got into an airplane they remembered to wind up, I did," the general said.

"Anything go wrong, Davis?" MacMillan asked.

"Everything is laid out, MacMillan," the aide-de-camp replied, coldly. There was no love lost between Captain MacMillan and Lieutenant Davis. Davis was painfully aware that before MacMillan had shown up, he was in line to become General Waterford's senior aide-de-camp. He had naturally expected to be named senior aide after doing his time as junior aide, and he had been cheated out of it. He was still the junior aide, doing dog robbers' tasks.

Like most general officers, General Waterford used his aides-de-camp in dual roles. The junior aides saw to the general's personal comfort and attended to his social duties. The senior aide attended the general officially. The idea was that being close to the commanding general in all sorts of situations would give him insight into the problems and functioning of a high command which would be useful in his own career. Davis had dog-robbed without complaint, biding his time until he would become senior aide. But MacMillan had been named senior aide, and Davis still did the dirty work.

"Well, Davis," the general said. "Where are my polo players?"

"Right this way, General," MacMillan replied for Davis. "I think the general will be reasonably pleased with what I've come up with."

"I better be, Mac," the general said. "I better be."

With MacMillan and Davis just behind, General Peterson K. Waterford, slapping his riding boot with his crop at every third step, marched across the field. A line of a dozen men came to attention at his approach. They were wearing GI riding breeches, except for one middle-aged man who wore officer pink riding breeches.

They came to attention without command. "Good to see you, Charley," the general said to the middle-aged officer at the end of the line. "Fat and all. Well, we'll get that off you in no time."

"Nice to see you again, General," the middle-aged officer said.

"Let's get that straight right now," the general said, raising his voice so that everybody could clearly hear him. "We are here to play polo, not fight a war. You are ordered to forget that you are playing with a man who can, with a snap of his fingers, ruin your military careers. There will be no rank on the field. You will consider yourselves sportsmen first and soldiers second. I will address you by your Christian names, and you will call me—" he paused—"sir."

He got the laughter he expected, and turned to the next man in the rank.

"Frank Dailey, sir," he said.

"You played much polo, Frank?" the general asked. "You rated?"

"One goal, sir," Frank Dailey said.

He went down the line, going through essentially the same questioning. He came to the end of the line, to a tall, muscular, rather handsome young man.

"Craig Lowell, sir," the young man said.

"No offense, Craig, but you don't look old enough to have played much polo. I don't suppose you're rated, are you, Son?"

"Three goals, sir," Craig Lowell said.

"Where did you play, Craig?" the general asked, gently.

"West Palm, sir, Ramapo, Houston, Los Angeles."

"You know Bryce Taylor?"

"Yes, sir, I do," Craig Lowell replied.

"And how is he, these days?" the general asked, idly.

"Rather poorly, sir, I'm afraid," Lowell said. "I think he may even be dead. My grandfather wrote he'd spoken to Mrs. Taylor..."

"You come with me and keep me company, Craig," the general said. "While I get out of my shirt."

The general winked at MacMillan. Goddamn, he had at least a three-goal rated player. With Fat Charley, who was rated at two before the war, and that ugly man halfway down the line, he just might be able to field a team that could take the frogs. A three-goal player was more than he had hoped for. The general was rated at seven.

The general bounded up the folding metal stairs of a van. The inside was plush, ornate. The general had crossed Europe in this vehicle. His rolling home and command post. There was coffee steaming in a pot, a jug with ice water, a plate of sandwiches covered with a towel.

"Help yourself, Craig," he said. "And tell me the bad news about Bryce."

The general pulled off the leather jacket, and the pink uniform shirt beneath it, and a sleeveless silk undershirt under that. He pulled on a GI T-shirt, on which had been neatly lettered, front and back, with the numeral 1.

Craig Lowell told him what he had learned from his grandfather about the terminal illness of Bryce Taylor.

"What did you say your grandfather's name was?" General Waterford asked.

"Geoffrey Craig, sir."

"Oh," Waterford said. "You're a Craig."

"My mother's name is Craig," Lowell said.

"That's right, you're a Lowell. The Cabots speak only to the Lowells, and the Lowells speak only to God. Boston, right?"

"No, sir," Lowell said. "New York."

"But you have the Harvard accent," the general said.

"I went to Harvard, sir."

"Yes," the general said, pleased with himself. "Of course you did." Then he turned to look at MacMillan.

"I want you to find out about my old friend Bryce Taylor, Mac," the general said. "(A) If he's dead. If he is dead, write a nice letter of condolence. Get the address from Craig here. (B) If he's still alive, find out where and in what condition, and what I can do."

"Yes, sir," MacMillan said.

"Where do you usually play, Craig?" the general asked, unzipping his fly, tucking the T-shirt in, and grunting as he fastened the tight trouser band against his middle.

"Three, sir."

"OK, we'll try it that way. Go tell the others to mark their shirts. But you'll play number three against me. Tell Fat Charley he's number one with you. We need to get some of that high-living fat off him."

"Yes, sir," Craig Lowell said. He walked back out of the van and crossed the field. A sergeant had led four ponies up the van. They weren't much, in Lowell's judgment, as a string. But they were the best available, and they had been reserved for the general. What were left over for the others to play were worse.

They played two "fool-around chukkers," as the general put

it, and then they played a game, six chukkers. Blues, led by the general, won 7–4.

The general accepted a large glass of heavily sweetened iced-coffee, and drank it quickly. He was in a very good mood.

"Gentlemen," he said, "MacMillan has arranged accommodations for us in one of the Bad Nauheim Kurhotels. The Germans, among other odd notions, apparently believed that the foul water in this bucolic Dorf had medicinal qualities. What we are going to do now is load into the staff cars, go have a bath, and get something to drink. Mac has imported the water to mix with the whiskey."

The general and Fat Charley got into a Ford staff car. MacMillan rode in front with the driver. The others, with one exception, got into other staff cars. The procession started off.

"Stop the goddamned car!" the general shouted. The driver slammed on the brakes. The cars behind almost ran into his car. "Where the *hell* is he going?" the general demanded rhetorically. He rolled down the window.

"Craig, goddamnit, where are you going?" he shouted.

"To walk the horses, sir," Craig Lowell replied.

"Goddamnit, we have enlisted men to do that."

"General," MacMillan said, "I didn't have time, the way the general sort of rushed out there on the field, to . . ."

"What are you telling me, Mac?" the general asked, slowly.

"Sir, that's Private Lowell."

The general waved at Private Craig Lowell, rolled up the window, and gestured for the driver to move on.

"Mac, goddamnit, you shouldn't have done that to me. I embarrassed that boy."

"No excuse, sir," MacMillan said.

"Goddamn it, I told you to round me up every polo player in the division, and in division support troops," the general said.

"Yes, sir. That's exactly what the general said."

"What the hell is a three-goal polo player doing in the goddamned ranks?" the general asked. "And he's a gentleman, too, Mac, goddamnit. He's a Lowell *and* a Craig. You heard what he said. For Christ's sake! What the hell is he doing as a goddamned private?"

"He's on the division golf team, General," Mac replied,

taking the question literally.

"The golf team! The *golf team!*"

"Yes, sir," Mac said. "He's a jock."

"I didn't think you'd go rooting around in the goddamned Form 20s, for God's sake. Sometimes, Mac, you're just too *goddamned* efficient a dog robber."

"May I have the general's permission to explain, Sir?"

"You can try, Mac. Right now my first thought is to send you back there to help him shovel the horseshit," the general said.

"With the general's permission, sir, it happened this way. When the general laid this requirement on me, I was faced with the problem of not knowing very much about polo."

"Or about much else, either," the general said.

"I asked around if anyone happened to know anything about polo. Lowell did, and he helped me out. He really knows a good deal about the game, General."

"I saw that," the general said. "If Fat Charley had been able to get his ass out of dead low gear, the Reds would have won. He set you up half a dozen times, Charley, and you blew it."

"I'm a little out of shape, sir," Fat Charley said.

"That's the understatement of the week. Go on, Mac."

"General, I brought Private Lowell along just to be prepared," MacMillan said. "All the other players are officers."

"Mac," the general said. "(A) In six weeks and two days, my polo team is going to play the team of the Deuxième Division Mécanique of the French Army, under General Quillier. (B) Because the French do not socialize with enlisted men, my team will be made up solely of officers. (C) My team will win. (D) My team cannot win without that Lowell boy as my number three."

"I believe I take the General's meaning, sir," Lieutenant MacMillan said.

(Five)
Bad Nauheim, Germany
12 May 1946

After Private Craig W. Lowell, working with the German stableboys, had walked the horses, he got in his privately owned black jeep and drove across town to the Constabulary golf course, where he was billeted in an attic room over the pro shop.

He fantasized about being stopped by one of the Constabulary MPs, or better yet, by one of the more chickenshit young officers of the Constabulary.

"Trooper," he would be challenged. The Constabulary was playing cavalry, and soldiers were "troopers" not soldiers. "Trooper, where the hell did you get so dirty?"

"Actually," he could then reply, "I've been playing polo with General Waterford. And the provost marshal."

He was not stopped. He parked the jeep behind the pro shop and climbed the narrow stairs to his tiny room. The only thing that could really be said for his special billet was that it was away from the barracks. He was left alone. If they wanted him, they had to send for him, and that was generally too much trouble, so some other "trooper" would be grabbed and given an unpleasant task to perform.

He pulled off his boots, and then stripped out of the sweat-soaked breeches, shirt, and underwear. The general had run their asses off. If the others were as tired as he was, he thought with a certain satisfaction, the officers and gentlemen with whom he had played must really be dragging their asses. All of them except the general, he thought. The general was the only one who had not looked to be on the edge of exhaustion when the jeep horn signaled the end of the last chukker.

Lowell had been as surprised to find that General Waterford was a first-rate polo player as the general had been surprised to learn that Craig was a private.

Naked, Lowell bent over and examined his inner legs. He was tall and well muscled, not like a football player, but with something of the same suggestion of great strength and endurance. He was chapped, slightly, or that was heat rash. Nothing serious.

He wrapped a towel around his middle and went down the stairs to the men's locker room and took a shower. He took his razor with him, and shaved under the streaming hot water. His beard was as light as his hair, but for some reason, more than eight hours' growth stood out on his skin as much as if it had been jet black. The Constab was big on clean-shaven troopers.

Lowell was mildly concerned about what would happen now that Major General Peterson K. Waterford had learned of his enlisted status. But he was more curious than worried. For one thing, he certainly hadn't tried to pass himself off as anything but a private. Lieutenant MacMillan knew he was a private. If the general decided to send lightning bolts of rage, his target would be MacMillan. Privates were invisible to generals.

In any event Lowell thought it unlikely that MacMillan would be struck by a lightning bolt and toppled. Craig Lowell had realized—while eavesdropping on the conversations of majors and colonels at the nineteenth hole of the Bad Nauheim golf course—that they had erred in their assessment of Lt. MacMillan. It was generally believed that MacMillan was the jester in the court of King Waterford. A pleasant fool who had somehow won the Medal. MacMillan's third-person manner of speaking to the general and other very senior officers was probably close to the official division joke.

But it was Private Craig Lowell's assessment of MacMillan that if he wasn't the *Éminence Gris* behind the throne, then he was at least a Knight Companion of the Bath. Not a simple dog robber and not a jester. Lowell had nothing really concrete on which to base this opinion, except for a combination of small things. There was a certain look in the general's eye, a certain shading of his behavior, when, for some reason, MacMillan was not at his side, and a certain relaxation when he showed up.

Lowell also had gotten to know Mrs. Waterford. She was a tall, thin, gray-haired woman, not at all the counterpart of her flamboyant husband. When she called the golf club, she asked when it would be convenient for her to play. The two other generals' wives, Mrs. Deputy Commanding General, and Mrs. Chief of Staff, as well as the senior colonels' wives, Mesdames G-1, G-2, G-3, and G-4, even Mrs. Division Surgeon, called to announce when they intended to play.

Mrs. Waterford asked when she could play, and she generally played very early in the morning, and invariably with Mrs. Rudolph G. (Roxy) MacMillan, a redheaded, buxom woman with a hearty belly laugh. There were seven children between them. Mrs. Waterford was twice a grandmother.

The first time Lowell had met Mrs. Waterford, she had

understandably come to the conclusion that he was German. She had overheard him talking to the caddies in German. The only thing lower on the social scale than a private was a kraut.

"Good morning," Mrs. Waterford had said, graciously, in rather badly accented German in the belief he was a kraut. "Isn't it a lovely morning?"

"A beautiful morning, Frau General," Lowell had replied, and then switched to English. "I'm Private Lowell, the caddy master."

"And you're also the best golfer in the division, according to Lieutenant MacMillan," she replied, without missing a stroke. "Do you think you could play with us? We could kill two birds with one stone. God knows, we need golf instruction. Mrs. MacMillan and I are ashamed to play with anybody but each other. And we both need practice in conversational German."

"Oh, do we need you!" Mrs. MacMillan said. She put out her hand. "I'm Roxy MacMillan."

By the time they had finished the first round, Lowell decided he liked both of them very much. Mrs. Waterford was a lady who reminded him of his late grandmother, and Mrs. MacMillan was—he thought of the old-fashioned phrase his grandmother had used to describe nice people who were rather simple—"a diamond in the rough."

The role of golf in the army had surprised Lowell when he had first come to Bad Nauheim and the U.S. Constabulary. He had always thought golf to be the sport of the middle and upper classes, not at all the sort of thing sergeants (who were the yeomen in the military social hierarchy) would do. But apparently, before the war, everybody in the army over the grade of corporal had been out there swatting balls. He finally realized that it was because the government paid for the upkeep of the courses, and that in order to justify the expense, and thus their own playing, the brass had had to encourage the yeomen to get out there and knock the ball around.

Lieutenant MacMillan, whom Lowell at first had also pegged as one of the yeomen, played every Wednesday afternoon, usually with the Constabulary finance officer, Major Emmons. They were joined infrequently by the general, but normally it was just MacMillan and Major Emmons. They played nine holes, and then spent a couple of hours at the nineteenth hole, eating hamburgers and drinking beer.

Several weeks after Lowell had begun to play with Mrs. Waterford and Mrs. MacMillan on a more or less regular basis, MacMillan had come up to Lowell when Lowell had been leaning against the wall of the caddy house and pro shop, devoutly hoping not to be pressed into service as a golf instructor. When MacMillan walked up to him, he handed Lowell a dollar in script.

"Get us a couple of beers and meet me in the locker room," he said. He spoke pleasantly enough, but it was a command, not an invitation.

When Lowell brought the beer into the locker room MacMillan was coming out of the shower, a towel wrapped around his middle. MacMillan turned his back, dropped the towel, and pulled on a pair of jockey shorts.

"I understand you've been giving my wife golf lessons," he said, his back still to Lowell.

"Yes, sir," Lowell replied.

"And German lessons," MacMillan pursued, as he turned around.

"Yes, sir."

"Where did you learn to speak German?" MacMillan asked. He did not like Lowell's type. He was generally suspicious of handsome young men, and this handsome young man was also charming, had a hoity-toity manner of speaking, and was a draftee to boot.

"A lady who took care of me when I was a kid was German," Craig replied.

"What do you want out of the army, Lowell?" Mac asked.

"I don't quite understand you, sir."

"Military government is always looking for people who speak German," he said. "You could make buck sergeant in six months, probably staff before your time is over."

"Well, if I have a choice, sir, I'd rather stay right here."

"That's right, you don't need the money, do you?" MacMillan said.

"No, sir, I don't." Lowell wondered how MacMillan had found out about that; but he was not surprised that he had.

"My wife thinks you're a very nice young man," MacMillan

said. "If you change your mind, let me know."

"Thank you, sir."

"I was a jock myself before the war," MacMillan offered. "I was Hawaiian Department light-heavyweight champ." He opened the beer bottle, drained it, and finished dressing. Lowell couldn't think of anything to say.

"I don't think you're a nice young man," MacMillan said to him, finally. "I think you're a goddamn feather merchant." When he saw that this had sort of stunned Lowell, he went on. "A word of advice, feather merchant: Don't try to take advantage of being the general's lady's golf pro and instructor in kraut."

Lowell flushed, but said nothing.

"I know, of course, that that had never entered your mind, Private Lowell," MacMillan said. Then he walked out of the locker room.

A month after that, MacMillan sought him out again.

"I've got a question for you, feather merchant," he said. "What do you know about polo?"

"What would you like to know?"

"What would I like to know, *sir*," MacMillan corrected him.

"Yes, sir," Lowell said. He had just noticed that Mac-Millan's lieutenant's bar had been replaced with the railroad tracks of a captain. "I wasn't trying to be disrespectful."

"I don't suppose you were," MacMillan said, after looking at him for a moment. "But I'll tell you something, Lowell. That's the way you come across. As if you think everybody in the army is a horse's ass."

"I don't mean to do that," Lowell said, sincerely.

"But you do think that we're a bunch of horse's asses, don't you?"

"I don't think *you* are," Lowell replied, without thinking. MacMillan's eyes tightened, and his eyebrows went up. Lowell remembered only a moment later to add, "Captain."

"I'm flattered," MacMillan said, sarcastically. But it was evident to Lowell that the sarcasm was pro forma. MacMillan had recognized the truth when he heard it, and he was flattered.

"Speaking of horse's asses," MacMillan said, "tell me about polo."

"What would you like to know?"

"Everything. All I know is that you play it riding on horses."

"Sir, it would help if I knew why you want to know."

"The general has decided to play polo," MacMillan said. "What the hell is a seven-goal player?"

"One hell of a polo player," Lowell said. "Sir."

"The general is a seven-goal polo player," MacMillan said. "What does it mean?"

"It's a handicap," Lowell explained. He explained the handicap system and the game of polo. MacMillan asked several questions, but Lowell never had to explain something twice.

"Between now and 0600 tomorrow morning, Lowell, I want you to make up a list of all the equipment we're going to need to field a polo team. Everything, from boots to horseshoes. I've found horses in Austria. There's a warehouse full of equipment at Fort Riley, and I've got an old buddy there who'll ship us what we need. But I'll need to know what. Decide exactly what you'll need. And then triple the quantities."

"Sir, I'm charge of quarters tonight."

"No, you're not. As of an hour ago, you're working for me. I've already fixed it with headquarters company. The general wants a polo team, Lowell, and you and I are going to see that he gets one."

Two days after that, Craig Lowell found himself a passenger in one of the Constabulary's Stinson L-5s, flown by the Constabulary aviation officer himself, Major Robert Robbins. Robbins flew him to the Alps near Salzburg, Austria, where military government held nearly five hundred horses captured from the Germans. There had originally been thousands, but the draft animals had been quickly released to the German and Austrian economies to till the land.

The horses still held were obviously not livestock but thoroughbred animals. They were kept as valuable property, which the Germans had presumably obtained illegally and which the authorities intended to return to their rightful owners.

A week after that, a ten-truck convoy of open flatbed trailers appeared at the horse farm and loaded the seventy animals Craig Lowell had chosen for the trip back to Germany. There wasn't a polo pony among them. But there were some fine saddle horses (a German groom told Craig they had come from

Hungary in the last days of the war) which could, with work, be trained for polo.

It was a five-day trip to Bad Nauheim. The horses survived the journey. The German grooms had had a good deal of experience in moving animals under worse conditions. When they arrived in Bad Nauheim, Captain MacMillan had everything waiting, from stables and food to a polo field in the municipal park and accommodations for the grooms. In the stables were two dozen wooden crates shipped from Fort Riley, Kansas, by air. Each crate was stenciled: PRIORITY AIR SHIPMENT. VETERINARY SUPPLIES. PERISHABLE. DO NOT DELAY.

The crates were full of saddles, horseshoes, tack, polo mallets, riding breeches, everything Craig Lowell had asked for and more. The day after the horses arrived, players began to arrive from all over the Constabulary. And two days after that, Private Craig Lowell met Major General Peterson K. Waterford and informed him that their mutual acquaintance, Bryce Taylor, was ill of terminal cancer.

(Six)

The problem of how to get Pvt. Lowell onto the polo field as a commissioned officer remained. MacMillan went through his service record. Lowell had been thrown out of college. College graduates, under certain circumstances, could be directly commissioned. MacMillan toyed with the idea of making certain "corrections" to Lowell's service record but decided against it; he was only nineteen years old, and there was no way he could correct that, too. Two "corrections" of that magnitude would be too noticeable.

Next, MacMillan went and had a talk with Major William C. Emmons, the Constab's finance officer. They were friends in the sense that they both had been stationed at Fort Riley before the war. MacMillan could not honestly remember ever having seen Specialist Six Emmons at Riley, but they had talked, and they remembered other people together. Sergeant MacMillan had had little to do with the pencil-pushers in the old days, and the pencil-pushers had had little to do with the troops. On Pearl Harbor Day, Major Emmons had been a Specialist Six, a PFC with three three-year hash marks, drawing the same pay as a first sergeant (Pay Grade Six) because of his specialist's skill in the intricacies of army finance. A month later, he had been directly commissioned as a first lieutenant of the Finance Corps, and had spent the entire war in the Prudential Insurance Company Building in Newark, N.J., in command of an army of civilian clerks who made up and mailed out allotment checks and insurance checks to dependents and the deceased's next of kin. He had ultimately risen to major doing that.

Major Emmons not only knew the army game and understood MacMillan's problem, but offered a solution to it. It was understood between them that MacMillan owed Emmons a Big One. There was no swap, no tit for tat, just an understanding between them that when Major Emmons wanted something, Captain MacMillan, senior aide to the commanding general, would make a genuine effort to see that he got it.

Pvt. Craig Lowell, who was either playing polo or training the polo ponies from sunup to sundown, had no idea that the wheels of army administration were grinding in his behalf.

HEADQUARTERS

UNITED STATES CONSTABULARY

APO 109   NEW YORK NY

SPECIAL ORDERS   19 May 1946
NUMBER 134

EXTRACT

****

35. PVT LOWELL, Craig W. US32667099 MOS 7745 Hq & Hq Co U.S. Constab APO 109 relvd, trfd in gr WP Svc Co Hq U.S. Constab APO 109 for dy with U.S. Constab Finance Office. No tvl involved. PCS. AUTH: Ltr, Hq U.S. Constab, 7 Jan 46, Subj: "Critical Shortage Enl Finance Personnel."

****

BY COMMAND OF
MAJOR GENERAL WATERFORD
Charles A. Webster
Colonel, AGC
Adjutant General

HEADQUARTERS

OFFICE OF THE FINANCE OFFICER
UNITED STATES CONSTABULARY

APO 109   US FORCES

19 May 1946

SUBJECT: Critical Shortage of Commissioned Finance Officers
THRU: Commanding General
                  U.S. Constabulary
                  APO 109, US Forces
TO: Commanding General
                  US Forces, European Theater
                  APO 757, US Forces

1. Reference is made to Letter, Subject as Above, Hq USFET, dated 3 April 1946.

2. The Finance Section, this Hq, is three (3) officers, MOS 1444 (Fiscal Accounting Officer) below authorized Table of Organization and Equipment strength, and has been advised that no replacement officers will be assigned from the Zone of the Interior for a minimum of six (6) months.

3. The Finance Section, this Hq, had been authorized to directly commission two (2) suitably qualified enlisted men as 2ND LT. FIN C USAR, to fill this critical shortage of personnel.

4. Reference Para 2 above: Request authority to directly commission one (1) additional qualified enlisted man as 2 LT FIN C USAR for a total of three (3).

William C. Emmons
Major, Finance Corps
Division Finance Officer

1st Ind

HQ U.S. CONSTAB APO 109 19 MAY 46

TO: COMMANDING GENERAL USFET APO 757 US FORCES

1. The Commanding General United States Constabulary is personally aware of the critical shortage of qualified commissioned financial officers, and of the serious threat this shortage poses to the operational status of this division.

2. The Commanding General strongly recommends approval.

BY COMMAND OF
MAJOR GENERAL WATERFORD
Charles A. Webster
Colonel, AGC
Adjutant General

2nd Ind

HQ USFET APO 757 22 MAY 1946

TO: COMMANDING GENERAL U.S. CONSTABU-LARY APO 109

Authority granted herewith to directly commission as 2nd Lt, Finance Corps, U.S. Army Reserve, one (1) additional highly qualified enlisted man.

BY COMMAND OF GENERAL CLAY
Edward K. MacNeel
Colonel, AGC
Adjutant General

3rd Ind

HQ US CONSTAB APO 109 23 MAY 1946

TO: FINANCE OFFICER, US CONSTAB
For compliance.

BY COMMAND OF
MAJOR GENERAL WATERFORD

Charles A. Webster
Colonel, AGC
Adjutant General

HEADQUARTERS

UNITED STATES CONSTABULARY

APO 109   NEW YORK NY

SPECIAL ORDERS   24 May 1946
NUMBER 137

EXTRACT

****

16. PVT LOWELL, CRAIG W. US32667099 Svc
Co U.S. Constabulary, APO 109, is relvd prs asgmt and
HON DISCH the mil service UP AR 615–365 (Con-
venience of the Govt) for purp of accept comm as officer.
EM auth transp at govt expense from New York NY to
home of record (Broadlawns, Glencove, LI NY) PCS.
S–99–999–999.

17. 2ND LT LOWELL, CRAIG W. FinC, 0–495302,
having reported on active duty Svc Co U.S. Constabulary
is asgd dy with Service Company, Finance Section. Off
auth transport at Govt Expense from home of record
(Broadlawns, Glencove, LI NY) to New York NY. PCS.
S–99–999–999.

18. 2ND LT LOWELL, CRAIG W. FinC, 0–495302,
Finance Sec Hq U.S. Constab, is detailed to Armor
Branch for pd of one yr for dy w/troops. (Auth: Letter,
Hq War Dept, Subj: "Asgmt of newly comm off of tech
services to combat arms for dy w/trps.) No tvl included.

19. 2nd LT LOWELL, CRAIG W. 0–495302 FinC
(Det/ARM) Finance Sec Hq U.S. Constab, trfd in gr WP
Hq Sq 17th Armd Cav Squadron APO 117 for dy w/
troops. In Compl with Msg, Hq U.S. Constab, Subj:
"Asgmt of Armor/Armored Cav Off to Provisional Horse
Platoon." Off is further placed on TDY, WP Hq 40th
Horse Platoon (Prov) for dy. TDN. TCS. S–99–999–999.

****

BY COMMAND OF
MAJOR GENERAL WATERFORD
Charles A. Webster
Colonel, AGC
Adjutant General

(Seven)
40th Horse Platoon (Prov)
U.S. Constabulary
Bad Nauheim, Germany

Private Craig W. Lowell drove up to the stables of the 40th
Horse Platoon in his black, privately owned jeep and blew the
horn. In a moment, the left of the huge matching doors, large
enough to pass the jeep, was opened by one of the German
grooms, and Lowell drove through it.

After Lowell had passed through the door, the groom closed
it again and walked to where Lowell had stopped next to the
stairwell leading to the second floor of the stables. He then
helped Private Lowell unload what he had beneath a scrap of
tent canvas in the back seat.

There was a Zenith Transoceanic portable radio still in its
carton. There were two jumbo-sized boxes of Rinso; a half
dozen bars of Ivory soap; three cartons of Camel cigarettes;
two boxes of Dutch Masters cigars; a case of Coca-Cola; a case
of Schlitz beer, in cans; a carton of Hershey chocolate bars
(plain) and a carton of Hershey chocolate bars (with almonds);
and six large cans of Nescafé instant coffee.

Private Lowell had been shopping at the PX.

"Put the radio, the beer, and the cigars in my room," Private
Lowell directed the groom, in German. "You know what to
do with the rest of it."

"Jawohl, Herr Rittmeister," the groom said. Literally translated, "Rittmeister" meant "Riding Master." It had also been
a rank in the German cavalry, corresponding to captain, as well
as a rank in the minor German nobility. All the grooms had
taken to referring to him as the "Herr Rittmeister" and Lowell
thought it rather amusing.

Before he went to his apartment, he inspected both wings of the stable, all the horses in their stalls, the tack room, and the dressing room where the polo players kept their riding equipment. He had had a little trouble at the very beginning with the grooms, but that had quickly passed when they learned that not only did the young soldier speak fluent German, but he knew horses. Lowell found nothing to complain about in the condition of the animals, the cleanliness of the stables, or the saddle-soaping of the tack and saddles, and he saw that the open lockers in the dressing room each contained two complete, freshly laundered and pressed riding costumes.

Then he went up the stairs to his apartment. He had known about the rooms over the stables from the very beginning and had immediately concluded that they offered much nicer accommodations than his tiny room over the pro shop at the golf course.

The morning after the first time he had played polo with General Waterford, he had made his move.

"Captain," he had said to MacMillan. "There's a place I can sleep over the stables. Could I move over there?"

"Where are you sleeping now?"

"Over the pro shop."

"Go ahead."

All the grooms were supposed to be equal. They were hired by the army as laborers for a minimum wage, given one hot meal a day, and provided with died-black army fatigues as work clothes. One of them, Ludwig, was more equal than the others, sort of a straw boss.

Ludwig arranged for the furnishing of the two rooms and bath over the stables. Overnight, a bed (as opposed to a GI steel cot) appeared. As did two upholstered chairs, a desk, a table, an insulated box full of ice, two floor lamps, a desk lamp, a lamp that clipped onto the headboard of the bed, and a carpet for the floor. The next night, there was an extension telephone sitting on a small table between one of the upholstered armchairs and the bed. Private Lowell could now take calls without having to rush downstairs to the telephone in the stable office.

When he got to his room, he saw that his laundry had been delivered, and that his other OD uniform was crisply pressed and hanging in the wardrobe. His riding costume was hanging beside it, and his boots, freshly polished, were at the foot of the bed. He took off his Ike jacket, pulled his necktie down, took a cold beer from the ice-filled insulated box, and then unpacked the Zenith Transoceanic portable radio.

He read the instruction book that came with it, opened the back, installed the large, heavy storage battery that had come as an accessory, and turned it on. He tuned in AFN-Frankfurt, the American radio station, and picked up Burns and Allen. With his feet on an upholstered footstool, a can of beer in his hands, and half listening to George's running battle with Gracie, he began to study the Transoceanic's operating instructions.

There was a knock at the door.

"Who's that?" he called, in German.

"Captain MacMillan."

"Come in," Lowell said. Shit. The last person Lowell expected to see at the door of his apartment was Captain Rudolph G. MacMillan. He had thought it was one of the grooms, who made predictable trips to his room to report on the condition of the horses in the certain knowledge they would be offered both a beer and a package of cigarettes.

Lowell had come to the conclusion that he was the only member of the Army of Occupation who was buying cigarettes on the black market. Every other mother's son was selling not only their ration, but having them shipped from the States to sell as well.

Lowell had considered writing his mother and telling her to send him a case of cigarettes. He did not. His mother would not understand. He would either get a carton of cigarettes, or, more likely, a cigarette case, suitably monogrammed. It wasn't worth the effort. He could afford to buy three cartons a week here and dispense them judiciously among the German grooms, in exchange for having his dirty clothing washed and pressed and his boots polished, and for having the assurance that the animals and tack were in impeccable condition when they were led to the field for the officers to ride. This was a better job than being caddy master. He intended to do what he could to keep it.

MacMillan made no secret of his dislike for him, and it was

entirely possible that when he saw the apartment, he would order Lowell to move back into the barracks with the other peasants.

MacMillan came into the room and looked around.

"Very nice," he said.

"Thank you, sir," Lowell said.

"You got another one of those beers?" MacMillan asked.

"Yes, sir," Lowell said. "Of course."

MacMillan walked around the apartment, opening the door to the bathroom, and then the door to the wardrobe.

"Very nice," he repeated. "Even an icebox. Like I said, Lowell, you're a survivor."

He was caught now. There was nothing to do but take a chance.

"My company commander thinks I'm sleeping on straw in a sleeping bag," he said, handing MacMillan a can of Schlitz, then a metal church key, and finally a glass.

"Very classy," MacMillian said. "Crystal, isn't it?"

"Yes, it is. Bohemian, about 1880, according to the markings. I looked it up in the library."

"You're interested in crystal?" MacMillan asked. His concern was evident. An interest in crystal was tantamount to a public announcement of homosexuality. MacMillan didn't think that was likely, but now that he thought about it, it wasn't beyond possibility either. Shit.

"Not really. When I was offered this by one of the grooms, he told me it was quite good. I was checking up on him more than anything else. The beer tastes the same."

MacMillan chuckled. Lowell thought that it was entirely possible that MacMillan was going to permit him to continue living in comfort.

"You got hot plans for tonight?" MacMillan asked.

"I was going to lie here and listen to my radio," Lowell said, nodding toward the new Transoceanic. "I just bought it."

"How would you like to come to my house for supper?" MacMillan said. When Lowell was obviously reluctant to reply, MacMillan went on. "Come on, Roxy's been wanting to have you over."

"That's very kind of you, Captain," Lowell said. "And I appreciate it, but . . ."

"What the hell's the matter with you?" MacMillan snapped.

"Look, I mean it. I do appreciate what you're doing. Take care of the lonely troops. I really appreciate it. But I'm sure that as seldom as you get to spend a night at home, Mrs. MacMillan would really rather spend it alone with you, instead of entertaining one of your troops."

MacMillan didn't say anything.

"Honest, Captain. I'm used to being alone, and I like it. And I really appreciate the thought."

"Take a shave," MacMillan ordered. "I'll wait. That a fresh uniform?"

"Yes, sir," Lowell said.

"Wear it," Captain MacMillan ordered.

(Eight)

Captain and Mrs. Rudolph G. MacMillan had been assigned a fourteen-room villa on the slope of the Tanaus Mountains looking down on the resort town itself. Lowell thought that it looked very much like the house his cousin Porter Lowell had built in East Hampton. He wondered where the Germans who owned it were now living.

He parked his jeep beside MacMillan's Buick and followed him up the brick stairs to the door. A German maid opened the door, but Roxy, in a white blouse, unbuttoned blue sweater, and pleated skirt, came rushing out of the living room.

She grabbed Lowell's arm, planted a kiss on his cheek, and said, "Congratulations, I'm so happy for you!"

He had no idea what that was all about, and he was aware that MacMillan had signaled his wife to shut up.

"Ooops," Roxy said. "Me and my big mouth. What do you drink, Craig? We got it all."

"I'll have a beer if you have one," Craig said.

"Good, that'll go with the steaks," Roxy said. She looked at her husband. "Oh, for Christ's sake, Mac, why don't you tell him?"

"Yes, indeed, please, Captain, sir, tell me," Craig said.

"Get us a beer, Roxy, and bring it out on the porch," MacMillan said.

The "porch" was actually a veranda, a thirty-by-eighty-foot

area paved in red flagstone, along the edges of which a two-and-a-half-foot tall, foot-thick brick wall had been laid. Bad Nauheim was spread out below them. Craig could see the six-story white brick and glass headquarters building, the only modern building in town. And the municipal park, and the polo field, and even, he thought, the red tile roof of his stable.

"It's beautiful," he said.

Roxy came onto the veranda and handed him a beer.

"It's a long way from the chicken coop, I'll say that," she said. She banged the neck of her beer bottle against his. "Mud in your eye, kid."

"The chicken coop?" Lowell asked, smiling.

"Our first home," Roxy said. "Mac and I got married in Manhattan. That's Manhattan, *Kansas*. Outside Riley. We lived with my folks, at first, and then Mac went airborne, and we went to Benning. Some redneck farmer had decided he could make more money gouging GIs than he could raising eggs, so he hosed out his chicken coop and turned it into three apartments. Plywood walls, and a two-holer fifty yards away. He charged us fifty bucks a month and Mac was drawing a hundred and fifty-two eighty, including jump pay. And we were glad to get it."

"Well, *this* is lovely," Lowell said, sincerely, gesturing around the patio and up at the house itself.

"It's supposed to be field grade," Roxy said. "But Mac pulled a couple of favors in."

Lowell didn't know what to say, so he just smiled.

"Have you told him? For Christ's sake, tell him, so we can start the party."

"Jesus, Roxy, you can really screw things up," Mac said.

"You want me to tell him? OK, I'll tell him," Roxy said.

"I'll tell him," MacMillan said. "I'll tell him." Lowell looked at him expectantly.

"Have you ever thought of becoming an officer?" Mac-Millan said.

"Not for long," Lowell said. "They wanted me to go to OCS in Basic . . ."

"You should have," Roxy said.

"I really don't mean to be rude, Mrs. MacMillan," Lowell said, "but I was in the army about three days when I realized that I didn't belong in the army."

"That's only because all you've seen of the army is the crap," Roxy said. "It's a good life, you'll see." He wondered what the hell she meant by that. But she was a good woman, and he would have been incapable of saying anything to hurt her feelings, even if he hadn't been afraid of her husband.

He smiled at her. "You have fifteen months and eleven days to convince me," he said.

"Tomorrow morning at 0800," MacMillan announced in a flat voice, "you're going to be sworn in as a second lieutenant."

"I beg your pardon?" Lowell asked.

"You heard what I said," MacMillan said. He was smiling at Lowell's discomfiture.

"I heard what you said, Captain," Lowell said. "But I can't believe it."

"Believe it. You got it from me. You can believe it," MacMillan said.

"Now we can party," Roxy MacMillan said, and kissed him again, wetly, on the cheek.

"Now just a moment," Lowell said. "I don't think I want to be an officer."

"What the hell kind of talk is that?" Roxy said. "What's the matter with you?"

"Let me spell it out for you, Lowell," MacMillan said. "The general wants to beat the frogs in a polo game. Now I don't know why that's important to him, and I don't care. I'll tell you this, though: it's more than wanting to beat them at a game on horses."

"I was an enlisted wife," Roxy said. "I know what it's like. And it's a hell of a lot better on officers' row."

"Roxy, for Christ's sake, will you shut up?" Rudy MacMillan said.

She gave him a dirty look.

"The general thinks the only way he can beat the frogs is if you're playing polo," MacMillan said to Lowell. "And frog officers don't play polo with enlisted men. The general says you will play. You with me so far?"

Lowell nodded, but said nothing.

"So tomorrow you get sworn in as a second lieutenant," MacMillan said. "You don't know enough about the army, about soldiering, to make a pimple on a good corporal's ass, much less a good officer. I know that, and you know that, but that's not the point. The point is that you *will be* an officer and a gentleman, and you will get on your horse and play polo. You got that?"

"And what happens at the end of polo season?" Lowell asked.

"The general's sure to get another star, and pretty soon. That means going back to the States. You keep your nose clean, and I give you my word we'll take that gold bar off you as quick as we put it on."

"And I go back to being a private?"

"You get out," MacMillan said, his voice hard. "I will see to it that your application for relief from active duty for hardship reasons is approved."

"This isn't the way I thought this was going to be at all," Roxy said. "I thought he was just getting a commission. I don't think I like this."

"How soon can I expect to get out?" Lowell asked.

"In six months, you'll be out. You can believe that. You got it from me."

"OK," Lowell said.

"You little shit," MacMillan said, angrily. "When I was your age, I would have given my left nut for a commission."

"May I be excused, Captain?" Lowell said, getting to his feet.

"Now wait just a minute!" Roxy said. "Mac, you stop this crap right now. This is *my* party. *I* asked Craig here for a party, and we're going to have a party. You guys just leave your differences at the goddamn door."

"No, you can't be excused," MacMillan said. "The general and Mrs. Waterford are due here in ten minutes. You will stay here, and you will act like you're having a good time. You understand me?"

"Now there's a direct order if I ever heard one," General Waterford said from the edge of the veranda. "But I don't see how you could possibly enforce it, Mac."

Lowell and MacMillan stood up.

"Good evening, Craig," Mrs. Waterford said. She walked up to him and gave him her hand. "How nice to see you."

"Good evening," Lowell said. He wondered how much of the exchange the Waterfords had heard. There were no signs that they had heard any of it except the last angry remark MacMillan had made.

"I understand that you're to be commissioned," Mrs. Waterford said. "Congratulations. I think you'll make a fine officer."

He looked at her, wondering if she was simply being gracious, or whether she actually meant what she was saying.

"Thank you," he said.

A cut-in-half, fifty-five-gallon barrel on legs was carried onto the veranda by two German maids. Major General Peterson K. Waterford removed his tunic, his necktie, and rolled up his sleeves. He put on a large white apron, on the front of which was stenciled the face of a jolly chef in a chef's hat and the legend, CHIEF COOK AND BOTTLEWASHER. Next he built a charcoal fire, and then personally broiled steaks. While he was cooking, he drank several bottles of beer, from the neck.

The steaks were excellent, thick, charred on the outside and pink in the middle. Roxy MacMillan provided baked potatoes, a huge salad, and garlic bread.

They talked polo. MacMillan, who knew nothing about polo, had nothing to say, and this pleased Lowell.

What the fuck, Lowell thought, sometime during the evening. I will play polo, and I will get out of the army six months early, and in the meantime I will be an officer. What have I got to complain about?

V

(One)
Bad Nauheim, Germany
24 May 1946

The Army of Occupation, recognizing the need for personal vehicles, and unwilling to pay what it would cost to ship tens of thousands of civilian automobiles from the States, had run excess-to-needs jeeps through the Griesheim ordnance depot. These were rebuilt to military specifications, except that the vehicles were painted black rather than olive-drab. They were sold to the post exchange for the cost of rebuilding $430, and resold to enlisted personnel who had expressed a desire to purchase such a vehicle for private transportation and who had been lucky enough to have their name drawn from a drum usually employed for bingo games at the service club. Private Craig Lowell's first (and as it turned out, his last) visit to the service club had been to witness the raffle. His had been one of ten names drawn.

Private Craig Lowell, in a Class "A" OD uniform, parked his black jeep behind division headquarters and met Captain Rudy MacMillan in the basement coffee shop. MacMillan told him to take off his Ike jacket. When Lowell had handed over his jacket, MacMillan laid it on the table, and unpinned the enlisted man's insignia (a U.S. and a representation of a World War I tank stamped on round brass discs) from the lapels. He reached out his hand and dropped them into Lowell's hand.

"Souvenir," he said. Then he ripped open small cardboard packages. He pinned small, unbacked, U.S. insignia to the upper lapels, a representation of a World War I tank to the lower lapels, and a single golden bar on the epaulets of the Ike jacket. He handed the jacket back to Lowell. By the time Lowell had shrugged into it, MacMillan had pinned a gold bar to the front of a gabardine overseas cap with officer's braid sewn along its seams.

He tossed Lowell's woolen enlisted man's overseas cap into the wastebasket.

"You won't need that anymore," he said. He handed Lowell the officer's cap. "You tuck that under your belt," he said. "You do not tuck it in your epaulet."

"Yes, sir."

He led Lowell back through the coffee shop, into a corridor, and to an elevator. They rode up to the fourth floor, walked down a hotel corridor, and came to a corner suite, converted into offices.

"Good morning, Sergeant," MacMillan said to a master sergeant behind a desk. "I believe Colonel Webster expects us."

"Oh, he expects you all right," the master sergeant said. "You've really made his whole day with this, Captain."

"Yours not to reason why, Sergeant," MacMillan said. "Yours but to have everything all typed out."

"He called the general, you know," the sergeant said.

"I thought he might," MacMillan said. "I'm sure that the general reassured the colonel of Lowell's splendid, all-around qualifications to become an officer."

The sergeant looked at Lowell with amused contempt. He shook his head, then picked up the telephone.

Fuck you, Lowell thought. *Fifteen minutes from now, you will have to call me "sir."*

"Captain MacMillan is here, Colonel," he said. There was a reply. "Yes, sir."

He hung up the telephone.

"I gather the colonel is composing himself," he said, wryly. "He said to get everything signed."

MacMillan nodded. The sergeant got up. "You'd better sit down," he said to Lowell. "There's a lot of paperwork."

He handed Lowell a pen and handed him the first of an inch-thick stack of forms, each of which had to be signed. Lowell's fingers actually became cramped before he was finished, and by the time he was done, his signature, never very legible, had deteriorated into a scrawl.

There was a five-minute wait after all the papers had been signed. The sergeant major and MacMillan discussed someone Lowell had never heard of, an old friend from long ago. The telephone rang.

"Yes, sir," the sergeant said. He listened. "Yes, sir," he repeated, and hung up the telephone.

"Gentlemen," he said, "the colonel will see you now." He stood up and held open the door.

Lowell marched into the large room on MacMillan's heels. When MacMillan stopped, he stopped. When MacMillan saluted, he saluted.

"Good morning, Colonel," MacMillan said. The colonel ignored him.

"You are Craig W. Lowell?" the colonel said to Lowell.

"Yes, sir."

There was a look of utter loathing in the colonel's eyes. He hadn't liked it when the army had directly commissioned engineers, transportation experts, college professors, and other professionals in War II. He was furious with the idea of this young pup being made an officer simply because General Waterford wanted to play polo with him.

"I thank you for your opinion, Colonel," the general had said, when he telephoned him to protest. "But I want him commissioned."

Colonel Webster, a portly, dignified man, stood up.

"Come to attention," he said. "Raise your right hand and repeat after me: 'I, your name...'"

"I, Craig W. Lowell..."

"Do solemnly swear, or affirm..."

"Do solemnly swear, or affirm," Lowell parroted, "that I

will defend and protect the Constitution of the United States against all enemies, foreign and domestic; that I will bear true faith and allegiance to them; that I will obey all orders of the President of the United States and the officers appointed over me, according to the regulations and the Uniform Code of Justice; and that I will faithfully discharge the duties of the office which I am about to assume. So help me, God."

The colonel lowered his hand. With infinite contempt, he said, "Congratulations, Lieutenant, you are now a member of the officer corps of the United States Army. You are dismissed."

MacMillan saluted, and Craig Lowell saluted. They performed an about-face. They started to march out of the office.

"I'm going to have your ass for this, MacMillan," the colonel said.

MacMillan did not respond. They marched out of the outer office and went back down the corridor to the elevator. MacMillan didn't say a word until they were back in the basement.

"The general," he said, "will be free about 1430. Adjust your schedule accordingly."

"Yes, sir," Lowell said.

"Until you get your feet on the ground, I suggest you keep your ass out of the line of fire," MacMillan said.

Lowell nodded his understanding.

"Don't look so goddamn scared," MacMillan said. "You're a survivor. You'll be able to handle this with no sweat."

Lowell nodded his head, because he knew MacMillan expected him to. In point of fact, however, he was not scared. Colonel Webster was obviously furious that he had been commissioned, and obviously held him in contempt; but Webster understood that Lowell hadn't had any more choice in the matter than he did. MacMillan's ass was in the line of fire, not his.

As he walked across the parking lot to his jeep, a technical sergeant threw him a crisp salute, and barked, "Good morning, sir."

Second Lieutenant Lowell returned the salute.

"How are you today, Sergeant?" he said.

I'll be a sonofabitch, he thought. I did that splendidly.

When Lowell drove back to the stable, climbed the stairs to his rooms, and pushed open the door, the bed had been stripped of sheets. When he opened his wall locker, it was empty. He turned around in confusion and found himself facing Ludwig, the groom, who was smiling broadly.

"I have taken the liberty of having the lieutenant's luggage packed and sent to the bachelor officer's hotel," Ludwig said to him. The lieutenant will find his boots and breeches in the officer's locker room."

"The word got around quickly, didn't it?" Lowell asked.

"Will the lieutenant accept the best wishes for a long and distinguished career from a former Rittmeister of the 17th Westphalian Cavalry?"

"Is that what you were, Ludwig?" Lowell asked.

Ludwig nodded.

"Well, thank you," Lowell said. "But I'm afraid my 'long and distinguished career' is liable to end as quickly as it began. When, for example, the French ride all over us."

"I think you're going to do very well," Ludwig said. "The ponies are coming along very well. And they're eighty percent of the game."

"You've played, haven't you?" Lowell asked, with sudden insight.

"Yes," Ludwig said. "And one day, perhaps, I will be able to play again." He was trying, Lowell realized, to sound more cheerful than he felt.

"For God's sake, don't let the general hear you say that," Lowell said, "or you'll wind up as a second lieutenant."

"I would be happy to be a second lieutenant," Ludwig said. "That sounds so much better than Unterwachtmeister."

"What the hell is that?"

"I have been accepted by the Grenzpolizei, the border police, as an Unterwachtmeister. The same thing as a PFC."

"I don't understand that," Lowell said. "What are you talking about?"

"I'm a soldier, as you are a soldier, Lieutenant," Ludwig said. "For me it was either the French Foreign Legion or the border police. The Legion is full of Nazis, so it's the border police."

"You're wrong about that, Ludwig. I'm no soldier."

Ludwig smiled at him, shook his head, then nodded. "Yes, you are," he said. "And I would suspect that in time you'll be a very good one."

Lowell changed the subject. Ludwig's compliment embarrassed him. Not for himself, because the notion that he would become a good officer was absurd, but for Ludwig, who had been a bona fide officer in a losing army, and was now reduced to a stable boy paying outrageous compliments to a nineteen year old.

"You're quitting? When?"

"I will stay until after you play the French," he said. "I would like very much to see my team beat the French." He held open the door, and bowed Lowell through it, half mockingly.

None of the other players said anything when Lowell walked into the locker room to change into riding clothes except to nod hello. If the Germans already knew of the change in his official status, Lowell thought, certainly the officers must know.

They don't want to burn their fingers, Lowell thought, by getting too close to the fire.

MacMillan is probably right, he thought, as he pulled on his boots. I am a survivor. He thought about what Ludwig had said about his being a soldier, and in time a very good soldier. It was a compliment, very flattering. And a blivet, which is defined as five pounds of horseshit in a one pound bag.

He walked out of the locker room and to his string.

"Guten Morgen, Herr Leutnant," the exercise boy said, smiling from ear to ear as he gave him a hand up on the chestnut mare.

(Two)

It was a brilliant, splendid spring day, ideal for polo, and they played until eleven, saving the better ponies for the afternoon session when the general would play. There were three polo players, Lowell decided: the general, Fat Charley, and Private Lowell. The others played at polo, and there was a difference.

He smiled. He corrected himself. The three polo players were the general, Fat Charley, and *Lieutenant* Lowell. He wondered why he had not just been equipped with a gold bar when it was time to play the French, and told to behave like an officer. On the surface, that would seem to be a lot simpler solution to the problem. Probably, Lowell decided, it was another example of contorted military ethics. Falsely identifying him as a commissioned officer and gentleman would not be gentlemanly; hanging a commission on him when he was wholly unqualified to be an officer was something else. There was no question, now that he thought about it, that he was in fact an officer. All those papers he had signed, and Colonel Webster's unconcealed rage as he had administered that very impressive oath, left no doubt.

Fat Charley, sweat-soaked, red-faced, finally called the session off. Lowell had just scored a goal, and was at the opposite end of the field from the grooms and the three-quarter-ton truck on which the Veterinary Corps officer and his troops, and the troops with the towels and the ice water, waited and watched. Lowell rested his mallet over his shoulder and started down the field at a walk.

Fat Charley cantered up to him, turned, and rode beside him.

"Nice shot, Lowell," he said.

"Luck," Lowell said, modestly, although it had been, in fact, a damned good shot, a full stroke at the gallop that had connected squarely and sent the ball through the goalposts like a bullet.

"Could I catch a ride to lunch with you?" Fat Charley asked. "I've got to stop by my office a moment."

"Certainly, sir," Lowell said. Fat Charley, Lowell had learned by eavesdropping on his fellow polo players, had been with General Waterford in the war. He was an armor officer. But he had been detailed to the Corps of Military Police, and was the Constabulary's provost marshal. The idea was that he would become provost marshal general, which called for a major general. There was no way the establishment was going to let some asshole cop commissioned from civilian life be named a general officer.

There was an exception to that, Lowell had also learned. The European Command provost marshal was Brigadier General H. Norman Schwartzkopf, formerly Colonel Schwartzkopf of the New Jersey State Police. Schwartzkopf had been the man who had caught the kidnapper of Colonel Charles A. Lindbergh's baby, and was second in fame only to J. Edgar Hoover. The next provost marshal of the U.S. Army would be Schwartzkopf, and Fat Charley would be his replacement.

Only after Fat Charley had asked him for a ride to lunch did Lowell consider that as an officer he could no longer eat as a transient in the enlisted mess of the Signal Battalion, which was near the stables. And only a moment after that did he realize that Fat Charley had thought of that before he had and was helping him to ease the problem of transition.

Whether Fat Charley really had business at his office (a one-and-a-half-story brown stone building that reminded Lowell of a gas station) or whether that had simply been an excuse to have Lowell accompany him, he was in the building no more than three minutes.

He came out and heaved himself into the jeep beside Lowell, leaning back on the seat, his right booted leg outside of the jeep body and resting on the horizontal rear portion of the fender.

"The Bayrischen Hof," Fat Charley began without preliminaries, "is one of three hotels for bachelor officers, most of them company grade. Most senior officers are both married and have their dependents here. At lunch, the dining room feeds the married men who don't want to go home for lunch. Some of them stop in the bar for a drink or two on the way home. Dinner, and the bar afterward, is generally for the bachelors and transients. Now that the antifraternization ban has been lifted, you generally find frauleins, of all kinds, from the wholly respectable to the other end of the spectrum, in the dining room and bar."

Lowell nodded. He didn't say anything, because he didn't know what to say.

"It seems to have been decided," Fat Charley went on, "that if young officers are going to get falling down drunk and make asses of themselves over girls who are available for a pound of coffee or a couple pairs of stockings, it's better to have them do it where they're out of sight of the troops."

They were at the Bayrischen Hof by the time he'd made his little speech. Fat Charley pointed the way to the parking lot, and then led the way through the rear door of the four-story

Victorian hotel to the dining room. He walked to a table occupied by a military police captain, who stood up at his approach.

"Have you room for a couple of old horse soldiers?" Fat Charley said, slipping into a chair. "Captain Winslow, Lieutenant Lowell."

They shook hands. A German waitress immediately served coffee, and laid a mimeographed menu before them. Lowell saw, a little disappointed, that the food was the same food served in the enlisted mess. When Fat Charley left beside his plate thirty-five cents in the paper script they used for money, Lowell did likewise.

"Lowell," Fat Charley said, when they had finished eating, "if you want to make sure you're properly checked in, I'll have another cup of coffee with Captain Winslow."

"Thank you, sir," Lowell said. "Nice to have met you, Captain."

"I'll see you tonight, probably," Captain Winslow said. "I live here, too."

As he walked across the dining room, he heard Fat Charley say to Winslow that he had "just arrived. Nice boy. Fine polo player."

The sergeant at the desk went with him to his room, a pleasant, airy double room on the top floor. He told him how the laundry was handled, and advised him to make sure he locked up his cigarettes and other goodies, because the krauts would sure as hell steal anything that wasn't nailed down.

Fat Charley was waiting in the lobby when he came down from his room.

(Three)

The general showed up, with MacMillan, in a liaison aircraft precisely at 1430. His polo players were waiting for him, with the better ponies; and ten minutes after the general landed, the first chukker began.

At one point in the game, when the jeep horn sounded the end of the fourth chukker, Lowell found himself alone with General Waterford at the far end of the field. They walked their mounts back together.

"It's you, Fat Charley, and me," the general said. "Think

it over, and then tell me who else we should play with."

By God, Lowell thought, here I am, on my first day as a second lieutenant, and the general is already asking my advice.

When the game was over, there were cocktails at the general's van, served by the general's orderlies and attended by such officer's ladies as happened to be in the area. He was introduced to Mrs. Fat Charley. She was very much like Mrs. Waterford, Lowell thought.

Afterward, Lowell drove to the Bayrischen Hof, and went to his room. He took a leisurely shower and then spent the hour and a half until the bar opened reading the *Stars & Stripes* and listening to his radio.

The other polo players, when they came in, acknowledged his presence in the bar with a nod or a word, but none joined him where he sat at the end of the bar, and he was not invited to join any of the groups at their tables.

They're afraid of me, Lowell realized, or at least they don't know what to do with me. It is easier to stay away from me.

At six o'clock, after two beers, he went into the dining room and ate alone. Then he got in the jeep and drove across the park to the municipal auditorium, which like most of the useful buildings in Bad Nauheim, had been requisitioned by the army. He bought a ticket for twenty-five cents, and sat in the officer's loge, and watched a Humphrey Bogart movie.

After he'd returned to the Bayrischen Hof, he intended to go right to his room; but Captain Winslow, to whom he had been introduced at lunch, saw him passing through the lobby and called out to him. After Winslow had bought him a beer and he had bought Winslow a beer, Winslow offered the information that Fat Charley and the general and Winslow's father had been classmates at West Point.

Soon after that Lowell's eyes fell upon a tall, blond, dark-eyed fur-line at a table with another fur-line and two officers. The officer with her groped her, or tried to, under the table. His reaction was ambivalent. He thought that his new status would give him opportunity to rent a little pussy himself, something as good looking as that, something he had been reluctant to do so far because he had nearly been nauseated by the technicolor VD movie he'd been shown on arrival in Germany. Renting one of the fur-lines on the street for a box of Hershey chocolate bars or two boxes of Rinso was something a reasonable man just did not do. Renting one in an officer's hotel, however, might be something else again. Certainly, he reasoned, the army must take some measures to insure that the officer corps in an official officer's billet did not contact gonorrhea, syphilis, or even crabs.

He was also offended and angry that a nice-looking young girl like that should have to permit herself to be pawed by a drunken oaf like the captain at the table.

Then he told himself that it was none of his business, and said good night to Captain Winslow, who seemed to be a decent sort, and went to bed.

At midnight, there were sounds of crashing glass, and a feminine scream, and shouted male oaths, and of opening and slamming doors. He got out of bed and went to the door and stuck his head out.

The girl he had seen being groped in the bar was huddled against the wall at the end of the corridor, hurriedly fastening her clothes. Her blond hair, which she had worn in a bun at her neck, was now hanging loose and mussed. It made her look very young; and her wide blue eyes showed terror. The oaf Lowell had seen pawing her in the bar, dressed in only his skivvies, was being urged back into his room by two other officers and the sergeant from the desk downstairs.

As soon as they had the oaf inside his room, the room next to Lowell's, the sergeant turned to the girl and in broken German told her to get her hustling little ass out of the hotel, right goddamn now, and don't come back.

She scurried like a frightened animal down the corridor, past Lowell. There was shame and anger and terror and helplessness all at once in her eyes. She was entirely too good looking, Lowell thought, to be a whore. Whores are supposed to look lewd, lascivious, and tough. This one looked like somebody's kid sister. He thought about that. She looked like Cushman Cuming's little sister. What the hell was her name? The one he always mispronounced: Penelope. He had once seen Pen-ell-oh-pee Cumings in her nightgown with her boobs pushing out in front.

He watched as the whore fled down the stairs beside the elevator.

Lowell closed his door. He could hear, but not completely understand, the drunken outrage of the oaf next door. For some reason, he was as excited as he had been when he had seen Cush's kid sister in her nightgown in Spring Lake. He had been ashamed when that had given him a hard-on, and he was embarrassed now that what had just happened had also given him a hard-on.

He walked to the French windows and opened them, then looked out the window to the street below.

In a moment the fur-line came out of the hotel, walking quickly. She stopped on the sidewalk, looked both ways, and then hurried across the street into the municipal park. She disappeared into the shrubbery. She was probably taking a short cut through the park, Lowell thought. And then he saw that she had stopped twenty yards inside the park and was leaning on a tree.

What she is going to do, Lowell decided, is wait for a GI or an officer to come down the street, and offer herself. Strangely excited, he decided he would watch.

Two soldiers came down the sidewalk. The girl didn't move from her tree. Then an officer walking from another of the hotels to the Bayrischen Hof walked past her. She didn't approach him either.

There was a tightness in Lowell's chest, an excitement. He turned from the window, took his trousers from the chair where he'd laid them, and began to dress. He ran down the stairwell and walked past the knowing eyes of the sergeant on duty at the desk and into the street.

He entered the park. She wasn't leaning on the tree where he had last seen her, and for a moment he felt like a fool. Then he saw the edge of her dress behind the tree. She had seen him coming and was avoiding him.

"Guten Abend," Lowell said. She stepped from behind the tree, and stood clutching her purse against her chest. She smiled at him, a smile so forced it gave him a pain in the stomach. He saw that she had combed her hair. It was now hanging down past her shoulders. Damn it, she did look like Cush's sister.

"Guten Abend," she said, softly, barely audibly.

"He was drunk," Lowell said. She said nothing. "Are you all right?" She said nothing. "Can I take you home?" Lowell asked.

"I am very expensive," she said, after a moment's hesitation, in English, as if she was embarrassed.

Lowell was suddenly enraged. He had meant what he said; it was not a euphemistic phrase for "Wanna fuck? How much?" He had been offering to *take her home*. *Period*. He reached in his pocket, took what paper script his hand found, and thrust it at her.

She took it, counted it, nodded, her head bent, and jammed the money into her leather purse. He found himself looking at the purse. It was an alligator purse, a good one. But it was a woman's purse, not a girl's. It was obviously not hers. He counted the money as she counted it. He had given her fifty-five dollars, five or ten times the going rate.

She looked at him, met his eyes. There was defiance in them. Defiance and fear.

"Even for that much money," she said, in English, "I will not do anything with the mouth." She spoke decent rather than GI English, he realized. The partially understood complaints of the oaf suddenly came into focus. He had wanted her to blow him; she had refused. He turned around and started to walk out of the park.

"Where do you go?" she asked.

"To get my jeep," he said. "To take you home."

"It would be better that we go to your room," she said.

He had been torn between wanting to screw her, wanting to help a young woman in distress, and wanting to confirm his own wisdom and righteousness by telling himself he wouldn't touch a syphed-up kraut slut like that with a ten-foot pole.

Now he wanted to fuck her. He desperately wanted to fuck her. To impale her. To fuck the ass off her. Was it, he wondered, because she looked so much like Cush's practically certified virginal sister? That was a pretty disgusting thing to consider. Was he really, deep down, some sort of pervert, who wanted to mess around with little girls?

This was not a little girl, he reassured himself, no matter what she looked like. She might look about sixteen years old, with those blue eyes and that innocent little face, but she was as much a certified whore as Cush's sister Penelope was a certified virgin.

He waited until she caught up with him, then took her arm

and hustled her across the street and into the hotel. The sergeant at the desk looked up, recognized the girl, and started to say something.

"Stay out of this, Sergeant," Lowell heard himself say, surprised at his boldness.

"I don't want any more trouble in here tonight, Lieutenant," the sergeant said, backing down.

"There will be no trouble," Lowell said. He got the girl in the elevator, down the corridor past the oaf's door, and into his room.

She looked around the room. She looked at him, very intently. She went into the bathroom, and he heard the water running and the toilet flushing, and when she came out, she was naked save for a pair of cheap cotton underpants. Her breasts weren't very large, he saw, and he could hardly make out the nipples, but they stood out erectly in front of her. She was pale, and thin, but she had very feminine hips.

She walked to the bed, flipped the covers down, and lay down on it. He looked at her. She reached down and hooked her hands in her pants and raised her hips and slipped them down. The tuft of hair at her groin was no wider than his thumb. She met his eyes, and then turned her head to the side.

She just remembered to act modest and shy, Lowell decided. He had no way of knowing, of course, that she had just told herself that she was glad, now she was about to do it, that the first time she did it would be with a young man, and a good-looking young man, too, and not the captain who had wanted to commit a perversion with her, and had beaten her when she refused.

Lowell stripped standing where he was, letting his clothes fall into a pile on the floor. When he was naked, he went to the bed and lay down beside her.

She would not look at him. He put his hand to her breast. It was as firm and warmed as it looked. By now, he thought, his hard-on should be tickling his chin. But it hadn't even started to thicken, much less stand up.

He slid his hand down her body to her crotch. There was no response in her, either. He might as well be patting a dog. He put his hand to her breast again. She rolled over on her back and spread her legs. He got between them. Nothing. He had a limp, useless dick.

He rolled off her, out of the bed, went to the bathroom and pumped himself furiously. Nothing. He stayed in the bathroom five minutes, thinking lewd thoughts, manipulating himself, all to no avail.

What it was, he thought, was shame for thinking that way about Cush's sister. Jesus Christ, for his first whore, why did he have to pick one who looked like a nice girl, and made him feel like a slobbering pervert?

He didn't know what to say to her when he came out. When he finally did open the bathroom door, she was gone.

Humiliated, furious, he tried to go to sleep. He tossed and turned for forty-five minutes, got out of bed, went to the bathroom, and began to masturbate. His penis thickened instantly, and immediately afterward, he felt the birth of his orgasm. He came all over the back of the toilet seat and the floor, and before he was able to go to bed, he had to get down on his hands and knees and wipe it all up with toilet paper.

(Four)

The girl came into the bar of the Bayrischen Hof the next night, ten minutes after Lieutenant Lowell had come in. He had spent the afternoon being measured for pink-and-green uniforms, which would be made to order. ODs from the quartermaster officer's store would be altered to fit him perfectly. He had bought additional items of uniform. A leather-brimmed, fur-felt officer's cap. A gabardine trench coat. Three pairs of pebble-grained chukka boots. Two pairs of tanker's boots. After he had bought the jeep, he had been out of money. He'd wired home, asking for a thousand dollars. The reply, a telegraphic authorization to draw a thousand dollars from the American Express office, had come within forty-eight hours. It had been in his pocket, uncashed, during the hectic form-a-polo team days. He had taken it to be cashed that afternoon.

When he presented it, at first he thought something was wrong. The clerk had taken the telegram and gone into a rear office. The manager had come out, smiling.

"Forgive me," he said. "But this cable draft is to *Private* Lowell."

"I've just been commissioned," Lowell said. "I've got an ID card..."

"That won't be necessary at all, Lieutenant Lowell," the manager said. "But there is something else."

He handed him another telegram.

J. FRANKLIN POTTS
GENERAL MANAGER
AMERICAN EXPRESS ACTIVITY GERMANY

INFO COPY
AMEXCO BAD NAUHEIM

IN RECEIPT GUARANTEE OF HONOR DRAFTS UP TO $1000.00 PER CALENDAR MONTH ISSUED BY PRIVATE CRAIG W. LOWELL HQ US CONSTABULARY BAD NAUHEIM AGAINST US, MORGAN GUARANTY NEWYORK OR CRAIG POWELL KENYON AND DAWES, NEWYORK. UNDERSTAND LOWELL IS GRANDSON OF GEOFFREY CRAIG, CHAIRMAN OF BOARD, CRAIG POWELL KENYON AND DAWES. TELETYPE CONSTITUTES AUTHORITY TO DO SO.

ELLWORTH FELLOWS
GENERAL MANAGER, AMEXCO, EUROPE, PARIS

"If there is anything we can ever do for you, Lieutenant Lowell, please don't hesitate to ask."

"That's very kind of you," Lowell said.

"As I said, anything that we can do, anything at all."

Lieutenant Craig Lowell smiled smugly to himself as he walked out of the AMEXCO office toward the PX. Grandpa was passing out a thousand a month because he was under the impression Craig was being a well-behaved little private. Wait till the old man found out he was an officer.

That started him thinking of home. He thought there was six hours' difference between Bad Nauheim and Cambridge. That meant it was eight o'clock in the morning in Cambridge.

His peers, his chums from St. Mark's, his new friends from Harvard—those the provost had decided were Harvard material "worth salvaging," unlike those like himself who were not—were at that very moment lined up in their ROTC uniforms on the grass about to do a little close-order drill. If he should somehow manage to have himself miraculously transported to

Cambridge, they would have to come to attention, salute, and call him "sir."

How amusing.

He decided he would have a photograph taken and send it to someone, Bunky Stevens, probably. "Having lovely time, wish you were here."

As he was fitted for his pinks and greens, and waited for change to be made after paying the bill, he daydreamed of home. He had not allowed himself to dwell on that subject very often. The cold truth of the matter was, he had been quite terrified of the army. The power of the corporals in basic training over him had been the most frightening thing to happen to him in his entire life, including the death of his father. From the moment he had raised his hand in the induction center, the previous February, five months ago, he had ceased being who he was, a Lowell, and had become, as indeed the corporal had lost no time at all in telling him, a miserable pissant. He had been advised to give his soul to Jesus, because his ass now belonged to the army.

He had been so terrified of basic training that for the first time in his life he had made a conscious, consistent effort to behave and to deliver what was expected of him. He had become, if not a model soldier, then the next best thing, a nearly invisible one. He had not called attention to himself. He had neither talked back nor whined. On the rifle range, at the last moment, he had remembered to miss. If he shot High Expert, of which he was perfectly capable, he knew that he would have been taken out of the pipeline at the end of training and made into a marksmanship instructor.

Eight hours a day of Garand rifles going off in one's ear for the indeterminate future would be an awful way to pass one's penal servitude. He had been terrified on receipt of orders to proceed to Camp Kilmer for further shipment to Germany, and had spent his entire seven days' delay-en-route leave at Broadlawns on Long Island, half drunk, refusing to think about the future.

The troopship to Bremerhaven had been a floating Dante's inferno, a two-week horror. Only when he had arrived in Bad Nauheim and been assigned to the Constab as a clerk-typist had life begun to resemble at all the life he had known, and that similarity was limited to having sheets on the bunk, a place to take a bath, and food served on plates.

He had been in Germany only a week, and at the Constab only two days, when he came to understand that the venereal disease rate among the troops seemed to be the constant preoccupation of the Army of Occupation. Even the army radio station had commercials.

A GI solemnly pronounced: "Six fifteen hours, Central European Time. Remember, soldier! VD walks the streets tonight! And penicillin fails once in seven times!"

The army's solution to the problem was clean and wholesome sports, apparently in the theory that the troops would be exhausted to the point where they would not be interested in fornicating with frauleins. Every sport known to Western civilization was played, on command. Including, to his surprise, golf.

He had gone out for golf. At home, on the lawns of Broadlawns, which connected with the fairways of Turtle Creek Country Club, he had been whacking the ball around since he learned how to walk. The first time he played the Constab links, with some really awful clubs, he'd gone around the nine-hole course in 35, one under par. He had been posted to the golf team, and eventually named caddy master.

That was the turning point. He had moved out of the barracks into the golf course clubhouse. Slightly more civilized living. And then the polo came along. And now he was an officer and a gentleman.

He was a little annoyed with himself for his fear and concern. There was no reason why things should be different in the army—it was, after all, nothing more than a reflection of the society it served. He was what he was, a Lowell, and eventually he would come out on top.

Other people might have to spend their time washing tanks, or digging holes, or whatever; other people might have to wait, as the sign in the American Express office said in large letters, for a THREE WEEK OR MORE DELAY TO CASH PERSONAL CHECKS. He would spend his time playing golf and polo, as an officer, and would have his bank drafts honored at sight.

And soon it would be over, and he could go home. Certainly, as an officer, there would be a cabin on the returning troop ship, not a sheet of canvas between pipes in a hold thirty feet beneath the waterline.

He would, of course, wear his uniform when he got home. For a couple of days, until his civvies caught up with him. Pinks and greens, of course. Perhaps even the riding crop, or would that be a bit much? The pinks and greens, he decided. No riding crop. At Jack and Charley's 21 Club. Bunky Stevens would still be a college boy, down from Cambridge. He would be an officer, returned from overseas.

Second Lieutenant Craig W. Lowell moved his beer glass on the bar in the officer's mess of the Bayrischen Hotel, making little circles, dreaming of home.

"May I zit here?" the whore from the night before said timidly.

Goddamn, the last person in the entire fucking *world* I want to see right now!

He looked at her, met her eyes. Jesus Christ, how can she be a whore? She's even better looking than Cush's little sister. She's a goddamned certified beauty, that's all there is to it.

"Yes, of course, you may zit dere," Craig Lowell said, getting to his feet. He immediately regretted mocking her English and was relieved that she hadn't seemed to notice.

"Zank you," the whore said.

"Well," Craig Lowell said.

"I vaited in duh park undil I see you come in."

"Would you be more comfortable in German?" Craig Lowell said, in German.

"Oh, yes," she said, and she looked at him, and there was gratitude in her eyes. "I thought that you had spoken German last night, but I wasn't sure. I was so upset."

"May I offer you a drink?" he asked.

"A Goke-a-Gola, *bitte schön,*" she said.

What do I say now? How did a nice girl like you wind up in a place like this?

He ordered the Coca-Cola from the bartender, in German.

"Jawohl, Herr Leutnant," the bartender said.

"Do you live here?" he asked. Do you like Radcliffe?

"I used to live not far," she said. "Marburg. A very lovely little university city. You must see it before you go home."

She sounds like the goddamned Chamber of Commerce.

He looked at her and saw her naked in his bed, with the thumb-sized tuft of pubic hair. He closed his eyes.

"I vill go," she said. "I am you making uncomfortable."

"No!" the refusal burst out of him. "You will stay. You will have dinner with me." That seemed to scare her. He smiled. "We agreed to speak German, don't you remember?"

"Yes," she said.

The oaf, the captain from the night before, sat across the dining room from them and sneered at Lowell's naiveté. What kind of a whore was it that wouldn't give you a blow job?

He asked her if she would like to go to the movies. She accepted. It was the same Humphrey Bogart movie. He sat beside her and once took her hand. It was limp and cold in his.

In the jeep, when he reached for the ignition switch, she stayed his hand.

"We must talk," she said.

"About what?"

"I will go with you," she said. "But not just for one night. You understand?"

"No."

"I must do what I must do," she said. "But not for one night."

"Why must you do it?"

"My father is missing," she said. "There is no work. The state has taken over my home."

"What about your home?"

"My home has been requisitioned," she said.

"Where's your mother?"

"My mother no longer lives," she said. "She did not want to live, the way things are now."

Lowell decided he didn't want to know what she meant by that.

"I must have money, and I cannot get a job," she went on. "I have nobody. So I will do what I must do. But not for one night." He didn't answer. "After a while, perhaps, I will do what you like with my mouth."

"Oh, for Christ's sake!" Craig Lowell said. She was offering to blow him.

"But we must have an arrangement," she said.

"What kind of an arrangement?"

"You will give me one hundred dollars a month, and you will buy me things in the PX that I can sell on the black market," she said. She looked at him. "I will be good to you," she said.

He didn't reply.

"You have already given me $55," she said. "For only $45 more, and the things from the PX, you can have me for a month."

"You can keep the money I gave you," Craig Lowell said. "And I'll take you home." This had gone far enough. He was getting in over his head in an impossible situation.

"I don't have anyplace to go," she said, and there was desperation, even something close to terror, in her voice.

"What do you mean, you have no place to go? Where did you go last night?" Christ, if she's playing on my sympathies, she's doing one hell of a good job of it. How can a gentleman, like myself, fail to respond to a homeless waif? And then he was ashamed of himself for mocking her.

"To the park," she said, matter-of-factly.

"You spent the night in the park?"

She nodded, lowered her head. "If you want, I will do it with the mouth." It was total resignation, utter submission. And he knew she was telling the truth about the park.

"Shut up, goddamnit!" he said. He started the jeep and turned it around furiously. "I'll tell you what I'm going to do. I'm going to let you spend the night with me. Nothing will happen between us. I'll give you some more money. Tomorrow, you find someplace to stay. And I will see what I can do about getting you a job."

She wept silently, wiping her eyes.

When they came close to the Bayrischen Hof, she told him to stop the jeep. She jumped out and ran into the park. He waited, sure somehow that she was coming, unable to do what his logic told him to do, unable to put the fucking jeep in gear and get out of here.

She came back with a suitcase. Like her purse, it was a quality piece of goods. It was old, but it was good leather, and there was even the vestiges of gold initials.

"I had it hung in a tree," she said.

Craig Lowell had never felt before the humiliation he felt marching through the lobby of the Bayrischen Hof with his fur-line and her worn-out pigskin suitcase, before the eyes of the officers, before the eyes of the desk clerk sergeant who had thrown her out the night before.

In the room, she asked if she might take a bath. He nodded.

The prick in him, as he thought of it, came out when he had a mental image of her naked in his bathtub. He was paying for it; goddamnit, he had the right to see her in her bathtub. He had the right to do anything he goddamned pleased with her. She had even *offered* to blow him!

He did not enter the bathroom.

He put on clean underwear (he usually slept naked) and a cotton bathrobe. He waited until she came out, in a nightgown that went down to her ankles.

He went to his trousers and gave her five twenty-dollar script certificates.

"Tomorrow, you will find someplace to live," he said. "And this will carry you through until you've straightened yourself out."

Tears ran down her cheeks. She took the money.

"Zank you very much," she said. "God bless you!"

Oh, shit! That's all I had to hear!

They got in bed. They both faced outward, their backs to each other. After a long time, he went to sleep. He was not going to screw her. For one thing, she probably had syphylis, gonorrhea, an army of crabs, and God alone knows what else. For another, he was a Lowell, and a gentleman, and gentlemen did not take advantage of women in distress.

He woke up slowly, halfway into a wet dream. He had been touching Marjorie Carter's magnificent breasts, and suddenly he was awake and in bed with a real woman.

Her. He was really awake now, and excited. Her nightgown had riden up over her hips. He had wrapped his arm around her in her sleep. His hand was resting against her stomach. He had the World's Prize-Winning Number One Hard-On.

He very carefully lifted his arm and withdrew it.

"I'm awake," she said, softly, in German.

"Huh?" Craig Lowell said.

She rolled onto her back.

"I said I'm awake," she said. She looked up at him, and spread her legs.

He crawled between her legs. This time it didn't go down. This time it was ready. But it wouldn't go in. Where the hell was her hole? He spit on his fingers, rubbed it on the head, used it as a probe, felt it slip in.

He gave a massive thrust. It went all the way in. She yelped, softly, her hand in her mouth, biting her knuckle. It was easier now. It went in and out, in and out. She was making grunting sounds in her throat, half groans, half whimpers. Her midsection began to respond to him. She took her hand from her mouth and locked her arm around his neck, nearly choking him. She thrashed under him, calling upon Jesus, Mary, and Joseph.

He came.

He rolled off her and ran into the bathroom and washed himself, as he had been instructed to do in the technicolor VD movies. Now he was going to have clap and syphylis and crabs and Christ knows what else.

When he went back in the bedroom, she was curled up in a fetal position, not looking at him. When he got in bed, she got out, and he heard her doing whatever it is women do in the bathroom afterward. Then she came back and very quietly got into bed.

At first light, it happened again. Same goddamn thing. He woke up with his thing as rampant as it had ever been, pressed up against the crack of her ass.

The second time, he found the hole without much trouble, and she moved against him even more frenziedly, and she didn't make those yelping noises. And the second time, he told himself, what the fuck, I've already caught it. He didn't jump off her and go and wash his privates.

She said, when she had stopped breathing hard, "What is your name?"

"Craig," he said.

"I am Ilse," she said. "Ilse Berg."

When she had gone to the Civilian Personnel (Indigent Personnel) Office of the U.S. Constabulary to seek a job as a translator, the American had asked her her name, and she had told him Greiffenberg. He had asked her to spell it, and he couldn't understand her pronunciation, so finally he said, "Fuck it. From now on, fraulein, your name is Berg."

He wrote Berg down on her application, and she was afraid to correct him. Maybe he would, as he said, let her know in a month or two about a job. It didn't matter what her name was anymore.

She put out her hand to Craig, in the European manner, and shook his. She told herself that she had really been lucky. She had found an Ami who was kind and gentle. He was a nice person, she thought, and she thought that he acted a lot younger than he really was. He acted as if he was no more than eighteen or nineteen, and he must be older than that, for he was an officer. She promised herself that for as long as he kept her, she would do her best to live up to her end of the bargain.

It was preposterous, of course, to think that anything could come between them.

When he came back from the polo field that afternoon, she was waiting across the street from the Bayrischen Hof for him. When he stopped, she came gaily tripping across the street and got in the jeep and directed him three miles out of Bad Nauheim to a farm. She had rented a tiny two-room apartment. There was a tiny table. Somewhere she had found a rose, and put it in a small vase. There was a bed. She showed it to him proudly, and then turned. They looked at each other for a moment, and then, without a word, they started taking off their clothes.

(Five)
Baden-Baden
Zone Francaise de L'Armée de L'Occupation d'Allemagne
4 July 1946

The polo field was in sight of the Grand Hotel, and it was one of the oldest polo fields on the Continent, built to accommodate the English aristocracy whom had brought the game from India and then taken it with them to the Continent. It had been turned into a vegetable garden during the war, and the grass wasn't anything like either General Waterford or General Paul-Marie Antoine Quillier, his French counterpart, remembered from before the war, but it was, Waterford realized, a much better field than the field at Bad Nauheim.

The French, of course, had tried to get them drunk the night before at a dinner in the hotel, and afterward at a bar; but Waterford had seen that coming, and the only one who had defied his edict to stay sober was young Lowell.

He had decided to forgive Lowell. For one thing, Lowell was young; and there really wasn't much else for him to do with his elders around but drink. Primarily he was forgiving Lowell because the boy was playing better with what certainly must be a classic hangover than the others were playing in their physical prime.

They were five goals up on the French in the fourth chukker, when the French number three, with an offside neck shot, sent the ball toward the American goal. A good shot, twenty yards in the air, bouncing along the field for another ten yards and then picked up by the French number one, General Quillier, with an offside foreshot, which drove it another forty yards toward the American goal.

The players galloped past the spectators, past the band of the U.S. Constabulary in their chrome-plated helmets—its three trumpeters on their feet with instruments near their mouths—past the band of the Deuxième Division Mécanique of the French—with its bass drums draped in leopard skins, its Algerian mountain goats with gilded horns—past the tents set up to serve lunch and champagne, past the limousines of the generals, the staff cars, the personal automobiles, toward the American goal, behind which sat the L-5 Stinsons.

The American number four, Fat Charley, galloped up behind General Quillier. Leaning forward, standing in his stirrups, he passed him, raised his mallet over his head and swung it in a wide arc, a beautiful backhand that stopped the bouncing ball and sent it shooting in the other direction.

The American number three, Lieutenant Lowell, spun around in his headlong charge, changed direction, and galloped at the bouncing willow ball. He raised his mallet, then swept it down in a vicious arc so swift the whistling sound of the mallet was audible over the clatter of the pounding hooves. He drove the ball toward the French goal.

There was a muted round of applause from the ladies and gentlemen.

The three trumpeters of the U.S. Constabulary band, their

eyes on their general, sounded the charge.

The American number one, Major General Peterson K. Waterford, coming from across the field at a gallop, misjudged the speed of the bouncing ball. He almost overrode it, but saved his shot by making an offside tail stroke, his mallet coming from the far side of his mount under the tail, as he galloped past it. The ball was twenty yards ahead of him almost immediately, just time for him to raise his mallet for an offside foreshot. It was a clean blow. The ball went ahead of him in a straight line, hit the grass, rolled, stopped.

He raised his mallet again, urged his mount to go even faster. The trumpeters sounded the charge again. His mallet came down again in a swift arc. The crack of the maple head of his mallet on the willow ball was clear and crisp.

He watched the trajectory of the ball, then looked over his shoulder. In perfect position to back him up, in case he missed, was his number three, at a gallop, his mallet resting casually over his shoulder. He wasn't going to miss the sonofabitch.

He raised his mallet, heard his trumpeters sound the charge again, then swung his mallet and connected. He looked up to see the ball heading straight for the unprotected goal. He spurred his pony into pursuit.

Major General Peterson K. Waterford appeared to have lost his stirrup. He fell forward against the neck of his mount, as if he had lost his balance. The pony, still at the gallop, went through the goalposts.

The bell rang. Good goal.

The general's pony, at the last moment before running into the nearest of the Stinsons, veered to the right. General Peterson K. Waterford was unhorsed. He fell heavily to the ground, landing on his shoulder, skidding on his face.

His number three, Lieutenant Lowell, made what appeared to be an impatient shake of his hand, twisting his wrist free of the mallet loop. He reined in his galloping mount and was off the animal before it recovered from its abrupt stop. He ran the ten feet to General Waterford, knelt beside him, and rolled him over on his back. He saw that although General Waterford's eyes were on him, they didn't see him.

General Quillier was next to arrive, dismounting as quickly as had Lowell. He took one look at General Waterford's eyes

and crossed himself. Then some of the others came up, with
Fat Charley nearly last. And finally, on foot, red-faced, puffing
from the exertion, Captain Rudolph G. MacMillan.

QUARTIER GENERAL DE L'ARMEE DE L'OCCUPATION DE ALLEG-
MAGNE 4 JULY 1946

TO: HEADQUARTERS
UNITED STATES ARMY FORCES, EUROPE
FOLLOWING FROM BADEN-BADEN

MAJOR GENERAL PETERSON K. WATERFORD DIED SUDDENLY AT
1508 HOURS PRESUMABLY HEART ATTACK MORE FOLLOWS.

MACMILLAN, CAPT.

OPERATIONAL IMMEDIATE
HQ USFET
WAR DEPT WASH ATTN CHIEF OF STAFF
INFO HQ U.S. CONSTABULARY

IN RECEIPT UNCONFIRMED REPORT SIGNED MACMILLAN CAPT
THAT MAJOR GENERAL PETERSON K. WATERFORD DECEASED 1508
HOURS THIS DATE AT BADEN-BADEN.

CLAY, GENERAL

OPERATIONAL IMMEDIATE
HQ USFET
WAR DEPT WASH ATTN CHIEF OF STAFF
INFO HQ U.S. CONSTABULARY

DEATH OF MAJOR GENERAL PETERSON K. WATERFORD CON-
FIRMED AS OF 1530 HOURS. GENERAL WATERFORD SUFFERED COR-
ONARY FAILURE WHILE PLAYING POLO AT BADEN-BADEN. MRS.
WATERFORD PRESENT. FURTHER DETAILS WILL BE FURNISHED AS
AVAILABLE.

CLAY, GENERAL

(Six)
Bad Nauheim, Germany
4 July 1946

HEADQUARTERS

UNITED STATES CONSTABULARY

APO 109 US FORCES

GENERAL ORDERS 4 July 1946
NUMBER 66

The undersigned herewith assumes command of the United States Constabulary as of 1615 hours this date.

Richard M. Walls
Brigadier General, USA

General Walls had been known as "the Wall" when he had played football for the Academy because there had been few people ever able to push past him on the football field. He had weighed 220 pounds then. He was, twenty-five years later, ten pounds heavier. He was the Constab's artillery commander, and upon official notification of the demise of the commanding general, he had acceded to temporary command by virtue of his date of rank.

He was at the headquarters airstrip when the first L-5 Stinson from Baden-Baden arrived. Captain MacMillan hauled himself out of the front seat of the little airplane, straightened his uniform, and marched over to the Chevrolet staff car. He saluted crisply.

General Walls did not smile when he returned MacMillan's salute.

"All right, MacMillan," he said. "Let's have it."

"The general seemed all right through the first three chukkers, sir," MacMillan said. "In the last few moments of the fourth chukker, he appeared to have lost his balance, and then he fell off the horse. When I reached him, sir, he was dead."

"Mrs. Waterford?"

"Mrs. Waterford was among the spectators, sir. As soon as

possible, sir, I had the frogs TWX USFET."

"Subject to Mrs. Waterford's approval, of course, Captain, it is my intention to hold a memorial service for General Waterford at 1400 hours tomorrow."

"Yes, sir."

"How is Mrs. Waterford bearing up?"

"Very well, sir. Fat Charley . . . Colonel Lunsford is with her. They were classmates, sir, as I'm sure the general knows."

"I have spoken with General Clay," General Walls said. "The Air Corps has made available a C-54 to take Mrs. Waterford to the States. And the general's remains, if that is her wish."

"I believe Mrs. Waterford wishes the general to be buried at West Point, sir," MacMillan said.

"You've already asked, have you? You are an efficient sonofabitch, aren't you, MacMillan?" General Walls said. "All right, Captain, here it is. As a token of my respect for General Waterford, and my personal regard for Mrs. Waterford, you may consider yourself in charge of all arrangements until the general's remains leave the command."

"Thank you very much, sir."

"And then find yourself a new home, Captain," the general said.

"Sir?"

"You hear well, Captain," the general said. "General Waterford may have found you amusing, or useful, but I don't."

"Would the general care to be specific?" MacMillan, standing now at rigid attention, asked.

"The list of your outrages, MacMillan, is a long one. What comes to mind at the moment is that golf player you arranged to have commissioned. Shall I go on?"

"No, sir, that won't be necessary."

"I won't have someone like you in any outfit I command. In my judgment, medal or no goddamned medal, you are unfit to wear an officer's uniform. You are a scoundrel, MacMillan. A commissioned guardhouse lawyer. Is that clear enough for you?"

"Yes, sir, the general has made his point."

VI

Major Robert F. Bellmon, Assistant Branch Chief, Heavy Drop Loads Division of the Airborne Board, Fort Bragg, North Carolina, was regarded by his peers, and by the four bird colonels and sixteen lieutenant colonels senior to him, with suspicion and even contempt. He had been reduced to major in one of the first personnel cutbacks—"without prejudice"—but everyone knew that not all officers promoted beyond their age and length of service had been reduced in grade.

But even if he had just been caught in a rollback and was a good armor officer, what was such a good armor officer doing volunteering for airborne? Why would armor permit a good armor officer to go to Parachute School and then on to Ranger School? The answer was clear, and the proof was his assignment to the Airborne Board as the armor specialist.

There was nothing that anyone could put a finger on to *prove* their suspicions of Bellmon—he certainly did his work well enough—but two things about him were perfectly clear. There was nothing that airborne was planning to do that wouldn't be known to Fort Knox immediately. He was armor's spy in the airborne camp. That was perfectly clear. Airborne had their spies at Knox, too. That was the way the game was played. The second thing that was clear was that Bellmon was not, and would never be, one of them.

He went through the things that were expected of him: membership in the Airborne Association, wearing his parachutist's wings when no other qualification badge adorned his uniform, and as sort of a symbolic gesture that he wasn't really armor, having himself detailed to the General Staff Corps for the duration of his assignment to the Board.

They suspected, however, and they were correct, that he was laughing at them.

Major Bellmon thought a lot of things in the army were laughable. He had once gotten himself in trouble as a young captain by laughing out loud at the uniform General George Patton had designed for armor troops. He had once enraged one of the members of Eisenhower's SHAEF staff by pronouncing *Shayfe* as *Sheef,* and then going onto explain that a sheef was something somebody who lisped put on when he wished to diddle somebody.

A photograph had been circulated among senior airborne officers. The commanding officer of the Parachute School at Fort Benning, as a courtesy to a field-grade officer, had sent a photographer aloft in the C-47 to chronicle Major Bellmon's fifth (qualifying) jump. Instead of grim determination and great seriousness, the photographer had returned with a print of Major Bellmon going out the door holding his nose, his eyes tightly shut, his right hand over his head . . . a small boy jumping into deep water.

And he was amused now, although he kept his thoughts to himself. He was sitting in a jeep (another of his idiosyncracies was that he drove his own jeep; the assigned driver had to perch in the back seat) at Drop Zone Carentan. Other jeeps and trucks were gathered at the edge of the drop zone. There were a half dozen officers and twenty-five enlisted men. They all wore field jackets. The Airborne Board, like the Armor Board, the Artillery Board, and the Infantry Board, was a subordinate command of Army Ground Forces. The insignia of Army Ground Forces was a circle with three horizontal bands of color, blue for infantry, gold for armor, and red for artillery. But since all the personnel of the Airborne Board were airborne qualified, they sewed above this insignia a patch lettered *Airborne*. All this amused Major Bellmon.

A captain walked over to the jeep.

"The aircraft is airborne at Pope Field, Major," he said.

"Thank you," Bellmon said.

The test today was to drop, from a specially modified C-113 aircraft, an M24 light tank. The tank was firmly chained to a specially built platform, which in turn was chained to the floor of the C-113. When the aircraft appeared over the drop zone, the chains fastening the tank platform to the floor of the aircraft would be removed. A drogue parachute would be deployed from the rear of the airplane. When its canopy filled, it would pull the tank on its platform out of the rear of the aircraft. Then three enormous cargo parachutes would be deployed. They would, in theory, float the tank and its platform to the ground. On ground contact, the platform was designed to absorb shock by collapsing. The chains holding the tank to the platform would then be removed, and the tank driven off.

One of the weaknesses of a vertical envelopment was that you couldn't drop the necessary tanks, large-bore artillery, or engineer and other heavy equipment. This weakness was in the process of being rectified. Bellmon thought they had as much chance of solving the problem as they did of becoming ballet dancers.

Three minutes after the captain announced the aircraft was airborne, Bellmon got out of his jeep and walked to the drop zone. He saw that there were still and motion-picture cameras in place. And an ambulance. And even a three-man tank crew, to drive the tank away once it had landed.

He walked over to the tank crew. They came to attention.

"Stand at ease," he said. "How are you?"

"Good morning, Major," they chorused.

"What are you giving in the way of odds?" Bellmon asked.

"Not a fucking chance in hell, sir," the tank commander said.

"Oh, ye of little faith!" Bellmon said.

The airplane, a twin-boom, squatish aircraft whose boxlike fuselage had given it the name "Flying Boxcar," appeared in the distance. It approached and made a low-level pass. Someone set off a smoke grenade to indicate the direction and velocity of the wind. The aircraft made a low, slow turn and approached again, descending to a precise 2,000 feet altitude over the ground.

Bellmon raised his binoculars to his eyes and watched. The drogue chute came out the tail. Then the tank on its wooden platform. One by one, three huge cargo chutes filled with air and snapped open. The tank swung beneath them.

"Well, that much worked," Major Bellmon said.

One of the three parachutes began to flutter, and then lost its hemispherical shape.

"Sonofabitch ripped," one of the tank crewmen said. "I coulda told them that."

A second parachute ripped. The tank, which had been suspended horizontally, now hung from only one chute and was heading for the earth vertically. The third chute failed.

There was absolute silence as the tank plummeted toward the ground, trailing three shredded parachutes. It landed on its rear with one loud crash, and then fell over, right side up.

"I don't think you'll be needed today, fellas," Major Bellmon said. He walked quickly away. He sensed that the tankers were about to be hysterical, and he didn't want to be in the position of having to make them stop. He walked to his jeep, got behind the wheel, and drove out to where the tank had fallen.

The tank cannon had been in its travel position: turned to the rear and locked in place over the engine compartment. Some force, either of being jerked out of the airplane, or the opening shock of the cargo chutes, had torn it free from the mount. When the tank had hit, the high-tensile-strength steel in the gun barrel had been bent in a "U."

It was too much for Major Bellmon. As he reached for the jeep's ignition switch, he started to snicker, then to giggle, and finally he laughed out loud. It took him a long time to get the jeep started and moving.

"Get on the horn, Tommy," he said to the driver, as the jeep turned onto the dirt road leading back to Fort Bragg. "And tell them we're on our way back in."

The driver turned to the radio, mounted above the right rear wheel well, and communicated with the Airborne Board.

"Major," he said, in a moment. "The post commander wants to see you as soon as possible."

"The *post* commander?"

"Yes, sir."

"Do you think somebody already told him that I was laughing?" Major Bellmon asked.

Post headquarters was in one of a line of three-story brick buildings that Bellmon remembered from before the war as enlisted men's barracks. He parked his jeep, told the driver to get himself a cup of coffee, and entered the building from the rear.

The commanding general's office overlooked the post theater and senior officer's brick quarters. Bellmon, after announcing himself to the general's secretary, peered out the window of the anteroom to see what was playing at the movies, convinced that it would be at least fifteen minutes before the general would see him.

"Come on in, Bob," the general said, behind him. That was unusual, too. Normally an aide would tell him that the general would see him. The general did not welcome visitors personally. "Where the hell have you been anyway?" the general asked, touching his arm as they entered the office.

Bellmon started to snicker.

"Something funny?"

"Forgive me, sir," Bellmon said. "They were dropping an M24. It landed right on the tube, and bent it into a 'U.' I guess I have a perverse sense of humor."

The general didn't reply to that.

"The reason I asked, Bob, is that you had a call from the chief of staff, and nobody could find you."

"Sir," Bellmon said, "if I've caused you any inconvenience . . ."

"Not my chief of staff, Bob. *The* chief of staff."

"I don't understand, sir."

"When he couldn't get you, he got me. It is thus my sad duty, Bob, to inform you that Major General Peterson K. Waterford died suddenly at 1500 hours, German time, yesterday. We were old friends. I'm sorry."

"Do you know what happened, sir?"

"Heart attack," the general said. "Playing polo against the French. At his age."

"Jesus Christ!"

"I thought perhaps you would like to tell Barbara yourself. I'd be happy to..."

"I'll tell her, sir," Bellmon said. "Thank you."

"I've alerted Caroline. I thought I would give you a few minutes with Barbara and then send her in."

"Thank you very much, sir."

"Well, I guess he went the way he would have wanted to go. Playing polo."

"I was thinking just that, sir."

"My aide is laying on your plane reservations, and he'll be in touch. I'll come up for the funeral, of course."

"Thank you, again, General," Bellmon said.

"He was a little unusual, Porky Waterford," the general said, and his voice broke, and there were tears in his eyes, "But goddamn him, he was one *hell* of a soldier!"

(Two)

The president of the Airborne Board walked into Major Bellmon's small office to find him standing with a coffee cup in his hand and looking out of the window.

"Bob, I called your quarters and they said you were here. First of all, I'm terribly sorry; and secondly, I certainly didn't expect to see you here."

"Thank you, sir," Bellmon said. "Caroline, the chief of staff's wife, is with her. She's something like an adopted aunt to her... wanted me out of the house. And then there was a call from the Air Corps, General Deese, who was a classmate of General Waterford. He's sending his plane. He insisted we take it. So I had time to kill, and this seemed to be a good way to kill it."

"Anything we can do, of course. I've sent Janice over to your place."

"A soldier's death, sort of," Bellmon said. "Playing polo. *Polo!*"

"A soldier should die with the last bullet fired in the last battle," the colonel said. "I guess this is close. Why don't we have a drink?"

"I've got the Ranger honor graduates coming in," Bellmon said. "I don't want to breathe booze all over them."

"I'll take them," the Airborne Board president volunteered.

"If you don't mind, sir, I'd rather handle it. It's either that, or look out the window."

"I understand," the president of the Board said. "However, if you change your mind, I'll be in the building most of the afternoon."

"Thank you, sir."

"I understand the M24 drop was a failure," the president said. "Any ideas?"

"I think we better find a better way of air-landing our tanks," Major Bellmon said.

"Let me have your thoughts in a memo, Bob," he said. "When all this is over, of course."

"Yes, sir."

Bellmon's secretary, a civilian woman whose services he shared with three other officers, put her head in his door and knocked on the door frame. Bellmon looked at her.

"You've got five lieutenants to see you, Major."

"I'll get out of your hair, Bob," the president said. "Again, I'm very sorry."

"Thank you, sir," Bellmon said. He nodded at his secretary. "Send the first one in, please."

First Lieutenant Sanford Felter, Infantry, United States Army, his cap tucked under his upper left arm, marched into Major Robert F. Bellmon's office, stopped three feet from his desk, saluted crisply, and announced: "Lieutenant Felter reporting to Major Bellmon as ordered, sir."

Bellmon smiled as he returned the salute, but there was no recognition on his face or in his eyes.

"Sit down, Felter," he said, indicating a straight-backed, upholstered chair. "How do you take your coffee?"

"Black, sir, please," Felter said.

Bellmon looked much better than the last time Felter had seen him. His face and his body had filled out, and the unhealthy brightness was gone from his eyes. Bellmon filled a china cup from a restaurant-style coffee pot and walked around his desk and handed it to Felter.

"Congratulations, obviously, are in order," Bellmon said. "I was nowhere near being the honor graduate when I went through the course. As a matter of fact, I was way down the numerical list."

"One of my classmates, sir," Felter said, "developed a theory that small people, having less weight to carry around, should be handicapped."

Bellmon laughed, and looked at Felter with new interest. That wasn't the sort of remark he expected from a young leiutenant. It wasn't flip, or arrogant, but self-confident.

"He has a point," Bellmon said, chuckling. "What I'm going to do, now, Felter, is take a quick look at your record. I'm telling you that, because I don't want you to think I'm waging psychological warfare by making you wait for me as I do it. I just didn't have a chance to do it before."

"Yes, sir," Felter said.

Bellmon found the service record interesting. Even fascinating. He would never have suspected that this little man, this little Jew, had ever marched in the Long Gray Line. But there it was, the first entry on his service recrod:

1Jan45 Hon Disch f/Corps of Cadets USMA (Class of 46) for purp of accpt comm.

2Jan45 Comm 2ndLt Inf AUS Asgd Trans Off Det, USMA West Point NY

2Jan45—19Jan45 En Route 40 US Armd Div, APO 40, NYNY

19Jan 45 40MP Co, 40 US Arm Div (Dy as Asst O-in-C POW Interrogation Div)

23Apr45 Ofc of Mil Govt For Bavaria (Dy as Captured Documents Evaluation Off)

3Jul45 Prom 1st Lt, Inf AUS DOR 1Jul45 (Compl 6 mos satis comm svc)

17Aug45—4Oct45 En Route ZI (Incl 40 Dys Ret from OS lv)

5Oct45 Basic Inf Off Crs, USA Inf School, Ft Benning Ga

2Apr46 Dist Grad, Basic Off Crs USA Inf School Ft Benning Ga

21Apr46 Qual as Prchst, USA Inf School, Ft Benning Ga
23Apr46 USA Ranger School, Ft Bragg NC
2Jul46 Honor Grad USA Ranger School, Ft Bragg,
NC

"I see you were with Hell's Circus," Bellmon said. Felter
was not wearing the division patch on his right shoulder, as
his wartime service entitled him to do.

"Yes, sir."

"Did you ever happen to meet General Waterford?" Bellmon
asked.

"One time, sir, for about fifteen minutes."

"I'm sorry to tell you, Lieutenant," Bellmon said. "that
General Waterford died yesterday. Playing polo, of all things."

"I'm sorry to hear that, sir," Felter said.

Bellmon had a sudden urge to challenge this self-confident
little Jew.

"Why do you say that?" he demanded. "If you only saw
him once for fifteen minutes, why would you have any feeling
about his death, one way or the other?"

"I suppose I was considering what his loss means to the
army, sir," Felter said. "General Waterford was recognized to
be one of the better large armored force commanders."

Bellmon nodded, impressed that the reply had come without
thinking, that Felter had not been offering condolences to curry
favor.

"Yes, he was," he said. "I'm curious to hear your plans for
your career, Felter. Do you plan to stay? Are you going to
apply for regular army?"

"Yes, sir," Felter said.

"Since you left the Academy, you don't have a college
degree. What do you plan to do about that?"

"I am enrolled in the Extension Department of the University
of Chicago, sir. I hope to have my degree in a few months."

"You're talking about getting a degree by correspondence?
Through the mail?"

"Yes, sir. I'm going for a degree in political science."

"Commendable," Bellmon said, dryly. The little bastard had
an answer for everything. Then he suddenly realized that he
was being hard on him for no good reason. Because he was

a Jew? Or because his own father-in-law, who he really liked, maybe even loved, had just dropped dead, and he was upset by that?

"Felter, I apologize," Bellmon said. "I've been picking on you. For what it's worth, I have just had a death in the family. That's no excuse for picking on you, but that's what happened. I'm sorry."

Felter did not reply.

"Lieutenant," Bellmon said, smiling at him, "in token of the U.S. Army's profound appreciation of the splendid showing you have made at John Wayne High School, also known as the U.S. Army Ranger School, an effort, a real effort, will be made to give you your choice of assignment. There are about twenty-five different vacancies."

"Yes, sir," Felter said.

"You seem neither outraged nor amused at my somewhat irreverent reference to the Ranger School," Bellmon said.

"I've heard it called that before, sir," Felter said.

"And what was your reaction? Amusement, or outrage at the mocking of the sacred?"

"Amusement, sir," Felter said. He ran his hand over his closely cropped hair, which was already starting to thin. The movement served to shade his face. Bellmon looked at him very closely.

"And are you amused now, Felter?" Bellmon asked, and there was ice in his voice. He was furious with himself for not having recognized Felter immediately.

"Sir?"

"Do you find this situation amusing?"

"I don't quite know what you mean, sir," Felter said.

"You know precisely what I mean, Lieutenant. We have met before, haven't we?"

"Yes, sir."

"You did not elect to remind me," Bellmon said. "May I ask why?"

"I was offering the major the option of remembering me," Felter said. He paused, then added: "Or not."

"What happened to you when we got back?" Bellmon asked, after a moment. He ran his hand nervously over his head.

"I was ordered not to discuss Task Force Parker," Felter

said. "And then I was sent to Munich."

"Did you hear what happened to me?"

"I heard the major was hospitalized," Felter said.

"In the nut ward," Bellmon said. "Did you hear that?"

Felter just perceptibly nodded his head.

"Did you elect not to remind me of our previous meeting because you believe I was temporarily bereft of my senses at the time?"

"I have examined the Katyn material," Felter said. "I believe the Russians executed the Polish prisoners."

"Where did you examine it?" Bellmon asked, surprised.

"The Polish government-in-exile, what used to be the Polish government-in-exile, presented it to Congress. The hearings are a matter of public record."

"But you took the trouble . . ." Bellmon said.

"I was interested," Felter said.

"And have you discussed either the Katyn business or Task Force Parker with anyone?"

"Not until today, sir."

"Not even with your wife?"

"No, sir. My wife is a sensitive woman."

"Similarly, Lieutenant Felter, I have not discussed what happened with anyone."

"Yes, sir."

"I was reduced in grade shortly after the war ended, Felter. That might have been because I was too young for the grade I held. I have been led to believe that my name is number fourteen on the next promotion list to lieutenant colonel. I will still be a rather young lieutenant colonel. Does that suggest anything to you?"

"It would suggest that there is no question concerning the major's stability," Felter said. "Or his discretion."

"There are some things, Felter, which should not be discussed unless one is absolutely sure of the audience."

"Yes, sir."

"You and I are not alone, Felter," Bellmon said.

"Yes, sir."

"You demonstrate a rather unusual understanding for someone of your rank and length of service," Bellmon said. He let that sink in. Then he smiled. "You may even be able to grasp what a crock of shit the ranger philosophy is."

Felter smiled.

"Well, I owe you one, anyway, for keeping me from getting blown away the day I was liberated. Tell me what you've been thinking about your career."

"I don't know quite what to say, sir," Felter said.

"Where do you want to be twenty years from now? In 1966? By then you should be a major, possibly even a lieutenant colonel. Battalion exec? What?"

"Sir," Felter said. "I think I would be suited to be an intelligence officer."

"Why?"

"I have a flair for languages. I speak German and Polish and Russian. And a little French."

"Russian?"

"My mother's family, sir."

"There is more to intelligence than linguistics," Bellmon said. He had just realized that while he had planned to kill some time by making the expected remarks to a bunch of dumb lieutenants, he was now faced with the opportunity to offer some genuine advice to a lieutenant who was obviously anything but dumb, and to whom, in fact, he owed his life.

"Yes, sir, I understand that," Felter said.

"The truth of the matter, Felter, is that most of the good intelligence officers in the last war—and I would suppose in all wars—were civilians in uniform. The mental training which makes for a good regular officer in peacetime is not often valuable in the intelligence business. What I'm saying, I suppose, is that we need very bright people to be intelligence officers, but that there is no place in the peacetime army for a bona fide intellectual."

"Sir, are we going to have a peacetime army?"

"Take that further, Felter," Bellmon said. "Explain yourself."

"I saw in the newspaper last week that we've taken over for the English in Greece, sir," Felter said. "That's hardly garrison duty."

There was a moment's silence as Bellmon sifted through a manila folder on the desk before him.

TELECON MEMO

Record of Telecon Between G-1 This Hq and Office of
the Adjutant General, War Dept (Col J C McKee & Lt
Col Kenneth Oates)

Colonel Oates stated that the Chief of Staff had approved
a request from the Commanding General, United States
Army Military Advisory Group, (USAMAG-G) for 86
company grade combat arms officers to serve as advisors
to the Royal Greek Army. If possible, such officers
should have a knowledge of the Greek language, combat
experience, and be willing to serve a minimum tour of
one year in hardship conditions. A levy of two officers
has been laid upon Fort Bragg (including all subordinate
units). Col. Oates further states that he must have the
names of selected officers within 24 hours. Volunteers
will proceed as soon as possible via mil air to Frankfurt,
Germany, for transshipment to Athens.

"Where else in the world do you see trouble spots, Felter?"
Major Bellmon asked. "Just for conversation, of course."

"Sir, I think I'm talking too much," Felter said.

"Where else, Lieutenant?" Bellmon said. "If you haven't
learned by now, it's high time you did, that when you open
your mouth, you better be prepared to finish what you started
to say."

"Yes, sir," Felter said. "India, sir. With their independence.
Indochina, against French colonialism. China, where the communists are probably going to win. That may have implications
for Indochina, too. Korea. The Philippines. Palestine, I don't
want to forget that."

"Tell me about Palestine," Bellmon said.

"The Zionists are not going to give up. And neither are the
Arabs. They will not tolerate a Jewish state."

"Whose side are you on?" Bellmon said.

Felter was sure now that his mouth had got him in trouble.

"I'm Jewish, as well as a Jew," he said. "My sympathies
lie with the idea of a Jewish state."

"And if you were ordered to Palestine, on the side of the
English, for example, against the Zionists?"

"I don't know, sir. I would probably resign."

"Don't say that to anyone else, Felter," Bellmon said. "Never let the enemy know of your options until you have to." He paused. "A classmate of mine is over there. Resigned his commission. Fighting for the Zionists."

"And you don't approve, sir?"

"No, Lieutenant, I don't," Bellmon said. "Does that make me in your eyes a bigot? An anti-Semite?"

"No, sir. But it illustrates my point about Palestine being a trouble spot. There's very little room for reason on either side. In a way like northern Ireland, which is another trouble spot."

"I hadn't even thought about Ireland," Bellmon confessed.

Having said that, he realized that Felter's assessment of the world was very much like his own. Charitably, it was realistic; or cynical. Like his own.

"Your next assignment will be with troops," Bellmon said, formally. "Junior officers need the responsibility of command. The following are vacancies available to you: 1st Cavalry Division, Dismounted, Kyushu, Japan; 187th Regimental Combat Team, Airborne Hokkaido, Japan; 24th Infantry Division, Hawaii; 5th Infantry Division, Fort Riley, Kansas; 82nd Airborne Division, here at Bragg; Any of the infantry basic training centers; 1st Infantry Division, Germany; Trieste United States Troops . . . that's the old 88th Mountain Division . . . in Trieste. They call it TRUST. Those are your options, Lieutenant."

"Sir, I heard that we're going to send company-grade officers to Greece. Would that be considered duty with troops?"

"Where did you hear that?"

"From some of the men in class, sir. A number of them have volunteered."

"Volunteers are apparently being solicited from officers with combat experience," Bellmon said. "You have none. At least officially."

"If I have to spend time with troops, sir," Felter said, "as part of my education, I would prefer to spend time with troops who are engaged."

"What are you after, Felter, a reputation as someone spoiling for a confrontation with the Godless Red Hordes?"

"I believe it is an officer's duty to learn as much as possible about potential enemies," Felter said.

"It is, of course," Bellmon said. "The trouble, historically, is that few people have been able to identify the next enemy in time to do anything about it. What if you're wrong?"

"You and I, Major," Felter said, "already know the Soviet Union is our enemy."

"Watch who you say things like that to, Felter," Bellmon said. "A lot of people think the Soviet Union is just a friendly bear."

Felter nodded.

"It's a hardship tour, Felter," Bellmon went on. "No dependents. Your wife will be denied the opportunity to live high on the hog in an Army of Occupation."

"I understand, sir," Felter said.

Bellmon picked up his telephone and told his secretary to get Colonel McKee on the line. When, a moment later, the telephone rang, Bellmon turned the receiver from his ear so that Felter could hear both sides of the conversation.

"Sir, this is Major Bellmon. I have one of your two company grades for Greece."

"Who's that?"

"A lieutenant named Felter. He was honor grad of the ranger school. He wants to go, and I think we should send him."

"I don't think so, Bob," Colonel McKee said. "For one thing, I've already got a couple of people who were 'encouraged' to volunteer. What did your guy do wrong?"

"Nothing, sir. As I said, he was honor grad of the ranger course. He wants to go."

"Bob, I'm not getting through to you. We're dumping people to Greece, not awarding it as a prize. It's a lousy assignment."

"Lieutenant Felter wants to go, Colonel. As honor grad, he is more or less entitled to pick his assignment."

"There's something you're not telling me, Bellmon. But I'm not going to ask. OK, you want this guy shanghaied to Greece, consider him shanghaied. Give me his full name, rank, and serial number."

(Three)
West Point, New York
9 July 1946

Major General Peterson K. Waterford was laid to his final rest in the cemetery of the United States Military Academy at West Point. When the volleys had been fired, when the trumpeter had sounded the last taps, when the flag, folded into a triangle with no red showing, had been placed in Mrs. Waterford's hands by the Chief of Staff of the United States Army, the funeral party moved to the quarters of the Commandant for refreshments.

Major Robert F. Bellmon sought out Captain Rudolph G. MacMillan.

"I haven't had the chance before, Mac," he said, "to express my thanks. My mother-in-law's told me what a help you've been."

"What the hell, I was awful fond of the general," MacMillan said, embarrassed.

"And he of you," Bellmon said.

The Chief of Staff of the United States Army walked up and joined them.

"I've got to be getting back, Bob," he said. "But I didn't want to leave without saying good-bye and God bless, and without thanking you, Captain MacMillan, for all you've done for Mrs. Waterford."

"My privilege, sir," Mac said.

"You were with Porky a long time, weren't you?" the Chief of Staff said. He was a tall thin man, one of the few four-star generals then entitled to wear a Combat Infantry Badge, which General of the Army Omar Bradley insisted should go only to soldiers who had functioned well in ground combat. More than one general who'd been awarded one by orders he had signed himself had been told to take it off.

"No, sir," MacMillan said. "Not long at all. But Colonel . . . I'm sorry, *Major* Bellmon and I go back a long way."

"Mac and I were in the stalag, together, General," Bellmon said.

"Oh, of course. I knew there was something." His eyes dropped to the blue-starred ribbon topping MacMillan's display of fruit salad. "You are *the* MacMillan."

"The one and only," Bellmon laughed.

"And now what happens to you?" the Chief of Staff asked. "You're sort of left hanging, aren't you? Where would you like to go?"

"Anywhere they send me, sir, of course," MacMillan said.

"Oh, come on, MacMillan. The army owes you something," the Chief of Staff said.

"Sir, now that you bring it up," MacMillan said, "I was about to ask Major Bellmon if he could find a home for a battered old soldier."

"You got a spot for MacMillan, Bob? Where are you . . . oh, yeah. The Airborne Board. I *heard* about that."

"I think, sir," Major Bellmon said, "that we could find something to keep Mac occupied."

"I also heard—out of school, of course—that you're not going to be at Bragg much longer," the Chief of Staff said. "Among other things, I. D. White wants you at Knox. Why don't I just—?" He stopped in midsentence and made a barely perceptible movement of his head. A brigadier general walked over. He was a distinguished-looking officer with silver hair, and he wore the gold cord of an aide-de-camp.

"Tom, Major Bellmon will call you with the details," the Chief of Staff said. "The idea is to have Captain MacMillan assigned to Knox. Tell the G-1 to find something suitable for him to do there, will you?"

"Sir," MacMillan said, "the minute I get near personnel types, they want me to make speeches. Can it be arranged to sneak me into Knox?"

The Chief of Staff laughed.

"Sneak him into Knox yourself, Tom. I understand the captain's problem."

"Yes, sir," the aide-de-camp said. "Sir, we're going to have to be moving on."

"Let me say good-bye to Mrs. Waterford," the Chief of Staff said. "Get the car."

(Four)
McGuire Air Base
Wrightstown, New Jersey
10 July 1946

Sharon Lavinsky Felter was ashamed of herself because she hated her husband on the very day he was going away.

It wasn't that she didn't love him. She loved him as she had loved him for as long as she could remember. But it was possible, she had learned, to love and hate the same man at the same time.

She hated Sandy when he was being an officer, when he was giving orders she had to obey, and not listening to her, or even caring what she thought about anything.

They had ridden to McGuire, she and Sandy, and her mother and father, and Mama and Papa Felter, in a brand-new Buick Super two door. Now especially, with him going away, she needed a brand-new Buick Super two door like she needed a third leg. For one thing, she wasn't that good a driver, and for another, the Buick seemed to want to get away from her almost as if it had a mind of its own.

She had had no say about the Buick at all. He couldn't tell her father or his, or especially his mother what he'd told her ("The question is not open for discussion"), so he'd listened to their objections: All that money. Sharon didn't *need* a car. There was the Lavinsky's perfectly good 1938 Plymouth to carry her anywhere the Old Warsaw Baker's Dodge panel truck couldn't take her. If he had to have a rich man's car, he could buy one when he came to his senses and came home.

He heard the objections and ignored them.

"Try to understand this, Sharon," he said to her. "I'm getting a little tired of repeating it. I am a regular army officer."

He had told her that thirty-five times. She didn't really understand what that meant, but he had been very pleased with himself when the letter had come in the mail. They'd had to waste one whole day going down to Fort Dix, where he got another physical examination, and then was sworn in. But he was still a first lieutenant, and he wasn't going to get any more money, and the only difference she could see was that they gave him a new, shorter serial number.

Regular army officers, she tried to understand, had different obligations from reserve officers on extended active duty. And for reasons she could not understand, one of these was apparently that they had to have a rich man's car, a new one, just sitting around so that in case one was needed in a hurry, there it would be.

"We can afford it. For the couple of hundred extra dollars, I would rather have the reliability of a Buick. If I didn't think we needed it, or I didn't think we could afford it, we wouldn't buy it. Now let it be, Sharon."

He made her drive from Newark to McGuire Air Base, although that was the last thing she wanted to do. "Otherwise," he said. "You would never drive it. And I want you to know that you can."

It was crowded in the Buick, as big as it was, with Sharon and Sandy and Papa Felter in the front, and Sharon's mother and father and Mama Felter in the back. And with Sandy's luggage in the trunk, the front of the Buick was high up and Sharon had trouble seeing over the bull's-eye ornament on the hood.

And there was a lot of tension in the car, although everybody naturally tried to hide it. The Felters and the Lavinskys were really angry with Sandy, angry and hurt by his behavior and confused by it.

So far as they were concerned, he had done his part by going off to the war when he could have stayed safe and sound at West Point. Then when he had, thank God, come home in one piece, he had done more than his part by not taking the honorable discharge he had been offered.

Sharon had agreed with everything Mama Felter had said to Sandy, when she really laid it into him. Sandy could be anything he wanted to in life. God had given him the brains to be a doctor or a lawyer, or anything else he wanted to be. There was the GI Bill of Rights, which would pay for his education; and the bakery was coming along nicely, so there would be money for them to get a little apartment of their own and maybe even start a family while he was still in school, if that's what he and Sharon wanted to do. He had everything a reasonable man could ask for, and he was throwing it all away like a little boy running off to the circus. A soldier! Who did he think he was, Napoleon, because he was so short?

Papa Felter tried to shut Mama Felter up and calm things down. What Sandy was doing, he said, was proving himself, because he was small. After a while, he would come to his senses; he wasn't old yet. He said that Sandy had never had the time to sow any wild oats, the way he'd gone off to the war. Papa Felter said they should stop worrying, and be glad that he hadn't started drinking, or gambling, or chasing women, or whatever, the way most young men did.

After a while, Papa Felter said, Sandy would see things for what they were, and he would come to his senses. He had every confidence in that. For the time being, if it made Sandy happy to jump out of airplanes, and eat snakes in the jungle the way they made him do in ranger school, they would just have to go along with him.

That was all very nice, but it wasn't much help to Sharon. She wasn't asking much. She had been perfectly content in their room in Columbus, Georgia, outside Fort Benning, and in the little apartment in Fayetteville, North Carolina, outside Fort Bragg. As it said in the *Bible*, "Whither thou goest, I will go." If Sandy had wanted her to go with him to the North Pole, she would have gone and been happy, but that wasn't this. This was a whole year, maybe more, with her working in the bakery and Sandy doing God alone knows what in Greece. *Greece!*

Everybody in the car was torn between being mad at Sandy and feeling sorry for Sharon, and feeling sorry for the both of them.

When they got to McGuire Air Force Base, Sandy directed her to park the Buick Super in an area designated DEPARTING PERSONNEL PARKING.

He picked up his two heavy Valv-Paks and walked into the passenger terminal with his wife and his parents and his wife's parents trailing reluctantly behind him.

"Well, look who's here," he said, softly, as much to himself as to Sharon when he stepped inside the door.

"Who's here, Sandy?" Sharon asked.

"Some of my classmates," he said. "I heard about that. They report in early, and then take another two weeks in Germany when they get there."

She didn't know what he was talking about, but she could

see who he was talking about. There were twenty second lieutenants in the waiting room wearing Class "A" tropical worsted
summer uniforms—shirt, tunic, trousers, and brimmed cap—
and twenty young women, all dressed up with flowers pinned
to their dresses and suits, looking like brides.

Sharon deeply loved her husband, and wouldn't have
swapped him for any man in the world, but being honest about
it, when you looked at him in his khakis, Sandy looked like
somebody delivering from the delicatessen.

"Honey, why didn't you wear your TWs?" Sharon asked.

"If you're going to have to spend eighteen hours in an
airplane seat in a uniform," he said, just a trifle smugly, "you
wear khakis."

He picked up the two Valv-Paks and walked across to the
desk. Sharon trailed after him.

"Lieutenant," the sergeant said, scornfully, looking at the
heavy Valv-Paks, "you're going to be way over weight."

"Take a look at my orders, Sergeant," Sandy said, unpleas-
antly.

The sergeant read the orders Sandy handed him.

"OK, Lieutenant," he said. "My mistake."

Sharon became aware that several of the second lieutenants
were looking at them. She thought it was because Sandy was
wearing khakis.

"It'll be just a couple of minutes, Lieutenant," the sergeant
said. "Stick around the waiting room."

"Thank you," Sandy said. Then he took Sharon's arm and
marched her over to the second lieutenants and their wives.

"Hello, Nesbit," Sandy said. "Pierce. O'Connor."

"I'll be damned, Felter," one of them said. "It is you."

"You'll be damned, *sir*," one of the others said. "Note the
silver bar." He put out his hand.

The third one smiled broadly, and said, "Sir Mouse, sir,
may I present my wife?"

"How do you do?" Sandy said. "And may I present mine?"

One of them, as they were all shaking hands, told his wife
that "Lieutenant Felter was with us at the Academy for a while."
Sharon saw the explanation confused the wife. And she didn't
like it when people called Sandy "Mouse," even though he told
her he didn't mind.

"Deutschland bound, are you, Mouse?" one of them asked.

"Greece," Sandy said.

"Greece?" he responded, incredulously.

"There's a Military Advisory Group there," Sandy said.

"I didn't know that," he said.

Despite the fact that she knew Sandy was right that there was no sense in mussing a tropical worsted uniform on an airplane, Sharon wished that Sandy had worn his anyway. Or at least put on his other insignia. All he was wearing was his silver lieutenant's bar on one collar and the infantry rifles on the other. He was wearing regular shoes, even though he was entitled to wear paratrooper boots. He wasn't even wearing his parachutists' wings and boots or his Ranger patch.

Sharon could tell from the way the others talked to him, the way they looked at him, that they didn't think very much of him, either. Sad Sack Felter is what he looked like, two pastrami on rye and a side order of cucumber salad, double cream in the coffee. And meeting the young West Pointers and their wives confirmed what Sharon had suspected. Sandy said going to Greece was a great opportunity for him. The others didn't think it was such a great opportunity; they didn't even know the United States had soldiers in Greece. They were going to the 1st Division and the Constabulary in Germany.

And they were taking their wives with them. Right on the same plane.

When she and Sandy walked over to their parents, Sharon sensed that the West Pointers were whispering about them.

Then the plane was announced.

Sharon's mother and Mama Felter started to cry out loud when Sandy kissed them. Sharon kept her tears back until Sandy climbed the stairs and disappeared inside the plane. Then she cried on her mother's bosom.

In the car on the way home, Papa said something terrible. He didn't know he said it. He was just thinking aloud. Papa said, "I suppose if you have to send somebody to get shot, it's better to send a Jew."

Sharon told herself that Sandy was the smartest boy she had ever met. If she believed that, she would have to believe that he would come to realize that what he was doing was the wrong thing for him, for them; and then he would come home and they could build a life together.

When he missed her, Sharon decided, that's when he would decide he was wrong.

(Five)
Bad Nauheim, Germany
11 July 1946

Colonel Charles A. Webster, the Constabulary's adjutant general, entered the office of the commanding general, Brigadier General Richard M. Walls, to bring certain personnel actions to the general's attention. General Walls had received no word regarding his future. He did not know if he would be given command of the Constab permanently or whether a major general would be sent in to take General Waterford's place. He had therefore been commanding the Constab from the same office from which he had commanded the Constab artillery, rather than moving into Waterford's office at Constabulary headquarters.

"I'm afraid I've let this slip, sir," Webster confessed, handing General Walls a teletype message. "I sort of hoped they would just forget us."

"What is it?"

"USFET laid a requirement on us for two combat-qualified officers to send to Greece. They also have to speak Greek."

"And?"

"I found people with those qualifications, but their commanders don't want to give them up."

"What the hell is going on in Greece?"

"I really don't know, sir. As I said, I thought if I just let it slip, they'd forget us."

"And what's the problem?" Walls asked. He read the TWX from USFET:

PRIORITY
FROM USFET 10 JULY 1946
COMMANDING GENERAL U.S. CONSTABULARY
ATTN: ADJUTANT GENERAL.

(1.) REFERENCE TWX 55098. 27 MAY 1946.
(2.) YOU WILL IMMEDIATELY FURNISH NAMES OF TWO OFFICERS

SELECTED FOR TRANSFER TO US ARMY MILITARY ADVISORY GROUP, GREECE, REQUESTED IN REFERENCED TWX.

(3.) YOUR ATTENTION IS INVITED TO REQUIREMENTS SPECIFIED IN REFERENCED TWX. SELECTED OFFICERS SHOULD BE OF COMBAT ARMS, GREEK SPEAKING, AND AVAILABLE FOR HARDSHIP TOUR OF NOT LESS THAN ONE YEAR. VOLUNTEERS ARE PREFERRED.

BY COMMAND OF GENERAL CLAY

After General Walls read the TWX, he pushed it back to Colonel Webster. "Let me think about it a minute, Charley," he said. "I really hate to give up officers with combat experience. If the balloon should go up with the goddamned Russians, how the hell am I expected to fight with an officer corps that never heard a shot fired in anger?"

"That brings us to Lieutenant Lowell, sir," Webster said. "Does the general intend to bring him before a board of officers for dismissal from the service?"

"That fancy-pantsed sonofabitch hasn't been an officer long enough for us to make that judgment," General Walls said. "Not to speak ill of the dead, that was really going too far, even for Waterford. Where's MacMillan? Did he find a new home?"

"Yes, sir. We got a TWX yesterday. He's assigned to Knox. He won't even be coming back."

"I would like to be able to send that sonofabitch to Greece," General Walls said. He looked up at Colonel Webster. An idea had been born. He reread the TWX.

"As I read this thing, Colonel," he said, "it says volunteers are preferred. 'Preferred' is not the same thing as 'required,' is it? And it also says that officers 'should be' of combat arms, Greek speaking, and available for a hardship tour. I would say that Lieutenant Lowell is available for a hardship tour, wouldn't you, Colonel?"

"Yes, sir, I would," Webster replied. "If the general decides not to board him out of the service."

"And he is presently detailed to a combat arm, isn't he?" General Walls asked. There was a pleased tone in his voice.

"Yes, sir, he is."

"Pity he doesn't speak Greek, but two out of three isn't bad, is it, Colonel?"

"Not bad at all, sir."

"Who else can you think of, offhand, Colonel, who also meets these requirements?"

"I heard from the CID, General, that there's a captain in the 19th they think isn't entirely all man, if you follow me."

"Anybody else?"

"There's a lieutenant in Combat Command A who's been writing some rubber checks."

"Send the fairy," the general said. "Anything else, Colonel Webster?"

"Not a thing, sir. That takes care of all the loose ends I can think of."

"Get both of them out of the Constabulary this afternoon, Colonel," General Walls said.

(Six)

The military police duty officer came into Fat Charley's office in the provost marshal's building that Craig Lowell thought looked like a gas station.

"I thought I should bring this to the colonel's attention, sir," he said.

"What is it?"

"Colonel Webster just called, and said he was speaking for the general, and I was to send every available man to locate and arrest Lieutenant Lowell and bring him to his office."

Fat Charley thought a moment, and then he dialed Colonel Webster's number.

"Charley, what is this business about an arrest order on Lieutenant Lowell?"

"The general wants him out of the Constabulary this afternoon, Colonel."

"Where's he going?"

"He has been selected for assignment to Greece," Webster said, somewhat triumphantly.

"For Christ's sake, Charley, I saw that TWX. It says combat-experienced officers who speak Greek. It's not that boy's fault Waterford handed him a commission."

"Would you care to discuss it with the general, Colonel?"

"No," Fat Charley said. "I'll have him at your office in an hour, Colonel."

"Thank you for your cooperation, Colonel," Colonel Webster said.

Fat Charley hung up the telephone. He reached for his hat. "Is your driver outside?"

"Yes, sir. You know where to find Lowell?"

"I think so," Fat Charley said. "Have you issued an arrest order?"

"The duty sergeant put one out before I got this," he said. "Should I cancel it, sir?"

"No, you better let it stand," Fat Charley said. "I'm on Walls's shit list enough as it is without making things worse."

(Seven)

Forty-five minutes later Lieutenant Craig W. Lowell marched into Colonel Webster's office.

"Sir," he said, saluting. "Lieutenant Lowell reporting to Colonel Webster as ordered."

"You may stand at ease, lieutenant," Colonel Webster said. "Lieutenant, this interview will constitute official notice to you of inter-theater movement orders. Regulations state that personnel notified of such orders be further informed that failure to comply with such orders constitutes desertion. Do you understand the implication of what I have just told you?"

"Yes, sir."

"By command of General Clay, Lieutenant, you are relieved of your assignment to the U.S. Constabulary, and are transferred to Headquarters, United States Army Military Advisory Group, Greece, effective this date. You will take with you such fatigue uniforms, field gear, and shade 33 uniforms as are necessary for an extended period of duty in the field. Shade 51 uniforms, and any household goods you may have, to include any personal vehicles, will be turned into the quartermaster. Such items will be stored for you at no expense to you at the U.S. Army Terminal, Brooklyn, New York, until such time as you complete your assignment, or request other disposition of them. You will procede from here to Rhine-Main

Air Corps Base so as to arrive there for shipment by military air no later than 1800 hours this date."

"Yes, sir."

"Have you any questions?"

"Sir, I'm a little short of cash. May I have time to stop by American Express?"

"As part of your out-processing, Lieutenant, a partial payment of $100 will be made."

"Sir, I don't believe that will be enough money."

"You won't need money where you're going, Lieutenant," Colonel Webster said. "Any other questions?"

"No, sir."

"Captain Young, of my staff, will accompany you through your out-processing. If you have no further questions, that will be all, Lieutenant."

"Yes, sir."

Lowell saluted, did an about-face, and marched out of Colonel Webster's office.

Captain Roland Young, Adjutant General's Corps, who had rather relished the notion of personally running this disgrace to the uniform the hell out of the Constab, was annoyed and frustrated when he led Lowell into the corridor outside the adjutant general's office and found the provost marshal waiting for them. He could hardly tell the provost marshal to fuck off, even if the word was out that the provost marshal, like other members of Waterford's palace guard, was in hot water himself.

"I've sent a jeep for Ilse," the provost marshal said to Lowell. "They should have her here in a couple of minutes."

Captain Young thought that Colonel Webster would be very interested to hear that the provost marshal, in direct contravention of Constab (and for that matter, Theater) regulations, had ordered the transport of a German female in an official army vehicle.

"Thank you, sir," Lowell said. What the hell was he going to do about Ilse?

"What is the lieutenant's schedule, Captain?" Fat Charley asked.

"The lieutenant, sir, is to report to Rhine-Main no later than 1800 hours," Captain Young said.

"Amazing how efficient you paper-pushers can be when you want to," Fat Charley said.

Captain Young thought that Colonel Webster would be interested in that sarcastic remark, too.

"Is there anything I may do for the colonel, sir?" Captain Young asked. "There's not much time to go through the processing."

"I don't have anything else to do, Captain," Fat Charley said. "I think I'll just tag along with you."

The saddest part, Fat Charley thought later, was that in Lowell's room in the Bayrischen Hof, the two of them had looked like Romeo and Juliet. She cried and Lowell was teary-eyed, and they exchanged promises. They even dragged him into it. He offered to forward letters to Lowell, and to receive them for Ilse from Greece. And he assured Lowell, man to man, that he would keep an eye on her.

He would keep an eye on her, all right. He was convinced that what that eye would see—despite her tearful promises, despite the three hundred dollars Lowell had borrowed from him and handed over to her, despite what she probably believed herself at the moment—was that in two weeks she would be sharing some other junior officer's bed.

(Eight)
Rhine-Main Air Base
Frankfurt am Main, Germany
11 July 1946

Military Air Transport Flight 624, a passenger-configured C-54, landed at Rhine-Main twenty-two hours after takeoff from McGuire Air Base at Fort Dix, and after fuel stops at Gander, Newfoundland, and Prestwick, Scotland.

There was a welcoming delegation of officers and their ladies for the officers who were being assigned to Germany, and Transportation Corps people to handle those who were going beyond Frankfurt. Felter's khaki uniform was mussed, and he needed a shower, but clean uniforms and a bath were not among the facilities offered.

Felter was informed that the Athens plane was scheduled for departure at 1800 hours. It was 1500, three in the afternoon,

German time. That meant he had at least three hours to kill. He could take the shuttle bus running from Rhine-Main to the Hauptbahnhof in Frankfurt, have a couple of hours in Frankfurt, and return to Rhine-Main with plenty of time to make the flight.

The last time he had seen Frankfurt, he thought as the bus took him into town, it had still been smoldering, and he had been riding in the sidecar of a "liberated" Wehrmacht motorcycle.

When he got off the bus, he saw a white-and-black GI sign on a German hotel, the *Am Bahnhof,* identifying it as a bachelor officer's quarters. It followed that a BOQ in a hotel would have a mess. There had been an in-flight lunch between McGuire and Gander (a balogna sandwich, an apple, and a container of milk) and another (identical) between Gander and Prestwick. He had had nothing to eat since Prestwick.

He had just about reached the door of the *bahnhof* when a nattily attired MP stepped in front of him and saluted.

"One moment, please, sir," he said. "May I see your identification, please?"

Felter handed it over.

"Would the lieutenant please come with me, please?" the MP said.

"What's this all about?"

"You are being detained, sir, for being in violation of USFET uniform regulations."

"I'm in transit," Felter said.

"Would the lieutenant please come with me, sir?" the MP said; and with movements as stiff as the Chocolate Soldier, he indicated the bahnhof. Inside the bahnhof was an MP station commanded by a first lieutenant.

The MP lieutenant wore parachutist's wings and the insignia of the 82nd Airborne Division. Felter remembered that the 82nd had left in Europe one regiment, the 508th, to guard the headquarters of the Army of Occupation. He now noticed that the lieutenant wore crossed rifles, not crossed pistols. He was an airborne infantry officer pressed into service as an MP.

"Lieutenant, you're a mess," the paratrooper said to him. "Have you got some sort of excuse?"

"I'm en route from Bragg to Greece," Felter said.

That caused some interest. For a moment, Felter thought

he was going to be able to straighten this whole thing out.

"What were you doing at Bragg?"

"Ranger School," Felter said.

The lieutenant looked significantly at Felter's bare chest. Felter reached in his pocket and took his parachutist's wings from a collection of coins and held them up and smiled.

The lieutenant did not smile back.

Lieutenant Felter signed an acknowledgment that he was in receipt of a copy of a delinquency report, AG Form 102, the original of which would be sent through official channels to his commanding officer. He was delinquent in that he was in an unauthorized uniform, cotton khaki, where wool OD shade 33 or tropical worsted with blouse was specified. He was, moreover, without a necktie. He was not wearing qualification insignia (parachutist's) as required. In the Comments section, it was further pointed out that the uniform he was wearing was mussed and unmilitary, and that the subject officer was not freshly shaven.

A telephone call was made, and some senior military policeman decided that the thing to do with him, since he was in transit, was to transport him back to Rhine-Main, and turn him over to the air base duty officer, who could keep an eye on him until his plane left.

A Ford staff car was dispatched for that purpose.

It was, Felter thought, the first time that he'd been on report since he was a plebe.

The MP lieutenant marched him into the passenger terminal, where he telephoned for the duty officer, and then waited until he showed up and could sign for the "detainee," as if the detainee were a package. Then Felter was led to a small waiting room which held two other officers, a field artillery captain and an armored second lieutenant, tall, blond, muscular, in a superbly fitting uniform. He looked entirely too good to be true. He looked, Sanford Felter thought, like a model hired to pose for a recruiting poster.

"Keep your eye on this one, too, Captain," the duty officer said. "See that he gets on the Greasy Goddess." The captain nodded, but did not speak until the duty officer had left.

Then he said, "Sit down next to him, Lieutenant," and indicated the too handsome, too perfect lieutenant.

Felter did as he was told. The two lieutenants examined one another, and formed first impressions. While there were exceptions, of course, Felter had come to believe that officers who looked like movie stars seldom lived up to their appearance. Moreover, from the moment Major Bellmon had let him listen in to the telephone call at Bragg, when the officer Bellmon was speaking to thought that Bellmon wanted him shanghaied to Greece, Felter had come to understand that so far as most people in the army were concerned, an assignment to Greece was one step above being cashiered.

There was something in the field artillery captain's attitude that suggested that whatever had seen him assigned to the U.S. Army Military Advisory Group, Greece, it was not of his choosing, nor to his liking. He had, Felter was sure, been shanghaied. It was an easy step from there to conclude that the second lieutenant in the custom-tailored uniform and the handmade jodhpurs was also being shanghaied. It was not at all unusual for second lieutenants, even West Pointers, to go wild when they first became officers. Drinking generally got them, but there were variants of this. Fast cars, women, gambling. Or a combination of all those things and more. Even before he learned his name, it was Sanford Felter's first judgment of Craig W. Lowell, that Lowell had done something to outrage the system, and had been banished.

Lowell's assessment of Felter was equally nonflattering. Felter was not physically impressive. His hair was already thinning. His khaki uniform was baggy on him. He was, Lowell concluded, one of those Jewboys, who had scored 110 on the Army General Classification Test and qualified for Officer Candidate School. He had somehow managed to get through OCS (when there was a shortage of second lieutenants, it was difficult to flunk out) and had been commissioned. Once assigned as an infantry officer, he had obviously been unable to cut the mustard, and they had gotten rid of him.

"Felter," Felter finally said, putting out his hand to Lowell.

"Lowell," Lowell replied, shaking his hand. Felter saw the field artillery captain get up and walk to the window, obviously to spare himself the business of introductions. He turned to look at Lowell again.

"I think you have just been snubbed," Lowell said.

Felter chuckled. "Where are you from?" he asked.

"New York," Lowell said.

"I'm from Newark," Felter volunteered.

"What did you do wrong?" Lowell asked.

"According to the DR," Felter said, "I have violated every known uniform regulation. And, in addition, went unshaved."

"I meant before," Lowell said. "Why are they sending you to Greece?"

"Actually, I volunteered for the assignment," Felter said.

Lowell didn't reply. Felter understood that Lowell didn't believe him.

"What about you?" he asked.

"Apparently things are terribly fucked up in Athens," Lowell said. "And General Clay decided I was the only man who could straighten things out."

Felter chuckled.

"What about you, Captain?" Lowell called across the room. "What shocking breach of military behavior did you commit?"

"When I have something to say to you, Lieutenant," the captain flared, "I'll let you know. Now you just sit there, and keep your goddamned mouth shut."

Lowell insolently clapped his hand over his mouth.

"Are you looking for trouble, Lieutenant?" the captain flared.

"What are you threatening, Captain?" Lowell said. "That you'll have me sent to Greece?"

The captain glared at him.

"Just shut the fuck up," he said, finally.

"Yes, sir," Lowell said, and started to say something else. Felter shook his head, "no." Lowell said nothing else.

A jeep came for them thirty minutes later, and carried them far down a taxiway to a Douglas C-47, which bore the insignia of the European Air Transport Command. Below the cockpit window was a well-executed painting of a nearly nude, large-breasted female and the words THE GREASY GODDESS II.

The aircraft had its nylon-and-pole seats folded against the walls of the fuselage to accommodate a half dozen large crates strapped to the floor. Forward, behind the door to the cockpit, was a pile of canvas mail bags. Running down the center of the fuselage ceiling was the cable to which static lines were hooked, and the red and green lights used to signal the jump-master were mounted by the door. The plane was equipped to drop parachutists. Felter wondered, idly, if it had been used for that purpose in the war.

The crew chief asked for their names, and wrote them on the manifest. He handed a copy of it to a ground crewman. He walked forward; and almost immediately, the plane shuddered as the engines were started. The crew chief came back, closed the door, and spoke to them briefly.

"When we get up, you can probably find a mail bag soft enough to sleep on," he said. He steadied himself by putting a hand, palm up, against the ceiling. The Gooney-Bird was already taxiing to the runway.

They refueled late at night in Naples, and then flew on through the blackness to Athens.

VII

(One)
Athens, Greece
12 July 1946

They landed at Elliniko Airfield as dawn broke. They were
met at the airport by an American sergeant who wore British
Army boots and who carried a Thompson submachine gun
slung over his shoulder. He led them to the first British Army
truck either of them had ever seen. The captain got in the front
seat and they got in the back of the truck and were driven into
Athens. Peering awkwardly out the back, Lowell saw a water-
front.

"We're on the coast," he announced. "What is that, the
Mediterranean?"

Felter shook his head.

"That's the Saronikos Koplos," he said.

"The *what?*" Lowell asked, chuckling.

"Saronikos Kolpos," Felter repeated. "Greece is sort of a
peninsula here between the Ionian Sea and the Aegean. At the
bottom is the Sea of Crete. What we're looking at is the Saronikos Kolpos."

"Lieutenant, sir," Lowell said, now actually laughing, "you are a fucking *fountain* of information."

Despite himself, Felter smiled at Lowell. Lowell was obviously a fuck-up, and Felter accepted as gospel that an officer was judged by his associates. He had intended to treat Lowell with correct remoteness—in other words ignore him, let him sense he didn't want to become a buddy. But he could not do that, and neither could he bring himself to pull rank on the handsome young second lieutenant.

"I know what that is," Lowell said a few minutes later, pointing out the rear of the truck at the Acropolis. "That's the Colosseum."

"Acropolis, stupid," Felter corrected him.

"Acropolis, Colosseum, what's the difference?"

"Culture as we know it comes from this one," Felter said, not really sure if he was having his leg pulled or not. "And they fed you Christians to the lions in the other one."

"I'll be *god*damned!" Lowell said, in mock awe.

They passed the Grande Bretagne Hotel, then drove to the rear of it and stopped. They entered the building through a rear door around which had been erected a sandbag barrier. A major was waiting for them. He showed them the dining room and told them where to find him after they had had breakfast.

Breakfast in the elegant but seedy dining room of the Grande Bretagne was coffee, bread, reconstituted dried scrambled eggs, and very salty bacon from 10-in-1 rations.

Afterward, they sought out the major, who turned them over to a florid-faced, middle-aged lieutenant colonel of artillery who didn't bother to disguise his disappointment in them. He told them they would receive their assignments later that day, after they had been "in-processed."

They were given some additional immunization injections and provided with a bottle of pills by an army doctor, a young captain, who warned them not to so much as brush their teeth in water that had not had a pill dissolved in it.

They were given a brief lecture by a major of the Signal Corps on the role of the United States Army Military Advisory Group, Greece. A captain of the Adjutant General's Corps, an old one, twice as old as the starchy little prick who had rushed Lowell out of the Constab with such relish, took from them their next of kin and home address, and provided them with a printed LAST WILL AND TESTAMENT.

The elderly AGC captain didn't say anything, just raised his eyebrows, when Craig Lowell elected to leave all his worldly goods to a fraulein named Ilse, in Germany. Fraulein Ilse, it was the captain's solemn judgment, would not be the only fur-line to be enriched by the death of some kid whose cherry she had copped. Fuck it, it was their life, and their money, and in the captain's judgment, there wasn't all that much difference between a kraut cunt and some greedy god-damned relative in the States.

However he had to tell Lowell there was no way the army would let him leave his GI insurance to a German lady; bene--ficiaries not next of kin had to be U.S. citizens.

They were then taken to the fourth floor of the Grande Bretagne, where a ballroom had been converted into a supply and arms room. They were issued British Army helmets, the notion being that the silhouette of standard U.S. Army helmets was too close to that of the Wehrmacht and Red Army helmets with which some of the communist guerrillas were equipped. There was no mistaking the silhouette of a British Army helmet. It resembled a flat-chested woman, the captain of ordnance in charge of the arms room told them.

They were given their choice of weapons.

There were M1 Garand .30–06 rifles and .303 British Lee-Enfields and 7.93 mm German Mausers, even a few 7.62 mm Russian Moissant Nagants.

There were U.S. .30 caliber carbines, M1 and M2.

There were .45 ACP Thompson submachine guns and 9 mm British Sten submachine guns.

There were standard issue .45 automatics, .455 Webley revolvers, .38 caliber Smith & Wesson revolvers, 9 mm Luger pistols, and even a half dozen .32 ACP Browning automatic pistols. These were made in Belgium but bore the Nazi swastika on their plastic grips right below the place where the words BROWNING BROS OGDEN UTAH USA had been stamped in the slide.

"Things are a little fucked up," the ordnance officer, an old leathery-faced chief warrant officer, told them. "Eventually, the Greeks will have all U.S. Army stuff, and there won't be any problem. But right now, what the troops have is English and captured kraut stuff. Lugers, Mauser rifles, Schmeisser machine pistols. Now that's the thing to get your hands on, if you can. Best goddamn machine pistol ever made. Naturally, none of them ever get back this far, and when they do, the brass grab them. The Sten gun isn't worth shit.

"The M1, the Garand, has it all over the Lee-Enfield .303, but there's goddamn little .30–06 ammo in clips up where you guys are going. Plenty of .30–06 for the machine guns, so if you want to try to reuse your clips, that's your option."

Lowell remembered trying without much success to reload the spring steel clips for the Garand on the rifle range at Fort Dix.

"I can give you all the clipped .30–06 you want here, but you're going to have to carry it with you," the old warrant officer went on. "Now the Webley .455 ain't worth a shit either, and that .38 S&W shoots a .38 *S&W* as opposed to a .38 *Special*. That's *really* not worth a shit. There's nothing beats an army .45 if you can shoot one, but there's Lugers if you want. Plenty of 9 mm all over."

"What do the regulations say we're supposed to draw?" Lieutenant Felter asked, politely.

"They haven't made up their mind yet, Lieutenant," the warrant officer said. "There's one school of thought that says you're a technical advisor and a noncombatant, and don't have to go armed at all. Nobody believes that shit. Now, if you should want to draw a U.S. Army weapon for protection against burglars, or whatever, you can have a .45 and either an M1 or a carbine or a Thompson. But you have to sign for them.

"You don't want to sign for a weapon, you can take your choice of anything else. One pistol and one rifle or a Sten. They're not on paper."

Lieutenant Felter took and signed for a Colt .45 and a Thompson submachine gun. The captain from the 19th Armored Field Artillery took and signed for a .45 and a carbine. Lowell had fired the Thompson "for familiarization" at Fort Dix and hadn't been able to keep it from climbing off the target. He was therefore afraid of it and signed for an M1 instead. Giving in to an impulse, he also took a 9 mm Luger. He had never held one in his hands before. For that matter, it was the second pistol he had ever held in his hands at all. He had also fired "for familiarization" the Colt .45 at Fort Dix and had been unable to hit a three-by-four target at twenty-five yards with it.

Had he wanted to, however, he could have fired High Expert with the Garand. He had been surprised at how he had taken to the Garand. The legendary recoil, which had frightened him and the other trainees, had turned out to be far less uncomfortable than that of the 12-bore Browning over-and-under his grandfather had given him for his twelvth birthday. He had spent long hours firing the Browning on the trap range his grandfather had built behind his house on the island. He had understood the Garand from about the fifth shot he had taken with it; and by the time their week on their range was over, he felt quite as comfortable with it as any gun he had ever fired. If he had to take a shot at somebody, which seemed beyond credibility, he would do it with a Garand. He took the Luger because he had always wanted one. It looked lethal. All self-respecting Nazi bad guys in the movies, and sometimes even Humphrey Bogart and Alan Ladd, used Lugers. But the idea that he would actually shoot it at somebody was as ludicrous as the grade B movies.

Lowell took a sealed oblong tin can marked "320 Rounds Caliber .30–06 Ball in Clips and Bandoliers" and two loose bandoliers of Garand ammunition. The ordnance warrant officer gave him two cardboard boxes of pistol ammunition. The printing on them was in German: *Fur Pistolen -08 9 mm deutsche Waffen und Munitionsfabrik, Berlin. 50 Patronen.*

It wasn't quite credible, despite the evidence in his hands, that the pistol and the ammunition for it had been intended for use by the German Army.

They were fed lunch, 10-in-1 ration Beef Chunks w/Gravy, in the elegant dining room of the Grande Bretagne. Afterward, they found their names on a mimeographed Special Order of Headquarters, U.S. Military Advisory Group, Greece, which had been slid under their door. Felter and Lowell had been assigned to share a room. The field artillery captain's rank had entitled him to a private room, next door.

"Shit," Lowell said, when, sitting down on the bed, he read his orders. His name and the captain's were on the orders together. They were being assigned to the Advisory Detachment, 27th Royal Hellenic Mountain Division. Felter had been assigned to Headquarters, USAMAG(G), to something called DAB, Operations Division.

"What the hell is DAB?" Lowell asked.

"I think it means Document Analysis," Felter replied. "Probably Document Analysis Branch." He could tell from the confused look on Lowell's face that Lowell knew no more than he had before his reply. "I'm sort of a linguist," Felter said.

"No kidding?"

"My parents came from Europe," Felter said. "I picked up German, and Russian, and Polish."

"I had a German governess," Lowell said, in German.

"They need people who speak German," Felter replied in German. "They told me most of the maps are German and that what I'll be doing is adapting them for us. Didn't you tell that AG captain you spoke it?"

"I told him I didn't speak it," Lowell said, still in German.

"Well, go tell him you can. You can stay here," Felter said. "You're going to get yourself killed with one of the divisions."

"Why do you say that?" Lowell asked.

"You don't really think that ROTC and Basic Officer's Course qualified you for what you'll be doing, do you?"

"I was directly commissioned," Lowell said. "I don't know what they teach in ROTC or Basic Officer's Course."

"Directly commissioned as what?" Felter asked.

"Actually, so that I could play polo on a general's team," Lowell said.

"Am I supposed to believe that?"

"It happens to be the truth," Lowell said.

"You've had no duty with troops?" Felter asked.

"I was thrown out of college, so the draft board got me," Lowell said. "And then I had basic training, and then I was the official golf pro for the U.S. Constabulary golf club, and then I played polo," Lowell said.

"You're absolutely unqualified for duty as an advisor to troops on the line," Felter said.

"And you are?" Lowell asked. Felter let that pass.

"You're liable to get killed. Don't you understand that?" Felter asked.

"Ever since I put on this officer's uniform," Lowell said, "with a rare exception here and there, people have gone out of their way to let me know they think I'm something of a joke as a man. I'm rather tired of it. I intend to see if I am, or not."

"You don't know what the hell you're saying," Felter said.

"You too, you see? Even you."

"I'm a professional soldier," Felter said, somewhat solemnly.

"*Sure* you are," Lowell said, sarcastically.

"Listen to me, stupid," Felter said. "I was at West Point. I was in on the last days of the war. For what it's worth, I'm even a Ranger."

"No shit?" Lowell asked. He was dumbfounded. "Christ, you don't look like it."

"Thanks a lot," Felter said. They smiled at each other. Felter got up.

"Where are you going?"

"I'm going to tell the adjutant you speak German," Felter said.

"No, you're not," Lowell said. "Leave things alone. It's important to me."

Felter, standing by the door, looked at him.

"If you're a West Pointer, and whatever else you said, a ranger, what are you doing here?" Lowell asked.

"I asked for this assignment," Felter said.

"Why?" Lowell asked.

"For the experience," Felter said.

"I want the experience, too," Lowell said. "Please mind your own business, Felter."

"Good God!" Felter said. "Have you got notions of glory, or what?"

"I just want to see what happens," Lowell said, simply. "And, figure it out. It would be your word against mine about whether or not I speak German."

Felter looked at him for a moment, and then walked to where Lowell had rested his M1 Garand against the wall beside the bed.

"Do you know how to use one of these?" he asked.

"Actually, I'm pretty good with one of them," Lowell said. "But I'd be grateful if you'd show me how that Luger works."

"Why did you take a Luger if you don't know how it works?" Felter asked, throwing up his hands.

"I already know I can't shoot a .45 worth a shit," Lowell said, simply. "And I thought the Luger was prettier."

"Jesus, you're insane!" Felter said. Then he picked up the Luger. "Come over here, Lieutenant. I will show you how this works."

"Thank you, sir. The lieutenant is very kind, sir." He smiled at Felter. "Are you really a ranger, you little bastard?"

"Yes, I am, you dumb shit," Felter said.

(Two)

At midnight, there was a boom. Lowell, who had been sleeping fitfully dreaming of Ilse, sat up in bed and turned the light on.

"Douse the light!" Felter ordered in a fierce whisper. Lowell saw him, .45 in hand, standing against the wall. He turned the light off and started to giggle before it sank in that the boom had been a shot and that they had been issued weapons and what the army called "live ammo" and that they were in Greece and there was a revolution going on.

He slid out of bed, and groped in the dark for the Garand. He found it in the corner of the room. He took an 8-round clip from the cloth bandolier and opened the action. It made an awful amount of noise. When he slipped the clip into the action, it sounded like a door slamming. His heard was pounding. He stood between the beds, the M1 at his shoulder, covering the door.

There was a rap on the door. Lowell's finger tightened on the trigger before he realized if somebody was going to burst in to murder them in their beds, it was unlikely he would knock first. He took his finger off the trigger, but kept it inside the stamped metal loop of the trigger guard, and kept the rifle at his shoulder.

"Duty officer!" a voice called.

Felter jerked the door open. Light from the corridor flooded the room.

The duty officer saw Lowell, and Felter, poised for action. He put his hands up, half mockingly, in surrender.

"I guess you heard it," he said. "Where did it come from?"

"Next door, I think," Felter said, lowering his pistol. Lowell had no idea where the sound had come from. The duty officer turned and walked further down the corridor. Felter went after him, and Lowell followed, feeling foolish, carrying the Garand at port arms.

There was no answer to the duty officer's knock at the field artillery captain's door. He pushed it open.

"Shit!" he said. He went into the room.

Lowell looked over Sanford Felter's head. The field artillery captain who had been kicked out of the Constab along with Lowell had lain down on his bed, put the muzzle of his .45 in his mouth, and blown the top of his head all over the brocade wallpaper of his room. His face bore a startled look. His eyes were wide open, as if he was looking at them.

Craig Lowell barely made it back to his room and the toilet bowl before throwing up.

He was still throwing up when the duty officer came into their room and picked up the telephone.

"Sorry to bother you at this hour, Colonel, but I think maybe you'd want to come up to 707. That new captain just blew his head off."

He looked in at Lowell, sprawled sick and scared on the floor.

"You all right?" he asked, and there was genuine concern in his voice.

Lowell nodded his head.

(Three)

A sergeant came to their table in the dining room the next morning and told Felter that the adjutant wanted to see him.

Felter and Lowell said good-bye, shaking hands.

"Be careful," Felter said. "For God's sake, don't do anything foolish."

"Same to you," Lowell said.

They were both aware of and surprised by the emotion they felt at parting.

Felter started to ask Lowell one final time if he wanted him to tell the adjutant he spoke German, but he decided against it. He would make up his mind when he saw the adjutant.

Thirty minutes later, Felter walked into the room where Lowell lay on the bed, waiting for word that it was time to leave. Lowell said nothing as Felter walked into the room. Felter went to the closet and took out his Valv-Paks.

"The army, in its infinite wisdom, has decided to save your ass," Felter said.

"Goddamn you, I told you to keep your mouth shut," Lowell said, angrily, sitting up on the bed.

"I have just been appointed a replacement for the captain," Felter said. "We're both going to the 27th Royal Hellenic Mountain Division . . . whatever the hell that is."

(Four)

It was almost exactly two hundred air miles from Athens to Ioannina on the northern shore of Lake Ioanninon. There the headquarters of the 27th Royal Hellenic Mountain Division was located. It was just over twice that distance by road. They averaged twenty-five miles per hour over the road in a Dodge three-quarter-ton weapons carrier. The road was mostly dirt, or more accurately, stones, and narrow; and it wound around one precipitous granite mountain after another. From time to time, they passed through small villages of whitewashed stone houses perched precariously to fit whatever flat space had been available when they had been built.

They were twenty-six hours on the road, stopping overnight at Preveza on the Ionian Sea, because, as the sergeant driving the truck told them, the commies held the roads at night.

Headquarters of the 27th Hellenic was in a two-story white-washed stone building with walls eighteen inches thick. It was further reinforced to the level of the second floor by a mound of sandbags tapering toward the top. A pair of swarthy-skinned, unshaven Greeks wearing British Army uniforms were on guard outside. British .303 Lee-Enfield rifles were slung over the shoulders. They watched without expression as Felter and Lowell removed their bedrolls, their packs, their luggage, and the cases of ammunition from the back of the truck.

A competent-looking American master sergeant in British

woolen battle trousers, a crumpled GI khaki shirt, and British hobnailed boots waved them inside the building. He did not salute.

"The colonel'll be back for supper," he said. "You want something to eat?"

When they nodded, he said, "We have Greek and GI rations. The Greek gives you the shits until you get used to it. The GI rations make you sick, period."

A Greek woman with a scarf around her head and in a voluminous black shirt served them lamb stew on tin plates, black coffee, and a large chunk of dark bread.

The colonel, when he showed up, turned out to be a wiry red-haired lieutenant colonel wearing the crossed flags of the Signal Corps.

"My name is Hanrahan," he said. "You'll be working for me." Then he switched to Greek and, watching them carefully, talked for about thirty seconds. Then he shook his head in disgust when it was obvious that neither of them understood a word he was saying.

"That was too much to expect, I guess," he said, in English. "There's probably five thousand officers, Greek-Americans, who would give their left nut to come over here. And what do I get? No offense, gentlemen, but this is a fucked-up war."

He showed them a map. They were thirty miles from the Albanian border. Numbers on the map indicated the height of various mountain peaks from 5,938 feet to 8,192 feet. Lowell knew they were high, but he hadn't thought that high.

"Our mission," Colonel Hanrahan said, "is to keep the bastards from shipping supplies from Albania into Greece. There's no way in hell we can block every goat path, but we can block the roads. We do this from emplacements on hilltops, like something in the *Lives of the Bengal Lancer*. Little forts. They have machine guns for self-protection and mortars to cover the roads.

"The way it's set up is that I'm the advisor to the division. There are three regiments, each of them with three American officers—two majors and a captain. Each battalion has an advisor, supposed to be a lieutenant, but most of them are noncoms. And there are noncoms with some of the companies.

"There's nothing we can tell these people about fighting.

They've really got a hard-on for the communists. Vice versa, of course. They learn quick, but most of them don't know diddly shit about vehicles, jeeps, trucks, and especially tracked vehicles. That's where you'll come in, Lieutenant."

"Sir, I don't know anything about tracked vehicles," Lowell confessed.

"That figures," the colonel said. "And what's your speciality, Lieutenant?"

"I just finished Ranger School," Felter said.

"Great. We need Rangers here about as much as we need armored officers who don't know anything about tracked vehicles."

"Sir, I can handle some tanks. Drive them, I mean," Felter said. "I've had familiarization training."

Hanrahan looked at Felter with renewed interest.

"Where did you get that?"

"At West Point, sir."

"You went to the Academy?" Hanrahan was now really interested.

"For two years, sir."

"Why did you march away from the Long Gray Line, Lieutenant?" Hanrahan asked, dryly.

"I was commissioned as a linguist, sir."

"What languages?"

"Slavic, mostly, Colonel. German. Some French."

"Greek?"

"No, sir. I hope to learn it here."

"You will," Hanrahan said. "I can use your Russian, Lieutenant."

Felter nodded, but said nothing.

"I have nothing against West Pointers, Lieutenant," Hanrahan said. "Despite the fact that I too am a product of Beast Barracks."

There was no reaction, though Hanrahan looked closely at Felter's face.

"We're getting a steady supply of ammunition for the 83 mm mortars, and for the 4.2 inchers," Colonel Hanrahan went on. "They fly it in by English seaplane, which can just about manage to land on the lake. We're building up supplies of American small arms ammunition. And we're starting to get some M1s. What I think I'm going to do with you guys is send you around to the companies, one at a time, with either a GI who speaks Greek, or a Greek who speaks English. You will instruct their officers and noncoms in the M1. They will instruct their men. When they know how to take it apart and put it together again, you bow out. They know all there is to know about shooting.

"We got a couple of armored sergeants here . . . all the noncoms are good men, by the way. You guys just leave them alone, understand? The sergeants will teach you what they can about the M8 armored car, Lieutenant. Keeping them running is your job from here in. Got it?"

"Yes, sir," Lowell said.

"Either of you have any questions?" the colonel asked.

Lowell said nothing. The colonel looked at Felter. "You look as if you have something on your mind, Felter. Let's have it."

"Sir," Felter said. "I just wondered about you being Signal Corps."

"I'm detailed infantry, Lieutenant, if that's what's bothering you. But I'm Signal Corps. I came to Greece in 1942 as a second john to operate a radio station for the OSS. And I stayed. And when the war was over I went home. And now they've sent me back, because I know these people, OK?"

"I didn't mean to sound out of line, sir," Felter said.

"Felter, when I think you're out of line, you'll know it," the colonel said. For the first time, he smiled at them. Lowell was warmed by it, and smiled back.

"If you knew what I was thinking, Lowell, I don't think you'd be smiling," the colonel said. "For what I was thinking was that instead of the trained, combat-experienced, Greek-speaking officers I was promised, I just inherited two lieutenants, one even dumber than the other."

"I would say, sir," Lowell said, "that that would be a reasonable statement of the situation."

"And I was smiling because it had just occurred to me that while Felter demonstrated his dumbness by asking what a flag waver is doing here, you were too dumb to notice anything was wrong."

But his smile was still warm.

"If you can remember that," he said, "that you *are* dumb, and keep your mouth shut and your eyes open until you see how things are, and if you can use that M1, you just might stay alive."

He reached into the drawer of his battered desk and came out with a strange-looking bottle and three small water glasses.

"The cocktail hour, gentlemen," he said. "The booze is known as uouzo. It tastes like licorice. After a while you get used to it."

He poured the liquid in glasses and handed each of them one.

(Five)

No. 12 Company, 113th Regiment, 27th Royal Hellenic Mountain Division consisted of a Greek captain, a pair of lieutenants, three sergeants, a half dozen corporals, sixty-three other ranks, and an Alabama-reared Greek-American sergeant. The force was just about equally divided between two rock fortresses on either side of a narrow road winding down a valley.

The Greek-American sergeant, who gave his name as Nick, was a pudgy young man in his mid-twenties with curly blond hair. He wore no helmet or any other headgear. He wore GI OD trousers, a GI sweater, and over that a British battle jacket. Like everybody else, he wore hobnailed British boots. On the shoulder of the British battle jacket was the Greek cross, above which were superimposed, in Greek and English, the words *America*. He had a .45 automatic jammed into his waistband; and a Browning automatic rifle was slung over his shoulder.

As the American sergeant walked over to the half-track in which Lieutenant Craig Lowell had driven up the mountainside, Lieutenant Lowell was quite as impressed with him as he had been with the corporal who had called him a "miserable pissant" on his first day of basic training.

The difference, Lowell realized, was that *I* have been sent up here to command *him*. A chain of thought ran through his mind, triggered by the .30–06 caliber Browning automatic rifle the sergeant had slung over his shoulder.

The BAR was actually a light machine gun which could

empty its 20-round magazine in the time it took to fart.

The weapon, in the hands of somebody who knew how to shoot it, was of the same quality as the Garand. In other words, one hell of a fine weapon. Private Lowell had taken a great deal of pleasure on the Fort Dix, New Jersey, rifle range in mastering the BAR; and his proficiency had both awed and annoyed the corporal who hated college boys generally and handsome college boys from Harvard in particular.

The BAR was a heavy sonofabitch, not the sort of thing one carried fifty feet further than one had to. Sergeant Nick Whateverhesaid was not carrying it around for the hell of it and certainly not to impress anybody. Furthermore, the sergeant had removed the bipod normally fitted to the barrel to steady the weapon when it was being fired. That suggested that he carried the BAR frequently and as a personal weapon. And *that* suggested two things: that the sergeant was really a soldier, and that there was something to shoot at.

For the first time, he realized the absurdity of his position. He had no business being here as a private soldier, and absolutely none as an officer. He wondered why he wasn't terrified. In fact, he was excited. They call that naiveté, he thought. Also known as stupidity.

The sergeant touched his hand to his eyebrow in sort of a salute, and Lowell returned it as casually. He had one further thought: that is the kind of salute an experienced sergeant throws a second lieutenant fresh from Officer Candidate School. If this sergeant had any idea that I know about ten percent of what the bottom man in any OCS class knows, he would be thumbing his nose at me.

The sergeant looked in the back of the half-track. There was a case of sixteen M1 rifles, plus cases of ammunition, cases of mortar shells, tin cans of .303 British ammunition, and cases of rations.

"Are those M1s for us?" the sergeant asked.

Lowell looked at the sergeant and wondered what would happen if he told him the truth: "See here, Sarge. Talk about fuck-ups. I don't know the first fucking thing about being an officer. What I would like to do is have you take over, tell me what to do, and see if you can keep me from getting hurt."

"Are those for us, Lieutenant?" the sergeant asked again.

"Right," Lieutenant Lowell said, getting out of the truck. "The idea is that I'm to give basic instruction to the officers." He didn't sound as unsure of himself as he thought he would.

"It's about time we gave these guys something to fight with," Nick said. "Come on in the CP; I'll introduce you to the officers." He took Lowell's arm and led him into a bunker built of sandbags laid around enormous granite boulders.

The commanding officer was an olive-skinned man with a flowing black mustache. There was a five-inch scar on his right cheek. He was the toughest-looking man Lowell had ever seen. This guy's going to see right through me, Lowell thought. When the captain offered his hand, his calloused grip was like steel. Incongruously, he smiled at Lowell as if he was really glad to see him.

The other officers were shy.

The captain with the black mustache put his hand on Lowell's shoulder and led him through the rear exit to the bunker. Outside was a mortar position, a 3.5 inch mortar with cases of ammo stacked for use. It was in a natural depression in the boulders, and like the bunker itself, reinforced with sandbags to fill in spaces between boulders. There were rifle-firing positions around its perimeter.

Still smiling broadly, the captain unslung his Lee-Enfield rifle.

"He says," Nick translated, "that this is what they have now, and would you care to try it?"

"Thank you," Lowell said, and took the Lee-Enfield and examined it. He had never seen one up close before he had seen them in the arms room in Athens.

The broadly smiling captain rattled off something else.

"He says he *wants* you to try it," Nick said.

"What am I supposed to shoot at?" Lowell asked.

The captain seemed to understand that. He took the Enfield back, dropped into an almost prone position in one of the firing positions and aimed down into the valley. There was a small concrete kilometer marker beside the road. Lowell thought it must be at least two hundred yards away.

With sign language, the captain indicated that that was what he meant. He lay down and very quickly pushed the safety off and fired. Lowell realized that around here people always carried a round in the chamber.

A chunk flew off the kilometer marker. The captain got to his feet, rapidly worked the action of the rifle, and handed it to Lowell with another of his broad smiles, which by now Lowell suspected were anything but sincere.

"I guess he wants to see if you know what the fuck you're talking about," Nick said.

Lowell lowered himself into the firing position.

I'm going to miss that goddamned thing, and then what the fuck am I going to do?

He fired. There was a puff of dust in the middle of the road. He had missed by six feet.

He furiously worked the action, chambering another round, and fired again. He missed again and was horribly humiliated. Both the American, Nick, and the Greek captain were smiling at him. He was supposed to be an expert, and he couldn't hit a foot square target at two hundred yards. He looked at the Enfield's sights, and realized he hadn't the faintest idea how to change them.

"Hand me my M1," he said. When he put the Garand to his shoulder and pushed the safety off, he thought for the first time that he had not fired it. It was not zeroed. It would have been better to have kept the Enfield and try to hit the goddamned kilometer marker with Kentucky windage.

It was too late for that now. He looked at the M1's receiver, twisting it slightly to examine the sight.

"I've never fired this sonofabitch before," he said, so that Nick could hear him.

Nick looked at him with contempt in his eyes. Lowell understood that he wasn't just humiliating himself but Nick, too, for he was an officer.

And then Lowell knew what to do. "Tell the captain," he said, handing the M1 to Nick, "that it would be too easy for me to use this weapon, because it is mine."

Nicks' eyebrows went up, and he said nothing.

"Tell him I am going to take an unfired M1 from the case," Lowell said, "and zero it with three shots, and then blow that goddamned marker away."

"I hope for both of us that you can produce," Nick said, and then he smiled confidently and spoke in Greek to the captain.

"Tell him to pick any of the rifles," Lowell said. Nick led

the captain to the crate of M1s. The captain looked over the four Garands in the top rack and picked one out. Then he handed it to Lowell. Lowell opened the action and peered down the barrel. It was thick with preserving oil.

Lowell set the elevation at two hundred yards.

"Tell the captain the barrel is oily," he said. "And that I will clean it by firing twice."

Nick repeated the message in Greek. Lowell put a clip in the Garand, pushed the safety off, and shot twice in the air. Then he took up a sitting position.

"Tell the captain that for a short distance and a target that large, it is not normally necessary to use the prone position."

"Use the prone position, for Christ's sake. Hit that fucking road marker," Nick said, wearing a broad smile. "Once these guys figure you for a phony or a candy-ass, you're finished."

"Tell him what I said, Sergeant," Lowell said, smiling warmly at Nick, and then decided to go for broke. "And tell him that a good shot normally doesn't have to use a sling."

Nick spoke to the Greek captain.

"Tell him I will now fire three rounds for zero," Lowell said. He aimed very carefully, let out half his breath, held it, and squeezed the trigger. By pure coincidence, the sights were almost in zero. The bullet strike was vertically on the target, but two feet to the right.

He aimed and fired the rifle again. The second strike was within a couple inches of the first.

Lowell motioned the captain over, pointed to the sight.

"Tell him that sometimes only two shots are necessary for zero," he said. Nick repeated the message. "Tell him that I am moving the sight to the right twelve clicks, and that each click, at that distance, moves the impact two inches." He held up his fingers to illustrate. The captain, smiling with transparent insincerity, listened to the translation and nodded his head.

"And now tell him that I am going to demonstrate how to remove a partially emptied clip from the weapon," Lowell said. Nick made the translation. Lowell ejected the unfired six cartridges and their clip and put a full clip in the weapon.

"Shit, Lieutenant," Nick said. "I hope you can pull this off."

Lowell put the Garand to his shoulder, lined up the sights, held his breath, and squeezed off the first round. Dead on. A chunk of concrete flew into the air. He then emptied the rifle, firing as quickly as he could line the sights up on the shattered remnants of the concrete road marker. When he was finished, it was difficult to see the road marker; horizontally, about half of it was shot away, and four more inches or so off the left side.

With an entirely delightful feeling of triumph, Lowell gave Nick an idiot grin and then stood up. With a ceremonious bow, he handed the Garand to the captain and then motioned him to sit down in the firing position. He knelt over him, and fed a clip into the weapon.

The captain fired one shot, and then the rest of the clip, rapid fire. He flashed another magnificent smile, got to his feet, and handed Lowell the M1.

"Sonabitch!" he said. He reached over, patted Lowell's cheek, and then kissed it. Then he weighed the Garand appreciatively in his hands.

"That don't mean nothing, Lieutenant," Nick said. "Shit, they even hold hands! You just impressed the shit out of him, is all."

The Greek captain smiled at the American lieutenant. The American lieutenant smiled back. He smiled so broadly his cheek muscles began to ache. The captain, with an elaborate bow, waved him back to the bunker. He said something else.

"He says he would be deeply honored if you would show him how the magnificent rifle works, so that he and his men may kill many godless communists with it," Nick said. He watched Lowell's face for his reaction.

"They mean that, Lieutenant," Nick said. "I'm glad you didn't think it was funny."

Lowell felt a strange exhilaration.

"Please tell the captain that I would be honored to attempt to show a magnificent shot such as he is how the U.S. Army rifle functions," he said.

(Six)
Coordinates C431/K003
Map, Greece, 1:250000
22 July 1946

To tell the truth, if it wasn't for Ilse he wouldn't mind this at all, Second Lieutenant Craig W. Lowell thought. It was like something out of the movies. The days were pleasantly warm, and the evenings were pleasantly cool, and there was nobody jumping on his ass at all.

The simple truth of the matter was that he liked being an officer. Not a polo-playing officer, but a real officer. He had been given a duty, a real military duty, and he took no small pleasure in being able to discharge it, in the realization that he was meeting his responsibility—and well.

It wasn't even as if he were a marksmanship instructor in basic training. He was teaching the teachers. Through him and him alone, first No. 12 Company, and ultimately the entire 113th Regiment, 27th Royal Hellenic Mountain Division, would be instructed in the proper use of the M1 Garand rifle.

Even Felter acknowledged that Lowell knew what he was doing, and Felter really was a West Pointer and a Ranger, even if he didn't look like it. Lowell was smugly proud that he had his company, No. 12 Company, completely qualified with the M1 when Felter was still taking his company's M1s out of their crates. Felter was a good man obviously (otherwise, how would he have gotten to be a Ranger?), but he wasn't a good teacher. Not a leader of men.

In all modesty, Craig Lowell believed that he had demonstrated his leadership ability by his courses of instruction in the M1. He had first demonstrated to each little group of trainees that with it he could blow the balls off a horsefly at two hundred yards. This established his personal credentials. Then he had blown away road markers firing the weapon as fast as it would fire, thus establishing the weapon's credibility. After that, with Nick standing beside him translating his short, simple sentences into Greek, it had been a snap. They wanted to learn, and they soaked up the information like a blotter. It was completely unlike basic training had been. Nobody in basic training had given a shit for the M1 rifle. That was, Craig Lowell decided, because it had not been presented to them properly. By the time they actually got to fire it, they were so sick of looking at it, cleaning it, and dry-firing it that they wouldn't have liked it if it had dispensed ice-cold beer.

Later Felter had needed Craig's help with his own company; and he'd been glad to give it. Then Felter had called Colonel

Hanrahan and told him that he was having trouble but Lowell was doing splendidly, and that it would seem to make sense to have Lowell continue doing what he did so well so that he could return to see about the tracked vehicles.

Hanrahan had gone along with the suggestion. And now Felter was back at Ioannina, while Lowell had the Garand rifle training of the whole regiment to himself. It was rather strange, Lowell thought, about Hanrahan and Felter both having gone to West Point. He had always associated West Pointers with people like General Waterford and Fat Charley. His kind of people, so to speak. There was no question that Hanrahan was a good officer, but he behaved less like Fat Charley than like an Irish police sergeant.

But there was no question about it, as difficult as it was to believe, both Hanrahan and Felter had at one time marched up and down the drill field at West Point in those funny hats with what looked like a pussy willow bouncing around on top.

Lowell had become rather close to Nick. If Nick suspected that Lowell's knowledge of the military had come entirely from basic training, he hadn't made that plain. Aware that he had impressed Nick just about as much as he had impressed the Greek captain with that first day's marksmanship exhibition, Lowell had decided that what Nick didn't know wouldn't hurt him.

They shared a stone hut in the No. 12 Company area, taking turns boiling their eggs for breakfast, but eating the rest of their meals with the Greek officers. At night they read by the hissing light of a Coleman lantern. Nick could read Greek, so he got to share the Greek newspapers that came up and a few Greek magazines and what few books there were. The only thing in English to read was an occasional week-old *Stars & Stripes* from Germany and a shelf of field and technical manuals. For lack of something else to read, Lowell read the field and technical manuals. Some of them had as much application to what they were doing as the *Saturday Evening Post*, but some of them Lowell found fascinating.

The Infantry Company in the Defense, for example, spelled out in minute detail what 230 officers and men were supposed to do from the emplacement of the .30 and .50 caliber machine guns to the number and placement and depth of "field sanitation facilities, or latrines." Much of the information didn't precisely apply here, but a surprising percentage of it did. Lowell discreetly checked and learned that No. 12 Company's machine-gun emplacements more than met the criteria established "by the book."

Nick saw nothing unusual in Lowell's spending his evenings reading field manuals. Nick probably presumed that officers ordinarily passed their free time expanding their professional knowledge. He did not, in other words, give any sign that he suspected Lowell was discovering for the first time the meaning of such terms as "beaten zones" and "fields of fire" and "ammunition units," and what, precisely, a foxhole was beyond being a hole in the ground in which one took shelter.

Their routine was fairly constant. Every day, late enough in the morning to be warm enough to take the open-jeep trip in relative comfort, Lowell and Nick visited another company along the line. There they'd instruct the officers and senior noncoms in the M1 rifle. Afterward they would share a late lunch with the officers of the company they were visiting, before returning to No. 12 Company. There Lowell would fool around with the Zenith Transoceanic radio (thank God I bought that, Lowell thought; I would go insane without it) or play a little chess to pass the time with the Greek officers.

Sometimes, not always, he could pick up the American Forces Network on the short-wave band. That always triggered memories of Ilse, which sometimes depressed him and sometimes cheered him. He missed her terribly and worried about her; and he had to keep pushing back the fear that she would find somebody else. Other times, he was able to tell himself that he had found the woman who would share his life. When his year here was over, he would be reassigned to Germany, and they would be together again for good.

God, did he miss her! He had a mental image of Ilse on the banks of the Lahn River. That was only three weeks ago! And there hadn't been one letter in all that time.

What was she doing now?

Telling some new guy that she cost a hundred a month, plus rent on their apartment, plus the stuff he could get out of the PX?

Spreading her legs for somebody else? Oh, *shit!*

He forced that thought from his mind. He had read a line from a biography of General George S. Patton: "Never take counsel of your fears." There was obviously a good deal of sense in that, Lowell thought, and reminded himself again that if he had to be in the army, this was the place to be. Broadening. That's what it was. A splendid learning experience.

There came the peculiar burrup-burrup ringing sound of a U.S. Army EE-8 field telephone. A head appeared at the door to the bunker, said something in excitement, pointed to the right.

The Greek captain ran to a firing position, dropped onto his belly, and put field glasses to his eyes. He peered intently, and then suddenly turned and gave orders.

"What the hell is going on?"

"They got a report of bearers," Nick said.

The enemy! It's about time!

"Sometimes they make a mistake and get seen," Nick said, as he walked quickly to a firing position. He set the Browning automatic rifle in place in one of the rifle-firing points and peered off at what appeared to Lowell to be a bare expanse of rock.

Then Lowell saw something move. It was five hundred yards away if it was an inch.

The captain said something that Lowell somehow understood meant, "there." He gave more orders. Soldiers were working on the 3.5 inch mortar now, shifting the weapon, moving its baseplate.

The captain gave another of his insurance man smiles to Lowell and waved him to an empty firing position.

There was more movement in the valley below, things flitting between the huge boulders, casting shadows. You had to look carefully the first time, but almost immediately your eyes began to catch small movements, and you could see there were people out there, coming down the side of a mountain, moving slowly, but *there*.

The enemy!

There was the crack of the captain's M1, followed a moment later by a sharper sound, the burst from Nick's BAR. Lowell found himself peering through the sights of his rifle. Goddamned fool. Even if he saw anybody out there, he couldn't hit them. But he put his left hand on the sight of the M1 and cranked the knob, and the sight clicked as it rose up.

If one were to be completely honest, he was willing to admit there was something just a bit frightening about all this. Presumably, they, the enemy, will shoot back.

There came the roar of the 3.5 mortar going off behind him, and he felt the blast and his ears hurt. When he looked through the sights again, swinging the rifle from side to side, seeing nothing, he was trembling.

Nick's BAR went off and there was another shot from a rifle. And then there was an explosion out there, the dull crump of the mortar round landing. He saw by the smoke that it was far wide of the mark. The captain said something viciously sarcastic, then turned to his Garand again.

There was suddenly an awful pain in Lowell's bladder. I absolutely have to take a piss, he realized.

There came the sound of bullets passing overhead, remembered from the pits of the rifle range at Fort Dix. It was all rather amusing then, because the greatest care had been taken to insure that the bullets whistling overhead, however thrilling, would be harmless. There was no such intent here. There was also the sound of ricochets, not unlike the sound in the movies, but infinitely more threatening.

There came the noise that a kitchen knife makes when a large fat Negro, smiling broadly, swings it from behind his head and slices a red ripe watermelon in one fell swoop. On the porch of the mess hall at Camp Kemper. The Negro cook's name had been Ellwood. That is what came to Craig Lowell's mind when he heard the noise.

He turned and saw Nick sprawled on his back on the sun-baked pebbles. He had a shattered watermelon for his head. Second Lieutenant Craig W. Lowell threw up, and when he had finished heaving, became aware that he had shit in his pants. A moment later he had also voided his bladder.

He pulled his arms over his head. I am going to die here. I am going to have *my* head blown off. Oh, those dirty *bastards!*

He pushed himself a half inch closer to the top of the rocks protecting him, then an inch, then four inches, to get his head over the top, to *see* them, the dirty bastards. He saw a flicker of yellow flame out of the corner of his eye, and turned his head. There were two of them, lying prone, behind a light machine gun. The gun was on a bipod with a shoulder stock, rather than on a tripod. They were sweeping the position with short bursts of fire, so as not to over heat the barrel.

Where the fuck is my rifle?

He slid down and then crawled backward to where he had dropped the M1, grabbed the muzzle, and pulled it up to him.

Two bullets hit the rocks in front of him, high. They sent splinters into his face, stinging him, before ricocheting with a low whistle. He had a faint impression that he could see one at the top of its apogee.

He slid up on the rocks, laying his hand on a flat spot, laying the forearm in his hand. Fecal matter slid down his inner thigh. *Shit!*

He placed his cheek on the stock. He couldn't see the fucking sights! He was crying. He took his hand from the pistol grip and the trigger and wiped his eyes with his knuckles, then with his fingers, and blinked. The sights came into focus.

The machine gunner paused and then started swinging the muzzle back toward Lowell's position. The M1 jumped against Lowell's face. The loader let go of the belt of ammunition and collapsed. The machine gunner looked down at him, and then got to his knees and scooped up the machine gun in both arms. Craig shot him as he stood erect; again, as he wobbled; again, as he went back on his knees; and then, finally, very deliberately, in the head.

That'll teach you, you sonofabitch!

The M1's action was open, smoking slightly, giving off a faint bitter smell of gunpowder and burned oil. Following the example of the Greeks, Craig had wedged the leather rifle strap between the two rows of cartridges in two clips. He pulled one of them loose. The cartridges came out and spilled against the rocks, making a clinking noise. Trembling, he pulled the second clip loose. The cartridges didn't fall out, but they were out of their proper position.

Fuck it!

He laid the empty M1 down and ran over to Nick. Nick's eyes were wide open, very bloodshot, and blood ran out of his nose, ears, and mouth. The rear of his skull was shattered open. Lowell bent over him and felt the bile rise in his throat.

He took BAR magazines from Nick's pouches and ran with them to the firing position. Then he went and got Nick's BAR and ran back, dragging it by the barrel, the stock banging on the rocks behind him. He dropped onto his belly, breathing heavily, eyes full of sweat again, and pulled the 20-round magazine from the BAR. Though there were cartridges in it, he threw it away anyway, and charged the BAR with a fresh magazine.

He rested the front end of the BAR where he had fired the M1. There were two more men at the machine gun now, one picking up the ammo cans, the other scooping up the machine gun itself.

The BAR jumped in his hands. Two short bursts. There were now four dead men at the machine gun. No. Three. One of the bastards was still alive! The BAR jumped again in his hands.

And then one more man came to the machine gun. Didn't you get the message, you sonofabitch? The BAR jumped again, and then stopped. Empty. Lowell ducked behind the rock, pulling the BAR down with him. He changed magazines, then got back in position.

Nothing moved. And there were no yellow flickering muzzle blasts. Just the bluish white clouds of smoke, followed a moment later by the *crump* as the sound of mortar shell's detonation reached them.

The shit was drying, caking, on his leg. He could smell it. He threw up again, dry. There was nothing left to come out of his stomach. He felt faint and rested his cheek on the rock, smelling the tung oil on the BAR stock as he stared at the empty .30–06 shell casings scattered around him.

When there was quiet, he carefully aligned eight cartridges in a clip and loaded the M1; and leaving the BAR where it was, he went back to Nick. He pulled off his Ike jacket and placed it over Nick's shattered head.

The Greek captain came over to him and made the sign of the cross over Nick, and then, with tears in his eyes, he held Craig Lowell's head against his chest, and very gently kissed the top of his head.

Lowell went to the stone hut he had shared with Nick, took out his bedroll, and took from it all his spare underwear. Then he went to the water barrel, and took off his boots and his pants and dipped a T-shirt in the water barrel and wiped the feces off his legs.

It took a long time. He thought that he was going to be sick again. Then one of the Greeks came up to him. He handed him a pair of Greek (actually English) woolen pants, well worn but clean. And then he handed him a British battle jacket. It had his second lieutenant's bar and his tank on the collar points.

"Thank you," he said. The Greek soldier nodded and pointed to the left epaulet. There was a cheap, gray metal pin pinned to it. The insignia of the 113th Regiment, 27th Royal Hellenic Mountain Division. The Greek, who was a pockmarked old fart who needed a shave, reached out and tenderly ran his rough hand over Lowell's face and said something to him. Lowell had no idea what he said, but he smiled and nodded his head. The Greek bent over and picked up the shitty trousers and skivvy shorts and the T-shirt Lowell had used as a shit wiper and carried them off.

(Seven)

Second Lieutenant Craig W. Lowell, wearing mostly a Greek uniform, was leaning on the stone and sandbag walls of his hut, puffing on his next to last cigar when Lt. Colonel Paul T. Hanrahan and First Lieutenant Sanford T. Felter drove into No. 12 Company's area. Hanrahan was driving.

When the weapons carrier stopped, Hanrahan got from behind the wheel and looked at Lowell, who made no move to get off the wall. Hanrahan glanced at the body, which was under a sheet of canvas now. A crucifix rested on top of the canvas. Then he walked toward Lowell.

When he was ten feet away, Lowell pushed himself off the sandbags and saluted. Hanrahan returned the salute as casually.

"You all right, Lieutenant?" Hanrahan asked.

"I'm alive, Colonel."

"What happened to your face?" Hanrahan asked. Lowell unconsciously put his fingers to the already formed scabs on his face.

"Stone splinters, I think," Lowell said.

Colonel Hanrahan put his finger out and touched the regimental insignia on his epaulet.

"They *give* that to you?" he asked. The implication was clear, Lowell thought. I am wearing something I should not be wearing.

The Greek captain, seeing what Hanrahan had done, came up and, taking him by the arm, led him behind the bunker where the dead of the engagement were laid out in two rows. On one side were the Greeks, under cheap cotton flags. On the other the enemy were on their backs with nothing covering them. Captured weapons and supplies were piled between them. The Greek captain led Hanrahan to the end of the line where five bodies lay in a group. A machine gun and some small arms and some supplies were at their feet.

Lowell had seen the bodies before, but only then, when he saw the captain indicating him, did he understand why these bodies and the machine gun were in a special group. These were the men he had killed.

I don't feel a fucking thing, he realized. Not one fucking thing. If I'm supposed to be all upset because I have taken human life, I'm not.

"The captain seems to think you're pretty hot stuff, Lowell," Lt. Colonel Hanrahan said, coming back to him. "A regular Sergeant York."

"We're going to need another interpreter up here, Colonel," Lowell said.

"There's one coming with the trucks to get the other bodies and this stuff," Hanrahan said. "I wanted to come get Nick myself."

They had brought with them in the weapons carrier an American flag and a locally made cheap pine coffin, which was already splitting. Lt. Col. Hanrahan and Lieutenant Felter carried it to the tarpaulin-covered body. Hanrahan and Lowell picked Nick up and put him in the coffin, and then Hanrahan got on his knees and nailed the flag to it. Finally, Hanrahan and Lowell hoisted the coffin into the weapons carrier.

"I'll take care of writing the next of kin," Hanrahan said. It was the first Lowell had even thought about that.

"Thank you, sir," he said.

"And I'll send you some clothes with the other trucks."

"Is the mail coming up with the trucks?" Lowell asked.

Hanrahan pointed to Lt. Sanford T. Felter, who, looking ashamed, handed Lowell his only mail. It was from the Constabulary officer's club. He owed a twenty-five dollar initiation fee and three months dues of ten dollars per month. Unless the bill was paid within seventy-two hours, it said, his commanding officer would be notified.

"The mail is terribly fouled up," Felter said, lamely.

"Yeah, sure it is," Lowell said.

(Eight)

After his junior officer had passed satisfactorily, more than satisfactorily, through his first engagement, Paul Hanrahan was not surprised that he immediately started going Greek. Although Hanrahan would never have said it out loud, it was the Brotherhood of Arms. Probably without knowing it, and certainly without thinking about it, Lowell had joined the tribe. The tribe happened to be Greek. He wanted to be like the others, so he dressed like them, thought like them, acted like them.

Within a month, to the disgust of many of the American officers at Ioaninna, Lowell was far over the line. He had helped himself to a supply of British uniforms from a building full of British surplus at Ioannina. A Greek mama washed it for him to get rid of the awful smell of the British antimoth preservative. He wore a second lieutenant's bar pinned to one collar point, and a U.S. was on the other. These were the only things that distinguished him from a Greek officer.

Under the battle jacket, he wore an open khaki shirt, a GI sweater, and a silk scarf. In one of the Greek companies he instructed, he had acquired a black leather belt and Luger holster—the Germans had left behind. The buckle was a solid brass affair, cast with the words GOTT MIT UNS in inch-high letters.

Probably to mock Felter's parachute wings, Hanrahan thought, he had moved the 113th Regimental pin above his breast pocket from his epaulet. Felter had gone Greek only in that he wore British boots and no necktie. Hanrahan sensed that the only reason Felter was wearing his parachutist's wings was that he had noticed Hanrahan wearing his own.

Felter was spending most of his time around the division

and regimental headquarters. His fluency in Russian fitted in perfectly with Hanrahan's personal obsession. Lt. Col. Red Hanrahan took personal umbrage at the Russian insistence that the Greek revolution was nothing more than an internal affair and that they had nothing to do with it. He was determined to capture one of their Russian counterparts (they could hear them on the radio) and personally take the sonofabitch to Athens.

Lowell got back to Ioannina once or twice a week to sleep overnight, to run messages and errands from the regimental advisors, and to get an American ration meal. And, Paul Hanrahan knew, to wait for a letter that never came.

Paul Hanrahan often thought that if he could get his hands on the little German bitch who had dumped Lowell, he could have cheerfully choked her.

Lowell had received two letters from his mother, both of them still addressed to Private Lowell. She wrote that she remembered Athens from her honeymoon, and she gave him the addresses of restaurants he simply shouldn't miss. While he was there, she wrote, he should take advantage of the opportunity and take a week's cruise among the Greek islands.

Lowell never got around to answering his mother's letters.

The letter he was waiting for took seven weeks to come. The civilian mail service between Greece and Germany was practically nonexistent, and the APO service apparently wasn't much better.

> Dear Craig,
>   After waiting for a month, I know why you haven't written to me. I understand completely. I want to thank you for being so kind to me, and I want you to know that I will ever remember you with most fond thoughts. Your little German friend.
>
>   Ilse.

Craig Lowell had no way of knowing, of course, that two weeks after he had left Germany, General Walls had called Fat Charley into his office and with great delight told him he stood relieved. When Lowell's letters to Ilse arrived in Germany, care of Fat Charley, they were duly forwarded by the Army

Postal Service, surface shipment, to Headquarters U.S. Army Recruiting District, Pittsburgh, Pennsylvania, to which Fat Charley would report for duty six weeks after landing in the States.

It was only the night that Craig finally got Ilse's letter that Sanford Felter heard the whole story about how Craig had met Ilse. He learned, too, that Lowell was only nineteen years old and had lasted at Harvard College only three months before being placed on indeterminate suspension.

Sanford Felter wrote Sharon about it the next day—after he'd sobered Lowell up and sent him out of Ioannina lying in the back of an ammo carrier.

He told her that he really felt sorry for Lowell because of the girl. The thing was, despite everything, despite his good looks and his wealthy background and all, and even the way he'd become almost famous for his icy courage under fire, Craig was really just a boy who had been taken in by a German girl. She obviously was interested in him only for what he could bring her from the PX.

He had offered a prayer for Lowell, Sanford wrote, because the kid was likely to do something very foolish in his mental condition. It made me realize, he added, how good God has been to me in giving me a fine woman.

He wrote, too, that he had come to really respect and admire Colonel Hanrahan; but, because he didn't think she would either understand or care, he hadn't gone into much detail.

Hanrahan had sought out Felter's company the night before. An ad hoc social night, Hanrahan thought privately, of the Ioannina Chapter, West Point Protective Association. He needed somebody to talk to; and he guessed correctly that he could talk to Felter in confidence.

In Felter's room, over a cup of tea, they talked of many things, what they were doing, their wives, the Greeks, and, of course, the Future of the Army.

He asked Felter, and Felter told him, why he had volunteered for Greece. And then Felter had put the question to him, and Hanrahan had enough ouzo aboard to answer him.

"What about you, Colonel?" Felter said. "Why are you here?"

"The function of an officer in peacetime," Hanrahan said,

"is to prepare to fight the next war. That seems pretty god-damned simple to me, but most people I know don't understand it."

"You don't mean that we're going to fight here," Felter replied, "nor that our next war is going to be a guerrilla war, do you?"

"Award the short lieutenant the cement bicycle," Hanrahan said. "No, I don't. What I'm talking about is leading other people's troops."

"Mercenaries? That's the reason the Roman Empire fell."

"I don't mean mercenaries. I mean helping people fight their own wars. Phrased simply, Felter, whether we like it or not, we're going to have to keep the Russians from taking the world over. And since there's no way we can match them man for man, we have to use other people's troops. We're the most sophisticated society in the world, and we have enough people to train other people."

"That's not mercenaries?"

"Pay attention. I said 'to fight their own wars.' It is to the Greeks' advantage to keep the Russians out. And their own men are doing just as good a job, probably a better one, than the 82nd Airborne could do. We give them the equipment, and we train them to use it."

"You think this is the future, then?"

"I want to be a general just as much as anybody else who went to school on the Hudson, Felter. And I am not noble. If I thought the way to get to be a general was to be at Bragg playing paratrooper again, that's where I would be. I intend to be *the* fucking expert when it comes to fighting other people's wars with other people's soldiers."

Then he realized that he was talking too much, even to Felter, and went to bed.

Neither did Sandy Felter tell Sharon that he had written a staff study for Colonel Hanrahan, an intelligence estimate actually, concerning the situation. He wasn't sure if Colonel Hanrahan would have the time to read it, and if he did read it, what he would think of it. He might just laugh at him.

Sanford Felter had taken the facts as he saw them and come up with what he thought was a very likely course of enemy action.

The thin line that the 27th Royal Hellenic Mountain Division had stretched across its portion of the Albanian border was growing more and more effective as time passed. Many pathways across the border from Albania had been dynamited and rendered impassable. All roads wide enough for trucks were now covered by mortars, machine guns, and even by 37 mm mountain cannon in a few places. The enemy was no longer able to infiltrate supplies across the border with reasonable impunity, or with a rate of losses he could afford to pay.

Behind the thin line of the mountain division, however, the same paths were open as they had been for thousands of years. The same paths and a great many caves.

If he were the enemy, Sanford Felter reasoned, rather than send supplies piecemeal across the line, he would breach the line. In a sudden attack, he would take out a couple of the little fortresses guarding the roads. Once they were out of the way, he would send truckloads of supplies through. The trucks would be lost, but if they penetrated a couple of miles behind the mountain division's lines, and guerrillas were waiting to hide the supplies in the mountains, the trucks could be considered expendable.

And certainly the Russian-supported guerrillas and, more importantly, the Red Army advisors on the other side of the border would be influenced by the basic Red Army tactic, which was massive attack. In this case, probably with mortars.

A massive, hour-long attack by mortars against positions which heretofore had not been subject to more than an occasional round, would probably succeed, the valor of the Greeks not withstanding.

To Sandy's immense pleasure, Colonel Hanrahan sent the study to Athens with the comment that he found it very interesting and was taking appropriate measures, within the limits of his assets, to help the mountain divisions resist such an attack.

There weren't very many assets available to the senior U.S. Army advisor to the 27th Royal Hellenic Mountain Divison. But he organized what he had as best he could—three M8 armored cars, six half-trucks, two six-by-sixes, and five weapons carriers—into a mobile light armored column *cum* ammo train.

The vehicles and the men were now set aside and parked, awaiting the attack Felter prophesied. They were identified, and on receipt of a signal, their drivers would be given orders to report to a designated location. There a basic combat load of ammunition for the vehicles and troops and a load of mortar and small arms ammunition to resupply the fortresses under attack had been cached.

Lt. Col. Hanrahan didn't actually make these arrangements himself. He received and approved the arrangements made by Lieutenant Felter. He had come to admire Felter, a process which began with something close to paternal amusement. Felter was the archetypical West Point lieutenant, taking himself and his mission very seriously. But unlike most young lieutenants, Felter made very few mistakes. He neither left important things out, nor had to be cut down to reality. It occurred to Hanrahan one day that the only thing wrong with Felter was that he looked like a mouse. Hanrahan was regularly furious with himself for not being able to remember his first name; he kept calling him Sidney. He thought of him as the Mouse, and had not been surprised to learn from Felter that they had called him "the Mouse" at the Academy.

Once he had given Mouse Felter the go-ahead to set up his relief column, Felter had presumed that he would be in command should it be necessary to actually employ the column. At first, Hanrahan had thought the idea ludicrous, but had not hurt Felter's feelings by telling him so. But as Felter's analysis of the enemy's intention seemed more and more plausible, the idea of letting the Mouse have the command seemed more logical. Felter had run several dry runs: gathering the vehicles together, loading them up, forming the column. He worked the kinks out, made alternative arrangements and additions (the incorporation of three ambulances, for example) and so turned an idea into a working arrangement.

And then Hanrahan got the failed ring-knocker, and that blew the Mouse out of the saddle.

Once a week, or perhaps every ten days, a Stinson L-5 flew into Ioannina and picked up Hanrahan and flew him to Athens. Sometimes they wanted to see him in Athens; more often he went to Athens to plead for more supplies. And sometimes he went and flew back the same day because that way he could pick up the mail sacks and maybe a couple of bottles of whiskey.

The ring-knocker was a captain, a large man with a mustache. Hanrahan had noticed him before they were introduced. The captain was standing beside his luggage in the lobby of the Grande Bretagne. He was obviously new because he was wearing a complete OD uniform, his trousers tucked into new GI combat boots. He was also wearing his ribbons, including something Colonel Hanrahan had never seen before. It was an Expert Combat Infantry Badge without the silver wreath. All the captain was wearing was the blue part with the flintlock.

They looked at each other with frank curiosity. Hanrahan had gone Greek. His only item of U.S. issue uniform from his Limey helmet to his Limey hobnailed boots was a khaki shirt, to whose collar points were pinned the silver oak leaf of his rank and the gold letters, U.S. Everything else was British. He carried a Schmeisser submachine gun in his hands, not because he thought he would need it in Athens, but because there was a possibility the puddle jumper might have to land en route. And some of the areas between Ioannina and Athens were firmly in the hands of the bad guys. The captain was armed with a .45 in a regulation web belt, and a .30 carbine rested against his canvas Valv-Pak.

Lt. Col. Hanrahan had the distinct impression that the captain did not approve of him. He was, obviously, out of uniform. Hanrahan smiled at the mental image of what had happened back in Germany when they'd gotten Felter's delinquency report back. It had come down through channels. From Frankfurt Military Post to Headquarters, U.S. Forces, European Theater; and then because the U.S. Army Military Advisory Group, Greece, was under the Deputy Chief of Staff for Operations, U.S. Army, in the Pentagon, it had gone to Washington. And then been flown to Greece.

One lousy little lieutenant had been caught in an improper uniform because he was halfway through a forty-hour plane trip from the States. And some chickenshit, nattily uniformed MP officer, for the sake of all that was sacred to the chairwarmers, in the name of General Clay, had ordered that the "subject officer's commanding officer report by endorsement hereon the specific corrective disciplinary action taken."

Van Fleet had thought it was funny. There was a note in his handwriting paper-clipped to the official "Your Attention Is Invited to the Previous Indorsement":

"Red. If you have enough wood for a gallows, hang him. Failing that, I suppose shooting to death by musketry will have to do. Van Fleet, LT GEN."

Red Hanrahan had not chuckled at the whole thing and thrown it in the wastebasket, as General Van Fleet obviously expected him to do. For some reason, he kept it. And a day after it arrived, he put it into his typewriter.

8th Ind

HQ US ARMY MILITARY ADVISORY DETACH-MENT
27th ROYAL HELLENIC MOUNTAIN DIVISION
IN THE FIELD

TO: HQ US ARMY MILITARY ADVISORY GROUP, GREECE
c/o U.S. EMBASSY
ATHENS, GREECE

1. The serious transgressions by First Lieutenant San-ford T. Felter against good order and discipline enu-merated in the basic communication have been consid-ered at length by this headquarters.

2. After due and solemn consideration, and acting upon the advice of my staff, I have decided to slap subject officer lightly upon each wrist.

Paul T. Hanrahan
Lt. Colonel, Signal Corps
Commanding

He sent it to Athens in the next mail bag, thinking it would give the general a chuckle, and that the general would then chuck the whole ludicrous thing away. But a week later, there came in the mail bag a carbon copy of the ninth indorsement:

9th Ind

HQ US ARMY MILITARY ADVISORY GROUP, GREECE
THE UNITED STATES EMBASSY
ATHENS, GREECE

TO: HEADQUARTERS, U.S. FORCES, EUROPEAN
THEATER
APO 757, US FORCES
PERSONAL ATTENTION GENERAL LUCIUS D.
CLAY

The commanding general, US Army Military Advisory Group, Greece, heartily concurs in the corrective disciplinary action re: 1st Lt S. T. Felter detailed in the previous indorsement.

BY COMMAND OF LIEUTENANT GENERAL
JAMES VAN FLEET
Ward F. Doudt
Colonel, General Staff
Adjutant General

Clay was going to have to do something about that, when he got it. And it was unlikely that he would try to lecture Big Jim Van Fleet about the necessity of having officers properly uniformed and closely shaven. What would probably happen would be that Clay would simply pass the "Your Attention Is Invited to the Previous Indorsement" back down to the chickenshit MP, and that, it was to be hoped, would cause the bastard to lose some sleep.

Lt. Col. Red Hanrahan went into see the G-1, the personnel officer, first thing. He could see no reason why the entire goddamned United States Army could not arrange to make an infrequent shipment of PX items to the 27th Royal Hellenic Mountain Division's advisors. All he wanted was razor blades, shaving cream, and maybe a couple of lousy boxes of Hershey bars.

The G-1 expected this routine complaint. He listened to it patiently, waited for it to end, promised again to do what he could, and then said: "Say, Paul. I just thought of something. I've got a new officer for you. And I don't think he's left yet." A sergeant was dispatched to the lobby and returned with Captain Daniel C. Watson, the officer Hanrahan had noticed earlier.

Hanrahan took a certain perverse pleasure in being introduced as the man Captain Watson would be working for. It changed the captain's attitude about 180 degrees.

"What is that thing on your chest, Captain?" he asked, with a smile.

He was informed that it was the Expert Infantry Badge, as opposed to the Expert Combat Infantry Badge. So far as Colonel Hanrahan was concerned, the CIB was the only medal that meant a shit. What this ring-knocker was wearing was a qualification badge. He could shoot every weapon in the infantry arsenal, jump over barbed wire, throw hand grenades at a target, and probably make a fire by rubbing two sticks together.

After the captain had gone (to be carried to Ioannina in a supply convoy), Hanrahan asked to look at his service record. The G-1 was a little reluctant, but finally produced it.

Captain Watson had gone ashore in North Africa with the 1st Division as a platoon leader in the 18th Infantry. He had next gone to a hospital. There was no record of a Purple Heart, and there was no award of the Expert Combat Infantry Badge. You got the CIB for ninety days in combat, or unless you were taken out of combat sooner by getting shot, in which case the CIB and the Purple Heart came automatically and together.

Hanrahan looked up from Captain Watson's service record and met the eyes of the G-1.

"Battle fatigue," the G-1 said.

"I don't want him," Hanrahan said. "I'll send him back, and you can find a job for him here."

"For Christ's sake, Paul," the G-1 said. "You know how that happens."

The G-1 wore both the CIB and the ring. Hanrahan knew that another ad hoc meeting of the West Point Protective Association had just been called into session.

"He paid for it," the G-1 went on. "He spent the war running basic trainees. He's still a captain. His classmates are all majors, at least, for Christ's sake. He deserves another chance."

"Why?" Hanrahan asked, simply.

"I can show you his 201 file if you like," the G-1 said. "Once a month, from the time he went to the hospital, he requested combat duty. Every goddamned month, Paul. A career shouldn't be ruined by one incident."

Hanrahan suspected that that was a slip of the tongue. The G-1 hadn't used the word "incident" without some reason. The captain, Hanrahan decided, had either cowered in a hole, or run. The Association of Graduates of the United States Military Academy at West Point had taken care of one of their own. He had been adjudged to be suffering from battle fatigue. If you just lose it, they don't use the word incident. What the hell, he had been close to running himself a dozen times.

"OK," Hanrahan said. "We'll give him a second chance."

"Let's go get some lunch," the personnel officer said. "I understand for a change that we're having gravy with meat chunks."

When Captain Watson reported to Ioannina the next day, the Expert Infantry Badge was missing from his breast. Hanrahan assigned him as assistant G-3 (Plan and Training), sending the captain who held that post up to one of the regiments. Watson worked like hell; Hanrahan was willing to grant him that. He lorded it over Felter, but Hanrahan figured not only that the Mouse could take it, but that two enthusiastic ring-knockers deserved each other.

In the next two months, Second Lieutenant Lowell had only one run-in that required Colonel Hanrahan's personal attention. Righteously indignant, Captain Watson had reported to Colonel Hanrahan that Lieutenant Lowell "in his cups" had told him to go fuck himself when Captain Watson had suggested that not only was he making a spectacle of himself in the officer's mess, but that he had never seen a dirtier, more disreputable uniform.

Hanrahan had jumped all over two asses about that. He told the Duke, as he had come to think of his gone-Greek handsome young lieutenant, that the next time he talked disrespectfully to a senior officer he would personally kick his ass; and he had explained to Captain Watson, with exquisite sarcasm, that it was his position as commanding officer to exercise a modicum of tolerance vis-à-vis the behavior of a nineteen-year-old officer who was almost daily exposed to enemy fire, and who by his personal valor had earned the respect and admiration of the 27th Royal Hellenic Mountain Division.

"The officer of whom we are speaking, Captain, manages to get back here about once a week. While I deplore, of course, any action on the part of any officer which might tend to bring discredit upon the officer corps of the United States Army, I must confess that if I hadn't had a bath or a decent meal in a week, I myself, might be tempted to take a little drink when I came back here."

Watson took the rebuke as if he had had his face slapped. Hanrahan, after a day or two, came to the conclusion that perhaps it was getting through to Captain Watson what the fuck the army was all about. After eight years in uniform.

The next week, Watson had come to him with the request that he be given responsibility for the armored supply column. The request came as a surprise, but the captain's arguments were soundly based. And if the bad guys did try to bust through the lines, Hanrahan would prefer to have the Mouse here, to listen to the Russian frequencies and perhaps hear something of interest.

The Mouse took the news of relief without a word, but there was a deep disappointment in his eyes that shamed Hanrahan. The next time Hanrahan had a couple of drinks too many he told the Mouse about Watson being given a second chance. In the morning, when he remembered what he had done, he was furious with himself.

Although he looked for it, he could not detect any change in the Mouse's attitude toward Captain Watson. He was, in fact, so helpful to Watson that Watson came and asked if Lieutenant Felter might not be assigned as his deputy. "In case the balloon does go up, it would be better to have a backup American officer."

So ordered.

VIII

(One)
The Greek-Albanian Border
6 September 1946

The balloon went up three weeks later. Hanrahan had felt in his bones that it was about to happen.

There had been intelligence reports from Athens about movements from the interior of Greece toward the Albanian-Yugoslavian borders—an unusual amount of donkey-wagon traffic. Line-crossers reported to Athens and Athens reported to Hanrahan that there was an unusual amount of truck traffic in Albania. The number of reported attempted (and successful) infiltrations declined.

The Mouse had hit it right on the head. Hanrahan wondered how much longer he himself would have taken to figure it out.

There were reports from all over the line, first of sniper fire, then of mortar fire. The same reports had come in for the past five days. Nothing had happened. The fire had simply died down. The Greeks felt that they were teaching the Reds a lesson with their counter-mortar fire. Granting the Greeks could drop a 76 mm mortar round in a latrine hole at 1,000 yards, Hanrahan didn't think this was the case.

And then Captain Watson had come into Colonel Hanrahan's room.

"Lieutenant Lowell is on the radio, sir," he said. "He wants to speak to you."

If Captain Watson was piqued that Lieutenant Lowell hadn't wanted to talk to him, he gave no sign.

What the hell was Lowell's radio code? Hanrahan couldn't remember.

"Duke, this is Pericles Six, go ahead."

"I'm with Pegasus Forward, Colonel. We're under heavy mortar attack."

Pegasus Forward was No. 12 Company, 113th Regiment. Ever since Nick had been killed, Lowell had sort of adopted No. 12 Company, and vice versa. He was technically assigned to the headquarters company of 113th Regiment, but he spent his nights at the front with No. 12 Company. Hanrahan had learned that through Lieutenant Lowell's dedicated efforts, No. 12 Company had more than its fair share of what creature comforts were available. These he'd mostly stolen from the American officers at division.

Hanrahan had not responded to the complaints. So far as he was concerned, the key to success in an operation like this was for distinctions between the Americans and the Greeks they were advising to disappear. This wasn't the British Indian Army; the Greeks were not second-class citizens. The Greeks had to believe that, within reason, their American advisors lived as they did. Lowell was doing that. It was possible that his behavior would shame some of the other American officers into copying him. Lowell was proof of the colonel's theory. He was the only junior officer in the division who matter-of-factly issued orders directly to Greek soldiers, and more important, had his orders obeyed. If Greek troops didn't like their American officer, they weren't insubordinate; they were simply unable to comprehend what the American wanted unless it was translated for them by one of their own officers. Yet they seemed to have no trouble whatever understanding what Lowell told them to do in his really awful, hundred-word Greek vocabulary.

Hanrahan stepped to the map, checking his memory that No. 12 Company's two rock fortresses were on either side of a truck-capable road.

"When did it begin?" Hanrahan asked.

"About twenty minutes ago," Lowell's voice crackled over the radio. "They took out our signal bunker."

"What are you using?" Hanrahan asked. Across the room, his eyes met those of Mouse Felter, who was standing, his arms folded on his chest, watching and listening.

"The M8 radio, Colonel," Lowell said. The Duke doesn't know diddly shit about proper radio security, Hanrahan thought. And then he thought that it didn't really matter. "Pericles Six" was obviously known to the Russians as the American advisor's radio code.

"What's your situation?"

"I'm holding," Lowell's voice replied. "But we're running through a lot of ammunition."

Goddamned Greeks, Hanrahan thought. They regarded an incoming mortar round as a slur on their masculine pride, that had to be answered with a barrage.

"*I'm* holding?" Hanrahan said, a little annoyed. Lowell was not the commanding officer. He was just the goddamned advisor.

"Captain Demosthatis bought it," Lowell said. "I assumed command."

"How many other casualties?"

"All the officers," Lowell said. "They've been hitting us pretty hard."

"Mount your operation, Captain Watson," Lt. Col. Hanrahan ordered. Then he pressed the microphone button: "Duke," he said, "give them tit for tat. I'll run some ammo up there to you." He spoke conversationally, calmly, although his stomach was in painful knots.

"We can't get out of here, Colonel," Lowell said, and even in the frequency-clipped voice that came over the radio, Hanrahan could hear fear, perhaps even terror in his voice. "They got the motor pool, and when I came out to use the radio in the M8, the tires were all blown."

"No sweat, Duke," Hanrahan replied. "They can't get through your mortars, and we'll get some ammo up to you right away. I've already given the order."

"You better send some officers, too," Lowell said. "I took a little shrapnel coming out to the M8."

Hanrahan's stomach twisted again.

"Well, boy, you just take it easy. We're on our way. What they're trying to do is get some trucks down your road. We know all about it, and we're ready for it."

"Annie Oakley clear with Pericles Six," Craig Lowell's voice, for the first time using the correct radio procedure, came over the radio.

"The cavalry's on the way, Duke," Hanrahan said. "I promise you. Pericles Six, out."

He wondered if the message had gotten through. He wondered why Lowell had suddenly broken off radio contact.

He looked around the room. Felter, having checked it, was loading a 30-round magazine into his Thompson submachine gun.

"Sidney," he said.

"Sir?"

"Nothing," Colonel Hanrahan said. "Get moving."

"Colonel, it's *Sanford*," Felter said, gently, shaming Hanrahan again. Then he put his Limey helmet on his head and left the G-3 office.

Carrying the Thompson under his right arm like a bird hunter, Felter trotted across the parking lot toward the sandbagged ammo bunker, where several vehicles had already shown up. They were being hurriedly loaded by Greek soldiers. He heard the peculiar sound of a half-track behind him. When he turned to look, he saw the driver's face peering out the windshield. The armor plate which could be lowered to protect the driver was in the propped-open position. Felter waved the half-track into position in the column line.

Next he saw the command jeep, an innovation of Captain Watson's that Lieutenant Felter did not approve. The jeep held their communications radios and had a .50 caliber machine gun mounted on a pedestal. Captain Watson apparently thought of it as his horse. He was going to lead his troops like Light-Horse Harry Lee. Bugler, sound the charge!

When the column had been Felter's, he had the third half-track in line as the command vehicle. The radios would be protected, and so would the commander. If the column were ambushed, the first thing they would take out would be the lead vehicle. The way Watson had it set up, they would lose their communications and their commander to the first bad guy with a machine gun or a grenade.

Felter had tried to set up another group of radios in his half-track, but Watson had caught him at it and told him it wasn't necessary. He had also taken the opportunity to pointedly remind Felter that he was the column leader, and that simple courtesy, as well as regulations, dictated that Felter consult with the commander before taking any action on his own. A fellow West Pointer should know that.

A General Motors six-by-six, and then another, appeared, and troops poured out the backs. They joined the lines of men handing ammo cases hand-to-hand from the bunkers. The trucks, which carried a 2.5 ton load (and for that reason were also known as "deuce-and-a-halfs") were "new." They had seen World War II, and had been rebuilt in ordnance shops in Germany. The American supply line was beginning to operate.

Felter didn't like the way Watson was running around, excited, almost hysterical. He reminded himself that he knew something about Captain Watson that he shouldn't know. He wished Colonel Hanrahan hadn't told him about the captain's record.

In ten minutes, the column was loaded and ready. Watson stood up in the front seat of his jeep and gave the forward sign.

"Charge!" Felter thought, sarcastically. The drivers of the vehicles behind him had been racing their engines for two minutes, ready to go. They would have followed Watson's jeep the moment it moved. They didn't need a hand signal.

The half-track jerked into motion. He felt like a fool. He was almost knocked off his feet, because he had been standing up like Watson himself.

He could hear the sound of the mortar barrage, even over the roar of the engines, long before they reached the site of No. 12 Company. As they grew closer, however, the blurred sounds became more distinct, and there were separate noises now, cracks, and crumps, and *barooms,* and the rattle of small arms fire. Felter thought they were "marching to the sound of the musketry," but he couldn't remember which famous general had said that.

They were close enough now to make out the differing sounds of Enfields, Mausers, and Garands, of .30 and .50 caliber machine guns; and they were close enough to be able to detect glowing light as mortars were fired and as their shells landed. There was a low-hanging yellow cloud of dust around the next curve of the road.

Felter leaned over and lowered the armor plate over the driver's windshield. The driver would now have to steer by peering through a slit in the plate. He started to lower the armor plate on his side, and was suddenly thrown against the windshield. The half-track had lurched to a stop.

When he regained his balance, he stood up on the seat. There was a small cloud of yellow-and-black smoke on the road, fifty yards in front of Captain Watson's jeep. That had been a long round, Felter knew, a fluke. Watson's jeep should now move on.

Watson's jeep did not move on. Watson jumped out of his jeep and ran to the side of the road, the down side, and stood behind a boulder taller than he was. He looked around for Felter, and when he saw him, signaled him to join him.

Felter left the half-track by climbing over the windshield onto the hood, and then down over the bumper and the winch in front. He carried the Thompson in his right hand. As he ran toward Captain Watson, another mortar round landed, thirty yards further down the slope from where Captain Watson stood, a hundred yards toward the firefight. Another wild round, the Mouse thought, wondering if he was going to get wiped out by a mistake made by some worker in an ammunition factory.

"We can obviously go no farther in this fire," Watson said. "I intend to set up a defense line at the ridge of that hill." He pointed to the rear.

"They're waiting for this ammunition, Captain," Felter said.

"They've been overrun," Captain Watson said. "Isn't that obvious?"

"I don't think so, sir," Felter said, politely. "I can hear their mortars and automatic weapons."

"Well, then, Lieutenant," Captain Watson said, sarcastically, "if you're so sure, why don't you just reconnoiter on your own?"

"Yes, sir," Felter replied, accepting the sarcasm as an order. He ran back onto the road, and signaled the driver of Captain Watson's jeep to pick him up. The half-track behind the jeep moved as soon as the jeep did. Felter held out his hand, ordering it to stop.

He jumped into the jeep.

"Felter!" Captain Watson shouted at him. "Come back here!"

Lieutenant Felter pretended not to hear him.

The jeep carried him three hundred yards down the road. The positions of No. 12 Company were under heavy fire, wrapped in smoke and dust. But they weren't overrun. He could see muzzle flashes, and somehow his eye caught a mortar round at the apogee of its arc. No. 12 Company was returning fire, all right.

Felter studied the two little fortresses and the road leading to them through his binoculars. The road had been literally hacked out of the mountainside. It was one-way, just wide enough to take a half-track. But there was an advantage to that. If a mortar shell hit above the road, the shrapnel would be thrown sideward and upward. If one hit the slope of the mountain below the road, only a small amount of shrapnel would be thrown so as to strike anything on the road.

It would take a direct hit to knock out one of the column's vehicles. Even if that happened, they could simply push the disabled vehicle off the road and out of the way.

When he was sure of his position, he ran back to his jeep. The driver already had it turned around.

Captain Watson was where he had left him. For some reason, he had drawn his .45 and was holding it in his right hand, limp, at his side.

Felter got out of the jeep and ran over to him.

"They're under fire, sir," Felter reported. "But they have not been overrun. And the amount of enemy fire actually landing on the road up there is negligible."

"If they have not yet been overrun," Captain Watson said, in a strained voice, as if forcing himself to speak, "it is just a matter of minutes until they are. And this column cannot survive the fire being brought upon the road."

"Yes, it can, Captain," Felter said, very calmly. "Everything's going to be all right, Captain." Captain Watson looked at him as if he had never seen him before. "We're expected up there, Captain," Felter said, talking slowly and reasonably. "The colonel told them we would be there. They need our ammo. Sir."

"I'm not going to be responsible for this column being wiped out in any childish display of heroics," Captain Watson said, very clearly, as if he had rehearsed what he was going to say.

The Greek captain who served as interpreter, and who rode in the first half-track, came running over.

"Is there something you can tell me to tell the men?" he asked. "Is something wrong?"

"Nothing's wrong, Captain," Felter said. "We're moving out."

"We are *not moving out!*" Captain Watson said, firmly, loudly. "We are withdrawing." The Greek captain looked from one to the other American.

"Captain, among others, Lieutenant Lowell is on that hilltop," Felter said.

"I'm sick of you, and everybody else, telling me about Lieutenant Lowell," Captain Watson said, his voice very intense. "Lieutenant Lowell this, Duke Lowell that."

Felter felt himself, despite everything, smiling. Captain Watson sounded like Sharon when she was angry.

"Don't you smile at me, Jewboy," Captain Watson said. "Don't you ever smile at me!"

"Sir, I respectfully request permission to take two of the tracks to the hill while you form a fall-back line," the Mouse said.

"Denied!" Captain Watson sputtered. He was waving his .45 around. "You have your orders, and you will carry them out. Tell the drivers to turn around!" he said to the interpreter.

The interpreter looked at Felter. There was contempt for Watson in his eyes.

"I'll ride in the first track," Felter said to the interpreter. "We'll leave the wheeled vehicles here until we see what the situation is."

"Felter, I give the orders!" Captain Watson said, almost a shout.

"Sir," Felter said, "I have been ordered by Colonel Hanrahan to reinforce Number 12 Company. I intend to carry out that order."

"You'll obey *my* orders!" Captain Watson said, and now his voice was shrill.

"Everything's going to be all right, Captain," Felter said, calmly. He raised his hand over his head and made a "wind-up" gesture. Starters on the tracks ground.

"Goddamn you, this is mutiny!" Captain Watson said.

Felter ignored him. He started back to the road.

There was the booming crack of a .45 going off. Felter kept walking. There was another shot, and this time Felter heard the bullet whirring beside his head. He stopped, paused motionless a moment, and then turned around.

"One more step and you would have been a dead man," Captain Watson said. He was holding the pistol in both hands, pointing it at Felter.

They looked at each other for a long moment. Finally Captain Watson got control of himself. Trembling, he lowered the pistol, fumbled to get it back in its holster.

"Get these goddamned vehicles turned around!" he said to the interpreter.

Lieutenant Felter raised the muzzle of his Thompson submachine gun and pulled the trigger. Captain Watson fell over backward, struck by six .45 caliber bullets traveling at approximately 830 feet per second. And then his body started to slide down the mountainside.

The interpreter looked at Felter.

"Pass the word to the drivers that if a vehicle is disabled, they are to push it off the road," Felter said.

"Yes, sir," the interpreter captain said.

(Two)

Lt. Colonel Paul T. Hanrahan leaned forward and held up the sheet of paper in his portable typewriter and read what he had written. He looked across his desk at Lieutenant Sanford T. Felter, who sat in a straight-backed chair, his fingers locked together in his lap, staring at nothing. Hanrahan felt very sorry for him, a pity mingled with a surprised admiration. It wasn't the sort of thing he would have expected from Felter. Then

Hanrahan ripped the sheet of paper out of the typewriter, took a pen from a pocket sewn to the upper sleeve of his British battle jacket, and signed his name.

"Sidney," he said. "Excuse me, *Sanford.*"

Lieutenant Felter stood up.

"Yes, sir?"

"Read this, Sanford," Lt. Col. Hanrahan said. "Read it aloud."

Felter took the sheet of paper, and started to read it.

"Aloud, Felter," Hanrahan said. "I said, 'read it aloud.'"

"Dear Mrs. Watson," Felter read, in a strained voice. "By now you have heard from the War Department about the death of your husband. Please forgive the bad typing, but I wanted to get this letter out to you as soon as possible. It will be flown out of here with a young officer who was wounded in the same engagement in which Captain Watson gave his life.

"Captain Watson was commanding a relief column dispatched to relieve a Greek Army unit under heavy enemy attack. Heedless of the personal danger to himself, Captain Watson elected to lead the column in a jeep. En route to the scene of action, the convoy was ambushed by guerrillas. Captain Watson was struck by automatic weapons fire which killed him instantly, and I am sure, painlessly.

"I'm sure you will take some small comfort in knowing that, inspired by Captain Watson's personal example of courage, the junior officer under him rallied his troops and saw the mission brought to a successful conclusion.

"Captain Watson's courage and personal example were an inspiration to his men. I know of no finer epitaph for a soldier than to say that he died leading his men into battle.

"The officers and men of both the 27th Royal Hellenic Mountain Division and the U.S. Military Detachment join me in expressing their sorrow at the loss of your husband and their comrade-in-arms. I have been advised that Captain Watson has been recommended for a decoration by the commanding general of the 27th RHMD.

"Sincerely yours, Paul W. Hanrahan, Lieutenant Colonel, Signal Corps, Commanding."

Felter looked at Lt. Col. Hanrahan.

"I'm not sure I can live with this, sir," he said.

"You will live with it, Lieutenant. You will live with it the rest of your life. As I will live with the knowledge that if I had done what I knew should be done and had refused to accept him up here, he would still be alive. The subject is closed, Felter. I don't wish to discuss it further."

There came the sound of a multiengined airplane.

"That must be the Sutherland," Colonel Hanrahan said. "I guess we better go say good-bye to the Duke."

"People know, Colonel," the Mouse said. "Captain Chrismanos saw me. Lowell was there when we brought the body back. He asked me what had happened and I told him."

"The subject is closed, Mouse," Hanrahan repeated. "Closed. Finished."

He took Felter's arm and led him out of his office. They walked over to the infirmary, another of the stone buildings reinforced with sandbags. There was a sign over the door: "The Mayo Clinic G&O Ward."

"How is he?" Hanrahan asked the young American doctor, as if Lowell weren't lying on the stretcher, awake.

"I'd like to get a little more blood in him," the surgeon said. "He lost a hell of a lot. We need some type O-Positive. I was about to have a look..."

"I'm O-Positive," Felter said.

"You look pretty shaken, Mouse," the doctor said. "I think you're right on the edge of shock."

"I'll give him the blood," Felter said. "I'm all right."

"You sure you got enough to give away?" Lowell asked.

"Get on with it, doctor," Hanrahan ordered. "They don't like to leave that Sutherland sitting here any longer than they have to."

Felter rolled up his sleeve and lay down on the operating table.

When they were connected and left alone for a moment, he looked down at Lowell, below him on the stretcher on the floor.

"If they send you home, will you go see Sharon?" Felter asked.

"You gutsy little sonofabitch," Lowell said. "I've been thinking about you blowing that yellow bastard away. I would never have thought you would have had the balls."

"What I'm afraid of is that I really shot him because he called me Jewboy," the Mouse said. "I shouldn't have done it."

"Christ, *I'm* glad you did," Lowell said. "I was scared shitless up there. Better him than me. What the hell is the matter with you?"

"Will you go see Sharon?" Felter asked again, to change the subject.

"They're not going to send me home. They're sending me to Frankfurt, for Christ's sake. I'll be back here in a month."

"But if they do, will you?"

"Yeah, sure."

"You've got the address?"

"Burned in my memory," Lowell said. "The Old Budapest Restaurant. How could I forget that?"

"Warsaw Bakery," Felter corrected him, even though he knew Lowell was pulling his leg. "Are you in pain, Craig?"

"No, believe it or not. It feels like it's asleep. Doc says it will start to hurt after a while. He gave me some pills."

"You'll be all right," Felter said. "You were very lucky, Craig."

The doc and the colonel came in and watched as the blood flowed between them. Then they were disconnected, and a couple of Greek soldiers picked up Lowell's stretcher and carried it to the wharf and manhandled it into a rowboat. The doc rode out with him in the rowboat to the Sutherland seaplane and saw that the crew chief knew what to do with him. He wasn't really in any danger. His arm and shoulder had been sliced open with shrapnel, and he'd lost a lot of blood, but the doc doubted that there would be any trouble once they got him in a bed and started a penicillin regimen and got some decent food in him.

When the doc got back to shore, the Mouse had passed out and was on the stretcher.

(Three)
New York City, N.Y.
8 September 1946

The very existence of the United States Army Advisory

Group, Greece, posed certain delicate administrative problems for the United States Army, especially when one of its members got himself shot up.

There was no war, ergo, there could be no wounds, no Purple Hearts. Personnel of USAMAG(G) were "injured" not "wounded."

The entire Standing Operating Procedure–Notification of Next of Kin, U.S. Army Military Advisory Group, Greece, Personnel, was classified CONFIDENTIAL. The next of kin were to be advised by the most expeditious means, by a notification team consisting of a chaplain and another commissioned officer. In the case of company-grade officers, where possible, the notification officers would be a grade senior to the injured officer. They would exercise judgment in imparting specific information to the next of kin. The implication was that the next of kin be told as little as possible beyond the fact that their next of kin had been "injured"; his condition; the prognosis; and the medical facility (normally the 97th General Hospital in Frankfurt) to which he had been sent for treatment.

A brand-new olive-drab Plymouth four-door sedan, driven by a sergeant and carrying a major of the Adjutant General's Corps and a lieutenant colonel of the Army Chaplain's Corps bounced off the Governors Island ferry and headed up past the Battery to the West Side Highway. It crossed Manhattan on 57th Street, past Carnegie Hall, and then turned up Park Avenue. It turned left on 60th Street, and left again on Fifth Avenue, and finally stopped before a large apartment building overlooking Central Park. The doorman of the building, after a moment's indecision, walked across the sidewalk and opened the door of the staff car.

"On whom are you calling, gentlemen?" he asked.

"Mrs. Frederick C. Lowell," the major said.

"You mean Mrs. Pretier," the doorman corrected him.

"No, I mean Mrs. Frederick C. Lowell," the AGC major insisted.

"Mrs. Frederick Lowell is now Mrs. Andre Pretier," the doorman said. "Does Mrs. Pretier expect you, gentlemen?"

"No, she does not," the AGC major said. "This is official business."

Mrs. Pretier could not come to the telephone—she was

dressing—but Mr. Pretier gave the doorman permission to pass the gentlemen through to the elevator.

Mr. Pretier, who despite his name was a sixth-generation American, came to the door on the heels of the maid.

"My name is Pretier, gentlemen," he said. "What is it you wished to speak to my wife about?"

"We would prefer, sir," the major said, "to speak to Mrs. Pretier personally."

"Well, if you insist, and it won't take long. We're on our way out, so to speak. Can I offer you something?" He raised his martini glass.

"No, thank you, sir," they said in unison, the chaplain a bit more sternly because he was a Southern Baptist and as such a total abstainer.

Mrs. Janice Craig Lowell Pretier entered the living room, which overlooked Central Park, a few moments later. She swirled through the door to show off her dress to her new husband, and stopped at the bar where she picked up a martini glass.

"Aren't you *darling*, Darling," she said. "Just what I need before I face those awful people."

Her eyes fell upon the two officers standing at the entrance to the thirty-five by fifty foot room holding their uniform hats in their hands. Both were impressed by the room and its furnishings, and made just a little uneasy by the opulence and what it represented.

"What's this?" Janice Pretier asked with one of her winning little smiles. "Oh, it's about the *jeep*," she added. "I thought someone would show up eventually about that."

"Ma'am?" the AGC major asked.

"Three weeks ago," Mrs. Pretier explained, "someone in the army in Brooklyn telephoned to say there was a jeep over there, and could I come for it. It must be my son's. He's a soldier, you know, but I haven't . . ."

"Ma'am," the AGC major said, "we're here about your son. Your son is Lieutenant Craig W. Lowell, is he not?"

"And that's something else strange I've wanted to ask somebody about. One day he's a private playing golf in Germany, and the next thing I hear is that he's a lieutenant in Greece. A lieutenant is an *officer*, isn't he?"

"Yes, ma'am," the AGC major said.

"Then what's this all about? My son is just a *boy*. You people really shouldn't have drafted him at all."

"Mrs. Pretier, your son has just been recommended for the award of the second highest medal the King of Greece can bestow."

"*Craig?* You must be mistaken. A medal? What for? You people must have your wires crossed or something."

"No, ma'am, if your son is Craig W. Lowell, there's no mistake," the major said. "And I'm afraid I have some disturbing news, as well," he added.

"Disturbing? What do you think this has been so far? What are you talking about?"

"I'm afraid, ma'am," the chaplain said, "that your boy has been injured. He's in no danger—"

"Injured? What do you *mean, injured?*"

"He's suffered some cuts on his shoulder and arm," the chaplain said. "He is in no danger."

"Surely, this must be some ghastly mistake," Mr. Pretier said.

"And how did that happen?" Mrs. Pretier asked, icily, no longer smiling, now holding the major and the chaplain personally responsible for damage to her baby.

"It seems that Craig," the chaplain said, "was wounded in action . . ."

"Wounded in *action?* What are you *talking* about? The war is *over*."

"There is a revolution in Greece, ma'am," the major said.

"What's that got to do with my Craig?" she asked.

"Your son is assigned to the American Military Advisory Group in Greece," the major said.

"I don't understand any of this," Mrs. Pretier said. "Andre, darling, get Daddy on the phone, like a dear, will you?"

He went to the telephone and dialed a number.

"Lieutenant Lowell had been flown to the 97th General Hospital in Frankfurt, Germany, for treatment," the major said. "It is one of the finest hospitals in the world. The treatment is unsurpassed."

"I still think this is some horrible mistake, a nightmare. You are actually standing there and telling me my son has been *shot*, and is in a hospital?"

Andre Pretier carried the telephone to his wife. She snatched the handset, which had a silver sheath over it, from his hand.

"Daddy? Daddy, there are two soldiers here in the apartment, and they've got some crazy story about Craig being shot and being in a hospital in Greece or Germany or someplace; and Daddy, here, you talk to them."

The chaplain was closest to her. She thrust the phone at him.

"This is Chaplain Foley of First Army Headquarters, sir. I understand that you are Lieutenant Craig Lowell's grandfather. Is that the case, sir?"

"I was going to go in the service myself," Andre Pretier said to the major from the Adjutant General's Corps. "But they found a heart murmur."

(Four)
Frankfurt am Main, Germany
9 September 1946

The ambulance, a civilian-type Packard rather than a GI ambulance, rolled without stopping past the guard at the gate of the 97th General U.S. Army Hospital on the eastern outskirts of Frankfurt.

The huge, attractive hospital was a rambling, four-story structure, built just before World War II. The ambulance drove to the Emergency entrance, turned around carefully, and backed in.

A nurse and two medics who had gone to Rhine-Main Air Base to meet the plane got out; and four medics, in hospital whites, rolled a stainless steel body cart out to the ambulance. Between them, they got the patient out of the ambulance and onto the cart and rolled him quickly through automatically opening glass doors.

An officer of the Medical Service Corps met them right inside the door. His eyes rose when he saw the patient was holding a holstered German luger against his chest with his one good hand.

"Have you got a permit for that gun?" the Medical Service Corps captain demanded. "Is it registered?"

"Registered?" Second Lieutenant Craig W. Lowell said, incredulously. He started to laugh, but it hurt. "Oh, shit,"

Lowell said, shaking his head.

"I'll have to ask you to give me that pistol, Lieutenant," the captain said.

"Fuck you," Craig W. Lowell said.

"Watch your language, Sonny boy," a middle-aged nurse dressed in operating room greens said, walking up to the wheeled cart. A green mask hung around her neck, a green cap covered most of her gray hair, and her feet were in hospital slippers.

Lowell looked up at her.

"There's a lady present," she said.

"Sorry," he said.

She put her fingers on his wrist, and took his pulse. She snapped her fingers, and a younger nurse pushed a flask of fresh blood on a wheeled stand up to the body cart. The older nurse snapped her fingers again, and one of the medics handed her an alcohol wipe. Moving with speed born of skill and experience, she found his artery, slipped a needle into it, and watched until the blood began to flow into him. Then she signaled for the medics to start wheeling the body cart.

"What about that pistol?" the Medical Service Corps captain asked.

There was no reply.

The middle-aged nurse walked rapidly down the highly polished linoleum of the corridor, past the emergency examining rooms, directing the cart with one hand behind her. They came to a bank of elevators. After a moment a door whooshed open. There were three people on it, one in whites, two in uniform.

"Out," the middle-aged nurse said, gesturing with her hand.

The body cart, and the fresh blood stand, and the nurse and the two medics pushing the cart got on the elevator. There was no room for the captain. When the door started to close automatically, he put out his hand and held it open.

"He can't bring that pistol in the hospital," he said to the middle-aged nurse, who was a major in the Nurses Corps.

"Not now, goddamn it," she said. "Not in his shape. I'll take care of it later. Let go of the door."

The door closed, and the elevator started to rise.

She looked down at Lieutenant Lowell.

"Relax," she said. "I just did that to get him off your back about the gun. How do you feel?"

"Shitty," he said, "now that you've asked."

"I'm going to give you a bath anyhow," the nurse said. "Washing your mouth out won't be much extra work."

"Sorry," he said.

The elevator stopped and the door whooshed open.

"What happens now?" Lowell asked, as they rolled down another corridor.

"Well, the first thing we're going to do is get that cruddy uniform off you," she said. "And give you a bath. And pump some blood in you."

"I'm hungry," he said.

"And then we'll see what else you need," she said.

"You're not going to knock me out," he said.

"We won't? Get this straight, Sonny boy: I'll do whatever I damned well please to you."

"I'm not going to let you knock me out and grab the pistol," he said.

"What's with that pistol, anyway?" she asked.

"It saved my ass, and I intend to keep it," he said.

She looked down at him with surprise in her eyes, but said nothing. The cart was rolled into a private room. The orderlies moved him from the cart onto the bed. She saw his face go white from the pain.

"We'll just cut that jacket off," she said to him. "It won't hurt that way."

"I want the jacket, too," he said. "I want the jacket and the pistol. The rest of it you can have."

What she should do, she knew, was give him something to knock him out. And cut his clothes off, and give him a bath, and take the pistol. He was probably going right up to the OR anyway.

"You've got a hard head," she said, and bent over him and pulled the intravenous needle from the inside of his wrist. Then she reached for the holstered pistol he clutched to his breast.

"I'll put it under your mattress," she said. The young nurse with the whole blood looked at her in surprise when she did exactly that.

"Help me to get his jacket off him," the operating room nurse said. "And then send for one of the Schwestern to help me undress him and give him a bath. For reasons I can't imagine, it embarrasses healthy young men to be undressed by a healthy young woman."

She was pleased when the boy in the filthy, blood-soaked uniform chuckled. She wondered what had happened to him.

"Major, really," the nurse in the crisp whites and the starched cap and the lieutenant's bar said.

"Good God," the operating room nurse said. "You're lousy. Where the hell have you been, anyway?" She looked at the young nurse. "He's going to have to be deloused before we do anything else."

The young nurse left the room. Two middle-aged German nurses, called Schwestern, sisters, came in and matter-of-factly, impersonally, efficiently, stripped him, deloused him, and then bathed him in alcohol. The major pulled off his bandages, looked, and put them back. The blood transfusion apparatus was hooked up again.

"You need a haircut and a shave, too," the major said. "But that can wait."

"I'm hungry," he repeated.

"If we have to put you under," the major said, "you'll just throw up all over the recovery room."

"I was sewn up at Ioannina."

She picked up the telephone and gave a number. She asked for a colonel, and then said, "OK," and hung up. A few moments later, a doctor in surgical whites pushed open the door.

"I thought you were going to prep him and bring him right up."

"It looks to me like the guy in Greece knew what he was doing," the major said. "I just called up to ask you to look at him."

"How do you feel, Son?" the doctor asked, very tenderly raising the loosened bandages and examining the sutures.

"I'm hungry," Lowell said.

"Well, that's a good sign."

"He was lousy," the major said.

"I don't see any point in opening him up now," the doctor said. "Not until we get some X rays, anyhow. And let's get some more blood in him. Are you in pain?"

"I feel like I was run over by a locomotive," Lowell said.

"What happened?"

"I forgot to duck," Lowell said.

"Let's get some more blood in him," the surgeon said. "And get him something to eat. We'll have another look in the morning. I asked if you were in pain. You want something for it?"

"Hell, yes."

The surgeon scribbled an order. He smiled down at the bed. "You're going to be all right," he said. "Sore, but all right."

The ward nurse, a captain, had come into the room. The surgeon handed her the orders. The immediate care of the patient was no longer the responsibility of the operating room nurse. She left the room, and started toward the elevators. Then she changed her mind, and turned around, and walked to the kitchen.

"Hello, Florence," the dietician said. "What brings you here?"

"You got a steak in the cooler?" she asked. The dietician, a captain, raised her eyebrows. "You're about to get an order for a high-protein, low-bulk meal for 505," the operating room nurse said. "505 is about thirteen years old. He came in lousy, skinny as a rail, just about out of blood, and stitched up like a baseball. I figure we can do better for him than a couple of poached eggs on toast."

"All right, Florence," the dietician said. "I'll see to it."

"Thank you," the operating room nurse said. She picked up the telephone and gave a number, and when it answered, she said, "This is Major Horter. If anybody wants me, I'll be with the multiple shrapnel case in 505."

Major Horter walked back down the corridor to the PX refreshment stand. She reached into the flap of her operating room whites and took a dollar in script from her brassiere and bought two Cokes from the attendant. Then she went to 505.

"Chow's on the way," she said, handing him one of the Cokes.

"Thank you," he said.

"There's a phone line to the States," she said. "You got a number, I'll call your mother or somebody and tell them you're all right."

"No," he said, immediately, firmly. Then he smiled. "Thanks, anyway."

"By now, she's going to have a telegram, or they sent somebody to tell her," Major Horter said. "She's liable to be worried."

"When Mother heard I was in Greece," he said, "she sent me a list of restaurants I shouldn't miss. The less she knows about all this, the better off she'll be."

The ward nurse came in carrying a tiny paper cup on a tray.

"What's that?" Major Horter asked. The ward nurse told her.

"I'll give it to him, after he's eaten."

"He's supposed to have it now," the ward nurse said.

"He's an emergency surgical patient, and I'm the Chief Emergency Surgical nurse," Major Horter said, flatly. "OK?"

"Yes, ma'am," the ward nurse said, snippily. She set the tray and the pill on the bedside table and marched out of the room.

"You're a real hard-nose, aren't you?" Lowell said to her.

"Takes one to know one," she said. "You want a cigarette?"

"I don't use them, thank you," he said. "I smoke cigars."

"You're not old enough to smoke cigars," she said.

He shrugged.

When the WAC from the kitchen brought him his steak, Major Horter cut it up for him, and fed it to him, piece by piece. When she asked him if he wanted the bedpan, he said he could make it to the toilet, and she realized that unless they put somebody in the room to hold him in bed, he was going to try it the minute he was alone, so she helped him to the john, and smoked a cigarette until he was finished, and then she helped him back in bed.

"You want me to clean your Luger?" she asked. He was surprised at the offer.

"It's not the first one I've ever seen, Sonny boy," she said. "I got one in a leather case with a shoulder stock. Captain from the 2nd Armored gave it to me. I know how to clean a Luger."

"Please," he said.

"Who'd you shoot with it?" she asked, idly.

"He was supposed to be a Greek. But he was blond. He was probably a Russian," he said. "Sonofabitch sneaked up behind us and started throwing grenades."

"Is that what happened to you? A grenade?"

"No," he said. "I'd been hit two hours before that."

She gave him his medication. Then she took the Luger from under the mattress and wrapped it up in his bloody, dirty British battle jacket. She stood by the side of the bed and waited until the narcotic got to him and his pupils dilated and his eyelids fell. Then she lowered the top of the bed, and walked out of the room.

She went to the dressing rooms for Operating Ampitheaters Four and Five, and put the battle jacket in the linen sterilizer, giving it fifteen minutes at 500 degrees to kill the lice and whatever else it was infested with. Then she took it and the Luger, now wrapped in surgical towels, to her rooms. She filled the bathub, added Lux and got down on her hands and knees and scrubbed the battle jacket. The rinse water was still dirty, so she filled the tub again, and left the jacket to soak overnight. She took her baths in the OR dressing room anyway.

Then she took the Luger and removed the magazine. There was one round in the magazine, and when she worked the action, another 9 mm case came flying out. Then she took it apart, cleaned it and oiled it, wrapped it again in the surgical towel, and put it in the top drawer of her dresser under her khaki shirts.

On the way to see him in the morning, she stopped by the PX and got a really weird look from the clerk when she handed him her ration card, and said she wanted a box of the best kind of cigars.

(Five)

"Dearest Sharon," the Mouse wrote from Ioannina, "you remember what Scott Fitzgerald wrote about the rich being different from you and me. I want you to remember that if Craig Lowell comes to see you. I don't know why I said 'if.' He said he would come to see you, and I think he will. I will be surprised and I guess hurt if he doesn't, because I have come to think of him as a friend, probably the best friend I have ever had, and I don't think he would have promised to come see you unless he meant it.

"What happened to him sounds like a movie starring John Wayne.

"I already wrote about him sort of adopting one of the Greek companies up near the border. I don't know if Colonel Hanrahan knew what he was doing or not. If he did know, he looked the other way when Craig stole anything that wasn't nailed down, as they say in the army, and carried it to 'his' company. Food, liquor, clothing, fuel, and even an oil heater from the senior (U.S.) officer's quarters here.

"He was up with 'his' company when there was a large attack on it. The communists were trying to overrun the forts. They used a lot of mortars; and a large number of people, including all the Greek officers, were killed or wounded. Craig was badly wounded himself. But he took command (which is really unusual, since the Greeks normally won't take orders from anyone but another Greek) and held out until we were able to get a relief force up to help. When they got there, there were only twenty-eight men left alive (out of 206), and they were nearly out of ammunition.

"When they got Craig back here, the doctor had to give him five pints of blood. He'd lost that much. They flew him out of here on a Royal Air Force seaplane to an army hospital in Germany. The doctor said he will be all right, but when I first saw him, I was frightened for him. He was gray.

"He thinks he'll be coming back here, but Colonel Hanrahan doesn't think so. Colonel Hanrahan thinks they will probably, eventually, ship him to the United States. Colonel Hanrahan is usually right, which means that you will probably soon get to meet the fellow I've written so much about. I don't want you to judge him by first impression, and I want you to warn Mama and Papa beforehand that he will certainly say something that will either hurt them or make them mad, or both. The language Craig uses—and sometimes it's really *raw,* honey, if you know what I mean—I guess is some kind of a defense mechanism, to hide his feelings, but you had better be prepared to be shocked. You'll have to remember that he doesn't mean anything by it. Tell Mama and Papa that.

"I want you all to be very nice to him. I don't think he has many friends, and not much of a family either. I really don't understand his relationship with his mother. He just doesn't seem to care about her at all. And she feels the same, from what I've seen, about him.

"That's all I have time for now, except to tell you that Colonel Hanrahan liked an intelligence analysis I drew up for him, and is going to put something about it in my efficiency report. I told him that I wanted to be an intelligence officer, and this will probably help me.

"And tell Papa that Colonel Hanrahan said he would have me flown to Athens for the Holy Days. And never forget even for a second, that I am

> Your *faithful* and loving husband,
>
> Sandy
> (also known as "the Mouse")
> (I don't even mind anymore.)

(Six)
Headquarters, War Department
Office of the Surgeon General
The Pentagon, Washington, D.C.
13 September 1946

"Within the hour," the surgeon general of the United States Army said, "I'm delighted to be of service, Senator." He broke the connection with his finger, and then tapped the phone to get his secretary on the line.

"Ask Colonel Furman to come in here right away, will you, please, Helen?"

Colonel William B. Furman, Medical Service Corps, Chief of Administrative Services, Office of the Surgeon General, appeared ninety seconds later.

"Get on the phone, Bill," the surgeon general said. "Call the 97th General Hospital in Frankfurt, and get me a complete rundown on the medical condition of a soldier named Craig W. Lowell."

"Do you have his rank and serial number, sir?"

"No serial number. But he's either a lieutenant or a private, if that's any help," the surgeon general said, smiling. And then he thought a moment. "And, Bill, when you get his rank and serial number, send a TWX. Medical condition permitting, space available, have him put on the next medical evacuation flight to Walter Reed."

"He's somebody important, I gather, sir?"

"I just had the senior senator from New York on the phone. He leads me to believe that Private Lowell, or Lieutenant Lowell, whatever he is, owns just about a square mile of downtown Manhattan Island," the surgeon general said.

"I'll get right on it, sir."

(Seven)

The commanding officer of the 97th General Hospital was an old friend of Major Florence Horter. They had served together three times before, and it was unofficial but rigid Standing Operating Procedure that when the hospital commander scheduled an operation, Major Florence Horter was scheduled as his gas-passer; and if the Medical Corps officers who were board-certified anesthesiologists felt slighted, tough teat.

Major Horter, in a green blouse and pink skirt, and wearing all of her ribbons, walked into his office.

"What the hell is going on, Flo?" the hospital commander asked.

"About what?"

"With you and this kid from Greece," he said. "Don't tell me May and December."

"Don't be a horse's ass," Major Horter exploded. "He's a nice kid, that's all."

"And that's why you're taking him off on a weekend pass? Two days after you tell me, and I TWX the surgeon general, that he shouldn't be airlifted for at least a week?"

"How'd you find out about that?" she asked, curiously.

"It doesn't matter," he said. "What the hell is going on?"

"OK. He's got a girlfriend. Or he had one. He can't find her, and we're going to look for her."

"A girlfriend, or a fraulein?"

"Both," she said.

"The policy of this command is to discourage emotional involvements between troops, especially officers, and frauleins."

"Tom," Major Horter said. "This boy is going to go look

for that girl whether or not the army likes it. You want to get involved with an AWOL charge?"

"I can call him in here and scare him a little," the hospital commander said.

"He won't scare," Major Horter sad. "Not only is he a boy who thinks he's in love, but he's a real hard-nose."

"Where are you going to look for the fraulein?"

"Bad Nauheim," she said.

"OK, Flo," he said. "But for Christ's sake, remember he's got friends in high places."

"I don't think he's got a friend in the world, except maybe me and this fraulein," she said. "You're forgiven for that May and December crack, Tom."

"What the hell was I supposed to think? All of a sudden, you start acting like a . . ."

"Maybe a frustrated mother, Tom," she interrupted him. "Leave it at that."

Major Florence Horter had a brand-new 1946 Packard Clipper two-door sedan. When she drove it up the curved road to the main entrance of the 97th General Hospital, Craig Lowell was standing there waiting for her, his arm in a sling, his Ike jacket worn over his shoulder. She thought again that he looked very, very young. Maybe not thirteen anymore. But his age. Nineteen was still a boy.

She dreaded what he was likely to find in Bad Nauheim. It wasn't that she blamed the German girls for jumping into bed with these kids. Under the circumstances, that was to be expected. Sex was all they had to get by. It wasn't the first time in history that had happened, nor would it be the last.

It was just that this damn fool of a young man really believed that he had found the exception that proved the rule. That *his* fraulein had been a virgin—he'd even told her that, and he obviously believed it—and that she was different from all the others.

What he was liable to find, if he found her at all, was that she had simply substituted some other young jackass for him, and that if she was everything he said she was, she had the new jackass convinced that he had been the first and that she was in love with him. Again, she didn't blame the girl. If she was one of these German kids who had lost everything in the war, and couldn't find a job, a young American officer with a ticket in his pants to the land of the big PX would look pretty appealing to her, too.

She just didn't like to think what being forced to face facts would do to Craig Lowell. She didn't care if Lowell was a personal friend of Harry S Truman himself, the bottom line was that he was the loneliest kid she had ever met and that he was betting his entire emotional bank account on one hell of a long shot. An impossible long shot. This race had been fixed, and Lowell had a ticket on the wrong horse.

When they got to Bad Nauheim, he directed her to the outskirts of town and down a dirt road to a farmer's house. She went with him to the door. She didn't speak German, but she understood enough to understand what the farmer and his wife told him. The girl was gone, had been gone for a long time, right after he had left, and they didn't know where she had gone.

Then they went back into Bad Nauheim, to the provost marshal's office. The provost marshal Craig Lowell was looking for was long gone. No one he asked had ever heard of a fur-line called Ilse Berg. Then they drove across Bad Nauheim to one of the BOQs, and they sat in the lobby and waited until the bar opened so he could ask the bartender. The bartender was new, and he couldn't remember a fraulein with that name—hell, he never got their names—or meeting the description Lowell gave him.

"There's one more thing we can try," he said, when they were in the Packard again. "She was from Marburg. She was always trying to get me to go to Marburg, and see the house she lived in before the war. She said it was a castle."

"Haven't you had enough?" Florence Horter said. "You're kicking a dead horse."

"I want to try it," he said. "If you don't want to take me, why don't you just take me to the railroad station?"

They drove to Marburg, and put up in a transient officer's hotel right in the middle of the medieval city. A smart-ass sergeant asked them if they wanted adjoining rooms.

In the morning, a sympathetic sergeant at military government called the German police, who told him there was no

Berg family with a daughter named Ilse in Stadt, Land, or Kreis Marburg. Then he went to the military government files and came up with a 1940 city register. There were seventeen Bergs, none of them with a female child named Ilse. And there was no castle named Berg. *All* castles, or most of them, anyway, were called "Berg Something."

"Like the Administration Building for the Kreis," the MG sergeant said. "That's Schloss Greiffen*berg.*"

"Thanks a lot," Lowell said. "I really appreciate your courtesy."

"How'd you hurt your shoulder, Lieutenant?" the sergeant asked.

"You know what they say, Sergeant," Lowell said, bitterly. "It's not sex that's bad for you. It's the running after it that kills you."

They started back to Frankfurt am Main. He didn't say anything at all until they were back on the autobahn; and when she stole looks at him, she saw that he was really thinking this whole mess through. The proof came when he told her about some little Jewish lieutenant in Greece, who had not only saved his ass on the hillside, but who had given him blood later.

"He was like you, Major," Lowell said. "He had my fraulein pegged and didn't know if he should tell me or not." He put a cigar in his mouth, and lit it with the cigarette lighter. He laid his head back against the seat and blew smoke rings. He looked, for a while, as if he might cry.

"She wasn't the first girl in your life," Florence Horter said. "She won't be the last."

"As a matter of fact," he said, "she was the first. But she won't be the last." He sat up, and jammed the cigar defiantly in the corner of his mouth.

"Now, don't go off half shot, chasing every skirt in sight just to prove you're a man," Florence Horter said.

He gave her a dirty look, and she thought she was about to be told off. He had to be mad at somebody, she decided, and it might as well be her.

But he surprised her. He chuckled.

"C. Lowell," he said, raising the arm in the sling. "One-armed broad chaser." Then he cursed. He had moved the arm too far.

"Watch the sutures, damn it," Major Horter said.

"Yes, ma'am," Lowell said. "Major, sir."

When they got to Frankfurt, a little after five thirty, and saw the curved white bulk of the I. G. Farben Building looming out of the rubble, Major Florence Horter took her hand from the wheel and pointed at the building which housed Headquarters, U.S. Forces, Europe Theater.

"How would you like to buy me a steak in the O Club?"

"I would be honored, ma'am," he said.

"If you stared soulfully into my eyes," she said, "and maybe held my hand a little, it'd give everybody something to talk about."

They attracted more than a little attention when they walked into the officer's club dining room, a large, glass-walled, high-ceilinged room. For one thing, she thought, Lowell was a rather spectacular sight with his arm in a sling and his Ike jacket worn over his shoulders like a Hungarian cavalryman. Even without that, he would have attracted attention simply for being a tall, handsome, muscular young man. And finally, here he was in the company of a frumpy field-grade nurse, nearly old enough to be his mother.

He was, she saw, totally oblivious to the looks they got.

She didn't like it when he gulped down the first scotch and water, and then had two more before he even opened the menu, but then she decided that maybe he was entitled to get a little drunk; and in his condition, she didn't think it would take much booze.

It took a lot more to get him high than she thought it would, and something else surprised her. He did not, as she expected, start either to feel sorry for himself about his fraulein or to get nasty about her. He ran off at the mouth a little, but there wasn't one self-pitying word about the fraulein.

They stayed in the officer's mess until it closed at midnight, and then drove back to the 97th General Hospital compound. It was only after she had dropped him in front of the main entrance that she remembered that his pass had expired at 2400. The door would be locked, and the OD would have to let him in and take his name. She figured she could talk the OD out of writing him up, but decided the hell with it. By the time it worked its way through channels, he would have been evacuated to the States. She parked her car and went to her room.

The duty officer had taken a chance and gone to bed right after midnight; and so he was annoyed to see the young second lieutenant standing outside the locked glass doors. He gave the kid verbal hell as well as writing him up for being AWOL.

When he handed Lowell his copy of the delinquency report, Lowell asked, very politely, whether he had been born chickenshit, or whether it was something he had learned in the army. The OD snatched the delinquency report from Lowell's hand.

"You will consider yourself under arrest, Lieutenant," he said.

"Fuck you," Lowell said, cheerfully.

The OD called the sergeant of the guard, a middle-aged sergeant-technician, and told him to "escort this officer to his ward and inform the nurse on duty that he is under arrest."

"Will you come with me, please, Lieutenant?" the sergeant asked, kindly.

"Certainly." Lowell said. "Anything to oblige."

When they were out of sight of the OD, the sergeant asked him what had happened.

"That wasn't too smart, Lieutenant," the sergeant said after Lowell had told him. "But I'm glad somebody finally told that sonofabitch off."

They walked up the wide, curving stairs to the mezzanine and the bank of elevators.

The German night maintenance force—the gnomes, as they were known—were scrubbing the marble floors on their hands and knees. They made Lowell uncomfortable. There was something degrading about it. He walked quickly to the elevators to avoid looking at them.

"Craig?" a soft voice asked hesitantly, disbelieving. He paused, but didn't completely stop walking.

"Craig," the voice said. "Oh, my God, you've been hurt!"

He stopped and turned.

"Yeah, I've been hurt," he said.

"Craig!" It was a wail now, of anguish.

Ilse was kneeling, erect, but kneeling, behind a bucket. She had a scrub brush in her hand. She was wearing a shapeless black smock of some kind, and there was a faded blue rag wrapped around her head.

"I'll be a sonofabitch," Craig Lowell said, unaware he had said it.

Ilse got awkwardly to her feet, putting the scrub brush in her bucket. She wiped her hands on her dress.

"I am happy to see you again," she said. "I didn't know that you were here, or perhaps I would have asked per..."

"Oh, Jesus Christ," he said, and it came from the depths of his soul. "What are you doing with that fucking bucket?"

He ran toward her, his eyes filled with tears, and he was drunk, and he slipped on the slippery wet marble and went crashing to the floor. He got the stitches in his chest and in his shoulder, and as he felt the blood warm his skin, he thought: They won't be able to put me on that fucking air evac plane now.

Ilse screamed and a nurse came running and took one look at him and said, "You opened your goddamned stitches."

Other people came running, a wardboy, and another nurse and a doctor.

When they got him onto a wheeled cart, he reached for Ilse's hand, and held it. She looked so terrified he was afraid she would faint.

The doctor said, "What's that all about?"

"This is my girl," Lowell said.

"She can't come with you now," the doctor said. "You're bleeding like a stuck pig."

"She either comes," Lowell said, "or I will wake up everyone in the fucking hospital."

"OK, Romeo," the doctor said. "If that's the way you want it." They were rolling him down the hospital corridor now, toward the elevator. "What were those stitches put in there for, anyway?" the doctor asked.

"I was hit in Greece," Lowell said.

"Oh, you're the multiple shrapnel case," the doctor said. "I've heard all about you."

They were in some kind of an emergency room now, and they stopped the cart and Lowell looked up at Ilse, who was crying and smiling at once, and he felt a pin prick and the next thing he knew he was in the hospital bed, with Major Florence Horter looking down at him. She was still in her Class "A" uniform skirt and khaki shirt.

"You're disaster prone, you know that?" she said. "A walking accident."

"I found my girl," he said. "She was here all the time, goddamnit. Scrubbing your goddamned floors."

Major Florence Horter just nodded. She didn't trust herself to speak.

(Eight)

HEADQUARTERS

WALTER REED US ARMY HOSPITAL

Washington, D.C.

SPECIAL ORDERS   27 Sept 1946
NUMBER 265

E X T R A C T

****

41. 2ND LT LOWELL, Craig W FinC (Det Armor) 0–495302, Det of Patients, WRUSAH, is plcd on CONVALESCENT LEAVE (not chargeable as Ord Lv) for pd of thirty (30) days, and WP Home of Record, 939 Fifth Avenue, New York City NY. Off auth per diem. Off auth tvl by personal auto. TCS. TDN. Off will report as req to U.S. Army Hosp, Governor's Island, New York, NY as nec for outpatient treatment. AUTH: VO, The Surgeon General.

****

FOR THE HOSPITAL COMMANDER
James C. Brailey
Colonel, Medical Service Corps
Adjutant

Lowell rode in a taxicab from Walter Reed to the station. His right arm was still in a sling, but he could bend it and get it into the sleeves of his shirt and Ike jacket. The wound on his chest had stopped suppurating, and while there was still some suppuration from the wound on his arm near the elbow—a slimy, bloody goo—all he had to do to it was to keep putting fresh bandages on it to keep it clean. He was to exercise it every day.

He had five twenty-dollar bills, crisp new ones, in the breast pocket of his jacket. No one seemed to know where his records were, so they had given him a partial payment and told him that he could get another from the finance officer on Governors Island by showing his orders and his ID card.

He had a canvas bag from Frankfurt, bought with the partial pay Florence Horter had arranged for him at the 97th General. The bag held two changes of underwear, two khaki shirts, a razor, a tube of shaving cream, and a styptic pencil. Over the underwear and below the shirts was the Luger. The German belt and holster had simply rotted away, but he had kept the GOTT MIT UNS brass buckle. The battle jacket was in Germany. Florence Horter had said there was no point in his taking it with him, and he had agreed.

He bought his ticket, boarded the train, and went to the club car. He was disappointed that they refused to serve drinks until the train left the station. A salesman came and sat down in the opposing chair and took out his briefcase and started to use it as a desk. Lowell was relieved; he would not be expected to talk.

When the train started moving, he ordered a bottle of ale from the waiter and drank most of it down immediately. He was parched. Some soldiers got on the train in Baltimore, but none came into the club car. A great many soldiers got on the train in Trenton, and a dozen came into the club car.

Lowell thought that it was almost exactly a year before that he had gotten on the train at Trenton, Private Craig W. Lowell, ordered from the U.S. Army Replacement Training Center (Infantry), Fort Dix, N.J., to the U.S. Army Overseas Personnel Station, Camp Kilmer, with seven days' delay-en-route leave.

Like these guys, probably.

A group of four troopers obviously fresh from basic took over a four-man table and called for drinks. One of them pulled down his tie, unbuttoned his jacket, and slumped down in the chair.

It must be the ale, Lowell thought. That trooper's behavior annoys me more than I am willing to bear in silence.

He got up and walked to the table.

"Pull up your tie, button your jacket, and act like a soldier," he heard himself say.

He was met with eight hostile, scornful eyes. Nobody moved.

"I won't tell you again," Lowell said.

"Yes, *sir!*" the one with the loose tie and open jacket said. There was a snicker from one of the others. But the tie was pulled up, and the jacket buttoned.

"Thank you," Lowell said. He returned to his seat. For some reason, he was very pleased with himself, even though he couldn't imagine why he had done what he did.

The train backed into Pennsylvania Station, so that the parlor cars and the club car were close to the end of the platform. Long before he could get up and get off the train, he saw his grandfather, a tall, heavy, mustachioed man in a chesterfield and homburg, standing just outside the wrought-iron gate. A man in gray chauffeur's livery stood beside him.

When he finally managed to leave the train, and his grandfather saw him, there was a smile on his face. He took his homburg off and held it in his hand as Craig walked up.

"Well," the Old Man said, "home is the soldier, home from the wars." He put his hand out. Craig Lowell hugged him. His grandfather, he thought, was the only one in the family worth a shit.

"You don't have any luggage?" his grandfather asked, rather ceremoniously putting the homburg on his head.

"Let me have that, sir," the chauffeur said, reaching for the canvas bag from the Frankfurt PX.

"I'll carry it, thank you," Lowell said.

The car, a 1940 Packard with a body by Derham, the front seat exposed to the elements, was parked in the 33rd Street entrance to the station. A policeman, standing near it, touched his cap as they approached. Lowell's grandfather waved Craig into the car first. Inside, it smelled of leather and cigars. His grandfather leaned forward in the car and took a cigar from a box mounted beneath the glass divider.

"May I have one of those?" Craig asked.

"Yes, of course," his grandfather said. He looked indecisive for a moment, and then handed him the cigar he held. "I've already clipped it," he said. "Would you like me to light it for you?"

"Just hand me the lighted match, please," Craig said. His grandfather struck a regular kitchen match on the sole of his shoe and handed the flaming match to Craig.

"How long have you been smoking cigars?" he asked.

"Since I was ten," Craig said. "My father caught me smoking a cigarette and made me smoke a cigar, so I would get sick. But I didn't get sick; I liked it. What he did was teach me to smoke cigars, not give up smoking."

"I didn't know that," his grandfather said.

"Where are we going?" Craig asked.

"I thought we'd have some lunch," his grandfather said. "Porter wanted us to come downtown, but I thought you would be going out to Broadlawns . . ."

"Porter?"

"I thought it would be appropriate, under the circumstances, to have Porter welcome you home. It's such a trip in from the Island that I didn't think you'd want your mother to endure it."

Lowell wondered if that meant his mother was drunk again, or flying high on her pills.

"I had hoped to have a talk with you alone," Lowell said.

"I was under the impression you liked Porter."

"Porter is an asshole," Lowell said.

"You're not in the company of soldiers now," the Old Man corrected him. "Watch your language, Craig."

"You told him to come," Craig said, an accusation.

"I telephoned to tell him you had returned to this country, and he said that I should by all means bring you to lunch when you got to New York."

"What is he doing downtown?" Lowell asked.

"Working for Morgan and Company," his grandfather said. "I thought he could use the experience."

Geoffrey Craig had had two children, a son and a daughter. Porter Craig was the son of his son, now deceased, and Craig Lowell the son of his daughter. There were no other children or grandchildren.

The Packard limousine pulled to the curb before a building

just off Fifth Avenue on 43rd Street. The chauffeur ran around the front and opened the passenger door. Geoffrey Craig got out, and then turned to help Craig. They walked up a shallow flight of stairs, and the older man held open a door for his grandson.

"Good afternoon, Mr. Craig," the porter said. He went to a large board which listed the names of every member of the club and had a little sliding tag device to indicate if they were in the building.

Lowell looked up at the board and saw *Craig, Porter* below *Craig, Geoffrey.*

"Porter belongs?" he asked. The Old Man nodded.

"I thought you had to be at least sixty," Craig said.

He got a withering look from his grandfather. Porter Craig at that moment walked into the foyer of the club. He was a slightly chubby man of indeterminate age. He was actually, Craig thought, twenty-nine or thirty. He could have passed for twenty-five or forty.

"Well, hello, Craig," he said, with forced joviality. "How the hell are you, boy?" He grabbed Lowell's shoulders.

"Watch the goddamn shoulder," Lowell said.

"Sorry," Porter Craig said, jerking his hands away.

The porter appeared with a claim check.

"I'll be happy to take that bag, sir," he said.

"I'll keep it, thank you," Lowell said.

"Does Craig have to sign the guest book?" Porter Craig asked.

"I believe he does," the older man said.

"Sign it for me, then, Porter," Lowell said.

"Yes, of course."

They walked up a wide flight of stairs and took chairs around a small table.

A waiter took their drink order.

"Ordinarily, I don't," Porter Craig said. "But this is rather a celebration, isn't it?"

When the drinks were served, a scotch sour for the Old Man, a scotch and soda for Porter, and a bottle of ale for Lowell, Porter Craig raised his glass and said, "Welcome home, Craig."

"Thank you," Lowell said. He wondered what Ilse was

doing at precisely that moment. It was half past one here. It was half past six, already getting dark, in Germany.

"Granddad tells me you're going out to Broadlawns and get your strength back," Porter Craig said.

"I don't know if I am or not," Lowell said.

"Because of Pretier, you mean?" his grandfather asked. "Actually, he's rather a decent sort, Craig."

"If he can put up with Mother," Lowell said, "he's either a saint or a masochist."

"That's a remark in extraordinarily bad taste," his grandfather said.

Lowell shrugged, but made no apology.

"Your mother expects you," his grandfather said. "You're going to have to go out there."

Lowell shrugged again, this time in agreement.

"I'll go see her," he said.

Lowell finished his ale, and looked around for the waiter.

"Is that good for you?" his grandfather asked.

Lowell looked at him and raised his eyebrows.

"I'm a big boy, now," he said.

"With a chip on your shoulder," Porter Craig said.

"Porter, Craig has just gone through a terrible experience," their grandfather began, and was interrupted when another guest stumbled over the canvas bag from the PX in Frankfurt. He didn't fall down, just lurched, regained his balance, and gave the trio a dirty look.

"What in the world do you have in that bag," Porter Craig asked, "that you refuse to check it?"

"A change of underwear, a razor, and a pistol," Craig said.

"What are you doing with a pistol?" his grandfather asked.

"You'll go to jail," Porter Craig said. "Didn't you ever hear of the Sullivan Law? Pistols are illegal."

"Not for an officer, they're not," Lowell said.

"I've been curious about that," Porter Craig said. "Are you really an officer? How did you become an officer? You're only nineteen. And you didn't finish school. The last I heard, you were expelled and drafted, and the next thing, you show up in an officer's uniform . . ."

"Just who the hell do you think you are, Porter, the FBI?" Lowell asked.

"Porter's curiosity is natural," their grandfather said. "I'm more than a little curious myself."

"You have a right to be," Lowell said. "So far as I know, that temporary guardianship order is still in effect."

"And I don't?" Porter Craig asked.

"Fuck off, Porter," Craig Lowell said, conversationally. Heads turned.

"Lower your voice," the Old Man said. "Porter, under the circumstances, I think that it might best if Craig and I talked privately."

Porter Craig, red-faced, tight-lipped, got to his feet and fled from the room. He didn't even say good-bye. Grandfather and grandson locked eyes.

"I realize now that bringing him here was a mistake," the older man said.

"I've never liked that sonofabitch," Craig said. "And one of the things that came to mind when he gave me the phony dear-cousin welcome downstairs was that I no longer have to put up with his bullshit."

"You have proved that you are a man," his grandfather said. "That language is unnecessary. Please remember that you are a guest in my club. A club to which your father belonged."

"I'm sorry," Craig said, sounding genuinely contrite.

"We'll say no more about it," his grandfather said. He took a wooden match and struck it and handed it to Craig, whose cigar had gone out. "Do you like that?"

"Really good."

"I've had some put down at Dunhill's," his grandfather said. "They make them in Nicaragua, of all places. I'll have some sent out to Broadlawns, or, if you like, you can stop by on your way to the Island and pick up whatever you need. I'm taking a cab downtown, so that you can have the Packard."

"Thank you," Lowell said.

"And now, I hope, we can conduct our conversation in a civilized manner," his grandfather said. "Do you feel like telling me what has happened to you?"

"All right," Lowell said, and he told his grandfather the whole story, leaving out any reference to Ilse.

"If I didn't think it would set off a stream of obscenity," the Old Man said, when he had finished, "I would tell you that

I am not only proud of you, Craig, but happy for you. You seem, finally, to have grown up."

Lowell smiled broadly.

"Is something funny?" his grandfather asked.

"Grandpa, you just fell into the spider's web," Lowell said.

"How do you mean?"

"I want my majority," Lowell said.

"I don't quite understand."

"I want to go back to court with you, and have that temporary guardianship order revoked, and then I want another order granting me my majority."

"Would you mind explaining why?"

"It's a little embarrassing for me, as an officer and a gentleman by act of Congress, to be legally a minor child."

"We can talk about this later," his grandfather said.

"No, we're going to talk about it now," Lowell said.

"Let's get something to eat first," his grandfather said.

"Fine. We can talk while we eat," Lowell said.

They walked out of the library into the dining room and ordered.

"Even if I were willing to go along with this majority business," his grandfather said, "what makes you think the court would?"

"For one thing," Lowell said, "you seem to generally get what you're after in court. And for another, according to the law of the State of New York, one of the times maturity can be granted is when the minor child is commissioned as an officer in the armed forces."

"You've consulted an attorney, I gather?" the Old Man said, dryly, looking at the plate of Dover sole the waiter had laid before him.

"I've asked one a couple of questions," Lowell said.

"The only possible motivation I can come up with is that you have the misguided notion you're qualified to manage your financial affairs, that you want your trust fund now."

"I didn't say that," Lowell said. "I don't know the first goddamned thing about money. I don't give a damn about managing the trust fund. I want some money from it, say another thousand a month, but that's all."

"They're making available a thousand a month now, aren't

they?" Lowell nodded. "And that's not enough?"

"I told you, Grandpa, I'm a big boy now. I don't need you or anyone else telling me how much money I need."

"And," the Old Man said, sharply, "if I don't think it's wise to go along with this idea of yours?"

"Then I'll just have to find some hungry shyster lawyer," Lowell said.

They locked eyes again. Finally, his grandfather snorted.

"And I think you'd do that," he said. "Let me understand what you're asking. You want your majority. You want an income of two thousand a month from the fund. Actually, it's funds, plural. And you will permit me to retain the management of the funds?"

"I'd be grateful to you if you would," Lowell said.

"You'd put that in writing, of course?"

"I'm prepared to trust you, as one gentleman to another," Lowell said, smiling at his grandfather. "But if you insist on having it in writing..."

"By God, you have grown up," his grandfather said, smiling back at him. "I'll have it in writing, though, since you don't mind."

"If you can't trust your own grandfather, who can you trust?" Lowell asked, in mock innocence. The Old Man laughed.

"It's a pleasure doing business with you, sir," he said, and laughed. Then he said: "It will take a couple of weeks. I'll look into it."

"All it takes is for us to show up the judge's chambers. I want it done this week," Lowell said.

There was one more locking of eyes. Then his grandfather shrugged his shoulders.

"If it's that important to you," he said, "I'll start the wheels rolling as soon as I get to the office."

Lowell thought that this confrontation between them was very different from their last. At that time, when an appeal to emotion had failed to achieve the desired result, the Old Man had resorted to shouts, arm-waving, and a threat that Lowell had known was empty (he'd seen his father's will) to cut him off without a dime. He would not be the only young man who had ever thrown away the advantages to which he had been born to die in the gutter, his grandfather had shouted.

Obviously the Old Man wanted something this time. What it was came out over the Brie and crackers with which they ended their meal. His grandfather told him that Andre Pretier was good for Craig's mother. She was off the bottle, he reported with surprising candor. She wasn't on pills. There had been few "incidents," and he wanted it kept that way. The way the Old Man put it, Lowell thought, it had been rather ungentlemanly of him to have caused the notification team to go to the apartment on Fifth Avenue and upset his mother.

The limousine was waiting for them at the curb when they went back out onto 43rd Street. Lowell had always wondered how the chauffeurs managed it, considering the traffic and the other limousines that had passengers at the same place.

"I can get a cab out to the Island," Craig said.

"Nonsense," his grandfather said. "Besides, you're going to stop at Dunhill's and get cigars."

"I would hate to have anything get in the way of your little chat with your legal counsel, Grandfather."

The Old Man chuckled. Then, seeing a cab, he put his fingers in his mouth and gave out with a whistle that pierced the noise and bustle of midtown Manhattan. The cab pulled to the curb, and his grandfather got in.

Then Lowell got into the limousine.

"Dunhill's and then Broadlawns, is it, sir?" the chauffeur asked.

Three weeks ago today, Lowell thought, I was living in a sandbagged hut in the mountains of Greece.

And three weeks ago today, Little Craig nearly got his little ass blown away.

"Please," he said to the chauffeur, and then reached for another of his grandfather's cigars.

(Nine)

Gardeners were at work wrapping the shrubbery in anticipation of the first frost when the Packard rolled through the gates of Broadlawns. The house itself was not visible from the road. He didn't see anybody in the gate house, but there must have been someone there, for his mother was standing on the veranda in front of the long, rambling, two-story brick house when they got there. Obviously expecting him. With a tall, rather elegant man standing beside her.

Andre Pretier. His mother's husband. Well, if she had to buy a husband, she had bought a good-looking one, a gentlemanly type.

When the chauffeur had to help him out of the car, his mother put her hand to her mouth. Her hair was solid gray, worn short. She had a ragged cashmere sweater over her shoulders.

"Oh, darling!" she said, when he walked up to her. "Are you all right?" She gave him her cheek to kiss. He remembered the smell of her perfume.

"Is that the best you can do?" she asked.

He embraced his mother somewhat gingerly. She had been drinking—he could smell the gin—but she was not drunk, and that was an improvement. She looked healthier, too.

"And this is Andre," she said.

Pretier gave him his hand.

"Welcome home, Craig," he said. "I hope that we can be real friends. I'd really like that."

"Thank you," Craig said.

"Let's get inside before we catch a cold," Craig's mother said.

A tall, light brown butler stood inside the door.

"Welcome home, sir," he said. "May I take your bag?"

"Thank you," Lowell said.

"I expect Craig would like a drink," Pretier said. "Come on in here," he said, gesturing toward the sitting room. "We've had a fire laid. First of the year. I always like a fire, don't you?"

Very handy, Lowell thought, to warm your shaving water.

The butler wheeled up a cart.

"What will you have to drink?" Pretier asked him.

"Ale, please," Lowell said.

"I don't believe we have any ale, sir," the butler said.

"We'll have to have some in the future," Andre Pretier ordered.

"Scotch and soda, please," Craig said.

"We have your little jeep," his mother said. "Andre went to Brooklyn and picked it up for you himself. That and your trunks."

"That was very nice of you," Craig said to Andre Pretier. "Thank you very much."

"I was happy to do it," Andre Pretier said. "I want you to feel welcome here, Craig."

"Thank you," Lowell said again, taking the drink from the butler.

He didn't recognize any of the servants. When she had been at the sauce, or on the pills, or both, she had run off a lot of servants. These were West Indians, blacks who spoke a British-accented English.

Lowell wondered if Andre Pretier knew that he wanted Craig to feel welcome in his own house. Lowell's father's will had given his mother use of the house for her lifetime, or until she remarried, whereupon it would pass to the Aforementioned Trust for the Benefit of Craig W. Lowell, together with all furnishings. She had married Pretier, and now all this was his.

"Well," Andre Pretier said. "As the Spanish say, my house is your house."

Craig looked at him, wondering if he meant what he was saying, and if so, why he had brought it up the moment he had walked in.

"You just let us know what you want, and we'll do our best to provide it," Pretier went on. "If you'd like to just lie about and do nothing, or if you'd rather get together with your friends, a party or a dinner or whatever, just speak up."

"We want you to be happy, dear," his mother said. "We're so glad to have you back after your accident." He was looking at Pretier when she said that, and Pretier winked at him. The message was clear. Let her think you had an accident.

"Thank you," Craig said.

"Did Grandpa give you lunch?" his mother asked.

"Yes," Craig said.

"Would you like something to eat now? A sandwich and a glass of milk?"

"No, thank you."

"Would you like a cigarette, Craig?"

"I'd like a cigar," he said. "Grandpa got some for me, from the humidor at Dunhill's."

"Oh, I'm afraid my baby is gone for all time," his mother said brightly. "Smoking cigars."

"We kept the boat, the power boat, in the water," Andre

Pretier said. "I thought you might feel up to using it. Some of the days are really quite warm."

"What boat?"

"My boat," Andre Pretier said. "I had her brought down from Bar Harbor."

"That would be very nice," Craig said.

"I've become quite the sailor," his mother said. "Haven't I, darling?"

"Yes, my darling, you have," Andre Pretier said.

When the butler handed him his scotch and soda, Craig said, "There was a package of cigars from Dunhill's in the car. Would you get me a box, please?"

"I've sent someone for them, sir," the butler said.

"I hope you're not smoking too many of them," his mother said.

"I understand that they're supposed to be better for you than cigarettes," Andre Pretier said.

"Don't be silly, darling," his mother said. "How could they be?"

Andre Pretier did not press the point.

"I don't mean to cast a pall on your welcome, Craig," he said, "but what are the arrangements for medical treatment?"

"I'm going to go into New York," Craig said. "To Governors Island. Tomorrow."

"Do you have to?" his mother asked. "There are perfectly good doctors we can call here."

"Craig is a soldier, darling," Andre Pretier said. "Soldiers do what they're ordered to do." He smiled at Craig. "I'll tell the chauffeur," he said. "Have him stand by, so to speak."

"You know, even with him sitting there in his soldier suit," his mother said, "I really can't believe that he is a soldier." She smiled at her son. "Do you have to wear it all the time?"

"No," he said. "As a matter of fact, I'd like to change out of it right now."

"I'm sure you would," she said. "But finish your drink, first."

The butler held out an open box of cigars to Craig. After he had taken one, the box was placed on the coffee table. Andre Pretier bent over him and held out a match.

"That's vulgar, darling," his mother said, when he bit the

end off and spat it out. "Grandpa has a little knife he uses. If you're going to smoke cigars, you really should get one of those little knives."

"They call them cutters, I think," Andre Pretier said.

"You should have gotten one when you were at Dunhill's," his mother said. "Why didn't you think of it?"

Craig drained his drink.

"I think I'll change clothing," he said. "Will you excuse me?"

"We've put your things in your old room, darling. Remember?" his mother said.

"Yes, of course," he said.

He walked up the thickly carpeted stairway to the second floor, and down a wide corridor toward his old room, actually two rooms, at the end of it. A maid was vacuuming the carpet. She shut the machine off and smiled at him shyly until he passed. He had a mental image of Ilse kneeling by her scrub bucket in the 97th General Hospital.

He went into the bedroom of the small suite and took the sling off very carefully. Then he took off his jacket and his necktie and his shirt and pulled off his T-shirt. The shirt stuck to dried whateveritwas leaking from the bandage at his elbow.

He rang for a servant.

The butler came right away. Craig told him to bring bandages and gauze and Mercurochrome.

When the butler came back, Andre Pretier was with him.

"Your mother thought I might be able to help," he said. When he saw the bandages, he said, "I'd rather your mother didn't see that."

"Me, too," Lowell said. He pulled the adhesive tape loose and held his arm out for the butler to rebandage.

"They said that if there was suppuration, they would probably keep me in the hospital on Governors Island for a couple of days," Craig said. "How do you want to handle that?"

"Why don't you just say you're spending a couple of days with friends?" Andre Pretier said. "That way she won't worry."

"Why don't you tell her I called and said that?" Craig said.

"I think that would be best," Andre Pretier said. "And now I'll go down and tell her that Kenneth is perfectly capable of helping you."

When Pretier had gone, Craig asked Kenneth to pack a bag for him, enough clothing for a week or ten days, one uniform, the rest civilian clothing, and to put it into the car he would be using in the morning.

He had breakfast alone the next morning. The Master and Madame, Kenneth told him, seldom rose before ten; and then they had breakfast in their room. After he had breakfast, he walked out the front door where the chauffeur was waiting, holding open the rear door of an ornately sculptured automobile Craig didn't recognize.

"What is this thing, anyway?" Craig asked.

"It is a Delahaye with a body by Fortin," the chauffeur said. "It is Mr. Pretier's automobile."

"Very nice," Craig said. "Have you been with Mr. Pretier long?"

"Oh, yes, sir."

Well, that seemed to confirm it. Pretier had money of his own. He had not married Craig's mother for her money. He wondered why he had married her.

"I want to go to the Morgan Guaranty Trust on 53rd Street first," Craig said. "And then to the Federal Building."

"And then to Governors Island, sir?"

"No. After the Federal Building, we're going to Newark," Craig said.

(Ten)

In Newark, after they'd driven past the Old Warsaw Bakery on the corner of Chancellor Avenue and Aldine Street and he knew he'd found what he was looking for, he told the chauffeur to drop him at the corner and that he wouldn't need him anymore.

There was a line of people waiting to buy bread and rolls; and two pictures of the Mouse were over the cash register, one in his cadet uniform, one in pinks and greens. Two little American flags were crossed proudly above them.

He set his bag down on the tile floor and after a moment sat on it. He waited there for about five minutes until the line went down. Then the slight, pleasant-faced, shy-appearing woman with her black hair in a bun, dressed in a too-large white baker's smock saw him for the first time.

She looked at him very strangely, and then she came from behind the glass display cases and walked up to him. He stood up.

"Craig?" she asked.

"Sharon?"

Sharon Lavinsky Felter stood on her tiptoes and kissed Craig Lowell on the cheek.

"Sandy wrote you'd come," she said. "I'm so glad you did."

A couch in Felter's flat over the bakery opened up into a double bed, and he slept in that.

Three days later, he took a cab from the Felters' flat back into New York, although Mr. Felter had offered to drive him anywhere in the world he wanted to go.

He met his grandfather at the Borough of Manhattan Court House, where a judge took about five minutes to declare him an adult in the eyes of the law. Next he went to the Federal Building and picked up his passport, then to LaGuardia Airport where he caught Trans-World Airlines Flight 307, a Lockheed Constellation, New York–Paris, with a stopover at Gander Field, Newfoundland.

He told the captain in the embassy in Paris who handled entry permits for the American Zone of Occupied Germany that he was a student who wished to visit his aunt, Major Florence Horter, at the 97th General Hospital in Frankfurt. The captain telephoned Major Horter to verify his story. She met him at the Hauptbahnhof in Frankfurt. She was alone.

"I wasn't sure that you were going to get away with this," she said. "And I didn't want Ilse to get upset."

"I said I'd be back in about a month," he said. "It's twenty-six days. I'm back. And anyway, Ilse's pretty tough."

"Ilse's four months' pregnant," Major Horter said. "Chew on that for a while, Sonny boy."

(Eleven)

Craig W. Lowell and Ilse von Greiffenberg were married by the pastor of St. Luke's Protestant (Lutheran) Church in Frankfurt am Main, with Major Florence Horter as their only attendant.

The pastor had mixed feelings about the whole thing. For one thing, the groom's great good spirits were at least partially inspired by alcohol. The bride was obviously pregnant. He had serious doubts if they had considered all the ramifications of marriage, temporal and spiritual.

But they seemed to be in love; and at least the American was trying to do the right thing. There were literally thousands of girls bearing the children of American soldiers who would not marry them.

After the wedding, the newly married couple went to Oberursel. There after a long and frustrating search, Ilse and Major Horter had found a small, but clean, apartment where Ilse would wait until her immigration papers were processed. The groom undressed, and Major Horter changed his dressings while the bride looked on, making little noises of sympathy.

Then Major Horter left the couple with her wedding gift to them, three bottles of Moët champagne, and a book, *So You're Going To Have a Baby?*

Before she left, Major Horter and Lieutenant Lowell went shopping in the Frankfurt post exchange for all the things Ilse would need while she waited to go to America. Ilse was a German national, and German nationals were prohibited by regulation from entering post exchanges. She waited in the car, nervously twisting the four-carat diamond ring on her finger. She knew it couldn't be real—where would Craig get that kind of money?—but she thought that it was beautiful anyway.

IX

(One)
Student Officer Company
The United States Armor School ☞
Fort Knox, Kentucky
30 October 1946

Student Officer Company, The Armor School (SOC-TAS) was a collection of two-story wooden barracks painted yellowish white with green shingled roofs. They were spread out to conform to the contours of the low hill on which they had been built, and were generally centered around a two-story administrative building and a single-story orderly room. The latter was two standard orderly rooms built together. A standard mess hall capable of seating 750 troops had been converted to form slightly more luxurious dining facilities for officers (instead of twelve-man plank tables, there were four-man tables covered with oilcloth). It was placed on the edge of the cluster of buildings overlooking the classroom buildings built on the flat land below.

Each of the student BOQs was identical. They were slightly longer than standard enlisted barracks. There were six suites

319

on each side of a corridor running down the center of the buildings. Each suite contained two bedrooms, each furnished with an iron bed, a chest of drawers, a desk, a straight-backed chair, and an armchair. A bath, consisting of a water closet, a double sink, and a tin-walled and concrete-floored shower, connected the two rooms of each suite. In each barrack, one of the two-room suites had been set aside for use as a "recreation room," which was a euphemism for bar.

Having been assigned to Room 16-A of Building T-455, Second Lieutenant Craig W. Lowell lifted his luggage—a canvas Valv-Pak and a nearly new leather suitcase, stamped with his father's initials—from the back seat of a Chevrolet sedan. He found Building T-455 and then, on the second floor, Room 16-A. He had some trouble making his key operate the lock on the door, but he finally managed to get it open. He walked into the room and looked around at the bed, the desk, and the armchair. He tossed the suitcases on the bed, and one by one unpacked them. He hung the uniform and the civilian clothing in the doorless closet, and then put his shirts and his linen in the chest of drawers. When the suitcases were empty, he put the suitcases in the closet.

He opened the door, found the bath, urinated, and then, after a moment's hesitation, knocked on the door opening to the other room.

"Come!" a deep voice called.

He stepped inside, smiling. He was surprised to see a very large, very black man lying on the iron bed, dressed only in a pair of white jockey shorts.

"Surprise, surprise!" the black man said to him. When Lowell didn't reply, he added, "You're not in the wrong place, white boy; but then, neither am I."

"My name is Craig Lowell," Lowell said.

"And I know what you're thinking, Craig Lowell," the black man said to him.

"Do you?"

"Hell, they put me in with a dinge!" the black man said.

"What I was actually thinking was that you're the biggest coon I've ever seen," Lowell said. "Excuse me, black boy." He pulled the door closed and went back through his room and outside. He got back in the Chevrolet and went to the PX and

bought a Zenith Transoceanic portable radio to replace the one
that had gotten blown away at No. 12 Company. That accomplished, he went through the PX scooping up things he thought
he would need, from shaving cream to shoe polish to half a
dozen paperbacks from the newsstand rack. He put everything
in the car and then found the liquor store. He bought scotch
and gin and vermouth and asked for ale, but there was none.
Then he went back to the PX and bought a carton labeled, "A
complete set of household glassware," and put it in the car.
Finally, he drove back to Room 16-A of Building T-455.

He put away the things he had bought, unpacked his complete collection of glasses, rinsed out one, and poured scotch
into it. There was probably ice around somewhere, he thought,
but he decided against going to look for it. He had grown used
to iceless whiskey in Greece. He diluted it with water from the
bathroom and then unpacked the Zenith from its box. He put
the empty glass carton and the empty radio carton in the hall
and pulled the desk across the floor next to the bed, so he could
put the radio on it. Then he plugged it in, went through the
broadcast band, found nothing he liked, and finally got some
classical music, fuzzy, with static, but listenable, on the 20-
meter band. He lay down on the bed and picked up one of the
paperbacks.

There was a knock at the bathroom door.

"Come," Lowell called.

The black man, still in his underwear, stepped inside the
room.

"You aren't the biggest white boy I've ever seen," he said.
"But you're not actually a midget, yourself." Lowell said nothing.

"Phil Parker," the black man said.

"Hello," Lowell said.

"I thought you went to ask for alternate accommodations,"
Parker said.

"I went to get booze," Lowell said. "You want scotch or
gin, help yourself."

"Thank you," Parker said. He poured scotch in a glass.
"You always drink it without ice?"

"I do when I don't have any ice," Lowell replied.

Parker picked up the pitcher which came with the complete

set of household glassware and walked out of the room. When he returned the pitcher was full of ice.

"You are a man of many talents, Phil Parker," Lowell said, holding up his glass. "Where did you get the ice?"

"There's a rec room, read bar, down the hall," Parker said, dropping two cubes into Lowell's glass. He met Lowell's eyes. "I would have gone to the Class Six myself, except I thought common decency required that I stick around until someone moved in here. In case, for some reason, having seen me, he might want to move out."

"You want to go half on a refrigerator?" Lowell asked. "I don't want to keep running down the hall for ice like a bellboy, and I do like a cold beer sometimes."

Parker looked at Lowell for a moment before replying. The easiest thing to do was take him at face value as a man who wasn't a bigot. But he had been down that road before. A belief in racial equality sometimes was a fragile thing in the face of peer pressure.

He decided to take a chance. There was something special about this guy.

"There's something you should know about me," Parker said. "Before we become bosom buddies."

"What's that?"

"I'm going to be the honor graduate of this course," Parker said.

"Why in the world would you want to do something like that?" Lowell replied, astonished.

"I'm dead serious, Lowell," Parker said. "That's what you do, if you're colored, and a regular army officer," Parker said. "You do better than the white guys, just to stay even with them."

"Regular army? Funny, you don't look stupid."

"Actually, I'm a near genius," Parker said. "But it may be necessary for me to study at night once in a while. I become violent when someone disturbs me when I am studying. I thought you should be forewarned."

"Do you know where we could buy a refrigerator?" Lowell asked. "The PX?"

"That's not the way it's done," Parker said.

"It's not?"

"Give me a minute to clothe my magnificent ebony body," Parker said. "And I will show you how an old soldier does it."

When Parker returned, he was in fatigues. They had been tailored to fit his body and were stiffly starched. They were not anywhere near new. His boots were highly polished. His insignia and his brass buckle gleamed. He looked, Lowell thought, as if he were ready to stand inspection. Then he changed his mind. He looked as if he were accustomed to wearing a uniform. He thought it was likely that Parker (it was hard to tell how old he was) was a former enlisted man, a career sergeant who had gone to OCS. That would explain both the old soldier's appearance, and his announced intention to be the honor graduate. Lowell thought of Nick.

He was convinced of the accuracy of his assessment of Lieutenant Parker both by Parker's car, a gleaming 1941 Cadillac sedan with a Fort Riley auto safety inspection decal on the windshield, and by what happened next. Parker drove them to the Class Six, the liquor store, where he bought scotch and gin and vermouth, and two bottles of good bourbon. In the car, he made Lowell pay for one of the bottles of bourbon.

Then they drove to the Post Quartermaster Household Goods Warehouse. Parker found the small office used by the noncom in charge of the warehouse.

"Can I help you, Lieutenant?" the sergeant asked.

"I hope so, Sergeant," Parker said to him, closing the office door and setting the two bottles of bourbon in their brown paper bags on the sergeant's desk. "I have a small problem."

"What would that be, Lieutenant?" the sergeant asked, pulling the paper bags down to see what kind of liquor they contained.

"My roommate here has an unusual medical condition," Parker said. "Unless he has a cold beer when he wakes up in the morning, he suffers from melancholy all day."

"I've heard about that disease," the sergeant said.

"So I thought, in the interests of the health of the junior officers, you might be able to see your way clear to issue him a means to keep his beer cool."

"I think something might be worked out, Lieutenant," the sergeant said. He slid the bottles of bourbon off the desk top and into a drawer. "You got wheels?"

They drove back to the Student Officer Company with a refrigerator precariously balanced in the open trunk of the Cadillac. They carried it upstairs to Parker's room.

"I don't think I will be having many visitors," Parker said. "And that means no one will see this refrigerator. If no one sees it, no one will ask any questions, such as, 'How come that lieutenant has got a refrigerator, and I don't?'"

Lowell chuckled. "What were you, Parker, before you were commissioned?"

Parker looked at him, as if surprised by the question.

"If you must know, I was cadet major," he said.

"West Point?" Lowell asked, in surprise.

"Bite your tongue!" Parker said. "Norwich."

"Norwich?"

"You've never heard of it," Parker said flatly. "I'm not surprised. But to widen your education, Norwich for a hundred years has provided the army with the bulk of its brighter cavalry, and now armor, officers."

"I've never heard of it," Lowell repeated.

"It is not, Lowell, what you're thinking," Parker said.

"What am I thinking?"

"It is not a Mechanical and Agricultural College for Negroes with an ROTC program," Parker said. "I was the only colored guy in my graduating class."

"Where is it?"

"Vermont," Parker said. "And where did you go to school? Yale?"

"Harvard."

"How come you're not artillery? I thought Harvard had artillery ROTC."

"I'm not ROTC," Lowell said.

"There is no way a slob like you could have gotten through OCS," Parker said.

"I was directly commissioned," Lowell said.

"What kind of an expert are you?" Parker asked.

"I know how to play polo," Lowell said.

"So why aren't you playing polo?" Parker asked. He didn't seem at all surprised at Lowell's announcement.

"The general I was playing for dropped dead," Lowell said.

"Waterford?" Parker said. "I heard about that. My father

and Waterford were pretty good friends."

"Your father was in the army?"

"Mah daddy, and mah gran'daddy, and mah gran'*daddy's* daddy," Parker said, in a mock Negro accent. "White boy, you now runnin' around with a bona fide member of the army establishment, Afro-American division."

"What the hell are you talking about?"

"If you don't know, then I can't explain it to you."

"Try."

"My antecedents have been slurping around in the army trough since, right after the Civil War, they chased the Indians around the plains. They used to call them the 'Buffalo Soldiers,'" Parker said. "My father and my grandfather retired as colonels. My great-grandfather was a master sergeant."

"I'm awed," Lowell said.

"So after fucking around with you for a while, wondering what to do with you, they decided to send you to Basic Officer's Course?"

"Yeah."

"Well, under my expert tutelage, Lieutenant," Parker said, "you may just be able to get through."

There was no overt act of racial discrimination from the first day. The 116 white second lieutenants in Basic Armor Officer's Course 46–3 simply ignored the five black, two Puerto Rican, six Filipino, and three Argentinian officers. And Lowell, the white one who lived with the big coon.

On his part, Parker ignored the four second lieutenants who were black, the Puerto Ricans, and three of the six Filipinos, the three who had gone to West Point. The other three he tolerated. The Argentinians stuck to themselves, eventually moving out of the BOQ entirely to rent an apartment in Elizabethtown, where many of the married second lieutenants also lived.

It was a week before Phil Parker saw Lowell without his T-shirt, and thus the scars, which resembled angry red zippers running up his chest and over his shoulder.

"What the hell happened to you?"

"I walked into a fan," Lowell replied.

"The hell you say," Parker replied.

(Two)

The day after Parker saw Lowell's fascinating and unexplained scars, Parker learned that Lowell was married, and to a German girl, and shocking him far more, that Lowell's Chevrolet was the Hertz rent-a-car he had picked up at the airport on his way to Fort Knox and simply kept.

It was a Saturday morning, and when Parker went into Lowell's room to wake him for breakfast, Lowell wasn't there. On the way to the mess hall, Parker saw the Chevrolet parked outside a building housing a dozen pay booths for the use of enlisted men undergoing basic training.

When he looked in the car, to make sure it was Lowell's (there was no question about that; Lowell's helmet liner and several of his books were on the back seat), he came across the rental documents from Hertz.

He went in the telephone building and found Lowell sitting on a couch, waiting for something.

."I'm calling my wife," Lowell volunteered when Parker crashed into the seat beside him.

"Why don't you call her collect from the phone in the BOQ?"

"She's in Germany," Lowell said, and while they waited for the international call to be completed, Lowell told him about Ilse.

"Hey, if there's anything I can do," Parker said, "like a little money for a plane ticket, or something. Just speak up. Unscrew your left arm at the elbow and the Friendly Phil Parker Small Loan Company will leap to aid you."

"Money's not the problem," Lowell said. "It's the fucking Immigration Service. They're waiting for the CIC to clear her. They have to be sure she wasn't a Nazi. For Christ's sake, she was sixteen when the war was over." He looked up at Parker. "But thanks, Phil. I appreciate that." There was such gratitude in Lowell's voice, in the look in his eyes, that Parker was embarrassed. He changed the subject.

(Three)

Craig Lowell was sitting on his bed dressed in his shorts with his back up against the headboard. He had a glass of scotch whiskey in his hand, a large black cigar in his mouth, and a copy of *The Infantry Company in the Defense* in his lap. He was no longer as awed by the manual as he had once been, and he had just concluded that if some unsuspecting neophyte placed his air-cooled .30s where the book said they should be placed "for optimum efficiency," he was going to get his ass rolled over the first time he faced an enemy equipped with grenade launchers. At that moment there was a knock at the door.

"Come!" he called.

"Are you decent?" a female voice called.

"I am neither decent nor clothed," he called back. "There is a difference. Wait a minute."

He got out of bed and went to the closet and wrapped himself in a silk dressing gown. Like the luggage, it had belonged to his father, and he had helped himself to it when he returned from Germany and spent his last two days of leave at Broadlawns. He had heard the female outside giggle at his remark, and that pleased him.

He had wondered what King Kong was doing about his sex life, and now he was about to find out.

When he pulled the door open, he was facing an attractive woman in her late twenties or early thirties. She was white, and that surprised him.

"Yes, ma'am?" he said.

"I'm Barbara Bellmon," she said. "I'm looking for Phil Parker."

She was wearing a wedding ring. What was a respectable-looking, even wholesome-looking, married white woman knocking on King Kong's door for? Whatever it was, it was none of his business.

"I'm sorry," he said. "Phil went over to the library. He should be back in an hour, or maybe longer."

"Oh, damn," she said. "Look, I'm an old friend of his. Could you give him a message for me?"

"Certainly."

"Message is simple and classified Top Secret," she said. "Message follows. Bob gets his silver leaf back effective Saturday. Party at the house at 1830. Appearance mandatory."

"Got it," Lowell said. "I'll tell him as soon as he gets back."

"Translated, that means my husband got promoted and I found out before he did," she said.

"How would one offer congratulations under those circumstances?"

"Very simply," she said. "Come to the party with Phil."

"You say you're an old friend of Phil's?"

"I used to baby-sit for him when he was in diapers," she said. "And his father and my husband are very close."

"That would be Colonel Parker," Lowell said, trying to put it all together.

"Colonel Parker and, as of Saturday, *Lt. Col.* Bellmon," she said. "We're all old friends."

"How nice for you," Lowell said.

"I didn't get your name," she said.

"Lowell," he said. "Craig Lowell."

"Well, Craig Lowell, you just tag along with Phil on Saturday night. All you can eat, and more important, all you can drink."

"That's very kind, but I'll be out of town," he said.

"Some other time, then," she said.

At the prescribed hour, Second Lieutenant Philip Sheridan Parker IV presented himself at the quarters of Bob and Barbara Bellmon, a small frame house near the main post, above which a large sign read: "Second-Chance Bellmon's Party."

Barbara Bellmon saw him first, and kissed him on the cheek.

"My, how you've grown, Little Philip," she said.

"And you're a colonel's lady now, again, and not supposed to go around kissing second johns before God and the world," he said.

"Where's John Barrymore?" she asked.

"Who?"

"Your roommate, the one with the silk dressing gown, Harvard accent, and stinking cigar."

"Lowell," Phil Parker said, grinning at the thought of an encounter between Barbara Bellmon and Lowell. "That's right, you met him, didn't you?"

"I invited him to the party."

"He didn't say anything to me," Parker replied.

"Strange man," she said. "Most second lieutenants jump at a chance of free booze."

"He's strange, but he's a good guy, Barbara," Parker said. "He's got money, I think."

"Doing his two years?"

"If he has to serve that long," Parker said.

Bob Bellmon saw him then.

"Jesus Christ, look at this! The last time I saw it, it wasn't an inch over six feet."

"Congratulations, Colonel," Parker said.

"I've been waiting for you," Bellmon said. "We're going to call your old man. If it wasn't for your old man, I wouldn't be here." He grabbed Phil's arm and led him into the crowded living room and to the telephone, and they placed a call to Colonel Philip Sheridan Parker III, Retired, in Manhattan, Kansas, and the name of Craig Lowell didn't come up again.

(Four)

The next Saturday, very early in the morning, Lieutenant Phil Parker was introduced to Ilse Lowell on the telephone. Later, over breakfast in the main post cafeteria, Lowell asked Parker if he had any plans, or whether he would be free to go to Louisville with him.

"What's in Louisville?"

"I've been thinking over what you said about getting a car."

"Perhaps you are not then quite as dense as the evidence suggests," Parker said. "You want to go look at cars?"

"No, I want to buy one," Lowell replied, as if the question was a strange one.

"What kind of car?"

"A Packard."

"A Packard? Packards are driven by movie stars and uppity niggers," Parker said.

"Somebody in Bad Nauheim had a Packard," he said. "A convertible. Ilse said it was the most beautiful automobile she had ever seen."

"Obviously the lady has taste," Parker said. "But have you got the pocketbook to support it?"

"Yeah, Phil," Lowell said, "as a matter of fact, I do."

They went into Louisville in uniform, because Parker had been informed that the Brown Hotel would serve colored officers in uniform. They dropped off the rental car at the airport, had lunch with several drinks in the Brown Hotel, and then went to the Packard dealership on Fourth Street.

The salesman on duty, fully aware that the basic pay of second lieutenants was just over $310 a month, didn't even bother to pitch the two young officers. They had obviously come in solely to gape the Rollson-bodied 1941 convertible on the showroom floor. They certainly couldn't afford a car like that; but on the other hand, they were officers, even if one of them was a nigger, and were unlikely to get the seats dirty or do something else to harm the car.

The 180 convertible had been turned in three months before on a new Packard Clipper by the proverbial Little Old Lady. It had been up on blocks during all of World War II, and there was only a little over 9,000 miles on the clock.

The sales manager had decided to hang on to it to draw customers into the showroom. They weren't making cars like that anymore, and Packard wasn't even going to have a convertible in the line until next year's lineup. The sales manager hung a $6,500 price on it, which was about a thousand more than the car had cost when it was new. He would take a chance, he said, that someone would walk in with more money than brains and pay it. If no one bought it for, say, three or four months, then he would decide what to do with it. In the meantime, it would draw potential customers to the showroom floor.

It was an enormous automobile, built on a 138-inch wheelbase, and was bright yellow, with the Packard stylized swan in chrome sitting on top of a massive grill. The headlights were separate, and the front fenders held spare tires.

The two young soldiers examined the car from front to rear for about three minutes, and then the white one walked over to where the salesman sat in an armchair.

"Can I help you?"

"I just might be interested in that," the white kid said.

"That's $6,500," the salesman said.

"I'll give you six even," the kid said.

"Have you got any idea what the payments would be?" the salesman said. "We'd need a third down, that's more than two thousand, and . . ."

"I'll give you a check for six thousand," the young lieutenant said, interrupting him.

He seemed perfectly serious. Since the sales manager normally didn't come in on Saturdays, the salesman called him at the golf course and told him he had a soldier from Fort Knox who was prepared to write a check right then for six grand for the convertible.

The check he offered was on the Morgan Guaranty Trust of New York. The price was all right, but there was a large question about a second lieutenant having enough cash in his checking account to cover the check. It was finally decided to accept his offer, and to tell him that the car would have to be "gotten ready" and unfortunately there was no one around on Saturday to do that. They would be happy to deliver the car out to Fort Knox on Monday after it had been "gotten ready." That would also give them a chance to call the Morgan Guaranty Trust and see if the check was any good, or whether, as the sales manager half suspected, it was just one more crazy soldier boy from Fort Knox just fucking around with half a load on.

The car was delivered Monday afternoon. It was waiting for Parker and Lowell when they came back to the BOQ to find the academic standings for the first two weeks of the course posted on the BOQ bulletin board.

Parker, Philip S IV was first, with an average of 98.7.

Lowell, Craig W was third, with an average of 97.9.

Parker was delighted. Lowell was amused. He understood why he was getting such good grades. For one thing, the course material was rather simple. It was, in effect, a basic training course for officers upon first entering the army. Lowell had had enlisted basic training, and for all intents and purposes he had been running a company in Greece. Parker had gone to Norwich, a military college. And they had studied, not very hard, nor very long, but apparently long enough and hard enough to be able to beat the tests.

They had a couple of drinks to celebrate and then decided to get a steak at the main post officer's club to "test" the yellow Packard convertible. They put the roof down, and snapped the boot in place, and then, for a joke, Parker insisted on riding in the back seat.

They were both astonished at how often and how snappily they were saluted. Not only by enlisted men, the only people required by military custom to salute second lieutenants, but by officers as well, even one full bird colonel.

It was obviously the car, they decided over their drinks and steaks; and they were correct but not in the way they thought.

Two weeks after the convertible was delivered, Lowell ran into Captain Rudolph G. MacMillan at the Class Six store.

Lowell was coming out of the store with his arms full of booze and ale. There was no way he could salute.

"Hello, Captain MacMillan," he said.

"I'll be damned," MacMillan said. "What the hell are you doing here?" He turned and followed Lowell into the parking lot. The Packard was parked next to a Ford coupe. MacMillan opened the door of the coupe, so that Lowell could unload his whiskey and beer. Lowell put the whiskey and beer in the Packard. He didn't have to have the door opened, for the top and windows were down.

"I don't know why I'm surprised, but I am," MacMillan said, when he realized his error. "That's the sort of thing I should have expected from you, rich boy."

"It's nice to see you, too, Captain," Lowell said.

"Why aren't you in Greece?" MacMillan asked.

"The real question, Captain, sir, is why am I still in the army. Do you remember telling me, sir, that you'd get me out of the service?"

"You know what happened," MacMillan said. "I asked you how come you're not in Greece?"

"I didn't like it there," Lowell said. "People were shooting at me."

"And so you pulled some strings and got out?"

"That sums it up neatly, sir," Lowell said.

"You're in Basic Officer's Course?"

"That's right," Lowell said.

"Maybe you'll learn something," MacMillan said.

"As you told me, Captain, I don't know enough about the army to make a pimple on a good corporal's ass. That was just before you told me I would be able to get out of the army."

"I hope they run your ass off over there," MacMillan said.

"Actually, sir, I'm number three in my class."

MacMillan's face flushed. He looked as if he was going to say something, but he simply turned around and walked away.

"Captain MacMillan," Lowell called; and when MacMillan ignored him, he called his name again so loudly that Mac-

Millan, aware others in the parking lot were looking, had no choice but to turn around.

Lowell saluted crisply. "It was very nice to see you again, Captain MacMillan," he said. "Please extend my best wishes to Mrs. MacMillan, sir."

MacMillan returned the salute and walked into the Class Six store.

It was a week after his meeting with MacMillan before Lowell understood why he and Phil Parker had been so enthusiastically saluted while riding around in the Packard and why MacMillan had made the crack about the car. The major general commanding Fort Knox also drove a Packard convertible. It was also yellow, but it was a 120, and not nearly so ostentatious as Lowell's 180. They had been saluted in the belief that the car was the commanding general's personal vehicle. It was now believed that Lieutenant Lowell was not only guilty of a breech of etiquette which decreed that lieutenants do not drive automobiles as expensive as the commanding general, but that he (and Parker) were intentionally mocking him (because Parker rode in the back seat with the roof down in the winter, grandly returning the salutes).

They stopped putting the top down, and when they went to the main post, they now went in Phil's old Cadillac; but the damage was done. They had been identified as smart-asses, and there was nothing they could do to alter that perception.

Lt. Col. Bob Bellmon, when he heard about the two wise-ass lieutenants in SOC, one of whom was a nigger who had gone to Norwich, called Phil Parker on the telephone.

"Phil," he said. "A word to the wise should be sufficient. Get yourself a new roommate. I'll speak to the SOC commander, if you like."

"With all respect, sir, I wish you wouldn't do that."

"Goddamn it, Phil, I know that you weren't mocking the general. But the general doesn't know that."

"Sir, neither was Lowell."

"Bullshit."

"Sir, Lowell is my friend."

"Your friend is a wise-ass, and he's going to hurt your career."

"I'll have to take that risk, sir."

"Your loyalty, Phil, is commendable," Bellmon said, dryly. "Don't say you weren't warned."

(Five)

Even the continued ranking of Second Lieutenants Parker and Lowell at or very near the head of their class did nothing to reduce their ostracism. The word was out that they were a couple of smart-asses, and that was that. They even had a goddamn refrigerator in their room; they thought they were too good to drink with everybody else in the rec room.

But what really pissed their classmates and their instructors was what happened at the retreat parade. There was a regular once-a-month formal retreat parade, at which people got medals and citations, and heard their retirement orders read. Student Officer Company marched over to the main post in formation, a hell of a long walk, especially since nobody in SOC was going to get a medal or a citation, or be retired.

When they had roll call in the SOC area, Lieutenant Lowell did not answer when his name was called. The tactical officer even asked the nigger if he knew where he was, and the nigger said, "No, sir."

So they marched over to the main post without him. While they were walking at route march, before they got near the main post and the tac officer started calling cadence, it was whispered about that the smart-ass nigger lover had finally fucked up. He should have known there would be roll call and that he would get caught ducking the formation. He'd have a hard time explaining by indorsement hereon (which is probably the way they would handle it) why he had absented himself without authorization from a scheduled formation.

But when they were all lined up, and the school commandant stood up in front and bellowed, "Persons to be decorated, Front and center, March!" there was the nigger lover, right at the head of the line. And when the adjutant stepped to the microphone and called, "Attention to orders," it was something none of them had ever heard before.

"His Most Gracious Majesty, Philip, by the Grace of God, King of the Hellenes, is pleased to bestow upon Lieutenant Craig W. Lowell, United States Army, the Order of St. George and St. Andrew with all the rights and privileges thereunto pertaining, in token of His Most Gracious Majesty's appreciation of Lieutenant Lowell's outstanding valor and military prowess while attached to the 27th Royal Hellenic Mountain Division."

It wasn't even a regular-sized medal. It was about the size of a coffee cup saucer, and the VIP from Washington didn't pin it on him, he hung it over his shoulder on a purple ribbon six inches wide.

"Hey," one of his classmates asked *sotto voce*, "who the fuck are the Hellenes?"

"The Greeks, you clod-kicking hillbilly," Lieutenant Parker informed him.

Smart-ass nigger.

For a couple of days, the citations for his medals (they'd also hung a U.S. medal on him, an unimportant one, the Army Commendation Medal, called the Green Hornet) were on the SOC-TAS bulletin board, and then somebody tore them down.

(Six)

When he finally got word that Ilse had her visa, Craig Lowell went to the orderly room and asked the Student Officer Company commander for a few days off. He wanted to look for an apartment for his wife, he said, and then he wanted to go to New York to meet her plane. He was sure, he said, that he could make up what academic work he would lose. His overall average so far was 98.4.

"You're in the army, Lowell," the major who was his company commander said. "Even if you don't seem to fully understand that. Don't let that goddamn medal go to your head. You can't just take off whenever you feel like it to handle your personal affairs. I can see no reason why an adult female can't get off one airplane and onto another by herself. And when she gets here, you'll be given two hours off, like everybody else, to go by post housing."

"Sir, I hadn't planned to live on the post," Lowell said.

"Quarters are available, Lieutenant. You will live on the post. Is there anything else?"

When he told Parker what that chickenshit sonofabitch had

said, Parker said it was what he should have expected for being a nigger lover. And he fixed the business about quarters (probably with a couple of bottles of bourbon; Lowell never knew how for sure). The day before Ilse was scheduled to arrive, he took him to the company-grade family housing area, where barracks had been converted into apartments. A neat little painted sign LT LOWELL was on the door of one of them. When they went inside, it was full of brand-new furniture from the quartermaster warehouse. All they had to do was push it around where it looked best.

Parker didn't go with him to meet Ilse at the airport in Louisville, and he was sort of glad that he didn't. Because when he saw Ilse coming awkwardly down the steps from the plane, as big as a house, looking frightened and pale, and when he hugged her, both of them cried, and he wouldn't have wanted Phil to see that.

Ilse told him that Sharon Felter and the elder Felters had met her plane. Then they had driven her to someplace called Newark and put her on the plane to Louisville.

He was disappointed with Ilse's reaction to the Packard. She said it was beautiful all right, but with her pregnant and his mother sick, he must be really out of his mind to think they could afford something like that.

"Liebchen," Lowell said. "I've got a lot of money. *We've* got a lot of money. Much more than most people do."

"I know," she said, and he understood that she didn't have the first faint idea what he meant. It was not the time to get into it, not now.

Ilse was pathetically pleased with the apartment and the furnishings, and he wondered how she would have reacted if he had gone through with his original notion to call Andre Pretier and tell him he was married, and would Andre either meet his wife's plane or at least send a chauffeur and a car and see that she got on the Louisville plane.

If Sharon hadn't seemed so delighted that she could go and meet the plane, he'd have had to do something like that; and if learning that her baby was married unduly upset his mother, fuck it. She was going to have to find out sooner or later anyway. She was about to be a grandmother.

But Sharon had really wanted to go meet the plane, and the

problem of how and when to tell his mother—and for that matter, his grandfather—about Ilse could be delayed for a while.

Ilse smiled, but she really didn't understand the flowers Parker had sent to the apartment—a huge horseshoe, with the words DEEPEST SYMPATHY in gold foil letters on a purple sash hung on it. Ilse didn't understand, if that was what Americans sent to a funeral, why Craig thought it was so funny.

Ilse's nearly joyous reaction to the crappy little apartment with its veneer furniture and thin rugs (Lowell thought the shag living room carpet looked like an enormous bath towel) made him face what he thought was an unpleasant truth about his wife. She wanted him to think she came from a good background—that *von* Greiffenberg bullshit—but when he pressed her for details, she didn't want to talk about her family. She'd tried once to tell him her father had been a count and a colonel, and that the castle in Marburg (it was more of a villa than a castle; didn't she know the difference?) was the house she had grown up in.

If that was so, why was she broke? Why was she in Bad Nauheim, doing what she was doing? The truth to be faced was that she was lying through her teeth about her father (or else he had been a Nazi, which was something else to consider). She was ashamed that she had been a whore (or at least that she had been willing to be a whore, and would have been one if he hadn't come along), and so she was making up stories. So what was wrong with that?

She probably thought, he decided, that he was telling her a lie, too, about having a lot of money.

The truth of the matter was that he didn't give a damn if she had been raised in a cave by pig farmers. And he hadn't exactly been honest with her, either, when he'd told her his mother was sick, and that that was the reason she couldn't meet the plane and her daughter-in-law. His mother didn't even know he was married. He had enough problems as it was, without having his mother flip her lid and causing trouble.

He had not completed an overseas tour, so he was eligible for one when he graduated from Basic Officer's Course. With a little bit of luck, he would be sent to Japan or Alaska, someplace where he could take her with him. But he could also be sent to Korea where you couldn't take dependents, or back to Germany, maybe even to the Constab. You couldn't have German nationals as dependents in Germany.

She might find herself as alone here as she had been in Germany.

The thing to do was say nothing that was liable to upset her. Especially now, just before the baby was to be born.

(Seven)

Mrs. Ilse von Greiffenberg Lowell was delivered of a seven-pound four-ounce son at the U.S. Army Hospital, Fort Knox, Kentucky, two days before her husband was graduated, third in his class, from Basic Officer's Course.

Ilse was so happy that she was afraid something would go wrong, she told her husband. She was so happy that she wept when a sterling silver teething cup was delivered to the hospital with a card reading, "Love, Mother Pretier." She didn't suspect at all that it had been sent by her husband.

All she cared was that the baby was healthy and that Craig wasn't going to be sent overseas, the way Phil Parker was. Craig had been assigned to the Armor School as an instructor in the Tank Gunnery Division. They were sending Phil all the way to Japan.

The child was christened at post chapel number three following the rite prescribed by the Episcopal Church. It was necessary to have two godfathers and one godmother. Because it was of obvious importance to Ilse, and because he didn't know anyone else he could ask, he called Roxy MacMillan and explained his problem. Roxy said that she would be delighted, and so would Mac, but when they got to the chapel, she said that Mac had been called away. So Peter-Paul Lowell's godfathers had the same name. His godfathers were Lt. Philip Sheridan Parker IV and Colonel (Retired) Philip Sheridan Parker III. Phil's father had come down to Knox from Kansas for the graduation parade. He remembered Knox, he said, when it had six buildings and four outhouses, and he wanted to see how it had changed.

Colonel Parker stayed with the Bellmons, and when Bob Bellmon told him of his concern about Phil's roommate, Parker said that he had actually rather liked Lowell, but in any event it was all over now.

(Eight)
Fort Knox, Kentucky
18 October 1947

First Lieutenant Sanford Felter returned from the U.S. Army Military Advisory Group, Greece, with two Green Hornets for his outstanding administrative skill (which was fairly routine for a first john who had spent his entire tour with one of the divisions,) and with the Legion of Merit, which was unusual. He was also decorated by the Greek government with the Order of Knight of St. Gregory, First Class.

In the Comments section of his last USAMAG-G efficiency report, he was described as "a small in stature, erect officer who has constantly demonstrated a grasp of military affairs beyond that expected of an officer of his grade and experience. He is unhesitatingly recommended for command in the grade of captain in combat. However, this officer has indicated a preference for a career in military intelligence and in the opinion of the rating officer would make an outstanding intelligence officer." The efficiency report was "enthusiastically endorsed" by Lt. Gen. James Van Fleet, USAMAG-G Commanding General.

On the morning of his fifth day in the apartment over the Old Warsaw Bakery on the corner of Aldine Street and Chancellor Avenue in Newark, N.J., the mailman delivered a thick manila envelope, registered, return receipt requested. It contained a hundred copies of Paragraph 33, Department of the Army General Order 101:

* * * * * * * * * *

33. FIRST LIEUTENANT SANFORD T. FELTER, 0-357861, INFANTRY, Transient Officer Detachment, Camp Kilmer, N.J., is placed on temporary duty and Will Proceed to U.S. Army Language School, the Presidio, San Francisco, Calif, to undergo Course No. 49-002 (Greek Language). Off will report no later than

5 January 1948. Upon completion of course of instruction, Off is further placed on TDY and WP to the Infantry
School, Fort Benning, Ga., to undergo Course No.
49–444 (Advanced Inf Off Course). Upon Completion
of course of instruction, Off is transferred in grade and
WP to the U.S. Army Counterintelligence Center, Camp
Holabird, 1019 Dundalk Avenue, Baltimore 19, Md. to
undergo Course No. 49–101 (Classified). Upon reporting to Fort Holabird, Off will be detailed Military Intelligence and all further personnel actions will be under
the Assistant Chief of Staff, G-2, Hq, Dept of the Army.
Off will be in per diem status while attending the Army
Language School. Off will be in Temporary Change of
Station status while attending the Inf School. Assgmt to
Fort Holabird is PCS. Off auth tvl by private auto. Off
is auth to be accompanied by dependents at no expense
to govt to the Presidio and the Infantry Center. Tvl of
dependents and household goods to Ft Holabird is auth
from Newark, N.J.

* * * * * * * * * *

FOR THE CHIEF OF STAFF
Edward Witsell
Major General, The Adjutant General

When he knew what his orders were, and after he had been
home two weeks, he and Sharon loaded all their clothes in the
Buick Super and started out for the Presidio, via Fort Knox,
where Craig Lowell was stationed.

Craig and Ilse and the baby (Peter-Paul, like the candy bar,
and called P.P. for a couple of reasons) were living in a converted barracks near Godman Field and driving an enormous
old yellow Packard convertible. Despite the car (which was,
after all, nearly six years old), Sandy wondered if maybe Craig
had just been telling stories about having a lot of money. Their
quarters were furnished with strictly GI furniture, and Ilse
didn't seem to be expensively dressed. But then the very first
night when they were playing gin rummy and the pencil broke,
Sandy went to the GI desk to get another. When he opened the
drawer he found five uncashed paychecks and a statement from

the Morgan Guaranty Trust in New York showing a checking balance of $11,502.85 and was a little ashamed of himself for doubting Craig.

He also saw a signature block on a training schedule for the Department of Tactics. Craig was a gunnery instructor in the Tank Gunnery Division of the Department of Tactics. The signature block was:

> Robert F. Bellmon
> Lt. Colonel, Armor
> Deputy Department Commander

He asked Craig what he looked like, and Craig described him.

"Why do you ask?" Craig then asked.

"I know him," Sandy said. "I was—" he stopped. "He's the officer I asked for the Greece assignment."

"That sounds like him, the chickenshit sonofabitch," Craig said, bitterly. "He's prick enough to let a dumb lieutenant volunteer to get his balls shot off."

Sharon and Ilse were embarrassed at the outburst, and especially at the language, and Sandy let it drop.

The next night, however, while Craig was off running a night-fire exercise (he would have liked to have seen that, but Craig told him that with Chickenshit Bob around, there was no chance), he took Sharon to the movies (Ilse didn't like to put P. P. in the officer's club nursery and begged off). When they came out, after he'd thought it over carefully, he decided it was the right and proper thing to do to pay a courtesy call on Colonel Bellmon.

Lt. Col. Bellmon had been assigned quarters near the parade ground on the main post, not far at all from the theater. They were two-story brick houses, looking like something from an Andy Hardy movie. Middletown, U.S.A.

Sharon was a little nervous. She really had no experience with the army at all, just the two dances she'd gone to at West Point. And the truth of the matter was that the only confidence that Sandy had was in the training he'd received at West Point in "Customs of the Service" as a yearling. Calls were required of junior officers upon their seniors when reporting for duty.

Cards, one corner turned up, were deposited on a tray provided for that purpose in the foyer of quarters. Calls were encouraged, but not required, upon senior officers with whom one was acquainted, when visiting officially, or unofficially, other posts and stations.

As he walked up the concrete walk between the closely cropped sections of lawn, Sandy suddenly remembered the rest of it. Wives were expected to wear gloves and hats. Sharon had a hat on, but no gloves. Well, it was too late to do anything about that.

He stood under the porch light and took a card from his wallet. It was a little smeared. He'd bought a hundred of them, but the only time he had ever used one was to put it on the mailbox at the bakery so he would be sure to get his mail.

But there was nothing he could do about that, either. He turned up the corner of the card the way you were supposed to and rang the bell.

A tall, attractive woman wearing a turtleneck sweater and slacks answered the door.

"Hello," she said cheerfully.

"Good evening," Felter replied and thrust the card at her. She smiled, and he saw tolerance in the smile. He was being gently laughed at.

"You're reporting in, Lieutenant . . ." She read the name. "Felter?"

"No, ma'am. I'm passing through. I just wanted to pay my respects to Colonel Bellmon."

She turned. "Bob!" It was a shout. "Come in, please. I'm Mrs. Bellmon."

They stood awkwardly in the foyer. Colonel Bellmon, a plaid sweater over his khaki shirt, a glass in his hand, came into the foyer. For a moment, Sandy was afraid he wouldn't remember him. Or wouldn't want to.

"Felter," Colonel Bellmon finally said. "I'll be damned."

"Yes, sir."

"Well, come in," Bellmon said. "I'm glad to see you. You've been assigned to Knox?"

"No, sir," Sandy said. "Sir, may I present my wife?"

"It's a pleasure to meet you, Mrs. Felter," Bellmon said. "I gather you've introduced yourself to Barbara? Barbara, Lieutenant Felter was in on Task Force Parker."

The women shook hands. Barbara Bellmon looked at Felter with new interest.

"You say you've been assigned here?" Bellmon said, leading them into a well-furnished living room. There was a silver-framed photograph on the mantelpiece of Major General Peterson K. Waterford sitting erect on a horse.

"No, sir, I'm just passing through. I'm on my way to the Presidio to the Language School."

"Well, I'm glad you stopped in to see me," Bellmon said, and he sounded perfectly sincere. "I often wondered what happened to you in Greece."

"It was a very interesting assignment, sir," Felter said. "That's why I came. To thank you."

"I'm glad to hear that," Bellmon said. He looked thoughtful. "I'm really not just saying that, Felter. I've often wondered about it. The truth of the matter is, I had learned an hour or so before I talked to you that my father-in-law had just dropped dead." He gestured toward the framed photograph on the mantelpiece. "I wondered if I was in full possession of my faculties, is what I'm saying."

"I think it was a good assignment, sir," Felter said.

"And now you're going to the Presidio. And from there, no doubt, to Dundalk High?"

It took Felter a moment to catch up on that, to remember that the U.S. Army Counterintelligence School was located at 1019 *Dundalk* Avenue, Baltimore 19, Maryland.

"Yes, sir," Felter said. "Via the Infantry School. Advanced Officer's Course."

"Fine, fine," Colonel Bellmon said. Mrs. Bellmon arrived surprisingly quickly, Sandy thought, with a tea tray. That made him feel better. If her husband were really not glad to see him, there would be no tea tray.

"And what brings you to Knox? Certainly not just to see me."

"No, sir, I have a friend here," Felter said.

"Who's that?"

"Lieutenant Craig Lowell, sir," Felter said. "I believe he works for you."

"I'm disappointed in you, Felter," Bellmon said. "Until you

said that, I had an image of you as one more responsible member of the Long Gray Line. You met him in Greece, I gather?"

"Yes, sir."

"The Duke is not one of Bob's favorite lieutenants, I'm afraid," Barbara Bellmon said, laughing.

"He has managed to antagonize just about everybody on the post," Bellmon said. "Me, most of all."

"I'm sorry to hear that," Felter said, realizing that it didn't surprise him. He regretted bringing up Lowell's name. "Can I ask what he's done?"

"What Bob cannot stand is being outwitted," Barbara Bellmon said, laughing. "It destroys his image of himself."

"I can't stand being mocked," Bellmon said. "I'm a soldier, and I don't like to see officers mock the army." Then he softened. "But you're right, honey, that bastard has outwitted me."

"Tell him what he did," Barbara Bellmon said. "You're making it sound as if he ran off with army funds."

"Do you know about the medal?" Bellmon asked. "The one he got the Greeks to give him?"

"Yes, sir," Felter said. "I was there when he earned it."

"You were? What's it for?"

"He assumed command of a Greek company after the Greek officers were killed," Sandy said. "And, although he was pretty badly wounded, he kept the communists from breaking through our lines."

"You know that for a fact?" Bellmon asked, sharply.

"Yes, sir. I was with the relief column."

"Goddamn it," Bellmon said. "He did it again. When I asked him where he got it, he said it was for his contribution to Greco-American relations."

Barbara Bellmon laughed heartily.

"Goddamnit, that's not funny," Bellmon said.

"I think it's hilarious," Barbara said.

"It is not funny to mock decorations for valor," Bellmon said. "That's not funny at all."

"You're being unfair, Bob," Barbara Bellmon said. "Tell them the whole story."

"OK," Bellmon said. "I'll tell you my assessment of your friend, Felter, and you correct me where I go wrong. Before he was assigned to me, he had already earned himself a reputation as a smart-ass while he was in Basic Officer's Course. The general is very proud of his Packard automobile. A yellow convertible. So your friend shows up in a bigger, fancier yellow Packard convertible. You can imagine how the general liked that."

"I thought it was funny," Barbara Bellmon said.

"The general didn't," Bellmon said. "And neither did I. If you think about it, that's a pretty expensive little mockery. I hate to think what his monthly payments were on that Packard."

"Sir?" Felter said, hesitantly, and Bellmon looked at him. "Sir, Lowell is well off. I mean, he's rich. He can afford a Packard or anything else he wants to drive."

"Oh," Bellmon said. "Well, that explains a lot, I suppose."

"Tell him about the medal," Barbara Bellmon said.

"Well, the general passed the word that he wanted your friend off the post ninety seconds after he finished Basic Officer's Course. He was going to send him to Korea. He was assigned to the Department of Tactics, and I put him to work as a gunnery instructor, having found out that he didn't know anything at all about tank gunnery. I figured that just might humble him."

"And it turns out, Lieutenant," Barbara Bellmon said, "that he seems to have some mysterious, otherworldy ability to control projectiles in flight. He *wills* a hit. He promptly became the darling of the enlisted men, those old sergeants who think second lieutenants are useless. His students have constantly done much better than any other lieutenant's students. But that's still not the story of the medal."

"But it is of the sergeants," Bellmon said. "Now, certainly, I don't hate all Germans. There are good Germans and I'm the first to admit it. But the facts are that the German girls who marry Americans are, by and large, looking for a meal ticket. So far as I know, Mrs. Lowell is a lady in every respect."

"I'm glad you said that," Barbara Bellmon said, icily.

"I like Ilse very much," Sharon said, suddenly. It was the first time she had opened her mouth. "I like her and I feel sorry for her. She lost her father in the war, and here she is all alone with a baby."

"I like her, too," Barbara Bellmon said. "What little I've

seen of her. Sometimes, Bob, you make me sick."

Felter picked up on that. It meant acceptance of them by Mrs. Bellmon. Otherwise she would have kept her mouth shut and told her husband off when they were alone.

"Be that as it may," Bellmon went on, obviously uncomfortable, "she is an officer's lady, and she is not supposed to find her friends from among the enlisted wives. And second lieutenants are not supposed to run around with the sergeants, either."

"Put yourself in that girl's shoes, Bob," Barbara Bellmon said. "How would you like to go to a party and have all the women make it pretty clear to you that they think you're a prostitute who latched on to an American meal ticket?"

"How terrible for her!" Sharon said.

"It's your job, Barbara," Bellmon said, "to stop that sort of thing."

"When I had the chance, I did what I could," Barbara Bellmon replied.

"The point is, she didn't give you the chance, because she didn't go to officer's ladies meetings. And your friend, Felter, never went to the officer's club or to official parties."

"And socialized with the enlisted men," Felter said. He wasn't surprised to hear that. In Ioannina, he could get away with that because of the circumstances. He could not get away with it in a garrison situation, where the customs of the service, the rigid distinctions between officers and enlisted men, were rigidly observed.

"I called him in," Bellmon went on, "and had a little talk with him. I didn't like his attitude at all, but there was nothing I could put my finger on. My father told me that before the 1928 Manual for Court-Martial, there was an offense called 'silent insolence.' If that was still in effect, I could have had him tried. All I could do, however, under the circumstances, was let him go. But then I wrote him a DF..."

"Excuse me?" Sharon interrupted. "A what?"

"A DF," Bellmon explained. "It stands for distribution form. The next stop down from an official letter, and one step up from a note."

"I'm sorry, I must sound stupid," Sharon said.

"Don't be silly," Barbara Bellmon said.

"Anyway, I wrote him a DF telling him that it was considered important for officers to participate in the social activities of his organization, and that I expected him to appear, in the prescribed uniform, at all subsequent such events."

"And he didn't show up?" Felter asked.

"Oh, did he show up!" Barbara Bellmon said. "General Dowbell-Howe of the British Royal Tank Corps was given an official dinner. The invitations said dress uniform with medals. That meant the general and the chief of staff and a couple of the senior colonels came in dress blues. Bob doesn't even have any. Everybody else came in pinks and greens. Your friend, Lieutenant, shows up in mess dress. God only knows where he got it, but he showed up in it. Wearing his medals. The Army of Occupation Medal, the Army Commendation Medal, and this enormous thing pinned to the jacket and a purple sash. His Greek medal. He looked like something out of Sigmund Romberg operetta."

"I don't know what mess dress is," Sharon said.

"A little jacket like a bartender's," Barbara said. "With a vest. White tie and stand-up collar. The trousers have colored stripes, gold for armor in his case. And a cape. With a yellow lining. God, he was spectacular!"

"I sent him home the moment I saw him and told him that I expected to have on my desk, in writing, at 0700 the next morning, his explanation for his conduct," Bellmon said. There was a touch of a smile at his face. "Why he was out of uniform."

"And your friend sent him a copy of the regulation which encouraged the optional wearing of mess dress at all official functions at which dress uniform was required."

"Sir, is it possible that he was trying to comply with his orders to the best of his ability?" Felter said, loyally. "I mean, where I would have to think a long time about buying mess dress uniform, Craig wouldn't have to worry about it. He'd just order it."

"I don't think so, Felter," Bellmon said. "He was doing it on purpose. He's a real guardhouse lawyer when he wants to be."

"Tell him about the pistol range, Bob," Barbara said. "That really did it."

"ARs, as you know, call for the annual qualification by

commissioned personnel with the .45," Bellmon said. "Lowell, as a token of the affection and respect in which he is held by his seniors, was named range officer for the Tactics Department."

"And he ran it exactly by the book," Barbara Bellmon said, chuckling.

"You really think he's funny, don't you?" Bellmon said.

"Honey, he reminds me of my father," Barbara said. "Think about it, you know he does. Fancy uniform. Always making waves."

"What your friend Lowell did, Felter, was certify that thirty-eight of the fifty-one officers of the Tactics Department had failed to qualify."

"Now, wait a minute," Barbara Bellmon said. "You stood up for him for that. You said you would have done the same thing, if you had the courage, when you were a lieutenant."

"I never had the smart-ass reputation Lowell does," Bellmon said. "When the colonel heard about it, he was furious. He'd already lost one full day's duty from fifty-one officers, and now he was going to lose a full day's duty from the thirty-eight who had failed to qualify. He was convinced Lowell had failed them on purpose."

"So he sent them back out and thirty-one failed the second time around," Barbara said.

"Mrs. Bellmon," Felter asked, "your father was General Waterford, wasn't he?"

"Why, yes, he was."

"Unless I'm mistaken, Mrs. Bellmon," Felter said, "it was General Waterford who commissioned Lowell."

"What did you say?" Col. Bellmon said.

"I said, I think General Waterford is the one who commissioned Lowell from the ranks."

"Your friend pulled some smart-ass guardhouse lawyer trick and had himself commissioned as a finance officer," Bellmon said. "I checked. I wondered where he got a commission."

"Why would my father do that?" Barbara Bellmon asked, visibly interested.

"As I understand it, Mrs. Bellmon," Felter said, "General Waterford wanted Lowell to play on his polo team. And he couldn't, because he was a private."

"Oh, that sounds like Daddy!" Barbara Bellmon said, and really started to laugh. "Call me Barbara, Lieutenant, please."

Bellmon jumped to his feet and went to a telephone on a small table by the door. He dialed a number. "Roxy," he said. "This is Bob Bellmon. Is Mac there?" There was a pause. "Sorry to bother you at home, Mac. But I have just heard an incredible story that I want to check out. What do you know about General Waterford commissioning Lieutenant Lowell?" There was a much longer pause. "I wish I had known this earlier, MacMillan," Colonel Bellmon said, coldly. "I can't imagine why you didn't think I would be interested." Then he hung up.

He nodded at Barbara, who laughed out loud again, and then he said to Felter: "Score one for you, Super Sleuth. And that damned MacMillan knew it all the time and never said a word to me."

"MacMillan," Barbara said, chuckling again, "knew of the high esteem in which you held Lieutenant Lowell. He wanted to put as much distance between himself and Lowell as he could. I think that is known, darling, as covering one's ass. And we know how good Mac is at that, don't we?"

Bellmon gave his wife a dirty look.

"Well, now," Barbara Bellmon went on, brightly. "Now that we know that he and Daddy were friends, we'll have to have Lieutenant and Mrs. Lowell to dinner, won't we? I wonder how that's going to go over with the colonel?"

Bellmon frowned a moment, and then smiled. "Since the colonel thinks your father was at least as infallible as the Pope, it should be very interesting." He reached over and patted Felter's knee.

"Felter, you never cease to amaze me," he said. "You're a fountain of information nobody else has."

(Nine)

Barbara Bellmon, who was the daughter and granddaughter of a general officer, and who regarded her present role in life as simply marking time until Bob got his stars, made up with great care the guest list for the "little dinner" she arranged for the lieutenants and their wives.

First of all, she wanted to do something nice for the Lowells, especially for the wife, who had been treated shabbily. And she knew that Bob liked Felter and Felter's wife and that he wanted to introduce him to the establishment here. It would be obvious to everyone that since the Felters and the Lowells would be the only junior officers present that they were someone of whom the Bellmons thought a great deal.

Captain and Mrs. Rudolph G. MacMillan were not on Barbara Bellmon's guest list. Barbara felt sorry for Roxy, who would quickly get the point of not being invited. Roxy was incapable of cutting someone or hurting someone's feelings. MacMillan had simply, with his usual skill, protected his ass. Lowell was on some people's s-list, and MacMillan didn't want to get splattered. Sometimes, Barbara could not stand MacMillan. He was supposed to be an officer and a gentleman. But he was only an officer, as he had proved here.

MacMillan, she knew, would work his way back into Bob's good graces. For one thing, he had a skin like an alligator. More important, she knew she would never be able to completely break him off from Bob. They'd been in the damned POW camp together, and Bob had some absurd notion that he had failed Mac when they were there. He would carry Mac on his back, get him out of scrapes, as long as they were in the army.

There was going to be an element of humor, too. Barbara could hardly wait until the colonel, who referred to Lieutenant Lowell as that "blond-headed pissant," found out the pissant had been a lot closer to her father than the Colonel had ever been.

There would be some dropped jaws from the other lieutenant colonels, too, when they saw Lowell and his German wife. And they would probably drop even further when they saw that the Bellmons were having as their guest of honor a slight, already balding little Jew, who would deliver a little talk after dinner on the functioning of the U.S. Army Military Advisory Group, Greece.

Barbara decided that she would call Lieutenant Lowell's quarters and ask his wife and Felter's to "help" her with the arrangements for the dinner. She didn't need any help, but if they came early, she could brief them on who was who at the party. Neither one of them, obviously, had had any experience at all in dealing with either the wives of senior officers or the senior officers themselves. And that was an important part of the army.

Barbara had no way of knowing that Craig Lowell's reaction to her request was that she had a lot of goddamned nerve asking her guests to help set up her stupid party. Fortunately, Sandy Felter correctly guessed Barbara Bellmon's motives, and he drove the women to the Bellmons' quarters at five in the afternoon and then spent from five fifteen to six forty-five, when it was time for them to go to the party, keeping Lowell from drinking.

After Barbara had finished her briefing, Bob Bellmon went out of his way to be charming to the young women. He complimented them on their looks and opened a bottle of Rhine wine for them, partly because Lowell's wife was German and partly out of concern that if he gave either of them anything stronger, they would get tight.

"What part of Germany are you from, Mrs. Lowell?" he asked, as he poured the Rhine wine.

"Hesse," Ilse said.

"Oh, I know Hesse," he said. "Where in Hesse?"

"A small city," Ilse replied. "Marburg an der Lahn."

Of course, he thought. Marburg was near Bad Nauheim, where she apparently had met Lowell. And then he thought of something else, and the thought pleased him.

"Oddly enough, Mrs. Lowell," he said, "both my wife's father, General Waterford, and myself, had a good friend from Marburg."

"Did you really?" Ilse asked.

"A German officer. He had gone to the French cavalry school at Samur with General Waterford; and when I was captured, he was the commandant of my prison camp. A really fine man. His name was von Greiffenberg."

"What did you say?" Ilse said, barely audibly.

"I said my friend's name was Peter-Paul von Greiffenberg," Bellmon repeated.

"*Herr Oberst Bellmon,*" Ilse said, "*Oberst Graf Peter-Paul von Greiffenberg war mein Vater.*"

"Oh, my God!" Bellmon said.

Sharon, thinking she had to translate, said, "She said the officer you said was your friend was her father, Colonel."

"I speak German," Bellmon said, more sharply than he intended. Then, much more loudly than he intended, he called his wife's name.

Barbara came quickly into the living room.

"What's the matter?" she asked. She saw the look on Ilse Lowell's face and on her husband's. Ilse was fighting back tears.

"Mrs. Lowell," Bellmon said, "would you please be good enough to tell my wife who your father was?"

"My father," Ilse said, speaking slowly and precisely in English, "was an officer the colonel tells me he knew and that your father knew."

Barbara looked at her husband.

"Von Greiffenberg," he said. He pointed his hand at Ilse. "That's Peter-Paul von Greiffenberg's daughter."

"My God!" Barbara said.

"Goddamnit, he did it to me again!" Bellmon said.

Barbara looked at him in confusion for a moment, until she took his meaning.

"Don't be an ass," she snapped. "How was he to know you knew him?" Then she saw the worried look on Ilse's face. "Ilse, honey," she said, "it's all right. It's just that Bob really admired your father, and he feels like a fool because you've been here so long, and so alone, and he didn't know who you were."

Lieutenants Lowell and Felter arrived at the Bellmon quarters at the same time as did the colonel and his lady. The colonel was surprised to see Lowell, but not nearly as surprised as he was by how Bellmon greeted them.

"My wife tells me, Lowell, that there was no reason for you to presume that I knew your father-in-law. Somewhat against my better judgment, I have decided to go along with her reasoning."

"I have no idea what you're talking about, Colonel," Lowell said.

"Colonel Graf Peter-Paul von Greiffenberg is who I'm talking about, Lieutenant," Bellmon said. "Your father-in-law. And one of the finest officers it has ever been my privilege to know."

Lowell looked at him and saw he was dead serious. So Ilse was telling the truth about her father being a colonel after all, he thought. I'll be goddamned!

Barbara heard his raised voice and came rushing up. She smiled broadly at the colonel and his lady.

"The most wonderful thing has just happened," she said. "We've just learned that Mrs. Lowell's father was an old and dear friend of my father's and of Bob's. He was the commandant of Bob's prison camp."

"Mrs. Lowell's father?"

"Was Colonel Count Peter-Paul von Greiffenberg!" Barbara said.

"Extraordinary," the colonel said. "Well, how about that!"

There were cocktails and then a sit-down dinner, after which Bob Bellmon, not feeling much pain, repeated the story of the extraordinary coincidence.

"As some of you know," he said, "I was liberated from Russian internment by Task Force Parker, Colonel Philip Sheridan Parker III. The man who located us, Lieutenant Sanford T. Felter, is the man we're honoring tonight. He's just returned from Greece, and I've asked him to tell us what's going on over there."

Lieutenant Felter, once he was called on, spoke with a surprising lucidity about the functioning of a military advisory group. With great skill he traced the Greek operation from the beginning until he had left it. Barbara decided that Bob was right. Felter was as smart as a whip, a far better officer than he looked capable of being.

She was worried about Lieutenant Lowell. He had had entirely too much to drink, from the predinner cocktails through the postdinner brandy, and was now sitting with the brandy bottle before him, leaning back on the legs of his chair, listening with what looked like interest to Felter's little speech.

And then Felter lit the fuse.

"My service in USAMAG-G was entirely on the staff," he said. "Lieutenant Lowell was on the line. I'm sure he could offer something of value to add to what I've said."

"You got it, Mouse," Lowell said, waving his hand drunkenly, deprecatingly. "I can't think of a thing to add. Thank you just the same."

One of the lieutenant colonels was drunk, too. Delighted

with his own wit, he said, "Since you've found fault with everything in the Department of Tactics, Lowell, I'm surprised you didn't find a good deal wrong with the way General Van Fleet ran the Greek operation."

"Van Fleet did a superb job with the crap they sent him," Lowell replied, matter-of-factly.

"General Van Fleet, you mean, Lieutenant," the lieutenant colonel snapped, before he was shushed by his wife.

"Big Jim," Lowell said, agreeably, helping himself to more brandy. *"That* Van Fleet. Superb officer."

"I would be interested in your assessment of the line, Lieutenant," the Colonel, Bob's boss, said. If Lowell was good enough for Porky Waterford, perhaps he had made too hasty a judgment of him. After all, the boy did get that fancy medal and was married to the daughter of a German officer who was an old friend of Waterford's.

"I don't think so," Lowell said, pleasantly.

Lowell let the chair fall forward onto its four legs. He drained his brandy glass and stood up. Barbara exchanged glances with Bob. There was nothing that could be done now except pray.

"There were, as I see it, two major errors in the way we handled Greece," Lowell began, now dead serious. "The first was that we tried to superimpose our ideas and our organization on theirs. We simply presume that we know all there is to know about organization and that everybody else is doing it wrong. Bullshit.

"The second error, which compounded the first, was in the selection of officers. I was rather typical of the officers we sent over there. I was absolutely unqualified, and I wasn't alone. We had a motley collection of incompetents other people were happy to get rid of. We had the failures, the ignorant, and the cowardly."

"See here, Lowell!" one of the guests protested.

"By the time I left," Lowell went on, undaunted, "and I wasn't there long, we had gotten rid of most of the incompetents. They had been shipped home, sometimes in a box or put to work counting rations, or shot for cowardice. Or, as in my case, somehow learned their job by doing it."

"Wisdom from the mouth of a babe," one of the colonels snorted.

"What did he say about getting shot for cowardice?" a wife asked in a loud whisper.

"The next time you gentlemen mount an operation like that," Lowell went on, "I respectfully suggest that you send your best officers, not your worst, officers whose knowledge of warfare goes beyond the field manuals." They were glowering at him. It was not the position of a second lieutenant to publicly challenge the conduct of a military operation.

Mimicking a lecturer at the Armor School, Lowell said, "I will now entertain questions until the end of the class period."

There was absolute silence for thirty seconds. Then the colonel, ice in his voice, said: "I can't let that comment about cowardice go unchallenged. On what do you base that allegation? You're not speaking from personal knowledge?"

"Yes, sir, I am," Lowell said.

"You felt someone was a coward? Is that what you're saying?"

"I *suspected* someone was a coward," Lowell said. "Another officer was forced to make that judgment."

"In what way?"

"In order to complete his mission, the officer to whom I refer—a West Pointer, by the way—felt it necessary to remove his cowardly commanding officer. Who was also, come to think of it, a West Pointer."

"What do you mean, *remove?*"

"He cut him down with a Thompson is what I mean, Colonel," Lowell said, very simply.

"I think," Lt. Col. Bellmon said, after a long moment in which he decided that Lowell was telling the truth and that the situation was about to get out of control, "that we should have a nightcap on the porch, gentlemen."

Later that night, sleeping on the fold-down bed in the living room of Lowell's apartment, Sharon softly asked Sandy if what Lowell had said about one officer shooting, *murdering,* another officer in cold blood was true.

"Yes, it was," the Mouse said. "But I don't think Craig did himself any good by telling those officers that story. Those things happen, honey, but you just don't talk about them." He had a mental image of the Thompson bucking in his hands, of Captain Watson tumbling down the mountainside.

Sandy Felter suddenly rolled on his side and grabbed Sharon

and pulled her to him, and despite her protests that they would wake the baby and Craig and Ilse and that she didn't *want* to, not *here,* he took her. He had never done anything like that before, and he was ashamed of himself, even if Sharon, afterward, thought it was kind of funny and teased him about not drinking any more brandy.

(Ten)

Shortly after the dinner at Lt. Col. Robert Bellmon's quarters, Second Lieutenant Craig W. Lowell was transferred from the Tank Gunnery Division of the Armor School to the U.S. Army Armor Board. The Board, which was on, but not subordinate to, Fort Knox, was the agency which tested new tanks and other armored force vehicles.

Lowell was now viewed by the establishment at Fort Knox in a different light. He was no longer a smart-ass guardhouse lawyer who'd managed to somehow wangle a commission and had thereafter thumbed his nose at the army. Despite his indiscreet remarks at the Bellmons' party, he was a young man from a very prominent family whose potential had been recognized by no one less than Porky Waterford himself. In addition, he was married to the daughter of a German aristocrat who had been a colonel and an old friend of Waterford.

And Porky's judgment about the boy's potential had certainly been vindicated. The medal the Greeks had given him was the second highest one they awarded. It was understandable that a young man who had commanded a company in combat would tend to be a little bored with Basic Officer's Course and would say things he really shouldn't have said. Under the circumstances, it certainly spoke well for him that he had done so well in Basic Officer's Course, graduating third, with a 98.4 grade average.

Bellmon had a little chat about Lowell with Colonel Kenneth J. McLean, president of the Armor Board. McLean had not been at the dinner at which Lowell had made the speech, but he had been in North Africa with General Waterford. Colonel McLean said he could always use a bright young buck like that. The commanding general approved the transfer.

Lowell was assigned as an assistant project officer on the

90 mm high-velocity tube project for the M26. The original M26, which was to eventually replace the M4A4 as the standard tank, had come with a 75 mm cannon. The army had learned a healthy respect for the German 88 mm cannon, and a U.S. 90 mm high-velocity tank tube was designed and manufactured and was now under test by the Armor Board. If successful, it would make the M26 the most powerfully armed tank in the world.

The testing was rather simple in nature. The tube was fired under all possible conditions to see what broke. At that point ordnance engineers, military and civilian, came up with a fix.

Three M26 tanks, each under a lieutenant and crewed by senior noncoms, were under the general supervision of a lieutenant colonel, who handled the engineering and the other paperwork. Lowell became one of the three lieutenants.

The other lieutenants had heard that the president of the Board had requested Lowell's transfer from the school. That spoke well of him. So far as the noncoms were concerned, a second john with a CIB who had been an enlisted man was hardly your standard candy-ass shavetail, and Lowell's subsequent behavior (no chickenshit) and performance (that sonofabitch really knows how to fire a tube) confirmed their judgment of him.

The officers' ladies of the Armor Board, having heard that Colonel McLean had requested Lowell's transfer from the school, and having seen Mrs. Lowell together with Mrs. Bellmon at the commissary and at lunch with her in the officer's club, concluded that Ilse Lowell was the exception that proved the rule about frauleins; and they went out of their way to welcome her to Board social activities.

Lowell himself was delighted with his new duties. The M26s he'd been firing at the school had had to be treated with the utmost care to prevent breakdowns. During their four-week course of instruction, each tank crew in training had fired precisely thirty-two rounds of 75 mm ammunition. It was incredibly expensive and tough on the tube itself, and every round had to count. The absolute reverse was true at the Board. He and his crew picked up a tank at the maintenance building in the morning, drove the sonofabitch as fast as it would go out to the firing ranges and the torture-rack testing area, and then fired as many (sometimes twice as many) rounds in a day as he had fired in the whole four-week course at the school.

One of their problems was the necessity to constantly replace the M4 tank hulks and the worn-out trucks used for targets. They literally blew them into little pieces.

For lunch, they would pile into jeeps and three-quarter-ton trucks and drive five miles through the woods to the Fort Knox Rod and Gun Club for hamburgers and beer. There they'd fill out the forms that Testing Evaluation Division gave them to gain data on the M26A2 (90 mm high-velocity tube).

They were generally finished for the day at half past two or a quarter to three; and by half past four, Lowell had returned to his apartment. He took a shower, played with P.P., maybe fooled around with Ilse a little, and then they went together to the commissary or the PX, and maybe took in a movie. P.P. was a good baby. You could take him to the movies, and you never heard a peep out of him.

Craig actually looked forward with regret to his coming release from active duty, at the completion of his two years of commissioned service. He had to get out, of course. For one thing, it made absolutely no sense to stay in. If he stayed, they wouldn't let him stay at the Board. They'd send his ass overseas and make him officer in charge of counting mess kits or something. He wasn't even sure he could have stayed if he wanted to. The army was cutting back on the number of reserve officers on active duty. The only way to stay was to go regular army; and to do that, you needed a college degree.

What he had, he realized, was a very pleasant way to spend the last six months of his service. He should be, and was, grateful for that.

On a Thursday afternoon, when he had about two months to go, Colonel McLean was waiting for him at the door of the cavernous maintenance building, when he came barrel-assing back to the barn from a day on the range.

He signaled the driver to stop when McLean put up his hand. He climbed down from the turret and signaled for the driver to go park the beast.

"Good afternoon, sir," he said to Colonel McLean. McLean put his hand on his arm.

"There's been some bad news for you, Craig," McLean

said. "Your grandfather's passed on. Your cousin Porter Craig telephoned."

It wasn't like the school where those chickenshit bastards wouldn't even let him go to New York to meet Ilse. By the time he got back to the barn, the Board had really taken care of him. He had leave orders and reservations on the plane. Mrs. McLean was in the apartment, Ilse had their bags packed, and all he had to do was take a shower and get dressed and go down and get in the colonel's car. That way he wouldn't have to worry about his car while he was gone. "Let us know when you're coming back, and we'll have somebody to meet you."

Mrs. McLean insisted on going into the airport with them, carrying the plastic bag filled with diapers and stuff for P.P. that Ilse normally carried over her shoulder.

"I have reservations," he said. "Two, round trip to New York. The name is Lowell.'

"Oh, Craig, I didn't think about money!" Ilse said. Mrs. McLean started to open her purse.

Lowell handed over his Air Travel card.

"First class," he said to the reservations clerk.

Ilse wanted to say something; but with Mrs. McLean there, she didn't.

"Do you have enough cash, Craig?" Mrs. McLean asked.

"I've got enough for a cab," he said. "That's all I'll need." Then he decided to hell with that, too. Truth time.

When he had the tickets, and knew when they would be in New York, he walked to a pay phone and called Broadlawns, collect.

Porter Craig finally came to the phone. He wondered what Porter was doing there. Was his mother on the sauce again with the Old Man dead?

"I'm leaving Louisville in about ten minutes, Porter," he said. "We get in at nine twenty. Will you have somebody meet me?"

"Why don't you just take a cab?" Porter said. "The house is full of people."

"Goddamnit, Porter, send a car and a chauffeur," he snapped. "Nine twenty. Eastern Airlines Flight 522." He hung up. He saw the look in Mrs. McLean's eyes and the bafflement in Ilse's.

P.P. acted up on the plane, probably sensing that something was wrong. All he wanted to do was be cradled in silence; everytime that Ilse started to talk, to ask questions, he started to fuss. Lowell was grateful. He didn't want to explain anything. He would explain afterward.

A chauffeur in gray livery was waiting at LaGuardia when the DC-6 landed.

"I've got to change him," Ilse said, as the chauffeur walked up to them.

"Lieutenant Lowell?" he asked, touching his cap.

"Is there somewhere Mrs. Lowell can change my son?" Lowell asked him.

Ilse looked at the chauffeur in confusion, in disbelief.

"Yes, sir," the chauffeur said. "If you'll follow me."

On the second floor of the terminal building, the chauffeur pushed open an unmarked door. Inside was a private lounge. There was a stewardess or somebody behind a desk. When she saw the young officer walk in, she stood up.

"May I help you, Lieutenant?" she asked, barring his way.

"This is Mr. Craig Lowell," the chauffeur said. The hostess looked at him. "Mr. Geoffrey Craig's grandson," the chauffeur said.

"Oh, please come in," the hostess said, "And this is Mrs. Lowell?"

"Mrs. Lowell has to change our son," Craig said.

"Right this way, Mrs. Lowell," the hostess said, and took Ilse's arm and led her away. Ilse looked actually frightened, Craig thought.

Lowell handed the chauffeur the baggage checks.

"The car is at entrance three, sir," the chauffeur said. "Would you like to meet me there? Or should I come back?"

"I'll meet you there." There was a bar in the VIP lounge. Craig ordered a double scotch and drank it neat.

The limousine was a Chrysler LeBaron with a stretched body. Craig wondered idly who it belonged to.

Ilse didn't ask questions on the way to Broadlawns. P.P. had upchucked, she said, and he had a fever. But when they passed inside the gate at Broadlawns, she asked where they were.

"They call this place 'Broadlawns,'" he said. "My mother lives here."

There were a half dozen cars on the circular drive before the house. Most of them were limousines, with their chauffeurs chatting in a group off to one side. When they walked up to the door, it was opened for them by the West Indian butler.

"Good evening, Mr. Lowell," he said. "Madam. The family is in the drawing room."

The family and some other vaguely remembered faces were scattered around the drawing room; but the center of attention was his mother, who was sitting on a couch facing the door to the foyer.

When she looked at him, he saw that she was drunk.

"Craig," she said, getting unsteadily to her feet, "Pop-Pop is gone."

The she saw Ilse standing behind him holding P.P. A look of confusion, of bafflement, clouded her face.

"I don't believe..." she began.

"Mother, this is Ilse," Craig said. "The baby is Peter-Paul. He's your grandson."

"I don't understand," his mother said, plaintively.

"My God!" Porter Craig said.

"This is my wife, Mother," Craig said. "And our son."

"But you never said anything," his mother said. She walked unsteadily over to Ilse and stared frankly at her.

"I'm sorry about your father, Mrs.... Mrs...." Ilse could not remember the name of the man Craig had told her his mother had married.

"You're foreign," Mrs. Andre Pretier accused.

"Ilse is German, Mother," Craig said.

"Yes, I can see she is," his mother said. She turned to face him. "How dare you? How could you do this to me?"

"For Christ's sake!" Craig said.

P.P. struggled, turned, and threw up what looked like a solid stream of vomitus that splashed on the carpet.

"My God!" Porter Craig said.

"Andre!" his mother shrieked, turning around to look desperately for her husband. When she located him, she screamed, "Do something."

"What, darling, would you like to have me do?"

"Get that goddamned woman and her squalling brat out of my house!" she screamed, and then ran into the corridor and up the stairs.

"Craig," Porter Craig said, "you really could have handled this whole thing better."

"When I want your fucking advice, Porter," Craig exploded, "I'll ask for it."

"Craig!" Ilse said. "I want to go."

"I really think that would be best," Andre Pretier said. "Under the circumstances. Until your mother has had a chance to adjust to this."

"Craig," Ilse repeated, just over the edge of tears, "I want to go."

"Everyone seems to forget that this is my house," Craig said. "I'll go if and when I goddamn please."

"Craig, for God's sake!" Porter Craig said. "What did you expect, when you just walked in like this, with that woman?"

"That woman, you pasty-faced cocksucker, is my wife!"

"You can't talk to me that way!" Porter said.

"Oh, my God, Craig, please," Ilse said. "Take me out of here."

"Go to the apartment," Andre Pretier said. "I'll call and tell them you're coming." Lowell glared at him. "Craig, you know your mother. Staying here will just make things worse."

"Where are they going to bury him from?" Craig asked.

"Saint Bartholomew's, of course," Porter Craig said. "He was on the vestry."

His mother reappeared at the doorway, hysterical.

"Get out, get out, get out!" she screamed, tears running down her cheeks.

"You see what you've done," Porter Craig said.

The butler was standing by the door across from his mother. His face was expressionless.

"Have the chauffeur put my things back in the car," Craig Lowell ordered. "And then telephone the Waldorf and get me a suite. Have them get me a doctor."

(Eleven)

Ilse whimpered all the way into New York City, and she refused to go either to the funeral home to see the body or to Saint Bartholomew's for the funeral service. He tried to tell her that his mother had nothing against her and that it could just as easily have gone the other way, that she could have welcomed Ilse and P. P. into the family. He tried to tell her that he had had no way of knowing which way his mother would go; and for that reason, he had put off the meeting until it could no longer be put off.

Ilse didn't seem to have been hurt by him, by what he had and had not done; and she certainly wasn't angry with him. She just wanted to get out of New York and go home, and she didn't want to see any of his family. He didn't blame her.

He sat next to his mother during the funeral, and he rode with her to the cemetery; but she didn't speak to him. She was on Cloud Nine, he realized. Tranquilized like a zombie.

When Andre Pretier and Porter Craig came to the suite in the Waldorf after the interment, Ilse fled into the bedroom and wouldn't come out.

They asked about the baby, and Craig told them the doctor said there was nothing wrong with him. He was teething, and the plane ride had upset him.

Andre Pretier said that if he had known who actually owned Broadlawns, he would have been in touch before to see what could be worked out in the way of renting it or, if Craig wished, having it appraised so that he could buy it.

Craig believed him.

"We can let Broadlawns ride," he said. "I was angry, and I shouldn't have said what I said."

"I understand there have been certain bequests in grandfather's will," Porter said.

"I understand, unless he was lying to me, that we split everything right down the middle," Craig said.

"We'll have to get together and talk things over," Porter Craig said.

"Steal what you can while you can, Porter," Craig said. "You've got two years."

"What is that supposed to mean?"

"Grandpa wanted me to go to Wharton, Porter," Lowell said. "I think I will. It's a two-year course. And then I'll be back."

"You're going to Wharton," Porter Craig said, tolerantly, patiently. "Wharton is a graduate school, Craig. You'll have to take a degree, Craig."

"Two things I learned in the army, Porter," Lowell said, even more dryly sarcastic, "is that 'when there's a will, there's a way' and 'there's an exception to every rule.' You ever think about that? Who knows? I just might be the next chairman of the board and chief executive officer."

X

(One)
Headquarters, The U.S. Army Counterintelligence Corps
Center
Camp Holabird
1019 Dundalk Avenue
Baltimore 19, Maryland
15 August 1948

First Lieutenant Sanford T. Felter spent the eighteen months following his visit to Craig Lowell at Fort Knox in school. First there was six months at the U.S. Army Language School at the Presidio of San Francisco. Next came six months at the Advanced Infantry Officer's Course at Fort Benning, Georgia. And finally there was to be six months at the CIC Center, "Dundalk High," in Baltimore.

The Army Language School was, and is, the best language school in the world. The instructors are persons wholly fluent in the language to be taught; and for many of them, the language they teach is their mother tongue.

From the first day, all instruction is in the language to be learned.

"Good morning, Lieutenant," Felter's advisor said. "What I have just said was in Greek, in case you didn't know. Henceforth, all instruction will be in Greek. The Greek phrase for 'repeat after me' is—" and he gave the phrase. "Repeat after me: Good morning, Major."

"Good morning, Major," Felter said in Greek.

"Very good," the major said in Greek. "That means very good."

"Yes, sir," Felter said in Greek. "I know. I picked up a lot of it while I was in Greece."

"Can you read it as well?"

"Yes, sir. I read it a little better than I speak it. I'm told I have a terrible accent."

Following a written and oral examination, Felter's service record was amended to add "Greek language proficiency: Fluent, written and oral." Permission was received from the adjutant general, with the concurrence of the assistant chief of staff G-2, to submit Lt. Felter to instruction in the Korean language, in lieu of Greek.

The Felters shared a neat little brick duplex with a Chinese-American lieutenant from Hawaii who was an instructor in Cantonese. Orally, there was a great difference between the two languages, but there was, Felter found, a strong similarity in their written forms.

Felter was graduated from the Korean language course "with distinction," and as a result of an examination, he was also determined to be "fluent" in written Cantonese and "semifluent" in spoken Cantonese.

They drove back across the country. Sharon was pregnant (it had probably happened *that* night at Fort Knox; the Mouse prayed that the alcohol in his blood would not affect the fetus), and the trip was punctuated by frequent stops for her to spend a day in a motel bed.

The quarters available to first lieutenants attending the Advanced Officer's Course at Fort Benning were nothing like the duplexes in the Presidio. And the philosophy of instruction seemed to be to physically exhaust the students in one overnight field training exercise after another. Finally, Sandy convinced

Sharon that it would be better for the baby if he moved into the BOQ and she went home to Newark.

The only pleasant memory the Mouse had of Fort Benning was the day he was called into the Student Officer Company orderly room and told by a visibly surprised major (who knew he was en route from the Army Language School to the Counterintelligence center and had logically concluded he was one more pencil-pushing Jewboy) that a general order from the Department of the Army had been received awarding him the Expert Combat Infantry Badge and the Bronze Star with "V" (for Valor) device for his service in Greece.

Years later, Felter learned that Big Jim Van Fleet had gone from Greece to Washington and patiently demanded over a period of six months, day after day, that the army owed those who served with divisions and regiments in Greece more than the hypocrisy of an Army Commendation Medal. He finally wore the bureaucracy down.

Camp Holabird was much nicer than Fort Benning. There were no quarters on the post for junior lieutenants, but Holabird was right in Baltimore in the Dundalk section, and he and Sharon and Sanford Felter, Jr., spent the time in a nice little rented apartment.

It was like going to civilian work, and the duty hours were eight to five. Baltimore was close enough to Newark so that his father and mother could drive down and spend an occasional weekend with them, or sometimes his mother would come alone on the train. And it was just a couple of hours from Philadelphia where Craig was enrolled in the Wharton School of Business; and so they saw a lot of the Lowells. When, his curiosity aroused, he asked Craig how he'd gotten into Wharton, without having an undergraduate degree, Craig had said they made an exception for people who owned banks.

Some of the things Felter learned in the CIC Center were fascinating, and some of them were sort of funny. Privately, he thought of parts of it as the Official U.S. Army Burglar and Safecracker School.

But the life was good. For one thing, there were a lot of Jews there. During the war and immediately afterward, there had been a lot of Jewish refugees from Hitler in the CIC; and even now there were still enough Jewish refugees from Germany getting drafted who spoke German and were needed in the CIC.

There were enough practicing Jews for a Sabbath service under a rabbi-chaplain at the post chapel, and the Mouse and Sharon also participated in the congregational activities. There weren't that many Jewish officers, but because most of the CIC people worked in civilian clothes or with the blue-triangle U.S. Civilian insignia on their uniform, there were far less restrictions against being friendly with enlisted personnel than there were at other places in the army.

For a while Sandy was worried that he had been categorized as a Jew and would wind up in Germany chasing Nazis and doing security checks on German girls who wanted to marry Americans. But in his fourth week of training, while the others were being instructed in the filing system of the National Socialist Democratic Worker's Party, he and a major who had never before spoken to him were taken to a small office and began a course which explained the inner administrative procedures of the Russian State Security Service.

He learned that the Jewish personnel who were bound for Germany and the de-Nazification program were referred to as "the temporary help" and was a little worried that it was an anti-Semitic comment. But he thought it through. That's all they really were. They were not involved in the business he was being trained for. What the temporary help were involved in was the punishment of the Nazis. The Nazis no longer posed a threat to the security of the United States. The communists did.

When he was graduated, he was given a special $350 allowance to buy civilian clothing and a little leather folder with a badge and his photograph on a plastic identification card that said, THE BEARER IS A SPECIAL AGENT OF THE UNITED STATES ARMY COUNTERINTELLIGENCE CORPS. They also issued him a five-shot Smith & Wesson. 38 Special revolver with a two-inch barrel.

He was first assigned to the 119th CIC Detachment, First Army, which was in an office building on West 57th Street in New York City. He wanted to rent an apartment in New York, but Sharon said there was no sense throwing money away.

They could live with his parents, and besides he would hurt his mother's feelings.

So every morning, early, he would ride the bus to Pennsylvania Station in Newark and take the commuter train to New York and the subway up to West 57th Street.

What the 119th CIC Detachment did mostly was run complete background investigations on people who wanted to get a Secret or a Top Secret security clearance. Special agents went around to where they lived and asked questions, and they went to their schools and talked to their teachers.

Felter did that for a couple of months, and then he was named deputy agent in charge of the detachment, which meant that he handled all the administration. There were thirty-six special agents, most of them sergeants, with a couple of warrant officers and one other officer. Everybody was in civilian clothes.

It wasn't what he had envisioned it would be like as an intelligence officer, and he began to wonder if he had been letting his imagination and his ego run away with him when he had thought he was going to do something important. Nevertheless, there didn't seem to be anything he could do about it.

And then, all of a sudden, he was called to a meeting at First Army Headquarters on Governors Island and introduced to a gray-haired man with an accent like Craig Lowell's. The man bought him lunch and talked German, Russian, and Polish to him. Felter knew he was being checked to see how well he spoke those languages, but he had no idea why.

And then the man said, "A friend of yours told me you can be a mean sonofabitch on occasion, Felter. Is that true?"

"I can't imagine who would say that about me," Felter said, truthfully.

"Paul Hanrahan," the man said, "is our mutual friend."

"Oh, Colonel Hanrahan. He said that about me?"

"He sends his best regards," the man said.

"Where is he now?" There was no reply to the question.

"Felter, how would you like to go to Berlin for a couple of years?" the man said.

"Oh, I'd like that," Felter said.

(Two)

Mr. and Mrs. Sanford T. Felter and little Sandy flew to Germany on Pan American Airways. As a Department of the Army civilian employee, accountant, GS-9 (equivalent, if he had been an officer, to captain), employed by something called the office of Production Analysis, Mr. Felter was entitled to company-grade officer quarters, a PX card, and other privileges, including access to the U.S. Army Hospital for himself and his family.

For three months he debriefed line-crossers from East Germany, at first with regard to the placement of Russian military formations. Then, as he acquired knowledge of East Germany and Poland, he began to specialize in information regarding the Volkspolizei, the paramilitary East German police force.

From there he moved naturally to a position immediately under the station chief himself. This entailed the recruitment of Germans and others who—because they hated the Russians, or else for the money—were willing to cross the border the other way to provide specific answers to his (or Washington's) questions regarding various facets of East German military and economic activity.

Sharon liked Berlin. Zehlendorf, where they lived, hadn't suffered the destruction other parts of the city had; and their quarters were the nicest they had had so far, even nicer than the duplex at the Presidio.

But she really didn't understand when he told her that he was sorry, but he wanted her to discourage the overtures of friendship from the wives of officers he had known at West Point. They would obviously be curious to know what he was doing and that awkward question could not be answered. Neither did Sharon understand why she had to have a driver for the car and was forbidden to leave the little compound in which they lived on foot, unless Sandy or the "driver" she had been assigned were with her.

"Karl is a very nice man," she said. "And I know he wasn't a Nazi. But he scares me. Why does he have to carry a gun, Sandy? Why are you carrying a gun, Sandy?"

He could hardly tell her that the reason that she had been assigned a "driver" and that he was never without a gun was that the bastards on the other side often expressed their displeasure with their American counterparts by staging hit-and-run automobile accidents or by throwing acid in their children's faces.

Sharon spoke German, of course, and that made it easier for her to make friends with the German women who worked with Sandy, and even with women she met when she shopped. She adjusted.

When it became evident that the East Germans had every intention of transforming their border guard and the purely military elements of the Volkspolizei into an army (as, indeed, the West was transforming the Grenzpolizei, the customs/border guard, into a new Wehrmacht, ultimately to be called the Bundeswehr), Felter, on his own initiative, began compiling a dossier on its potential officers. The station would also get one from the Gehlen Organization, of course. Felter thought it would be good to be able to compare the two.

Many of the officers would obviously come from the present officers of the Volkspolizei, but there were not enough of those to lead an army. That left the Russians with two options: They could promote beyond their abilities officers and noncoms presently serving in the Volkspolizei whose loyalties to communism generally and the Kremlin specifically were beyond question; or they could draw upon the pool of captured officers they still (despite weak, pro forma, denials to the contrary), held scattered all over the Soviet Union.

Felter made regular inquiries concerning these officers, for it would not have surprised him if Katyn had been repeated many times in the blank expanses of northern Russia. Though he was never able to pin anything down, he heard rumors of large-scale massacres; and that buttressed his belief that the Soviets had decided upon another plan of action. If a man were confined to hard labor for many years and then offered the chance to put on again an officer's uniform— and particularly if he were not required to take an oath of allegiance to a communist state per se, but simply to a German government— he could be quite valuable to the Soviets.

Such men couldn't be trusted with command, of course. That would take someone of sound ideology. But there were any number of staff positions that needed filling, and filling them with qualified officers would free ideologically sound officers for command.

The Soviets ran the risk, of course, that among these "nonpolitical officers" would be some whose imprisonment had politicized them against the Soviet Union and their East German vassals. Such officers would be susceptible to approach from the West, either for purely ideological reasons or purely selfish ones. The Russians would watch for such men carefully, but two, or ten, or a hundred would slip through their net. Sandy Felter was determined to catch as many of them as he could.

This sort of thing was technically the responsibility of the Gehlen Organization, and any activities in this area by Sandy were supposed to be coordinated with the Gehlen Organization. The prescribed channel to effect liaison was through his station chief to the Gehlen man serving as liaison with him. Sandy Felter, with nothing to go on but a gut feeling, did not trust the Gehlen Organization liaison man, although the man enjoyed the full support of the station chief.

Fully aware that what he was doing was twice forbidden (going out of channels and establishing what were known as "private files"), he began to collect the names of prisoners known to be alive in the Soviet Union. When he had the names of fifty-three such officers in the grades of major through colonel, he carried them with him to the Gehlen Organization's compound in the American Zone outside Munich. And then he took a chance. He gave them to a fat analyst who looked for all the world like a jolly butcher. He told him the names were from a private file and that he hoped to expand the file. The fat jolly German told him that he could not, of course, accept material out of channels, but if Felter would come back in fifteen minutes, he would return his list to him.

When he picked up his list, there was stapled to the back of it three pages—photocopied—of a similar list. Where the names on the added list were duplicated on Felter's list, there was a brief biography of the individual name and a file number.

In the months that followed, he furnished the jolly butcher with two hundred more names, and he received in return more than one hundred other names he did not have. One of the names rang a very loud bell.

Greiffenberg, Paul.(?) Oberstleutnant(?) NKVD # 88–234–017. Sicherheitsdienst Folio Berlin 343–1903. Camp No. 263, Kyrtymya(?) 18Mar46. (File 405–001–732).

He picked up the Berlin telephone book. There were twenty-two people (including all spelling variations) named Greiffenberg. Paul was Ilse's father's middle name. P.P.'s name was Peter-Paul, with a hyphen. It had been Oberst, not Oberstleutnant. It had been *von* Greiffenberg, not plain Greiffenberg, and there were twenty-two plain Greiffenbergs in Berlin, so the name was not uncommon. Most importantly, Bellmon had told him that Oberst Graf Peter-Paul von Greiffenberg had been shot down by the Russians outside Zwenkau. It was highly unlikely that what he had was anything more than a coincidence.

But he asked for File 405–001–732, a routine request for information from the Gehlen Organization, sent through his station chief to the Gehlen man.

The station chief didn't pay attention when the request was sent in, but when the file in due time arrived, he blew his top and ate Sandy's ass out. He told him to stick to what he was supposed to do, keep up on the Volkspolizei, and forget about long-time prisoners.

"For Christ's sake, Felter," the station chief concluded, "The last note on this guy is March 1946. By now he's probably been shot. They do that, you know."

Felter never got a chance to look at File 405–001–732; and the next time he got to the Gehlen Organization, the jolly fat butcher was not there. You did not ask where people were.

He kept building up his list, however; and whenever he had a chance to debrief a returned long-time prisoner, he always brought up the name of Colonel Graf Peter-Paul von Greiffenberg. Nobody had ever heard of him.

(Three)
Philadelphia, Pennsylvania
21 April 1949

Craig Lowell, in a tweed jacket, a tieless white button-down-collar shirt, gray flannel slacks, and loafers, walked across the campus of the University of Pennsylvania to the MG, Ilse's car, in the parking lot. The enormous old Packard had gone shortly after they'd come to Philadelphia. Ilse didn't like to drive it, for one thing, and for another, he rather disliked having people stop and stare at it when he drove it around town.

He bought a Jaguar. He wanted the Jaguar, but he didn't like the trade-in offer the dealer made, so he did something impulsive with the huge yellow automobile. He had it delivered to Broadlawns with a red ribbon tied to the hood ornament, and a card taped—along with the bill of sale—to the wheel:

> Dear Andre,
> Thanks for everything. Try to stay on the black stuff between the trees.
>
> Fondly,
> Craig.

Andre liked classic cars, and he had done well by his mother. Ilse thought that it was a very nice thing for him to do. Ilse was about as afraid of the Jaguar as she had been of the Packard. And one day, when he had the Jaguar in for service, Ilse had walked out of the showroom and stared into the adjacent showroom.

"That's sweet," she said. "Are they very expensive, Craig?" she said about the car on the showroom floor. So he'd bought her an MG-TC with wire wheels. It made you feel as if you were being dragged along the ground in a bucket.

Ilse was coming along well. He couldn't be happier. They took an apartment high up at 2601 Parkway, nothing fancy, just enough for them; and Ilse furnished it in something called Danish Modern. He didn't know or care about things like that, but if it made her happy, great.

The apartment had three bedrooms, a kitchen, and an enormous living room on two levels. He went to a used office furniture place and bought a huge desk, some bookcases, and a lamp that moved around on swivels. He also rented a typewriter from IBM. The bills for the apartment and the typewriter, and what the GI Bill didn't pay for at Wharton, went into his Trust. As a married veteran with two dependents the government sent him a check for $134.80 a month. He gave that to Ilse for pocket money. The estate of Geoffrey Craig sent him a check every month, and a much larger check every three

months. He played around with the stock market with the larger
check, what was left of it after it passed through the hands of
the accountant; and he lived on the monthly checks. When the
checking balance got out of hand, he put the excess in the
market, too.

He turned down business propositions from Porter Craig.
He told him he would wait to get into that until he was through
Wharton and in New York when he could look at everything
and see where things stood.

Porter had been obliging as hell from the time he'd seen
him in the Waldorf right after the funeral. He was obviously
kissing ass for his own reasons, but some of it was useful. For
instance, Porter had put him up for the Rose Tree Hunt, on the
Main Line. He didn't intend to hunt, but they played some
half-assed polo, and there were bridle paths.

Ilse was riding. And she rode well. And she gradually started
to tell stories about riding as a child in Germany with her father.
Not all the women at Rose Tree were horse's asses. Some of
them were actually rather nice, and Ilse had moved into those
circles. Unhappily, his fellow students at Wharton were generally a pain in the ass, fiercely ambitious pencil-pushers. But
he held his own against them academically, and he came to
form the nasty arrogant opinion that if those morons were the
competition he was going to have to face when he went to New
York, then he was not going to have a hell of a lot of trouble.

Giving Andre the Packard had been rather like casting bread
upon the waters. He was sure Andre was responsible for the
armed truce that now existed between him and his mother. His
mother and Andre had been to see them twice, once when they
first moved into the apartment, and next a couple of months
ago, when the Pretiers were on their way to the Palm Beach
place.

Ilse, who was as hardheaded as a rock, was never going to
completely forgive his mother for the scene at Broadlawns, but
she had decided that a baby needed a grandmother and possibly
vice versa, so she watched carefully as his mother would play—
briefly—with P.P. It was hardly a scene, Grandma and Child,
that would wind up on a cover of the *Saturday Evening Post*,
but it was something.

In the campus parking lot Craig Lowell stepped around a

panel truck and found himself six feet from the muzzle evacuator on a 90 mm tube on an M26. Somebody was moving the turret. It was the cleanest M26 he had ever seen. Behind the tank was the recovery vehicle that had obviously carried it onto the campus. And behind that was an M24 light tank, a couple of M8 armored cars, some trucks, and a couple of jeeps.

The Pennsylvania National Guard was recruiting on campus.

"You want to look inside?" a captain in ODs asked him.

Lowell smiled and shook his head, "no." But then, he decided, what the hell. He laid his briefcase on the fender and climbed up over the drive wheel. He waited until some potential recruit, smiling with delight, climbed out of the commander's turret, and then he swung his legs through the hatch and dropped inside.

They'd stationed a master sergeant inside. Christ, the inside was spotless. The paint wasn't even chipped. It must be brand new, or damned near brand new. The master sergeant showed him the breech of the tube, and the place where they stored the rounds and the driver's seat.

Craig sniffed and smelled the familiar smells, and then he smiled and hoisted himself out of the commander's hatch.

"Like to drive something like that?" the captain asked him, with a smile.

Craig smiled back and nodded, "yes."

"Give me two minutes of your time," the captain said, "and let me explain our program to you."

Somehow reluctant to get off the tank, Lowell nodded.

If he would enlist in the Guard—either in the Tank Company or the Reconnaissance Company, which also had vacancies—he would be trained to drive and operate a tank at the regular Tuesday evening meetings, half past seven to half past nine. Then in the summertime, there were two weeks active duty for training. During these two weeks he would receive the same pay and allowance the regular army got. After he had gone to enough Tuesday Evening meetings and had completed one summer camp, he would be eligible to enter Advanced ROTC; and on graduation he would be commissioned a second lieutenant in the army reserve.

"I've already got a reserve commission," Craig said.

"You do? As what?" the captain asked.

"First john," Craig replied. "Armor." He jerked his thumb

at the M26. "M26 platoon commander." He had been promoted to first john the day before he had been released from active duty.

"School training? You been through Knox?"

"I taught M4A4 gunnery at Knox," Lowell said.

"No experience on these, then?"

"I was an assistant project officer at the Armor Board for that 90 mm high-velocity tube," Lowell said. "I know a lot more about that hot noisy sonofabitch than I really want to."

"We can use you," the captain said.

"No, thanks," Craig said.

"Get you a promotion to captain," the captain said. "What the hell, it's a day pay for two hours on Tuesday."

"No, thanks," Craig repeated. "But thank you just the same."

The captain gave him his card and said he should think it over. No obligation, he said, just come by the armory on Broad Street some Tuesday and see what it's like.

The first sergeant was a Fairmount Park cop. None of the platoon leaders had ever served a day on active duty. They were graduates of the One Night a Week for a Year, Plus Two Weeks at Summer Camp PANG OCS. The supply sergeant was Colonel Gambino's brother. Colonel Gambino had served two years as a major and then light bird in War II. He had commanded a Transportation Corps truck battalion, after being directly commissioned because of his experience with heavy trucks. Gambino and Sons had for years had the garbage hauling contract for the north end of Philadelphia.

"I'll tell it to you straight," Colonel Gambino said. "I felt like a fucking fool at Indiantown Gap last summer. We had nine tanks, and we couldn't get one of the fuckers out to the firing range without the fucker breaking down."

"What about the one I saw out on the campus?"

"I borrowed it, and a guy to run it, from the 112th Infantry in Harrisburg."

"You got spare parts?"

"I got a fucking warehouse full of spare parts. What I don't have is anybody who ever saw a fucking M26 before. I did all right with the M4A4s we had."

"I think I can get the M26s running for you," Lowell said.

"You get them fuckers running, you're a captain."

"I'm a captain and Tank Company commander, and *then* I get them running," Lowell said.

"I already got a company commander. He's the S-4's brother-in-law. I can hardly fire him."

"If you want me to get your tanks running, Colonel," Craig Lowell had said, quite sure of himself, "you're going to have to."

HEADQUARTERS

111th INFANTRY REGIMENT

PENNSYLVANIA NATIONAL GUARD
305 North Broad Street
Philadelphia, Penna.

SPECIAL ORDERS   15 May 1949

Number 27

EXTRACT

* * * * * * * * * *

3. 1st Lt Craig W. LOWELL, 0–495302, Armor, U.S. Army Reserve (Apt. 2301, 2601 Parkway, Phila Penna) having joined, assigned Tank Company, 111th Inf. 28th Inf Div, PANG for dy.

4. 1st Lt. Craig W LOWELL, 0–495302, Armor PANG, is Promoted CAPT PANG with DOR 15 May 1949. (Auth: Letter, Hq, The Adjutant General PANG, Subj: One Grade Promotion of Officers to fill PANG vacancies, dtd 11 Feb 1949.)

* * * * * * * * * *

BY ORDER OF COLONEL GAMBINO
Max T. Solomon
Major, Armor, PANG
Adjutant

HEADQUARTERS

111th INFANTRY REGIMENT

PENNSYLVANIA NATIONAL GUARD
305 North Broad Street
Philadelphia, Penna.

GENERAL ORDERS   15 May 1949

Number 3

The undersigned assumes command effective this
date.

Craig W. Lowell
Captain, Armor, PANG

While it proved impossible to get all nine M26s ready for firing
in time for summer camp, Captain Lowell got all of them
running well enough to be driven from the armory to the railhead, and then from the railhead at Indiantown Gap to the
training area.

He found one competent mechanic and two half-assed me-
chanics in the company; and the four of them—Lowell happily
up to ears in grease—got the turrets and the traversing mech-
anisms and the range finders and the sights and the tubes themselves ready on three tanks. There was no way that all nine
tanks could be gotten into shape with the time and the people
he had.

There was a simple dishonest solution to that. He fired nine
functioning tanks by firing the same three functioning tanks
three times over. The regular army inspecting staff was so
surprised that any of the 111th Infantry's M26s ran and fired
at all that they didn't notice (or pretended not to) that the paint
on the vehicle identification numbers was fresh and a little
runny, as if the numbers underneath had been painted over.

Everybody was happy, from the division commander down
to Captain Lowell. When he came back from summer camp,
he loaded Ilse and P.P. in the car and they went down to Cape
May, N.J., and rented a cottage on the beach for the rest of
the summer until he went back to school. Every Tuesday night,

he got in the Jaguar and drove back to Philly for drill at the armory.

What he was thinking of doing, when he finished school in January and they moved to New York, was join the New York National Guard. What the hell, some people played tennis for a hobby and some played golf. What he would do for a hobby is play soldier.

He'd straightened out the Fairmount Park cop who was his first sergeant, and the first sergeant straightened out the platoon sergeants while Captain Lowell straightened out the platoon commanders. Tank Company, 111th Infantry, PANG, was arguably the sharpest company in the regiment, possibly even in the division; and Lowell could not remember anything else that had given him so much pleasure since he had taught the Greeks of No. 12 Company how to fire the Garand.

It might be a little childish, but so what? If he was going to spend the rest of his life computing potential return on capital investment, getting out in the fresh air and getting his hands dirty would probably be very good for him.

(Four)
The American Sector
Berlin, Germany
21 May 1950

Lieutenant Colonel Bob Bellmon came through Berlin as part of some visiting general's entourage and looked up Sandy Felter. Bellmon was now in the Pentagon, assigned to the Office of the Deputy Chief of Staff for Operations.

He called Felter and offered to take Sharon and Sandy out for dinner, but they had him instead to their quarters. Sandy offered to send a car to pick him up, but Bellmon said he had a car and it wouldn't be necessary.

Felter was curious about two things: How did Bellmon come into possession of his quarters' telephone number, which wasn't listed in the Berlin Military Post telephone directory, and how did he know where he and Sharon lived? The compound was not listed either.

Sharon, sensing that Sandy liked Bellmon and that Bellmon was important to their future, made a special dinner, and even arranged for one of the maids to take care of Little Sandy after he'd been shown off, so that he wouldn't be a nuisance. After dinner she tried to leave them alone twice, in case "they wanted to talk," but each time Bellmon made her stay. The third time she asked, Bellmon said, "I really would like a couple of minutes alone with him, Sharon."

Sharon said she'd go see how Little Sandy was doing.

Felter offered Bellmon a brandy and set the bottle in front of him.

"How'd you get my quarters' number, Colonel?" Sandy asked, aware that he was putting Bellmon on the defensive. I am no longer an innocent young lieutenant, he thought.

The telephone number had come from Red Hanrahan, Bellmon told him, and that amounted to an announcement that Hanrahan was also in Washington. Hanrahan, Bellmon said, sent his best wishes and had asked about Duke Lowell.

"I haven't heard from him since he got out," Bellmon said. "Have you?"

"Sharon hears from Ilse all the time," Felter said. "He made captain in the Pennsylvania National Guard."

"Oh, Jesus Christ!" Bellmon said. "God help the National Guard."

In the mistaken impression that Felter knew MacMillan, Bellmon said that Mac had gone to helicopter school, and that he had been assigned to Tokyo. "MacArthur likes the notion of having another Medal of Honor around, I suppose. They can exchange war stories."

"Is he working for MacArthur?"

"He's assigned to Supreme Headquarters," Bellmon said. "I think he's too smart to get close to MacArthur. Good Soldier Mac avoids getting too close to the flames if at all possible." Then he asked, surprisingly, "You like working in civilian clothing, Sandy?"

"It's all right." There was more to the question than idle curiosity. "Colonel Hanrahan ask you to ask me that?"

Colonel Bellmon ignored the question.

"How are you getting along with your station chief?" he asked, instead.

Felter didn't answer the question.

"He asked to have you replaced," Bellmon said. Felter wondered if the visit of Colonel Bellmon was social, if Hanrahan had known he was coming to Berlin and had asked him to have a word with him, or whether Bellmon's role with DCSOPS had an intelligence connection of its own, and he was here officially.

Whatever the case, Felter was sorry Bellmon had told him what he had. Not because the station chief had stuck a knife in him, but because it might tend to cloud his judgment about the station chief.

"If I were in a position to ask for his relief," Felter said, flatly, "I would. And I would be justified. He's not."

"The story is that you're putting your nose in the wrong places," Bellmon reported.

"An intelligence officer has to walk a narrow line between putting his nose every place he can and interfering with somebody else," Felter replied. It had just occurred to him (and he wondered why it hadn't occurred to him before) that the only two officers in the army to whom he could say exactly what was on his mind were Hanrahan and Bellmon. Hanrahan because of their Greek service, Bellmon because of Katyn and Task Force Parker.

"You don't think you've gone over the line?" Bellmon asked. Felter shook his head.

"The only time I came close to it was asking for a file on a Soviet prisoner, a man named Greiffenberg."

"Greiffenberg? Our Greiffenberg?"

"I don't know. The one I found is a lieutenant colonel," Felter said. "And plain, without the 'von.'"

"Do you think it's possible he's still alive?"

"About one chance in two hundred," Felter said. "I thought it was worth checking out. But I was very careful. The file I asked for was purely routine. I checked that out. It had been offered to everybody. CIC. DIA. Even the Office of Naval Intelligence."

"What was your information? Where is your Greiffenberg?"

"I had fairly reliable information that there was an Oberstleutnant Paul Greiffenberg at a labor camp in Siberia. There are twenty-two people with that name in the Berlin phone book."

"How did it come up?" Bellmon asked.

"I've been compiling a list, a private file, on potential East German Army staff officers. The reason I checked was obviously personal. Not really personal. A gut feeling. Sometimes I go on my gut feelings. Ilse Lowell's maiden name was Greiffenberg, and her father is missing."

"Ilse's father is dead," Bellmon said. "The Russians shot him the day before you and Phil Parker showed up at Zwenkau."

"You see the body?"

"They shot all the Germans," Bellmon said.

"The reason I asked is that I found out they usually didn't shoot Oberstleutnants and better. Not even the SS equivalent. Not right off, anyway, the way they blew your people away."

"I didn't see the body," Bellmon said. "I didn't want to see it. But I think other people did."

"The operative word is 'think,'" Felter said.

"You don't happen to have a photograph?"

"I never got to see the file," Felter said. "My station chief sent it back."

"Why did he do that?"

"I was being put in my place," Felter said.

"What would you do if you found out?" Bellmon asked.

"Tell Craig and let him decide," Felter said.

"If the Russians knew he knew about Katyn," Bellmon said, "he'd be dead."

"Yes, he would," Felter said.

"Does your station chief know you know about Katyn?"

"I've never discussed it with him."

"What's he got it in for you then for?"

"Maybe he doesn't like Jews," Felter said. "But it's probably because I make him nervous. He's not too bright. Just bright enough to know it. He relies pretty heavily on Gehlen's liaison man."

"And you don't?"

"No."

"You're not going to be replaced," Bellmon said. "Unless you want to be. You want to come work for me in the Pentagon?"

"Not right now, but thank you."

"Something you want to finish here?"

"Yes."

"I gather it's important?"

"I think so."

"Red thinks you're pretty levelheaded, Sandy," Bellmon said.

"I think I am, too."

"When you're ready to leave here, let me know. I can use you, and a Pentagon tour wouldn't hurt your career."

"I gather you're doing something interesting?"

"Something right down your line, as a matter of fact."

"Maybe a little later," Felter said.

"Doing something foolish now would be liable to ruin your career," Bellmon said.

"I could always go join the Pennsylvania National Guard," Felter said, and they laughed out loud; and that was the end of the conversation.

(Five)

Felter thought about it a good deal in the days that followed. The only way his station chief would have enough balls to actually ask that he be replaced would be if someone encouraged him to do so. And that meant the man from the Gehlen Organization. One more improbable, unreliable, gut feeling to add to the question. Reliability Factor: Zero.

He also had a gut feeling about his loss rate, but he really had nothing to go on there, either. So far as his loss rate went, he was losing fewer agents than was to be expected (he should have lost more), but he was suspicious about the *quality* of the people he did lose. He wasn't losing the quick-money people. He was losing the people who had too much experience to be casually rolled up the way it seemed to be happening.

In the most recent case, one of his German associates recruited a former Dresdener who had been a black marketer and who for a price was willing to go back to Dresden.

When Felter submitted the memorandum and request for funds to the station chief, he identified the Dresdener as a former captain of the Sicherheitsdienst who had been in Munich. The memorandum also gave the date when he would cross the line.

An agent-in-place reported to him three days later that the

agent had been rolled up in East Berlin as he boarded the bus for Dresden. They hadn't even asked for his papers. They had been expecting him. They knew what he looked like, and they knew where to look for him.

The station chief listened carefully and thoughtfully to Felter's analysis of the probable explanation for that and then told Felter there was no way *his* German associate, who had been vouched for by General Gehlen *personally*, was a double agent.

What had happened to Felter's Dresdener was just one of those things. For all Felter knew, they had been looking for him. It was against the law to be a black marketer in East Germany, too. "And in the future, Felter, just put the facts in your memorandums. I've been charged with making analyses."

The facts were, as Felter saw them:

(a) He had arranged for *his* German associate to be out of Berlin, and he was sure that he had stayed out, from the time he had brought the agent's name up. His associate had not known whether Felter had put the Dresdener to work or not.

(b) He had typed up the memorandum and request for funds himself, rather than have his clerk do it, and he had omitted to make the usual copies for the file, and he had personally carried it to the station chief.

(c) It was unlikely that the station chief was a double agent.

(d) His agent had been rolled up; they had expected him.

A month from the day Lieutenant Felter entertained Lt. Col. Bellmon at dinner, Colonel Luther Hollwitz, who despite his Germanic roots, was a native-born Soviet citizen at that time serving as deputy chief of station for the NKVD in Berlin, crossed into the American Zone at Check Point Charley, at the wheel of a 1940 Opel Kapitan. He drove to the subway station at the intersection of Beerenstrasse and Onkel Tom Allee in the West Berlin suburb of Zehlendorf in the American sector. He walked a block to the Hotel zum Fister, drank a glass of Berliner Kindl Pilsener in the small dining room, and then walked up the stairs to Room 13. Two minutes after he entered the room, he was joined by the liaison officer assigned to the Office of Production Analysis by the Gehlen Organization. They shook hands perfunctorily, in the European manner, and then sat down in facing, identical rattan armchairs.

Something came crashing through the window, which

opened onto a small fenced-in courtyard. Colonel Hollwitz and the liaison officer from the Gehlen Organization had just enough time to identify the object which had come flying through the windowpane. It was a World War II German Army field grenade, the kind the Americans called the "Potato Masher," because it looked like that kitchen utensil.

By the time he heard the dull explosion, Sandy Felter had already dropped from the fire escape to the ground, jumped onto his bicycle, and pedaled through the alley to the sidewalk in front of the Hotel zum Fister.

Like the other people on the sidewalk, he stopped when he heard the explosion. Like the other people on the sidewalk, he looked around, registered surprise and curiosity, and then, shrugging, went about his business. He eased his bicycle over the curb, and rode slowly away.

When the Kriminalpolizei investigated the incident, they located sixteen people who had been in the immediate vicinity of the Hotel zum Fister at the time of the explosion. Not one of them remembered the young man on the bicycle.

Within thirty-six hours, the bodies had been identified, and the decision made "at the highest levels" that the files of the Office of Production Analysis had been wholly compromised.

The station chief was immediately flown out of Berlin to the United States. The Office of Production Analysis was closed down. The entire contents of its office—personnel, files, desks, tables, even the telephones—were taken under Military Police escort to Templehof Field and loaded aboard three C-47 aircraft of the Military Airlift Command. They were flown to Munich and then trucked to Garmisch-Partenkirchen near the Austrian border. The U.S. Army maintained a recreational area there for its forces. Other agencies of the army and the United States government had taken over salt mines there—literally miles of labyrinthine passages—for other purposes.

The man who had bought Felter lunch at Governors Island was there also, ostensiby a Special Services Lt. Colonel in charge of the army's recreation area. And there too was Colonel Red Hanrahan.

"I'm a little disappointed in you, Felter," Hanrahan said. "Was that really necessary?"

"I thought so," Felter replied. "It was two lives versus thirteen. We would have had to give Hollwitz back. By the time I would have been able to make my case to my station chief, there is no telling what damage would have been done."

"Why a hand grenade?" the man who had bought him lunch inquired, with polite curiosity. "What if it had been a dud, as old as it was?"

"I rebuilt the detonator," Felter said. "And replaced the charge with C-4."

"How thoughtful of you," the man from Governors Island said dryly.

"What happens to me now?" Felter asked.

"You'd be surprised to know how far up this went," Hanrahan replied. "Before it was decided that you had done what had to be done, under the circumstances."

"That doesn't answer my question, sir, with all respect."

"Do you know how to ski, Felter?" the man from Governors Island asked.

"No, sir."

"You'll have plenty of opportunity to learn," the man from Governors Island said. "We're going to keep you here, on display, and wait and see if the NKVD has figured this out."

"What about my family?" Felter asked.

"I'm sure you considered that before you acted on your own," the man from Governors Island said. "To answer the specific question: If we shipped your family home, they would know for sure, wouldn't they?"

Hanrahan said: "That decision came from way up, too, Mouse."

"I think they're going to blame it on the Gehlen Organization," Felter said. "They know that we normally hire out this sort of thing. When they find out this wasn't done on a contract, they'll think Gehlen."

"Unless they've got somebody else inside Gehlen who knows different," the man from Governors Island said.

"The only man in Gehlen who knows they didn't do it is Gehlen himself," Hanrahan said. "He's very embarrassed by the whole affair."

"What am I going to be doing?" Felter asked.

"No matter what happens," Hanrahan said, "you can't work covert any more. So we're going to put the Sphinx on your lapels and put you to work overt in uniform. You'll get your promotion on time, next month I think. The standard procedure, what would normally happen to someone like you whose operation was blown.

"You could, of course, resign," the man from Governors Island said.

"Is that a suggestion, sir?" Felter asked.

"No, it's not," he said. "But it's an option you can consider. You mentioned your family."

"I believe," Felter repeated, "that they're going to blame it on Gehlen."

Lieutenant and Mrs. Felter were assigned quarters on the second floor of a two-family, steeply roofed villa in Garmisch-Partenkirchen. Lieutenant Felter was assigned duty as an instructor (Soviet Army Organization) at the European Command Intelligence School and Center.

The day after he received his promotion to captain (Sharon was very angry with him; she simply could not see why he had to pay for his own promotion party, which cost nearly three hundred dollars), he learned that the station chief had been struck and killed by a hit-and-run driver on Collins Avenue in Miami Beach, Florida.

(Six)

Captain Craig W. Lowell, Commanding, Tank Company 111th Infantry, PANG, submitted his resignation on 14 December 1949, to take effect 16 January 1950, the day after he would graduate from Wharton and move to New York. Colonel Gambino was sorry to see him go, and said that he would be happy to ask around and see about getting Lowell a job in Philly if he really wasn't dead set on living in New York.

Lowell thanked him, but said he had to go to New York.

When he went home that night from the armory, he stopped in a bar on North Broad Street and had a couple of drinks with his first sergeant, enough drinks so that when he got home he had enough courage to tell Ilse what he was really thinking.

He didn't want to go to New York, he said. Spending the rest of his life making money he didn't need, becoming another Porter Craig, was a frightening prospect that became more frightening as the time to go to New York came closer. Ilse said she didn't really want to go to New York either.

He gathered his courage and told her what he really wanted to do was go back in the army. What did she think about that?

She said that she thought he should do what he really wanted to do. She would be happy no matter what he decided.

He spent three days writing and rewriting and polishing a letter to the adjutant general. Subject: Application for Recall to Active Duty.

He included with it, as attachment one, a letter from the dean of students at the Wharton School of Business, stating that although he had been admitted as a special student, he had undergone the curricula prescribed for candidates for the degree of Master of Science, Business Administration. Had he had the requisite baccalaureate degree, he would have been graduated as an MBA, summa cum laude; and if, at any time within the next five years he acquired such a baccalaureate degree, the Wharton School of Business of the University of Pennsylvania would, on application, award the MBA degree to him.

He included a letter from Colonel Gambino, who wrote that Captain Lowell was the finest company-grade officer he had ever known, and that he recommended him without qualification as a superb leader of men, as an outstanding administrator, and as a maintenance officer of proven ability. Gambino didn't believe all of this bullshit, of course, and he suspected correctly that Lowell thought of him as a dumb wop. But fair's fair: The snotty fucker had taken over the fucked-up tank company, straightened it out, got the fucking tanks running and the tubes shooting, and brought back a fucking SUPERIOR rating from summer camp.

After thinking it over carefully for a day and a half, Lowell's letter to the adjutant general included this sentence:

"4. The undersigned is aware that he is underage in grade and is willing to accept a reduction to first lieutenant in the event this application for call to extended active duty is favorably acted upon."

When there was no reply, he went through with the move to New York. Porter Craig was helpful. He personally took Craig and Ilse around and showed them half a dozen apartments in properties owned by the estate. Ilse wasn't enthusiastic about any of them.

"I know," Porter said. "The Mews."

"What the hell is a Mews?" Craig asked.

Porter showed them. Ilse was enthusiastic. The Mews, a block off Washington Square in the Village, was a row of town houses on a cobblestone alley. The whole block was owned by the estate, which meant the alley itself was a private street, like Shubert Alley. A private security guard kept the public out. You could park your car in front of the place when you didn't want to put it in a garage.

Ilse thought it was a good omen that the Mews weren't quite finished. She could pick the color of paint she wanted and decorate it herself. Until it was ready, they moved into a suite at the Fifth Avenue Hotel, a block away.

Lowell went to work downtown. Porter Craig very gently suggested that he spend some time looking around, to get a feel of the operation, and see if some facet of it didn't really interest him. Porter had taken over Geoffrey Craig's office, but their grandfather's name was still on the door. What he was doing, Craig realized, was waiting until it became evident to Craig himself that Porter should assume the chairmanship of the board. Geoffrey Craig had been chairman of the board and chief executive officer. Porter was functioning as "acting" chairman of the board. Logically, since Porter knew more about what was going on than Craig did, he should become chairman, and they could give Craig a title, maybe president, which would reflect his share of the holdings, but leave Porter in charge.

Porter had obviously decided, and Craig rather admired him for it, that he should lean over backward to avoid an awkward confrontation. Craig had already come to the same conclusion, that Porter was obviously better qualified to run things than he was, and that a confrontation would be likely to cost both of them money. The thing to do, he decided, was let Porter have his way, but not to hand it to him on a silver platter. Let him sweat a little, first.

Craig went to the 169th Infantry, NYNG, to see what he could do about joining the New York Guard. They had their full complement of officers, he was told, fully qualified. They would enter his name on a waiting list, but frankly, Mr. Lowell, we just don't believe that any vacancies are going to occur for which you would be qualified as a captain. Your chances would be much better if you were willing to apply for a second lieutenant's table of organization position. We really feel that first lieutenants should have between three and seven years of commissioned service, and our junior captain has eight years. You have two years of active service, and a year in the Guard. You see my point, I'm sure.

When he told Porter, over lunch, about this, Porter laughed gently at him.

"You really should have come to me," Porter said. "If you really want to be a weekend warrior, I'll have a word with the governor."

"I need a recommendation from you to the governor?"

"All I would do, Craig," Porter said, "is remind the governor who you are."

"You mean who I am in terms of how much Grandpa left me?"

"All right, if that's the way you wish to put it."

"I'm a qualified armor officer," Craig said.

"By your own account, your qualifications didn't seem to awe Colonel Whatsisname."

"Fuck it," Lowell said. "To hell with it."

"If you change your mind, let me know," Porter said. "Although, for the life of me, I can't imagine why you would want to waste your time doing that."

"I said, fuck it, let it go," Craig said.

"If you're not going to be a soldier, don't you think it's time you cleaned up your language?" Porter asked.

Lowell looked at him, half angry. He smiled. "Very well," he said. "Diddle you, Porter."

"That's an improvement," Porter said, and they laughed together.

The army finally got around to answering the letter Craig had sent to the adjutant general.

HEADQUARTERS

DEPARTMENT OF THE ARMY

OFFICE OF THE ASSISTANT CHIEF OF STAFF FOR PERSONNEL

The Pentagon, Washington 25, D.C.

15 May 1950
201-LOWELL, Craig W Capt
O–495302

Mr. Craig W. Lowell
Apt 2301
2601 Parkway
Philadelphia, Penna.

Dear Mr. Lowell:

Thank you for your letter of 17 December 1949, volunteering for extended active duty.

A careful review of your records, and the personnel requirements of the Army for the foreseeable future has been conducted by this office.

Under present policy, no applications for extended active duty from commissioned officers who have not been awarded a bachelor's degree from a recognized college or university are being accepted.

Furthermore, your total commissioned service and time in grade as a first lieutenant does not meet the established criteria for your present grade of captain. Your records will be reviewed sometime during the next fiscal year by a panel of officers who will recommend to the Assistant Chief of Staff for Personnel whether or not you should be retained as captain, Army of the United States, in a reserve capacity, terminated, or offered a commission in a grade commensurate with your age, length of service, and other factors. You may expect to hear from them directly in approximately six (6) months.

Under these circumstances, obviously, your application for recall to extended active duty cannot be favorably considered.

Thank you for your interest in the United States Army.

Sincerely yours,
John D. Glover
Major, Adjutant General's Corps
Deputy Chief, Reserve Officer Branch
(Armor) ODCS-P

He was sorely tempted to write Major Glover and tell him to stick his commission up his anal orifice, but he decided, finally, fuck him. It wasn't worth the time or effort.

(Seven)
Garmisch-Partenkirchen, Germany
30 May 1950

Garmisch was nice, really beautiful, but there were some problems. There weren't very many permanent party personnel, and the commissary and PX were small. There was only a small medical detachment, known as the Broken Bones Squad, to handle skiing accidents; and there was not even a dentist.

What the permanent party did was drive into Munich, about one hundred kilometers (sixty miles) to the north. A U.S. Army General Hospital there provided pediatricians for Sanford, Jr., and obstetricians for Sharon now that she was that way again. There was also a huge commissary with a much wider selection than the one in Garmisch had; and, of course, the Munich Military Post PX was the largest in Germany.

Sandy arranged his classes so that he was free after 1100 on Fridays. That allowed him to get into Munich to the hospital by half past two. He had bought a 1950 Buick Roadmaster sedan, two months old, from a captain who had been a ski instructor. He'd broken his leg and been shipped home. Sandy got it at a good price, and he liked having a big car. The way some of the Germans drove, it was better to be in a big car in case of accident.

There was a standard routine when the Felters went to Munich. First, he dropped Sharon at the hospital and then he went to the commissary with the shopping list. Then he went back to the hospital and picked up Sharon and Little Sandy, and they went together to the PX. They spent the night in the Four Seasons Hotel, and then drove back to Garmisch late Saturday mornings. He didn't like to be on the roads at night if he could avoid it, and the Four Seasons was a good hotel—run by the army—where you could get a really fancy meal at a very reasonable price.

It was a Friday afternoon in early June, the first really nice spring day they'd had. Sandy dropped Sharon off at the hospital

(Little Sandy didn't need to see the pediatrician, so he had him with him), and then he drove to the commissary.

He parked the Buick, then got out and somewhat awkwardly locked it, holding Little Sandy in his arms so he wouldn't run around the parking lot in front of a car.

And the fat jolly butcher from the Gehlen Organization appeared out of nowhere and said: "Oh, what a pretty little boy!"

"Why, thank you," Sandy said. "I think so."

"He looks just like my grandson," the jolly fat butcher said, and took out his wallet and held it open for Sandy to look.

It wasn't a picture of a little boy. It was a picture of a tall, skinny man in worn work clothing.

"That was taken ten days ago," the butcher said. "At Vyritsa, near Leningrad. If nothing goes wrong, processing takes about ten days. We'll keep you posted."

"You're sure this is the one?"

"My dear Felter," the man said, "please believe me. That is Colonel Count Peter-Paul von Greiffenberg."

"No offense," Felter said. "But this is a little personal, too."

"So I understand," the jolly butcher said, enjoying Felter's surprise. "Our mutual friend thought that Colonel Robert F. Bellmon would be interested in the gentleman's homecoming, and asked me to ask you if you would be good enough to give him the word."

The fat jolly butcher put his wallet away, and started making cootchy-cootchy-coo sounds to Little Sandy. Then he said, "Our mutual friend would like both of you to know that while we make a mistake once in a while, most of the time we're pretty efficient."

Then he tipped his hat and walked away.

(Eight)
Marburg an der Lahn, Germany
24 June 1950

He was tall and skeletal. His eyes were sunken and his skin was gray, and he had other classical signs of prolonged malnutrition. The suit that Generalmajor (Retired) Gunther von Hamm had insisted on giving him in Bad Hersfeld to replace the rags he had from the Russians hung loosely on his shoulders and bagged over his buttocks, which were nothing more than muscle and bone. The shoes hurt his feet, although he couldn't understand why that should be. They were quality leather, even lined with leather. Gunther had said that the government was paying pensions again and that he really could afford to give him clothing, money, and whatever else he needed until his own retirement and back pay came through.

He had been riding in the dining car since lunch. He had felt a little faint, and he hadn't wanted to walk back to his second-class compartment. He'd asked the waiter if he could stay, and the waiter had been more than obliging. The waiter had seen returnees like him before. They made him uncomfortable, and if one of them wanted to sit at a dining car table, that seemed little enough to ask.

He had broken the rules. He was supposed to go to a returnee center in Cologne, but when the train had stopped at Kassel, the first stop after crossing the border, he had just gotten off. He had had enough of centers and processing. He'd hitchhiked to Bad Hersfeld and found Gunther and Greta by the simple expedient of looking for their name in the phone book.

Gunther had picked him up in his Volkswagen, and he could tell from the look in Gunther's eyes how bad he looked—and something else: Gunther did not have good news for him.

He got it that night: His wife was dead, a suicide. His daughter was believed to have gone to relatives in East Germany. Gunther said the Red Cross was very helpful in circumstances like these, in establishing contact across the East/West German borders.

He knew that Gunther didn't believe a word he was saying.

So he had come home to nothing.

He had felt too weak to go on just then, and so he imposed on Gunther's hospitality for four days. They fed him, and they tried to talk of pleasant things. And then he had announced, and he would not be dissuaded, that he was feeling fine now and wanted to go to Marburg. He had no place else to go, and there was no sense putting it off.

Kassel appeared to have really taken a beating. He remembered the Americans had come up north to Kassel through Giessen. Out of the foggy recesses of memory, he recalled seeing a communiqué. American armored forces had taken

Giessen and were proceeding in the direction of Kassel.

If they had done this to Kassel, what had they done to Marburg, which was on their only possible route north?

The train reached the Marburg railyards all of a sudden, surprising him. The area didn't seem to have suffered any damage at all.

He got up and picked up the cardboard suitcase, tied shut with strings. He remembered to leave a tip for the waiter. There was new money; deutsche marks had replaced reichsmarks. He really had no idea what they were worth. Gunther had given him five hundred deutsche marks, to be paid back when he got his affairs in order.

He looked at the money, and decided that five marks would be a suitable tip. There was a little strip of silver inlaid in the paper. He had noticed that with interest.

He laid the five marks on the table and got up and walked carefully out of the dining room and stood in the vestibule. The waiter came after him and gave him his five marks back.

"Welcome home, *mein Herr,*" he said.

"Thank you very much," he said. That was very touching. Do I look that bad?

He could see out the open vestibule window now. There *wasn't* much damage. People were playing soccer on the old soccer field. Whatever else had happened, the twin spires of St. Elizabeth's Church were there, rising above the trees.

Next the old city came into view. There was no damage. How incredible. It looked exactly as it had looked the day he left! As he had so often thought of it in memory.

And then they were in the station, and the train was slowing. He waited until it had completely stopped. He stepped between the cars into the vestibule from which the steps had been lowered, then got carefully, awkwardly off.

He was still holding the five marks in his hand. He put it into his jacket pocket, or tried to. The pocket was still sewn shut. He put it in his trousers pocket. Just having money was a strange feeling.

The people made him feel strange. They were all so fat, they were all so *rosy.*

There were two men on the platform, watching the arriving passengers go down the stairway to the tunnel leading to the station. Policemen. He knew a policeman when he saw one.

They were looking at something, probably a photograph, held in their hands.

They can't be expecting me, he thought. No one knows about me. No one knew about me coming until I arrived. My name wasn't even on the list of returned prisoners.

But the policemen, nevertheless, looked at him very intently when he walked past them and started down the stairs. Probably because I was so long a prisoner. Policemen don't like prisoners; whether they are criminals or prisoners of war, it makes no difference.

They know, he thought, with something close to terror. They know I didn't go to the center in Cologne, as I was ordered to do. They have come to arrest me.

He sensed, rather than saw, that the policemen were coming down the stairs behind him. There was a feeling of terror. So close, and am I to be arrested again? But why? There didn't have to be a reason. The state provided any reason it wanted. It was not necessary to satisfy a prisoner that he was being justly detained.

He went up the stairs into the station. The general outline of the station was familiar, but there was something new. He wondered about that. The glass, of course. The doors were now all glass. Before they had been wooden doors with glass panels. Now they were huge pieces of thick glass. Much nicer. The station had obviously been bombed; and when they'd rebuilt it, they had put in new doors, making them all glass.

He wondered why they didn't break, with all the use they obviously got.

He had probably been wrong about the policemen. They hadn't arrested him. Why should they? They had just happened to come down the stairs when he did.

He reached the glass doors. The door was automatic, and he watched it close. He put his hand out to push it open again. Before he touched it, the door opened away from him with a whoosh. How did they do that?

He stepped outside. Way down Bahnhofstrasse, he could see the Cafe Weitz. It was still in business. How interesting.

Somebody snapped their fingers behind him. He started, turned his head, and saw one of the policemen, with a subtle but unmistakable gesture, pointing him out to someone else, someone ahead of him.

What do they want to arrest me for?

How much can I be punished for not going to the center in Cologne?

Then he thought: It's probably nothing more than a debriefing. The military wants to debrief me on what I saw in Russia. I saw the inside of an office in a logging camp in a swamp and nothing more. I could tell them, "I saw nothing of military significance at all." But they wouldn't believe him. They would insist on a full interrogation, according to regulation.

He bristled then. They should have sent an officer to do this. I am entitled to that courtesy. They should have sent an officer in uniform, not policemen.

There was an enormous car at the curb. He read what was spelled out in chrome on the trunk lid. Ford Super Deluxe. It didn't look like the Ford automobiles he remembered.

A tall man who looked like a policeman was leaning on the car, and now he stood up straight and took off his hat and stepped in front of him.

"Herr Graf?" the man asked in a Berliner's accent. It had been a long time since he had been addressed as Herr Graf. He was afraid of the policeman.

"Herr Oberst Graf von Greiffenberg?" the policeman asked again.

"Yes," the Graf said. "I am the Graf, and formerly Oberst."

"Herr Oberst Graf, will you come with us, please?"

Resistance was obviously futile. There were three of them, and he was tired and weak. He got in the back of the Ford. One of the policeman got in beside him and the other one in the front.

With squeal of tires, the car made a U-turn and drove past the soccer field. Policemen always drove too fast, he thought.

"See if you can raise them from here, Ken," the driver of the car, the man in charge, said. He spoke in English. It had been a long time since he had heard English spoken.

The other man in the front seat picked up what looked like a telephone.

"Umpire, Umpire," he said. "This is Home Base. Do you read, over?"

"Home Base, this is Umpire. Read you five by five, go ahead."

"I'll be damned," the man driving said.

"Umpire, Home Base," the man with the telephone said. "We have the eagle in the bag. I say again, we have the eagle in the bag. Heading for the autobahn."

"You're Americans," he said.

"Yes, sir, Colonel," the man driving said. "We're American. We've been looking all over for you."

The radio went off again a few minutes later.

"Home Base, Umpire, do you read?"

"Go ahead, Umpire."

"You'll be met at the autobahn. Black Buick Roadmaster. Confirm."

"Understand black Buick at the autobahn."

"Roger, Roger. What's the eagle's condition?"

"Feathers are a little ruffled, that's about it."

"Umpire clear with Home Base."

There was an even more enormous automobile waiting for them at the autobahn. A little Jew got out of it and walked over to the Ford and opened the door. He put his hand out.

"My name is Felter, sir," the little Jew said. "I'm here to meet you at the request of an old comrade-in-arms. We've been looking all over for you, sir."

"Who would that be?" he said, stiffly. "What old comrade-in-arms?"

"Colonel Robert Bellmon, sir," the little man said.

The Graf straightened. So Bellmon had made it, had he?

"This is very kind of Colonel Bellmon," the Graf said. "But if it is permitted, I would prefer to be in Marburg."

"If you will, sir," the little Jew said, "please come with me. I have a car, here, sir," Captain Sanford T. Felter said.

The Graf was not used to arguing with authority.

"Very well," he said.

The Jew's Buick Roadmaster was the biggest automobile the Colonel Count von Greiffenberg had ever seen. The softness of the seats was incredible. They were like a very comfortable couch.

"May I be permitted to inquire where I am being taken?"

"Kronberg Castle, sir. Colonel Bellmon, and some others, are waiting for you there."

"Some others?"

The little Jew didn't answer that question.

"It'll take us just about an hour, sir," he said.

Colonel Graf Peter-Paul von Greiffenberg dozed off.

The last time Colonel Graf Peter-Paul von Greiffenberg had been to Kronberg Castle was at a reception given by Prince Philip of Hesse. Now, he was not very surprised to see, it had been taken over by the Americans. To judge by the officers he saw, they were using it as some sort of rest hotel for their senior officers.

The little Jew opened the door for him and led him into the hotel.

"If you'll come with me, please, sir," he said.

The inside of the castle was just as luxuriously furnished as it ever had been.

"Colonel, if you'll just sit here a moment, I'll go get Colonel Bellmon," the little Jew said, ushering him into an armchair.

"Get this gentleman whatever he wants," the little Jew said to a waiter.

"What can I get you, sir?" the waiter asked.

"Nothing, thank you," he said. "I think I'll walk around. If I may."

"Of course, sir."

He walked into what used to be the library. It was still the library, and through its French doors he could see the rolling lawn. He went to look out.

He saw Bellmon. Bellmon and a tall, good-looking young man were driving golf balls. The colonel was perversely pleased that the little Jew had not been able to find Bellmon. He considered walking through the French doors and just going up to him. And then he decided he had better wait. He was, in effect, Bellmon's guest.

There was a blond child, a boy, a beautiful little thing, being attended by a middle-aged woman in an army nurse's uniform, and a blond young woman, obviously the child's mother. The young woman looked too young to be a general's wife, but she had a coat, mink, he thought, and clothes and jewelry that made it plain she was not a junior officer's wife.

She belonged, the colonel decided, to the tall blond man driving golf balls with Colonel Bellmon. There was something about him that smelled of money and position.

Then the little Jew appeared and walked quickly over to Colonel Bellmon.

Bellmon dropped his golf club and started into the building. The young man went to the young woman. They started for the building. It must be Bellmon's son and daughter. That's who it had to be.

Colonel Count Peter-Paul von Greiffenberg turned and faced the door through which Bellmon would appear. He would, he told himself, not lose control of his emotions. He would be what he was, an officer and a gentleman.

Bellmon entered the room and saw him and, the colonel knew, recognized him. But he did not cross the room to him. Do I look that bad?

The young woman in the mink coat, clutching the child in her arms, came into the room. She gave the child to the handsome young man. And then she crossed the room, and looked into his eyes.

"Papa?" she asked.

At approximately 0500 Sunday, 25 June 1950, Koreans awakened Major George D. Kessler, USA, Korean Military Advisory Group advisor to the 10th Regiment at Samch'ok and told him a heavy North Korean attack was in progress at the 38th parallel.

> *U.S. Army*
> *in the Korean War, Vol. 1, p. 27.*
> *Office of the Chief of*
> *Military History, U.S. Army,*
> *Washington, 1961.*

ABOUT THE AUTHOR

W. E. B. Griffin, who was once a soldier, belongs to the Armor Association; Paris Post #1, The American Legion; and is a life member of the National Rifle Association and Gaston-Lee Post #5660, Veterans of Foreign Wars.

Bonded together in battle—
as they could never be in peace...
The Biggest War Saga of Them All!

BROTHERHOOD
OF
☆ WAR ☆

With all the majesty of *Once An Eagle,* all the
power of *War and Remembrance, Brotherhood of
War* is a brilliant new saga of heroes and lovers,
fighters and dreamers whose stories are told in
a series of unforgettable novels.

———— **BROTHERHOOD OF WAR I, THE LIEUTENANTS**
by W.E.B. Griffin 05643-X/$3.50

———— **BROTHERHOOD OF WAR II, THE CAPTAINS**
by W.E.B. Griffin 05644-8/$3.50

———— **BROTHERHOOD OF WAR III, THE MAJORS**
by W.E.B. Griffin 05645-6/$3.50

55